D0175339

THE EXTRA

Also by Elizabeth Sims

The Actress

Easy Street

Lucky Stiff

Damn Straight

Holy Hell

THE EXTRA

Elizabeth Sims

Minotaur Books
New York

This is a work of fiction. All of the characters, organizations, and events portrayed in this novel are either products of the author's imagination or are used fictitiously.

THE EXTRA. Copyright © 2009 by Elizabeth Sims. All rights reserved. Printed in the United States of America. For information, address St. Martin's Press, 175 Fifth Avenue, New York, N.Y. 10010.

www.minotaurbooks.com

Library of Congress Cataloging-in-Publication Data

Sims, Elizabeth, 1957–
  The extra / Elizabeth Sims.—1st ed.
    p. cm.
  ISBN-13: 978-0-312-37729-8
  ISBN-10: 0-312-37729-0
  1. Single mothers—Fiction. 2. Extras (Actors)—Fiction. 3. Los Angeles (Calif.)—Fiction.
I. Title.
  PS3619.I564E97 2009
  813'.6—dc22

                                                                              2009004501

First Edition: June 2009

10   9   8   7   6   5   4   3   2   1

THE EXTRA

ONE

The picket line surged again, and the police, already nervous, got panicky. I know my heart was pounding. Those of us not in riot gear stayed at the edges and tried to contain the crowd. It was near noon and very hot. One protester, a rangy young woman with flower-child green eyes, stepped up to my face, shook her fist, and sneered, "How do you sleep at night?"

As if I personally had taken a blowtorch to the earth to make it hotter. As if I personally had chained a Malaysian ten-year-old to a machine that dangerously stamped out American waffle irons.

All up and down the picket line the protesters were doing their mightiest to provoke the cops, yelling, swearing—everything short of actually striking us. I felt especially uneasy wearing an ordinary uniform, no helmet, no riot shield.

Someone behind the line threw a bottle. I watched it arc through the air, safely over the heads of the front-line protesters, and explode in shards against a riot shield. My goodness, that could have been recycled.

And on that signal, the protesters' fury amped into the red zone and they rushed us, blindly flailing their signs. Following orders, I stood my ground, narrowly missing getting brained by another bottle.

I heard the *phot! phot!* of tear gas canisters being fired, and more screaming. A plume of poupon-yellow smoke began to drift my way.

"Cut! Cut, goddamn it!"

The director flung his cap to the ground and almost hurled his bullhorn too. He leaned riskily over the scaffold railing and bellowed, "I didn't want the tear gas yet! The riot squad's supposed to move in as soon as the bottle breaks! Didn't you hear me? Where's Stuart? And *then* the tear gas *after* they pull back! You people look like a buncha drunken sheep down there! Where's Stuart?"

His orange cap, embroidered with what looked like a stylized Tweety Bird, lay crown up on the oozy asphalt. We were here on a little stub of Eighth Street near the Los Angeles River, not that the river had any cooling effect, running only a few inches deep. The director continued to holler. "And they've got to get in *front* of the non-riot police! Right away, as soon as that bottle—which by the way, good throw, see if you can do that again—breaks, because—"

A squeal of feedback cut him off as the first assistant climbed up the scaffolding with *his* bullhorn. I heard him say calmly to his boss, "Look, we need to rethink this." Then he announced, "Let's break for lunch, the caterers are ready. Everybody back on set in forty minutes."

2

I walked past the scaffold and the orange cap with the yellow bird, the logo for the movie we were all making: *The Canary Syndrome*, yet another conspiracy-theory film about who's to blame for the fact that we're all going to hell, and not soon enough. A lackey snatched up the cap and scampered up the scaffolding. Everyone was wearing the same cap; all the crew, that is.

Something clammy and protoplasmic nudged the back of my bare elbow. I turned to find a German shepherd the size of a minivan looking up (barely) at me. Panting cordially, he nudged me again with his nose. My friend Sylvan, in police costume as I was, held his leash.

"Hey, Rita," said Sylvan.

"Hey. Where were you guys? I didn't see you."

"We were about to attack the flank, over there. If he's going to get his money's worth out of us, he needs to shoot some stuff of the dogs taking people down well before the tear gas, so the tear gas will make sense."

"Man, you're sweating like a Coke bottle."

He laughed. Thick shouldered and at least six two, he said cheerfully, "It's the dog days." Perspiration poured from Sylvan's heavy brown face and darkened his uniform this August day. He was an animal wrangler who usually worked off-camera with the actors and critters, but sometimes he got roles handling dogs himself if he fit the scene. Big Black Fucker was the politically incorrect yet crystal-clear casting designation his agent used.

"Thanks again," I told him, "for helping me get this gig."

"Least I can do. You've helped me out plenty. Glad that rumor wasn't true about you being through with acting."

"Well, I am. Basically."

He looked at me.

3

"I am," I insisted. "I'm just doing little jobs here and there to help me get through law school."

He smiled. "Once an actress, always an actress."

I shrugged that off. "Are you doing just dogs on this one?" He handled rodents too.

"Just dogs, yeah. But me and a hundred mice start shooting tomorrow on a made-for-TV on Louis Pasteur."

"Oh?"

"Yeah, I read that he actually used dogs for his testing, but the producers think mice'll be cuter."

"Plus imagine the spin-off possibilities."

Sylvan laughed.

"Wanna do lunch?" I asked.

"Nah, I've got to water and feed this guy and the other burly boys. Come on, King."

The Canary Syndrome was supposed to be a labor of love for everybody involved (French for low budget), but at least the extras, which I was one of, got scale, almost two hundred dollars a day.

And as in all good low-budgets, they were making the few do for the many: there were only about forty protesters and fifteen cops, including Sylvan and the other two dog-handling officers. The cameraman had snaked through the scene with his handheld, guided by the belt by his assistant so it looked chaotic and tight-packed. The director shouted from above, one eye on the remote monitor that showed what the camera was seeing.

When Sylvan had phoned to give me a heads-up about the extras call, I thought I'd have a better chance if I dressed as a protester, given that I'm blond, fairly small, and, well—that clatter you're hearing is my false modesty falling to the ground—pretty. I thought I'd make an unconvincing cop, so I put on an angry-looking outfit of tight torn jeans and a hot pink top. But first thing I knew I was hired as Police Sergeant I / Nonarmored, I guess in the name of diversity.

When I touched that police uniform, a special feeling came over me. A sense of potency filled my body, inch by inch, as I pulled up the pants and fastened them. They felt bulletproof. "Wool?" I asked the mohawked dresser in surprise. "Yeah," she said, "it's a great fabric, wool gabardine. The LAPD's used it forever, that's why they look so good. The shirts are tropical weight. Here."

I drew on the short-sleeved shirt, with its badge and insignia, and it felt great. I put on the black socks and duty shoes, buckled the leather gun belt around my waist with the dresser's help, put on the hat, and looked in the mirror. There behind all that officialdom was little old Rita Farmer. But my expression was clear and authoritative, and I looked powerful and proud.

I slipped my own small wallet into my back pocket, not quite trusting the security of the wardrobe room, a messy space rented in the very building providing the façade for the shoot.

The belt was so heavy, what with all the stuff on it—handcuff case and so on—that I thought the gun was in the holster already. But no, I had to see the prop guy for my fake gun, which looked and felt totally real. It must have weighed two or three pounds.

"Are you left-handed?"

"No, right."

He made me take off my belt, and he found a right-handed holster to replace the left-handed one.

"It doesn't make any difference, you know," I said. "I'm not even going to draw it, much less—"

"It does matter," he said. "You'll look maybe two percent more natural, having the gun on your handed side. It'll feel different to you."

"Yeah?"

"And from my perspective all those two percents add up." He adjusted my cap with a quick tap, and I was done.

Man, did I feel good. I tried to imagine what I'd do if I were a real cop in some tough situation. Probably crap my pants.

Our tidbit of Eighth Street wasn't far from Skid Row and downtown. A shipping office that had escaped blight was dressed as the headquarters of some evil multinational company, and this was the location of our protest scene.

The food on a movie set is usually quite luxe, but they'd cut even that corner. The one measly lunch wagon was overwhelmed by the crowd, so the caterers resorted to throwing wrapped sandwiches and poly bags of vegetable sticks to the throng, refugee-style.

I caught a sandwich, grabbed a Diet Pepsi from an ice bin, and sat down on a curb. The sandwich looked OK—ham and avocado ciabatta type thing—but as my mouth approached for bite one, a bug appeared between ham and bread. Hiya, bug. I watched its head emerge, feelers waving in the sunshine. It wriggled all the way out and began crawling along the ridgeline of a ham slice. I tried to convince myself it wasn't a cockroach, merely some clean-living lettuce-dweller, because I was very hungry. But no, it was a roach, it was a roach—that disgusting oily brown carapace. As soon as I realized it I recoiled like a Winchester, the sandwich flying from my hand. "Oh, *God!*"

I almost dry heaved, but got a grip and forced myself to pick up the sandwich. The roach fell to the ground and zipped to a wad of gum for cover.

I'm not really afraid of bugs in general, although spiders aren't my favorite. The best thing about my married years was that my husband, although an abusive drunk, would kill the spiders. Being divorced, upon finding a spider in the apartment I either had to slaughter it or adopt it as a pet. I've heard tell of people who scoop them up and take them outdoors, but that is so not me. When I had to, I'd kill them with one of my slippers, using my Gramma Gladys's spider-killing chant: "Oh, little spider, got no mama, got no papa, wanna see God?" *Smack!* The key is not to hesitate. Do not hesitate.

I would have stomped on the roach for vengeance since they're not yet an endangered species, but it was gone. I threw the sandwich into a trash barrel and trotted down the sidewalk to find something decent to eat. As soon as I got away from the cables and lights and gawkers, the mean streets pressed in, bleak and broken. The very air vibrated with low serotonin. I saw ugly hostile tagging all over the place, as if even the skilled graf artists had moved on to Pasadena. I jogged and jogged, finally turning north on Mateo, at least a through street. Where the hell was a market, a party store, a goddamn vending machine? I cruised past steel gate after brick façade after dirty plywood, my heart lifting for one second at a gas station that turned out to serve *only* petroleum products, a garbage-strewn parking lot. A drop of perspiration rolled down the side of my face and evaporated in the dry street heat.

It was nice to be putting so much mileage between me and the roach-wich, but the farther I went, the more anxious I got, what with having to be back for the next take. The blocks flew by and my sense of futility increased in direct proportion to my hunger.

Maybe I should give up, I thought, but then my inner voice demanded, *Are you a quitter, then?*

No, I answered. *No quitter am I.*

I trotted on.

Ah! An old enameled Orange Crush sign was almost covered over by a poster for some new brand of malt liquor, and the sign up top said GROCERIA.

The Mexican shop was dim, the windows plastered over with vivid signs, PINTO 79C, CORONA 3.99, and so on. But the proprietor smiled and his fruit glowed in heaps like treasure. My mouth watered cautiously. A girl of about eleven stood gazing from the shop's doorway into the white glare of the street. She wore a turquoise cotton dress with yellow rickrack around the hem. Her face was dreamy.

A sign pointed to ready-made sandwiches in the cold case, but not wanting to tempt fate, I returned to the fruit and chose a nectarine and a banana, first examining them for bugs with careful paranoia. I saw a package of peanuts and picked up that too.

I got out my wallet to pay, but the storekeeper pushed the food to me saying, "No, no, you take. You take it, OK?"

"What?"

Suddenly the young girl cried out at something in the street. She grabbed my arm, pulled me to the door, yammering and pointing in Spanish.

On the opposite sidewalk a young black kid was trying to shield himself from blows coming from a couple of thugs, one fat-assed, the other lean, their faces shrouded deep under sweatshirt hoods. The fat-ass swung a length of two-by-four like an axe, overhand, pounding the kid's shoulders and then, as the kid curled himself into a ball on the sidewalk, his back and legs.

You see this kind of thing all the time in movies and TV, the violent clichés we all have a beer by, go to bed by, entertain our children by. Just a few minutes ago I watched the picketers slamming their breakaway polyethylene signs on the cops' helmets, and the cops unleash their spongy fake batons on their opponents. Everybody acted extremely fierce, with lots of grunting and wincing.

But this—this. The purposeful silence of the attackers. The sound of the blows in the suddenly quiet street, the sound so small compared to the amplified *thwack!* of movie blows, but so much more chilling, so much less tolerable: bone and muscle yielding to kiln-dried lumber. My spine contracted at each sick thud.

The other attacker was attempting to stomp the kid's head. Someone's son. A brown suitcase lay on its side next to him.

I had a mental flash of my own son. His trusting little face—had I packed his favorite dinosaur, the orange one, in his daybag this morning?

My blood pressure spiked and I found myself on the bright sidewalk. *Found myself* is exact: my legs took me there without any command from my brain. I heard more sickening blows and then the kid's muffled pleas. The first attacker lifted the piece of timber again.

"Stop it!" I barked.

The pair looked over at me. I rushed into the street, dodged sideways for a car, and by the time I reached the curb, the attackers had dropped the two-by-four and taken off, fast. They separated, one darting down an alley, the other continuing up the street, then disappearing around a building.

The boy rolled over on the sidewalk and sat up, blood pulsing from beneath a flap of scalp. He looked to be fifteen or sixteen years old. He struggled to get up. I said, "Wait, don't, you're hurt." Blood coursed down the side of his face, slick and so red in the L.A. sunshine.

He kept trying to stand. "Leave me alone," he mumbled. He

wore green camo pants and a white T-shirt, the shirt soaking up the blood like snow. Each of his breaths was torn with pain, but he spoke again. "They'll be back."

I looked around for help. A few passersby had stopped to stare; others hurried by.

The bleeding boy struggled, again, to stand. His eyes were confused. "Stay down!" I yelled in my mom voice. His skin was as smooth as boot leather and dark brown, his hair short-cropped.

"Hey, leave him alone!" a stranger shouted.

"Racist!" called another.

"What?" I said.

"No, she no touch him," contradicted someone else.

I comprehended none of this.

Automatically, I reached for my cell phone, always clipped to my waist, and found the prop gun in my hand instead. Surprised, I stared at it, its lethal-looking barrel leveled at the hearts of the bystanders.

The small crowd screamed and scattered.

The boy cowered on the sidewalk. "Don't shoot, please don't shoot," his voice a terrified rasp.

As I stood in that street holding the gun, everything came clear at once. In the heat of the moment I'd forgotten I was dressed as a police sergeant. The storekeeper had tried to give this new cop free food, the little girl saw violence and drew the cop to it, this inner-city black teen surely would fear a cop—blond and pixie-faced though she might be—and the crowd saw a black kid bleeding with a white cop standing over him yelling. Yes, everything came clear. Perception is reality, just like they say in acting school.

Where the hell's my cell phone? Oh yes, in my little changing basket, back in wardrobe.

The boy moaned. I knelt to him. "You'll be OK, honey. Please," I shouted, "someone call 911!"

But the street was empty now. Did the people here know what was about to happen?

"Hey, grocer!" I hollered.

The boy lurched from my arms and scrambled to his feet.

A dilapidated car pulled up to the curb.

Crak! I saw a flash inside. Photography? Paintball? I stupidly wondered. *Crak!* and again *crak-crak!* the sounds quick and flat in the silent street.

My young friend collapsed. The car sped away.

I felt a hot sting on my upper arm and flinched away from it but it stayed with me and I saw torn skin and blood starting down from my LAPD uniform shirt.

I knelt again to the boy. His eyelids fluttered. Blood seeped from a new wound in his side and poured, more ominously, from another in his neck. He tried to speak.

Supporting his neck with one hand, I pressed my other hand firmly over the bullet hole. "Help!" I shrieked.

Softly, the boy said, "I'm gonna die."

"No, honey, you are not gonna die. You hang on, you hear me?"

"Officer." He looked up at me, struggling to say something.

I bent my ear to his lips.

"Tell my grandmother I'm sorry."

His eyes closed.

TWO

George Rowe grasped the brass ring, lifted it, and let it fall solidly on the strike plate cast in the shape of a wolf's head. The wolf's mouth was closed.

A sharply dressed old man answered the door. "Mr. Rowe, I presume? Come in."

Rowe walked into the stone foyer of a house in Hancock Park.

Beginning in the 1920s, the old-money names of Los Angeles built mansions here of imported stone and fine brick, employing masons from Italy and Mexico to fit the basalt sills, build up the facings, and craft the chimneys.

This house was solid and nice, smaller than most in the neighborhood but with more stone.

"I'm Colonel Markovich." The man's face bore a wealth of small scars and spots of age. His eyebrows were like tiny white angel wings over his eyes, and the eyes were clear and blue. His bearing was straight. "I don't have a butler," he added.

"Then I guess he didn't do it," said Rowe.

"I beg your pardon?"

Rowe smiled. The old man made an I-get-it sound and smiled too.

Since he had left his job as an insurance investigator and gone into private practice, George Rowe had had plenty of work, some of it challenging, like tracking down the origin of counterfeit securities on behalf of a corporation that didn't want the word to get out, or finding a politician's stolen laptop. For the past few months, though, most of it had been pretty pedestrian: missing persons who'd clumsily run away from some crappy deal or another. This appointment, today, had the aroma of something different.

Markovich steered Rowe through an arch to a reception room, with leather furniture and books on the walls. Rowe stood waiting for what Markovich had to say.

"Do you like dogs, Mr. Rowe?"

"I like them all right."

"Drink?" Markovich indicated a sideboard with two crystal decanters and some glasses. "Whiskey, brandy?"

It was one in the afternoon. "I guess whiskey," said Rowe.

"A whiskey man, then." Markovich poured off about three fingers' worth for each of them.

A gently dangerous feeling hovered in the air; Rowe half expected a beautiful woman to stalk into the room smacking a riding crop against her palm.

After handing him his glass, Markovich led him to a sunroom that overlooked a smooth lawn.

"One thing, the grass is doing better now that Ernest is gone," he said.

"Who's Ernest?"

"That's why you're here. Have a seat."

There was an eagerness about Markovich, something more energetic than Rowe might have expected from a snowcapped fellow like this.

"Ernest is my dog. To say that: Ernest is my dog, is to make a gross understatement. He is my dog, but he is much more to me than that. To call him a person would be a slur. I've known so many people with hideous souls, Mr. Rowe."

"Yes," said Rowe.

"Ernest certainly transcends the animal kingdom, but his line is straight to enlightenment. Pure clear light, pure atomic essence."

This kind of talk made Rowe uncomfortable. He uncrossed his legs and made a move as if deciding whether to leave.

"Please, Mr. Rowe, I'm not a kook. I may be an odd sort, I grant that. But if you bear with me, you'll see how things are. I'm serious about hiring you."

Rowe sat back.

"Ernest disappeared two days ago." The Colonel sipped his whiskey. "Of course I notified the authorities. But you know how it is."

Rowe nodded.

"I need someone to find Ernest. A man like you: a serious investigator who gets results. Someone who isn't afraid to take bold action on behalf of a client. I read about the Tenaway case."

Rowe looked at him. "But my name barely made the—"

"I can read between the lines, Mr. Rowe."

That felt good. "OK. Well, what happened to the dog? Did he run away?"

Markovich laughed, a Sunday-matinee laugh, a you-are-quite-mistaken laugh. "Oh no, Mr. Rowe, Ernest did not run away."

"Have you checked the shelters?"

"He is not in any shelter. Hellholes. He is not in any animal rescue situation, not Ernest. When you begin your inquiry you'll soon see the shelters are not the place to look."

"Then—"

"Ernest was taken, Mr. Rowe." Blood rose up Markovich's neck, then into his jaw. He stopped and snapped open a white linen handkerchief. He wiped his face. "This has been the most upsetting occurrence of my life."

"You were very fond of the dog."

"Please don't use the past tense. Yes. I won't be so trite as to say I love him. Let's just say I hold him in the highest regard."

"So who did it? Any neighbors mad at you?"

"Your naïveté is almost cute, Mr. Rowe. Before I go into detail, are you interested in taking the case?"

"I'd like to learn a little more. Do you have, uh, a picture of Ernest?"

Markovich's eyes flicked to a painting that looked like an abstract bunch of blobs, but on closer look depicted a beagle emerging from a fog bank. Just the pattern of the coat and a pair of rich round eyes, set against a shimmering sea-coasty sort of background. "That is Ernest as seen through the eyes of a master." He named a painter Rowe had never heard of, not that that was saying much.

"But here," said the Colonel. He opened a photo album to a glossy color photo of a male beagle posed in a commanding stance on a judging platform. Ernest's full name, in black type in the border, was Ch. Ernest Jiggs Cognac V. The dog stood grandly, chin up, tail high, muscles poised.

"Good-looking dog," said Rowe. "Stud?"

"Exactly. I showed him for four years. He's eight now. He took seventeen all-breed best in shows, ninety-eight group wins, and hundreds of best of breeds. Do you know how valuable his semen is?"

"More than mine or even yours, I'd guess."

Markovich ghost-laughed. "Isn't that the way of it. Nine hundred dollars a shot. I used to charge only five hundred if I could take a puppy or two from the litter. Which I would do only if I thought the brood bitch was outstanding."

"A valuable dog, then."

"Yes."

"All pedigreed dogs have names like that, don't they?"

"Yes. Some find it silly, but that's the way it's done. To show the lineage."

"The way it's done" seemed to fit Markovich on many levels. He wore pressed gray slacks, a navy double-breasted blazer, and handsome black loafers. His grooming was impeccable. He was a type Rowe respected. But this dog thing.

Markovich flipped through a few more pictures. "He's a classic tri-color: white and tan, with a black saddle. Here's his face full-on, take a look. See this?"

Rowe perceived that the dog's muzzle was mostly white, except for a thin column of tan shooting straight up from the dog's nose, flaring out and ending in a horizontal line on the forehead, where the white took over again. It looked like a perfect Doric column, and gave the dog a most intelligent look.

"Yes, I see," he said.

"That's his distinctive mark, that tan-inside-white blaze. Of course he's microchipped too."

"OK, yes. Uh . . ."

Markovich said, "I sense you're not very familiar with the world of elite show dogs, Mr. Rowe."

"Yeah, dogcatcher wasn't what I had in mind when I came here." Rowe rubbed the side of his neck. He had taken a few sips of the whiskey and felt quite warm. "I really don't think—"

"I have enemies," Markovich said bluntly.

Rowe stopped. "Yeah?"

"*Yeah,* as you say. There is a man named Nicholas Polen. Nick Polen. He and I were friends once. We both showed beagles, but we had an unspoken agreement that I could have the United States, and he could have the rest of the world. He's a Pole living in Montreal. It worked well, until we both happened to fall in love with the same woman. Dreadful coincidence. She favored me. He challenged me to a duel. His Polish blood, you know. It was supposed to have been to the death. Should have been, anyway. We were almost middle-aged men by that time."

"Pistols?" asked Rowe, his pulse quickening, an enjoyable ripple in his veins.

"Knives."

"Knives? Not swords?"

"Daggers. Fighting knives."

Rowe went silent with interest. The old dude had taken all this time to get to the good part.

"Well," Markovich continued, "I won. I trained up for it, and you may be aware that back in '44 I was awarded—"

"The Distinguished Service Cross for taking out a dozen Nazis with a bayonet and the butt of your empty M1."

"Oh, so you did do a little homework on me."

"You made it possible for your company to regroup and capture more than forty enemy soldiers. What happened in the duel?"

"Nick Polen drew first blood, but I drew best. I got him in the chest, and he fell, and I thought that was the end of it. The man was dead—I saw the life leave his eyes—and I walked away immediately, which is what you do. But they revived him. He'd stashed a small field hospital in a corner of the neutral property we'd agreed to meet on—a game park in Virginia. Just in case! Can you imagine that? Hidden in a copse of trees. I had no idea. They brought him back. Still, that should have been the end of it, you know."

"Did you get the girl?"

"I did. We were married for thirty-six years."

"That's a good thing," said Rowe.

"She died of a heart attack last spring."

"I'm sorry, Colonel."

Markovich laced his fingers and looked at them, then unlaced them. His hands were as clean and straight as the rest of him, with coarse white hairs on the backs. He looked up. "I'm quite certain Nick Polen took Ernest."

"Why would he do that?"

"He's never forgiven me for besting him."

"Well, why would he bother you now, after all these years?"

"It's more than trying to get back at me, especially now that Emily's gone. He's fallen on hard times. Beagles are all he knows. And he knows them, believe me. Polen's a well-connected man, but he's made some major blunders on the dog circuit. Some litigation, some things went against him."

"As in . . . ?"

"He was accused of bribing a show judge."

"He got nailed?"

"No, he tapped himself out defending against it, and he beat it, but he never collected costs. I had nothing to do with that one. He's carried a grudge against me all these years. Here's his plan, I'm sure of it. He's got an outstanding beagle stud named Rondo, about the same age as Ernest. He's put by some of Rondo's semen, but it's a finite resource, you understand. Rumor has it Rondo's got cancer and isn't long for this world. Polen's plan is to disguise Ernest as Rondo, claim a cure, and go on breeding him. I just know it. If he plays it right, he could make good money, set himself up for some new venture. He's a bit younger than me, still in his seventies. I'm eighty-six."

"Hm," said Rowe. "Do you have any evidence of—"

"You wouldn't believe the intrigue in the show-dog world. I miss it terribly. But it wasn't good for my heart. Are you a military man yourself, by any chance? You look like you might have been."

"No," said Rowe. "Private security, corrections. Then insurance investigation, as you know."

"You keep yourself fit."

"Try to."

Rowe, though not tall, was built well, with sloping shoulders and a flat stomach. He wore his cinnamon hair in a crew cut and he favored short-sleeved shirts and leather shoes when on the job. He liked to wear nondescript clothing, it paid off so often. But he took pride in his body, running and lifting weights a few times a week. He liked morning calisthenics, and had followed the fitness routine of the Royal Canadian Air Force for years, after picking up a paperback book on it in high school.

"But what about DNA?" he asked. "Wouldn't—"

"Yes, there's DNA profiling. The AKC requires it if a dog is used more than a few times. But somebody's suspicions would have to be raised for a good reason, because you can tell pretty quickly when the puppies are young whether they're from good stock or not. Polen would simply breed Ernest—as Rondo—with a spay/neuter agreement, meaning that his progeny wouldn't be allowed to breed, therefore would never need to be DNA profiled. He can sell his own spayed or neutered puppies for a thousand dollars apiece. When you think about it, it's really the perfect dog crime."

Rowe considered. "What about ransom? Has he been in touch with you?"

"No, but I expect he might make contact. I've been reading the classifieds in case he's trying to send me an anonymous message."

Rowe searched the Colonel's eyes. The man returned his gaze with depth and calmness. "Mr. Rowe," he said, "there are many scenes out there. Most dog people are timid about breaking the law, though they'll do many things just short of it. And they're very credulous. Well, people in general are credulous. They want to believe they're special, they want to believe they're sharp, they want to believe there's a great deal waiting for them in the hands of a handsome stranger."

"Yes," said Rowe. "Is Ernest insured?"

"No."

"How much is he worth?"

"Hard to say. In the States I could sell him for perhaps twenty thousand dollars, tops. But I could likely get much more than that if I were to sell him overseas. Upwards of a hundred, I'm sure, especially in Japan, they're mad for champion show dogs. The Chinese now too."

"OK," said Rowe.

"Let me show you one more thing." Markovich took the private investigator outside. They walked across the plush green lawn. Rowe saw an empty fenced kennel, a doggie shower and outdoor grooming table, the table nicely carpeted, all beneath the shady branches of an arbutus tree. A chew ball lay sadly next to a root.

Rowe asked, "Is Ernest your only dog these days?"

"Yes, I sold off my other animals. I do miss the excitement of showing, but I'm just too old for it now. Six years ago a mastiff nudged me at a show, and I fell and broke my hip. Oh, the champions I've bred. I don't need any more money. Once in a while I breed Ernest, but only for someone special—for an old friend or two." The colonel mused, "Why not rob a bank, why not take candy from a baby if candy's what you want? If dogs are all you know, you're going to look for a way out of your troubles via dogs." They walked all the way to a vine-covered fence at the edge of the property. It was a white board fence with peaked finials on the posts, about eight feet high, Rowe judged. Jasmine vines crept over it, helped every so often by narrow trellises. Rowe saw a slab of unpainted plywood about two feet square nailed into the fence at ground level.

"That's where they cut their way in," said Markovich. "I had my gardener fix it like this until the fence man can come and repair it properly."

"Did it happen at night?" Rowe asked.

"Oh, no, Ernest sleeps indoors. This happened in broad daylight, when I let him out that afternoon. Polen must have lured him out with a piece of steak."

Rowe looked at the fence.

"I found meat scraps on the other side," Markovich added. "I'd give anything to get him back."

"If I find where he is, you won't have to pay ransom," said Rowe.

"Does that mean you'll take the case? I don't care about recovering any frozen semen that might have been collected from him. I just want Ernest. I'll pay your expenses and whatever your usual fee is. Plus a hundred thousand dollars extra if you bring Ernest home."

Rowe looked at the old man, the breeze riffling his white hair like the crest of a proud stork. He thought about the twelve dead Nazis and the knife-blade duel and the international world of purebred animals. And he thought about a hundred grand.

"I'll take the case."

THREE

"Hold still now." The emergency room doctor injected my left upper arm with anesthetic as I lay watching. Needles have never bothered me. She told me she was a resident specializing in trauma. "Never been shot before, have you?"

The outside of my biceps, more or less, was where my skin lay open in a diagonal line about four inches long, like half of a sergeant's chevron. The doctor was injecting lidocaine around its edges. The bleeding had slowed way down; the paramedics had bandaged it snugly for the ride in. It hurt like a large cut. I hadn't really needed to ride in an ambulance, I thought. Looking down, I realized that the skin along the projectile's path had been sort of vaporized along the way. Still, it didn't look all that bad.

"Well," I said, "this is hardly a *bullet wound,* I mean, it's just a—"

"You got creased. It is a wound and it was made by a bullet, so you might as well make the most of it." She wore black plastic Buddy Holly glasses and pink lip gloss. She pressed the syringe's plunger steadily.

"Come to think of it," I remarked, "my little boy would be very impressed. But I don't think I ought to tell him that a bad man shot Mommy."

"Oh, tell him! He'll think you're invincible for the rest of his life."

I thought of Petey, his five-year-old face and his wise eyes.

It was good to be off the hot, dirty street.

The doc reached for another syringe. The linens on the gurney and the gown they'd given me to cover my breasts smelled clean and cool.

I asked, "Is the young man who came in with me going to make it?"

"He's in surgery now, that's all I know."

She stepped out to let the anesthetic work, and a police detective came in to talk with me. The responding cops had questioned me quickly at the scene, but this detective, named Herrera, wanted to go over things more thoroughly.

"Ms. Farmer, we know you're not a real police officer." He smiled.

"Right, I never said I was."

"So the uniform?"

"I told the first cops, I—"

"Tell me, please."

This young detective wore his close-nipped black hair spiked down in front. His nose was flattened at the bridge and bulbous on the end, as if he'd been quite the brawler before giving in and joining the Academy.

24

"I'm an extra in a movie, we're shooting on Eighth Street by the river."

"What's the name of the movie?"

"The Canary Syndrome."

"What's it about?"

"Oh, global warming and globalization and probably gamma globulin, I don't know. I haven't seen the whole script, only like a page. There were a bunch of us fake cops. Plus all these angry protesters. Of course, there were real cops there as well, you guys always have to be on hand when a street's blocked off. So you should have some information from—"

"Yes, I know," interrupted Detective Herrera. "And what were you doing way up on Mateo from there?"

"Uh, well, there was this roach, you see." Suddenly I felt lightheaded. "This cockroach, because I think the budget for this one was a little *too* stingy, and this bug crawled right onto my ham, and I threw away the whole ciabatta. And I was so darn hungry. And, uh, then this little girl—"

"Back up. Where did you get the uniform?" His questions sounded harsh but his voice was not.

"From wardrobe. The wardrobe people. You can see it's fake, I'm sure, plus my fake gun and all that. Wherever it is." I realized the equipment belt had been taken off me, and I only had on the uniform pants.

"You know you're supposed to turn in your gun to props before leaving the set for any reason. What happened?"

"I forgot!"

I don't know if he was practicing interrogation techniques or what. His eyes kept moving over my face and hair and my covered-up chest. I began to doubt, however, if I ever would've convinced

25

him that I was a paid performer in cop garb, not some scammer impersonating a cop for nefarious reasons. But a uniformed officer stuck his head in and told him two of the movie guys had followed the ambulance and wanted to talk to him.

"Tell them to come in here."

I said, "I don't think that's a good—"

But there they were, crowding in, big fine Sylvan and little tweaky Stuart, the first AD. Sylvan gave me a wide smile and, after taking one glance at my arm, avoided looking at it. Stuart stared at it and turned gray.

"She's bleeding!"

"I'm OK, Stuart. Thank you for coming. Thanks, Sylvan."

"But aren't they going to *help* her?" Stuart's whole body trembled with empathy. If you can imagine a mutation between Peter Pan and Sylvia Plath, you've got Stuart.

Detective Herrera said, "They are helping her. Monday afternoons usually aren't too busy here."

"Where's a doctor?" Stuart's voice rose uncontrollably. "Get this person a *doctor*, for God's sake!"

Sylvan grasped him under the armpit in case he fainted. "Man up here, buddy. Come on. Deep breath here, buddy." Stuart clutched a sweaty sheaf of papers.

I told them, "The doctor'll be back in to sew me up in a jiffy." Brave smile.

Detective Herrera said to Stuart, "So she works for you?"

"Yes."

"As what?"

Sylvan prompted, "You have her on the list."

"Oh, yeah, here." Stuart unscrolled the damp papers and jabbed at my name with a shaking finger.

"And did she," asked the detective, stealing another look at my chest, tented over though it was, "have your authorization to leave the set in the uniform of the LAPD?"

"Uh," Stuart looked up at Sylvan like a mixed-up kid, afraid to say the wrong thing.

I spoke up. "It was my fault. I should have either stayed on set, or gotten out of costume before taking off to hunt for edible food."

"What?" said Stuart.

"There was a roach in my sandwich."

Sylvan threw back his head and laughed. He had a great laugh.

"You're kidding," said Stuart.

"No, there was."

Stuart slumped against Sylvan. "Oh, the liability!" he wailed. "I hope those bastards have insurance."

"You guys can go," said Detective Herrera.

"I'll drop off Stuart and come back to wait for you," said Sylvan.

They went out past a couple of badges idling in the curtained passage. Herrera told the cops something, and one of them said, "When I saw her standing there bleeding, I thought it was Annette. I swear to God, she looks exactly like her."

"She does," agreed Herrera.

"Who's Annette?" I asked, but they didn't hear me.

Then the other one said something about the kid being in surgery. Herrera said his name, Kip Cubitt.

"Cubitt?" I called from my table. "Is he related to Amaryllis B. Cubitt?"

Herrera stuck his head back in. "He's her grandson."

All of Los Angeles knew and respected Amaryllis B. Cubitt,

founder of the ABC Mission in South Central. Using volunteers and donations and her own two hands, she helped needy people and unwed teen mothers of all colors. Angelenos listened to her brisk contralto voice on the radio, where she gave ass-kicking advice for free. "You're paying a cable bill and you don't have money to feed your kids? Wait on that!"

She went by the fullness of Amaryllis B. Cubitt, which, besides the satisfying ABC of it, just seemed to fit, like Susan B. Anthony or William Jennings Bryan.

Politicians loved getting their picture taken with her. Movie stars especially adored her, I believe because they crave authenticity above all: an antidote to their tendency to overdose on their craft. Some of them adopted the ABC as a pet charity—excellent for publicity. The actors and actresses came and went, of course, while Amaryllis soldiered on consistently. The mission held generic Christian services on Sundays. Which the movie stars tended to avoid.

The doctor returned and nudged over a rolling stool with her foot. She settled herself and began to flush my wound with saline solution out of a squirt-gunny instrument. "Does that hurt?"

"No."

A nurse came in, saying, "I can give you a hand."

"Thanks, Lourdes," said the doctor.

So the nurse assisted, dabbing gauze and so on. Nurses in the movies dab their gauze daintily, as if they're afraid to hurt the person, but real ones dab it pretty firmly, I can tell you. The doctor breathed evenly as she worked, her eyes quick behind her glasses.

Detective Herrera came back. "You have a very protective friend out there." He smiled, amused. He was good-looking with that tough-guy nose, but I didn't have the energy.

I said, "You mean Sylvan?"

"Yes."

"He's a good man."

"The other one seemed pretty traumatized."

"Oh, yeah, Stuart. He has a delicate constitution."

Herrera laughed.

Feeling steadier, I told him about my quest for a reasonably sanitary lunch, the boy on the sidewalk, the thugs and the two-by-four.

"I didn't see their faces at all, unfortunately, what with the sweatshirt hoods."

He asked about their height and weight, and I did the best I could, remembering the one to be short and thick-butted, the other much taller, maybe six feet, and thin.

"How do you know they were guys?"

"I don't, I just got that impression. I can't even tell you their race. Or races."

"Did you see their hands?"

"Now that I think of it, they were wearing gloves. Yeah, like work gloves, leather work gloves. The heavier one's sweatshirt was black with a white graphic on the front."

Herrera took notes. "See any lettering?"

"No, I don't remember, it was so fast. The other one's sweatshirt was plain gray."

"Pants?"

"Uh, blue jeans on the big-butt, and different pants on the tall one, maybe brown or black? I don't remember."

"OK."

"Shoes?"

"Sneakers, I think. Yeah, sneakers, mostly white. I don't know what kind."

"Clean or dirty?"

"Clean."

"Go on with what happened."

"Well, it was like my maternal instinct kicked in or something—"

"You're a mother?"

"Yes, I have a five-year-old son, but I still get carded all the time. So yeah, I just yelled for them to drop it, and to my amazement, they did. I forgot about my costume. They took off running towards downtown on Mateo."

His cell phone rang. He flipped it open. "Yeah." He wanted me to hear him sounding tough and casual. "No," he said curtly. "I've only been here for"—he thrust out his arm and checked his watch—"twenty minutes. Can't somebody—"

He listened. "OK, I'll find out, but then I'm going to come back and finish this interview with the female."

He shut the phone. "Take your time," he said to the doctor. "Don't let her go anywhere, I'll be right back."

The doctor felt inside my wound with a gloved finger. All I felt was pressure. She said, "He likes you."

The nurse put in, "They like all the cute gunshot victims." She was fortyish and fairly pert.

The doctor used a forceps and a scalpel to cut away little bits of mashed skin. Competence radiated out of her. I watched without getting queasy, which made me proud.

One time I had, in utter desperation, turned to the ABC Mission. It was about two years ago, when Petey's and my chips were seriously down. Amaryllis B. Cubitt herself paid off my electric bill and then handed me a ten-dollar McDonald's card. Walking into that mission I felt like the lowest piece of crap ever to stumble the earth, but Amaryllis grabbed me by the scruff, as it were, and snapped me out of it.

"Don't be scared," she told me after listening to my angst. "You can come back if you need to. But judging by you," she laughed, "you aren't going to want to need to."

I looked at her.

She said, "I predict you're gonna get that commercial you just auditioned for. Either that, or I predict you're gonna go out and get a job waiting tables so PG&E doesn't ever again turn the lights out on you and your child. I also predict you're gonna get with DCSS and collect that child support you're owed."

"I intend to pay this back," I'd told her.

"Hmp," she growled skeptically. "Well, sister, I'll go ahead and predict you will."

It was that kind of clairvoyance that commanded the respect of the city.

On that occasion, I'd felt a resonance with this tall, beautiful, arresting woman. Not love, exactly, maybe not even affection, since her hard-assedness verged on belligerence, but something deep.

And I had, in fact, made a point of paying the money back, plus extra.

The doctor began to stitch inside the wound, and at this point I looked away. "You have to put stitches down inside?"

"Yes, I'm pulling together the fascia first, that's the sheathing around the muscle."

"I want to say *ow* but I don't really feel anything. Just, like, pulling."

"Good."

For the first time, I thought about how my arm would look later on. I asked, "Should I be worried about a big old scar? Will children at the beach scream and run from me?"

The doctor smiled. "You'll have a scar, but it should be quite a thin line, if you let it heal well. Do you model too?"

"A little, but I'm getting out of the whole business. Going to law school."

"Oh. Well, I suppose we could still call in one of the plastic fellows for a consult, if you're highly concerned about a scar."

"I don't know if it's that important to me."

"Do you have good insurance?"

"No."

"I'd forget it, then."

"OK."

"Your wound is fairly uncomplicated. I think you'll be pleased."

"OK."

She pulled each stitch carefully. I felt the tugging in a general, dull way. It was nice to just lie there and have someone take care of me.

I thought about Amaryllis's radio show. Whenever I caught a few minutes of it I'd remember how she'd made me feel: so much less like a loser, without even referring to God. You'd listen to her call-in program on Saturday mornings for the hell of it, for the pure entertainment of it. She was an anti–bleeding heart, which is to say she didn't pity the people she helped. Neither pitied them nor bought their bullshit.

"Well, you see," some sad sack would try to explain, "I can't work because I can't be away from my kids."

"That's a good excuse," Amaryllis would say breezily, "and you've used it for a long time, haven't you?"

"Well . . ."

"So long that you've even got yourself believing it. Let me assure you, you're the *only* one who *still* believes it. You got to get so you want that steady paycheck more than you want a knuckle-headed excuse. That's all."

She certainly was a fresh gust blowing through the shrillness of the city's cult-of-victimhood advocates who'd never gone a day without food in their lives.

"You come see me tomorrow if you decide to get serious, and I'll help you with the next step. I'll be able to tell right away if you're not serious, so don't waste my time, OK, sugar?"

The doctor began stitching my skin. The feeling of tugging got sharper. My stomach jumped and I took a deep breath.

The doctor stopped. "You OK?"

"Yeah."

She recommenced her sewing.

Detective Herrera came back, and I described the bullets popping out at the boy and me from the derelict sedan in the middle of the day.

"It was like a horrible dream, the way the car just slid over to the curb like a big fish and then these shots."

He questioned me closely about the shooters and the car. Again, I hadn't seen any faces. The car was an old Buick, I thought, in a crapped-out beige, and I had not seen the license plates. "Except I think they were California, that's just my impression. There was a driver, and somebody else in the backseat, but I don't know if they were the only people in the car."

As he questioned me, Herrera leaned in closer and closer. He wore a navy blue suit and a crisp white shirt, and I saw that his cuff links were brass discs stamped .45 ACP. Ammo-links.

At this point the doctor stopped and, continuing to breathe patiently, turned and looked at him over the tops of her glasses. She said in a nice voice, "You're interfering with my work."

Most people would back off, but this detective ignored her and told me, "We have a book of cars we'll show you when you come into the station. Can you come right after this?"

"Uh, I think so. You know, when the boy—"

The doctor interrupted, "Please lie still. Can you guys continue this interview later?" She sighed just the slightest, and bit her upper lip, and the nurse looked tense.

Herrera, irritated, said, "Fine. But let me ask you, can you tell about what caliber bullet that was?"

The doctor relaxed a little. "I can tell you it was a low-velocity civilian handgun load." She blinked and looked up at him.

"You mean like a twenty-two?"

"Or possibly a thirty-eight, but no bigger."

"How can you tell?"

"Anything bigger would have torn up her arm much worse. This is more like a simple laceration. I had to debride very little out of there." She turned back to me. "By the way, have you had a tetanus shot in the last five years?"

"No, I don't think so."

"Lourdes, order up one, OK?"

"Got it."

"Thanks," said the detective. He stalked out.

He left before I told him what Kip Cubitt said to me before he slipped into unconsciousness. I did not call him back to hear it, because suddenly I decided not to tell him. I guess it was wrong of me; the message could be terribly significant to the investigation. But I wanted to deliver my message to Amaryllis myself first.

As the doctor finished her work, I laid there and thought some more about Amaryllis.

People called her the Iron Angel, and invariably, the politically correct hand-wringers criticized her for being too tough. She'd give an individual help once or twice, say with drying out or getting a job, but if the person backslid more than once, that'd be the end of it. No more services, except for basic handouts like food and a cot in the shelter at night. She'd never see anyone starve.

Amaryllis defended herself against critics by simply saying, "There's too many folks need help, in line right behind that fool. There's no end to fools out there, but there's only one ABC Mission. Plenty of folks right behind who want to try harder." I always felt it had more to do with her belief in an individual. If you betrayed that belief, she took it personally.

She avoided government grant money, because she didn't want to answer to government regulations. Any donations that came her way—and there were many, every day—had to be made with no strings attached.

The ER doctor swiped up with a last pad of gauze, and told me she'd put in four stitches beneath the skin and eight on the outside.

"Wow, they're pretty widely spaced," I noted.

She explained, "I put in as few stitches as I could, because with a wound like this there's always a risk of infection. The less I put in there the better."

"I see."

She wrapped a soft bandage around my arm and taped it. "Keep it dry for two weeks until the stitches come out. See your family practitioner for that, OK? I'll write you a prescription for a pain reliever. And here's Lourdes with a tetanus booster for your other arm, so at least the pain will be symmetrical!"

I had felt drawn toward the Iron Angel, and after she helped me out, I'd half wished she and I could somehow become friends. Now I had a reason to go and see her.

FOUR

George Rowe walked down a spur of Eighth Street near the Los Angeles River. *River* seemed such an overstatement in this case. The watercourse was an over-engineered trickle most of the time, becoming an actual rolling, bounding main only during winter floods. Then it was not only capable of floating a skiff, but tearing up a full-grown tree if one happened to topple in.

Rowe went to the place *The Canary Syndrome* riot scene had been shot two days ago. It was Wednesday morning, and the sun was cutting through the midweek smog like a dull knife. He walked around, hearing his footfalls echo off the office building, noticing the chalk placemarks on the pavement where the actors and equipment had been. He looked up at the building, its windows clean and blank.

He walked west on Eighth and then turned right on Mateo, looking carefully at the buildings and the traffic and the people.

The bus station was around here somewhere. You get a lot of scuzz around bus stations, then there was Skid Row a few blocks northwest.

He found the grocery store across the street from where Rita and the young kid had been shot.

George Rowe was in love with Rita Farmer.

Not that she was in love with him.

He speculated she might be, but she insisted she wasn't. They had dated, and she'd broken it off, though she'd agreed to a minimalistic sort of relationship: they could keep in touch. And they did, by phone. She seemed to enjoy their friendly talks.

When she'd called last night to tell him what had happened, his guts almost fell out.

He crossed the street. Blood was easily visible on the pavement. No one had washed the sidewalk there, because the business that fronted it, a hairstyling school, was vacant. A small sign said, WE WILL MAKE YOU LOOK BEAUTEOUS. TEACHING HAIRCUTS $10. Nobody's business to clean up this blood.

Rowe squatted and looked at the sun-browned blood, now almost forty-eight hours old. Scattered around were scraps of bloody gauze and tubing the EMTs had left behind. The largest puddle of blood had flowed toward the curb—there had been enough of it to flow, not just spatter—in an accidental pattern that looked like a crown. The crown of the inner city, Rowe thought. He could smell the iron in it.

He turned toward the grocery store.

"THAT LOOKS LIKE a nice one," said Petey from the backseat of our lousy-but-still-running Honda Civic. I knew he was pointing even though I couldn't see his arm, him being secure in his car seat.

"Um-hm," I murmured noncommittally. This was the fourth day on the dog thing.

"You know how come I want a dog?" his little voice piped. "I'm bored."

Children need to be taught the concept *bored,* did you know that? They are born without the slightest clue of boredom. Some beastly little friend must have introduced him to the word.

I glanced to the side and saw a yellowish Chewbacca-looking thing lift its leg and pee on a spindly tree on Franklin Street. Pity urban trees everywhere, their trunks struggling to breathe under ceaseless showers of dog urine.

"Honey," I said, "I'll try and help you not be bored."

"A dog would be someone to do stuff with."

He'd started discussing this last weekend, and I feared an obsession was brewing.

"You have me," I reminded him. "You have your little guy and gal friends. You have Daniel, who's going to take you to swimming lessons this morning."

"But a dog would be with me all the time. Any time I want to do something, my dog'll be right there. We'd do so much stuff?"

"Well, honey, we're not getting a dog now. They're not allowed where we live."

"Let's move! Let's go live with Daniel!"

"No, honey."

"Well, I could really use a dog."

What you could really use is a dad. Well, Jeff was trying. Staying sober. Though he was still a careless asshole, living in an apartment in Torrance.

Petey had developed the idea, perfectly reasonable to him, that my best friend Daniel and I should get married. Great, except Daniel was looking for a steady *guy*. It was fun to compare notes on guys, and lucky that we went for different types.

It was now two days after the shooting. When Petey had asked about my bandage, I told him I'd been walking through the forest and a stick fell on me.

To Daniel I feigned nonchalance about having been grazed in a drive-by shooting in L.A. But I was damn freaked. Daniel was suitably aghast, and more concerned with me coming down with post-traumatic stress disorder than any future danger.

I'd lived in L.A. for years and walked down tough streets before. I'd been stuck on roadsides at night with flat tires (twice). I'd done wash in coin laundries a little tipsy at one in the morning. Never any trouble except stares and an unsavory remark or two.

Obviously the would-be killers had targeted Kip Cubitt. But what if—somehow, somewhere—they decided to come back for me, the only witness?

When I told my former boyfriend George about it, I could tell it frightened him too. He went quiet, then said he had to go.

"Don't do anything, George, OK?"

"I might look around, is all."

I dropped off Petey and drove across town and down—way down—toward the ABC Mission.

FIVE

A long the way, I thought about George, and the direction of my life.

There is true love, and there is false love, and running between the two is a *lot* of road. Then you throw in sex.

I don't consider myself a highly sexed person, but I'd turned thirty this year (prolonged scream of agony) and I knew about women losing their minds around this time, because our hormones are pumping fast and free. That last surge before premenopausal deceleration.

I thought about George Rowe a lot. We'd gone out for a few months, and I knew he was smitten. I enjoyed him, deeply, but I needed time to decide if he was really the one. Moreover, I couldn't devote as much of myself to the process—to *him*—as I felt he deserved, between Petey and law school and what acting work I could scrounge on the side. I believed then that I was finished with acting, except as it could help me get through law school.

I cared for George, and I admired him. He was straightforward, and rugged for real. A while back I'd dated a guy who tried to appear rugged by wearing safari shirts and a stubble, but all he did was whine about drafts and his diet. George, by contrast, wore ordinary grown-up clothing, shaved daily, and had once quelled a prison riot by walking up to a crazed inmate and grabbing a loaded shotgun away from him. And when a scorpion crawled onto Petey's backpack during a picnic in the Santa Susanas, he flicked it off with his bare hand. (Needless to say, Petey thought he was Jesus.) And oh yes, he had saved my life on an earlier occasion using a slingshot and raw cunning.

This is not the kind of man you take lightly.

What about sex? The thought of him could stir me almost any time of day, yet we are not all rational creatures when it comes to romance. He wanted, ultimately, to marry me. But being divorced from a guy I'd initially thought was perfect in every way, I hyperventilated just thinking about using the words *I* and *do* in the same sentence. Married at nineteen, a divorced single mom at twenty-six—that's a heavy trip.

I knew I ought to marry George, any idiot could see that, yet I couldn't commit. I just could not promise him. I was desperate to feel sure about some things. And I didn't know if I could ever completely trust a man again.

Since it wasn't fair to keep him waiting, I felt I had to take the risk of him being free for the time being.

I'd started in at UCLA's law school last year, amazingly having hammered the LSAT, helped by some great coaching by a lawyer on staff at the Los Angeles District Attorney's office (another story, another time).

I fully expected to have to wait a year to receive serious consideration, but I put in a late application for the hell of it. In terms of getting what you want, any university's such a bureaucracy, the closest things we have in America to communist-bloc countries— good old communist bloc. But somehow I vaulted over a raft of poor slobs on the fall wait list and got in.

I liked law school, and I got good grades that first year. But I didn't know then how critically important acting would again become in my life, and how soon.

AMARYLLIS B. CUBITT was baking bread. As soon as I, ushered by a female security guard named Wichita, walked into the mission's institutional kitchen, she dismissed her two floury helpers who had just turned an Everest-sized mass of dough onto a worktable.

She'd barely slept for two nights, but she was there, at eight in the morning. Her tall body was in a posture of emotional pain— a sort of writhe held to one side. But even the terrible calamity of her grandson taking two bullets, lying in the ICU, did not stop her from working at her mission. She had stayed at Kip's bedside until early this morning, when the boy's aunt and uncle had come in from Phoenix. They were sitting vigil now. Kip's mom and dad were, evidently, not in the picture.

"The daily bread must go on," she explained. "Nine in the morning's awful late to be starting on it, but my main baker called in sick."

The smell of young dough, tangy with yeast, was a comfort in that spotless, hard-lit kitchen. A commercial mixer hummed in one corner, its dough hook laboring in the tub.

Amaryllis was legendary for her perpetual motion: she'd give newspaper interviews while cleaning a row of sinks, hold meetings while sorting through clothing or even sweeping corridors.

She paused only to face me fully, wipe her hands on her apron, and shake my extended hand with a firm grip as I said my name. Her face was long and squared-off, with high cheekbones and a nose more beaked than broad. Native American blood, maybe Cajun. I remembered her eyes so well: inky-black and keen.

"Thank you for coming to see me, Rita Farmer." She pursed her lips as if trying to place me. "Wichita said you wanted to talk to me about what happened on Monday."

"Yes."

"Can you make biscuits?"

"Yes."

I watched her clip off a hamster-sized chunk of dough with the edge of her hand, lay it on a baking sheet, and press three fingers in to make it more or less uniformly thick. "Easier than rolling and cutting," she explained.

I joined in at her side, my fingers chopping dough from the mass on the table. Like pioneer women with fifteen more things to do before lunch, we worked fast. We laid out the biscuits in rows on long baking sheets. The work didn't really bother the stitches in my arm.

I asked how Kip was today.

"He's gonna make it, the doctors say."

"Will he . . . be OK?"

Quickly, through tight lips, she said, "He might be paralyzed. They don't know yet. You pray for him, OK?"

"OK." Not that I was much of a praying woman, but you don't explain things like that every time.

"I wish I could have saved Kip from getting shot," I began.

"The police say you broke up a fight he was in."

"I couldn't call it a fight. He was being attacked by two guys with a hunk of lumber. I was in a police costume from a movie I was working on a few blocks away. Those guys ran, then the car came and the shooting happened. I didn't get a look at who was in the car."

"It hardly matters, sister, it hardly matters. Just another testosterone-soaked day on the streets."

"Well, I wanted you to know your grandson wasn't doing any violence."

I don't know what it was, but the whole environment of the mission felt different to me this time. The guard, this woman named Wichita who had taken me to Amaryllis, was a hefty type who'd barely mumbled to me. Her hair was an unsettling greenish-bronze color, either a self-dye job that went wrong, or just a bad choice at the salon. Wearing a gray T-shirt with SECURITY lettered in red, she looked aggressive and a little insecure—a bad combination for a security guard, I thought, and definitely a bad combination for that part of town. And what was that part of town? Due south of the financial district by five miles and half a world: South Central, on Compton near the tracks and Slauson.

Bums had been sitting lethargically on the steps outside.

Even the energy in the lobby had felt different. People were still greeting each other "brother" and "sister," and saying Amen to everything in an active-listening way, and the schedule blackboard was crowded with writing, and there were the signs saying ZERO TOLERANCE FOR GUNS, DRUGS, ALCOHOL, AND TOBACCO. ONE HUNDRED PERCENT TOLERANCE FOR LOVE.

But there was—I don't know, an *ulterior* feeling to the place.

Amaryllis said, "They said you probably stopped him from bleeding out."

"Uh, I just used direct pressure until the EMTs came."

"Right there on the street."

"I hope Kip has a lot of life ahead of him." Our hands flew as we kept making biscuits.

"I thank you for coming to his aid."

"You're welcome."

I held back, for a few minutes more. "Do you remember that you helped me once? About two years ago."

She paused mid-dough-clip and looked at me again. We stood there holding our dough chunks. She was so tall—close to six feet, I'd say, and not lissome. Large joints, long bones, enough meat on them to enable her to sling around fifty-pound bags of sugar and flour. Beneath her apron she wore a white cotton blouse with lemon polka dots and a skirt that looked like it'd been cut from a canvas sail. She wore no jewelry at all. Beneath her gray-streaked natural, her brow bunched and her eyes sharpened in on me.

"Yes," she said at last. "PG&E bill. Yeah." Her eyes relaxed. "Actress. Commercials. Son named . . . Peter."

"Wow."

"I remember advising you to start a shoe fund."

I laughed. "You were right."

"Because," with an edge of grimness, "the feet's the last thing to stop growing."

"He's only five now."

"You're in for it, then."

We laid raw biscuit after raw biscuit on the rolled metal sheets. "Amaryllis, I'm very grateful to you for that day."

"You thanked me then, and you thanked me another time approximately one year later when you sent a letter and a check. You are thanked out."

"I'm in law school."

"Ha! Then you must be broke again." This with a wide smile. One of her upper side teeth was capped with gold. When it flashed it reminded me of my Gramma Gladys, who'd had a gold one up there.

"Fall term starts next month, my second year. Money's tight all right," I admitted, "but I'm not broke. You know how it is. When I said I'm grateful, I meant—I was very moved by you. Not just by your generosity. But by you as a person."

Amaryllis said nothing.

I went on, "I'd like to think Kip inherited that quality from you."

"Mm." Her eyes were far away.

"Do you have any idea who was after him?"

She heaved an impatient sigh. "Sister, the police asked me all that. Things happen in this life nobody can't explain."

"But—you'd like those people to be caught, right? When Kip gets better, maybe he'll be able to help the police."

"Sure," she said halfheartedly, and with an inflection that verged on irritation.

Did her indifference come from an ingrained skepticism about the justice system? Yet she seemed like such a play-by-the-rules person.

We worked some more. I asked, "Do you hire your security guards from outside?"

"No, we couldn't pay enough for that. Uniforms, benefits. *Benefits,*" she said contemptuously. "Our staff are folks who come here for help, then want to stay and work."

We had shaped about three hundred biscuits, covering all six long baking sheets. I opened the oven and Amaryllis rammed home the biscuits. "Shut that thing before the temperature kills us both." She punched a timer.

The way she stood there as she rested, shoulders down, eyes veiled, she was giving off the blues all over the place.

I leaned against the worktable. "Amaryllis, I'd like to help you. I know you have lots of volunteers, but is there anything I could do for you or Kip personally?"

Maybe she was unaccustomed to offers like that. After looking at the floor a long moment, she said, "No, honey."

"You seem troubled," I said bluntly.

She stared at me in surprise.

I added, groping, "Above and beyond what's currently going on."

She poured out a long breath. I waited. Her silence told me I was right about something. "Oh, sister," she said, "maybe we're finished talking. Is there anything else you want to tell me?"

Suddenly I wondered: "Are you mad I saved him?"

She opened her mouth but stood mute, considering what to say. Then, "You're asking me would I rather he be dead than impaired?"

"I wondered that just now."

"No, sister. I rejoice in Kip's life no matter what he is, no matter what he does. It's that—" She stopped, looking at the floor again. Wisps of flour lay like miniature snowdrifts along the hard gray tile. "It's just that there's no end to the grieving and the fear for your boys." She looked at me closely. "Are you holding something back from me?"

"Kip wanted me to tell you something."

She braced herself. "Go ahead."

"After they shot him, he said, 'Tell my grandmother I'm sorry.' "

Amaryllis cleared her throat and bowed her head. Her hands clenched. Then she lifted her head, fiery eyes not seeing me or the clean, productive kitchen. Her stare burned all the way through the ceiling tiles, through the floor above, and however many more floors of offices or whatever, all the way into the summer California sky, all the way up beyond that.

"You promised!" she shouted to God. "You promised. Praise, all right. Praise to you." Her tone fell. "But he's not the one who let us down."

Silently, I said an Our Father for Kip. In spite of this drama, I felt relief: I had done what I'd come to do. I should go now.

But I wanted to stay.

I waited patiently, quietly, then asked, "What did Kip mean?"

Amaryllis swallowed and came back to the kitchen. "Sometimes men like to trick the young ones. Like to get them in a corner. So many stunts, so much fear."

"What are you talking about?"

She shook her head.

I said, "You raised Kip?"

"From the age of five. His mother died at the time." She kept shaking her head.

I thought of Petey. Age five. I couldn't imagine him doing without me. But of course he would. My aunts back home would take him in. He'd go to Wisconsin and become a little cheese-head.

"Violence?" I asked. "Or—"

"Brain hemorrhage. No good reason, just one of those things. Natural you might ask that."

"I'm sorry. Was she your daughter?"

"No, my son Nathan Cubitt is Kip's father. Prison," she said in answer to my questioning look.

"Oh."

"Sister, what do you care?"

I was not put off by this roughness. "Amaryllis, I held your grandson in my arms. Our blood fell together in that street. I care."

"You mean you're curious."

"Sure I am. Is Nathan in for—good?"

"Oh, he's not a lifer. No, he ought to be out by New Year's, anyway. He pulled ten months for getting drunk at his own birth-day party." She stopped, waiting for me to give her the straight line.

Which I supplied. "Well, a man's got a right to get drunk on his birthday, doesn't he?"

"Except he got into his car and drove three blocks until a parked police cruiser got in his way."

"Oh, my."

"Totaled both cars, no one hurt, but the police—"

"Went and got all sore?"

She smiled sideways. "Amen. He wanted me to come get him out, you know."

My memory cells began firing. Something about this had made the papers, or else Amaryllis might have mentioned it on her radio show. "But you wouldn't post bail?"

50

Having rested enough, she now went over to the commercial mixer in the corner, peered at the dough, then flipped off the switch. "These are gonna be dinner rolls, for with their hot dog or soup tonight." She hauled that dough over to the worktable, and I thought we were going to set to chipping out rolls. But she stopped and put her hands on her hips. "I said to him and I said it publicly, 'You do the crime, you got to do the time.' No 'yo momma' on this one. I would have been mortified to bail him out."

"Sounds like he's not a bad guy."

Amaryllis's love for her son burst out all over her face. Her spine straightened. "He's a good boy. It's just that the brains skipped a generation."

My mouth fell open.

She added, "Sometimes you love the dumb ones more."

God, isn't gut-level candor like that refreshing? I gestured questioningly toward the dough.

"No," she said, "you've done enough. Time for you to run along."

She walked me toward the mission's cool tiled lobby. The building had originally been a junior high school. Rounding a corner to the main corridor, I saw Wichita talking with another security guard, in their red-lettered T-shirts. The other guard passed what looked like a thick roll of money to Wichita. They dropped their voices when they saw us, and Wichita crammed the roll into her jeans pocket.

I glanced sidelong at Amaryllis, who did not appear to have noticed. Looked odd to me, but what did I know of the inner workings of an urban rescue mission? Maybe there were special customs I was unaware of.

I stopped at the doors to say goodbye. I felt reluctant to leave.

Was I drawn to the Iron Angel's special spirit? Was I morbidly fascinated with the strange energy of the place? Carried away by my drama with Kip?

"Um, Amaryllis, maybe I could come back and do some work."

She took my hand in her warm, strong grip. "I told you, you've done enough."

"I don't feel I have."

She stared at me, hard. "Is God," she asked, "calling you to this place?"

I looked out to the white glaring street. "I don't know."

She lifted her shoulders in her polka-dotted blouse. She clasped her hands behind her and eased her spine. She straightened.

"Well then, you can come and serve soup Saturday noon. We're gonna be short that day."

SIX

The head-banging squeal of a garbage truck in the alley woke me at five the next morning. I got up and checked on Petey, who was profoundly sawing them off in his little bed, with Trikey, his stuffed triceratops, at his side. He had burned through his Spider-Man mania and gone on to dinosaurs just as most of the licensed Spider-Man merchandise I'd bought him was starting to wear out or get too small.

My son, I realized, was going to be a snorer. His five-year-old bronchial tubes were already configuring themselves that way, loosening from his chest wall, vibrating freely like the tailpipes on a tiny Harley. So be it.

I wondered if he'd start asking for dog pictures and models. The dog thing, I hoped, would pass soon, because I don't like dogs very much, not that I'm therefore a cat person. I tend to feel animals belong in the barn, or the woods.

When I splurged these days, I tended to spend on my son. It was good for my budget that at least his Spider-Man sheets had a decent amount of life left in them. Or so I thought until that moment, when Petey rolled over and his blanket fell away. Suddenly he looked like a little homeless man wrapped in a shredded rag, which I realized was his Spider-Man top sheet. That sheet had been fine yesterday, when I'd stripped his bed and tossed the linens in the hamper. Now it looked as if—well, as if a T. rex had flossed with it.

Silently, I crept closer and inspected the shredded percale, with its pattern of webs and heroism. It was a shade bluer than the bottom sheet—hmm. The raw cotton edges of the tatters were tinged with indigo.

I walked out to the living room where my older sister, Gina, slept.

Holding my temper before drinking even a single cup of coffee is not an easy thing for me to do.

Gina, three years my senior, lay like a mermaid in the sheets, her glossy brown hair arrayed as if by strong eddies, her body curved, feet together, beneath the flowing folds of the bedding. She'd come in quite late last night.

Back last spring, no sooner had I gotten a bigger place—an upgrade from Petey's and my cramped studio-plus to a real two-bedroom in the same building—than Gina phoned to say she was coming out for a visit.

"Wonderful!" I enthused, immediately on guard. "How long will we have you?"

She was vague on that. "I've just *got* to get out of Wisconsin! I just want to *see* you, it's been forever!" She was working as a secretary to some grain-elevator executive and told me this was vacation.

"Oh, for a week or two, then?"

"Um, yeah."

When she got here I put her on the fold-out after only briefly considering giving her my room. I knew her too well.

I showed her around L.A. on my time off from school and studying, and she helped with Petey. Within days, she'd begun to pick up certain California attitudes, like a strong sanctimoniousness against people whom she saw as behaving in an un-ecological manner.

"Look at the smoke belching out of that SUV. Call themselves patriotic. See that bumper sticker?"

"Yeah, yeah."

"But it's the people who drive electric cars who're truly patriotic, because they save energy. The solar people."

As the two-week mark approached, I asked Gina about her homebound flight. We were grocery shopping while Petey was doing a hike somewhere with Daniel.

"Well . . . ," she began, smiling brightly with pent-up optimism. "Well . . ."

"I knew it! I knew it!" I flung the radishes into the cart.

"I love it here!"

"What happened to your job?"

"I quit!" She tossed her bangs.

"You did not!"

"OK, so what, I was fired!"

"What for?" I pulled the cart over to a quiet spot in Fruit.

"My boss didn't understand that I need a grace period."

I sighed. "You mean you kept showing up late for work."

She sniffed a plum. "Plus he was a troll. Plus he caught me playing poker online."

"Once?"

Small voice. "No."

"Oh, Gina."

Her eyes got sly. "Well, he's crying the blues now, I assure you."

"What did you do."

"I slipped a motel key into his suit pocket and I think his wife found it."

"Good God!"

Her master plan finally came out: she wanted to stay with me just for a few weeks, in order to launch a career in Los Angeles as a torch singer. She'd start out singing in small clubs, and soon she'd be able to afford her own place, then after that it'd be onward and upward. Recording contract. Hey, world tours.

That was Gina. She was my sister. I loved her.

And I have to admit I was secretly glad she came to L.A. to pursue a dream. Only, I wanted her to *chase* the damn thing, not lie around my apartment. When she found out George occasionally played drums in a jazz combo, she thought he'd be able to get her gigs, but his group didn't want a singer, so all he could do was introduce her to a few other musicians and a club manager or two.

The plain fact is, anybody who wants to make it in L.A. has got to find out a lot for themselves.

The apartment was more tuneful with Gina around, I'll say that. She had a distinctive voice. Tone-wise, it was slightly nasal, but clear and true, like a traditional country singer—think June Carter or even Lynn Anderson. Yet she liked to sing the sad jazz ballads, which seem written for a cigarette-and-whiskey voice, or at least a throaty one, like Billie or Judy. Gina's voice singing those songs, bending around the blue notes, was arresting. Different.

And now here she was, crooning Petey to sleep with "The Man That Got Away" and "Blues in the Night." She'd haul the laundry down to the basement sobbing, "Love for sale."

At my insistence—"*Any* job!"—she found a position in a record store, up on Sunset, only nine blocks from our apartment on Curson, so she earned a little money, putting in about fifty dollars a week to the household fund. Which just about covered the "organic" label on the groceries she bought.

Thank God, though, she hadn't given up chocolate, which we shared a passion for. We loved the gourmet stuff—the Godivas and the Peruginas and so on, and I grooved on the local Mrs. See's— but mainly we were chocolate whores. Which was fortunate, due to our budget. Our roots were firmly anchored in Hershey bars and Three Musketeers.

Gina adored California, how progressive it was. She loved the concept of recycling, except she avoided the rinsing and sorting and stacking and hauling, leaving those little chores to Petey and me.

She loved the apartment. I'd furnished it from Ikea and junk shops with rugs to lie on while munching popcorn and listening to music, a couple of small bouncy sofas, plus some fun paintings Daniel had given me. He painted abstracts, which Petey kept trying to find order in. "See this part over here? I think it's supposed to be the inside of a dinosaur's stomach. In fact, I'm sure of it."

We got better daylight in this place too, thanks to a glass doorwall to a real patio, where I'd placed some herb pots for a bit of green.

As I knew she would, Gina shunned the unsexy bus system and acquired a car as soon as possible. A full-sized Jeep. Red.

"I need to get around, don't I?" she protested, before I could even open my mouth. "I mean, this is L.A.! And it's used! I only paid three Gs for it!" She was rapidly adopting the lingo.

"What, did you get under payments?"

"Yeah, they only wanted two hundred down."

"Not an electric car, huh?"

"My God no, those things are *expensive!*"

Confidence is great, and I was glad she had a pile of it, right next to her talent.

But talent is plentiful and dirt cheap. It really is, especially here. Talented people roll into Los Angeles every hour of every day, you can see them flowing over the passes like hopeful lemmings. The real key to success, if you've got talent, is to combine it with relentless hard work.

Now, as Gina slept, I continued to hold back the cresting flood of my temper. True, we're only talking about one ruined sheet, but how the hell did she do it?

I prepared a pot of coffee and mindlessly scanned the newspaper, when I was startled to see a picture of Amaryllis B. Cubitt and the headline DOT-COM PRINCE TO ENDOW ANGEL'S MISSION. Next to Amaryllis's photo was a smiling shot of Khani Emberton, a former gangbanger made good—very good. He was going to give the ABC Mission five million dollars to start a real foundation, something that would generate income for the mission's basic operating expenses, and more.

The *Times* recapped the story all of us Angelenos knew by heart: Emberton was the scion of a third-generation African-American welfare family from South Central. His mother was a drug addict, the all-too-typical story. Even she didn't know who his father was, let alone where.

Khani had plunged into gang life at the age of eight, following his brothers, all of whom were dead or in jail. After his umpteenth stint in juvenile hall, Amaryllis picked him up in one of her regular neighborhood stomp-arounds. "I could see the boy had sense, under all that do-rag and basketball pants," she said in the paper.

"She saved my life," Khani Emberton said simply.

She took him in and started walking him to school herself. She fed him good food, taught him the gospel, and encouraged him to work and put himself through junior college.

He studied hard, and before he graduated he'd started a software company that enabled old computers to talk to new ones. There was enough worldwide demand for his products to make him almost a billionaire.

And now he told the *Times* that he wanted to repay the woman who'd made it all possible, as he saw it.

They were going to throw a big presentation ceremony three weeks from Sunday, after service, on the front steps of the mission. The Christian rapper Malcolm Cross was to perform, there'd be dancing and more music from the Hybrids, the famous band from Detroit. Plus plenty of food, of course.

Emberton explained, "I'm not the only one who's done well from humble beginnings. Being public about this endowment is my way of telling my successful brothers and sisters they should do the same. It's too easy for us to forget our roots, when our roots seem so shabby to us."

The smell of the coffee finally penetrated Gina's brain stem.

"Hiya, hon!" she said cheerily, waking up quickly.

"Good morning."

She scooted into the bathroom and by the time she came out I heard Petey stirring.

Gina is the most cheerful morning person I've ever known. "Oh, coffee coffee coffee!" she said, smiling, reaching for my favorite mug, a thick yellow hand-thrown one I'd gotten at some craft fair. She liked it so much I'd ceded it to her, it was just easier. "How was your evening?"

"Look," I began—

"Mine was fairly productive! Sasha and I went to—mmm. You realize this coffee's better than from that old machine?"

"Yeah, fortunate that you broke it. While we're on the subject of—"

"Sasha took me to an art party, and—"

"They're called openings." Sasha was one of the handful of guys she'd met in jazz clubs and did stuff with.

"Gina, what happened to Petey's top sheet?"

"Plenty of wine and stuff, and all free. They had these mini quesadillas?"

"That's amazing. Did you hear what I asked you? You did the laundry yesterday before you went out."

"Oh. Yeah. I wondered what you'd say about that. The thing is, I was economizing. That's your favorite word, isn't it—economize?"

"God damn it."

"So, you know those old studded jeans of mine?"

"Those jeans aren't 'old,' you got them just last—"

"They're *vintage*."

"They're not even made of fabric, they're like chain mail or something. You threw those in the *wash*?"

"I didn't have a whole second load, so yeah, I put them in with that sheet. They didn't come out too well either, if that makes you feel any better. I found the dry-clean-only tag in the bottom of the washer."

"Gina, that set of sheets had a future, you know?"

Defensively, she said, "In case you didn't notice, the pillowcase and bottom sheet are fine, they went in with the underwear."

"I can't believe you actually made his bed that way."

Through this whole argument my sister kept doggedly drinking her coffee, getting that first dose down.

"What're you so upset about?" she demanded. "Just buy the kid new sheets. He doesn't like those ones anyway. He wants dinosaur ones, like they have at—"

"I'm not made of money!"

"You're starting to sound like Gramma Gladys."

"You're driving me to it!"

"You have plenty of money!"

I fixed her with a cold eye. "What do you know about my savings?"

She gazed into her coffee mug, swirling the dregs. "Almost thirty grand."

"You looked at my money market statement!"

"So what!"

I paused and breathed, trying to calm myself. Gina was perfectly serene. "Yes," I admitted quietly, "I have about thirty thousand dollars in that fund. But do you know how much UCLA costs? That's not even enough for a year's tuition. And I'm only working as an extra, plus with the temp service."

"But you're getting financial aid."

"I have to pay most of it back! Hardly half of it is scholarship money. The rest is loans."

Gina considered that. "Where'd you get all that money, anyway?"

"Some of it I saved up—I know that's a foreign concept to

you, so let me repeat the phrase: *saved up*. That's where you put money aside, where you live on less than you take in. And I received a reward from that insurance company, after the Tenaway thing."

"How much?"

"Forty-two."

"Forty-two thousand?!"

"George and I helped them recover millions, at the risk of our own—"

"OK, OK."

"I have to make that money last."

Petey ambled in, rubbing his belly. "You guys are loud."

I kissed him and fixed him a pre-breakfast slice of seven-grain bread and butter. He wolfed it, then went back into his room. We heard the *boopitty-boop* of his damn ScoreLad.

Gina said, "I'm sorry about the sheet. Maybe I could—" she cleared her throat and forced herself "—buy a . . . new one for him."

"OK," I agreed. "That would be really good, Gina."

Pleased to be finished with the quarrel, she poured herself more coffee, then together we folded her bedding and retracted the sofa. We made breakfast, fruit and eggs and more bread. She scrambled up the eggs beautifully, adding some parsley from the patio.

As we worked, I mused about my love life. I'd barely dated anybody since starting law school and breaking off with George.

"I'm thinking about sex a lot these days, you know?" I said. "I keep feeling guilty about George, and he's quite good in bed, I must say, but—"

"Let me reveal something to you, little sister." She turned the eggs onto a platter. "Lots of guys are a good lay. At least at first. After five years, no guy is a good lay."

"How do you know that?"

"Just trust me, I've known enough guys at different stages."

"I think you're just a nympho."

"So what if I am?" Gina placed the eggs on the table with a flourish.

"Petey!" I called. Then, dropping my voice, "Being a nympho's a liability in life, Gina. It is *clearly* not the road to—"

"Oh, I think it comes in handy enough."

SEVEN

George Rowe stripped off a piece of duct tape, tore it into fourths, and slapped up a color photograph of Ernest the missing beagle on a pole at the corner of Rossmore and Fourth. LOST DOG. REWARD. Rowe knew that if he put up a number, say $1,000, he'd be deluged with calls from people who'd gone out and stolen a beagle. He had already posted similar notices on lost-dog Internet sites, and he had phoned the shelters and clinics.

Methodically, sweating in the morning sun, he papered the intersections and supermarkets within a half mile of Markovich's house in Hancock Park. The skin on his fingers got raw from ripping tape. Today being Friday, people ought to be able to see the notice all weekend.

He wore his customary outfit of short-sleeved cotton shirt with a chest pocket (maroon plaid today), plain pants, and brown leather lace-ups. No tie today. With his crew cut, he looked forgettable, harmless.

As he worked he occasionally talked to people about the dog. He stopped in for a chat with the greenskeeper at the nearby Wilshire Country Club, with its rolling acreage and tempting rabbits.

After he finished with the posters, he got in his car and returned to the area of the shooting incident involving Rita and the Cubitt boy.

True, the police were investigating. But they had only so much time for things like this, even attempted murder, and much depended on how full their hands were.

Rowe knew he was a good investigator. And he was determined that no more harm must come to Rita. He zeroed in on a bar he'd noticed on his first trip.

The strange little den, half house, half industrial shed, had no sign; he'd simply noticed people going in and out, sometimes carrying a bottle in a bag. He went up the three concrete steps.

Entering a place like this where you don't belong, your impulse is to go slow. But you can't creep in, never; you stride right into the darkness and establish yourself before anyone has a chance to react poorly.

The bar was hardly larger than a home kitchen. Grime-streaked blankets covered the windows, but the front door was open to the street, letting in the white glare.

He placed a twenty-dollar bill on the bar and said to the narrow-eyed black dude behind it, "Relax, I don't even want a beer." The man's expression didn't change, but neither did he reach beneath the bar for his baseball bat or whatever. The bar top was white laminate with gold starbursts, coated with gray stickum from spilled beverages and elbow dirt. No stools.

Rowe said, "My name is George. If I were a plainclothes cop, I'd be wearing a jacket, right, with my gun under it?"

The man nodded. He wore a shiny black shirt and had a bushy beard pulled tightly into his lips. He folded his arms.

Rowe asked, "Did anybody talk about that drive-by last Monday to you? Or the beating of the kid before the shooting?"

The man's beard opened and he said slowly, "You've got to be kidding."

Two other men sat at the only table, back from the door. They had stopped talking when Rowe came in. The place smelled of rotten wine and tobacco spit.

"Might as well share around," said Rowe, stepping to the table and laying a twenty before each of the men. In some situations such a gesture would be an affront, but these men quickly slipped the money out of sight and looked hungrily at Rowe's pants pockets.

"Don't even think it," he said, although they looked too stoned to pull anything.

"Were the guys," Rowe asked, "that beat up the kid different from the guys that drove up shooting?"

"All I know," said the bartender, "they weren't from here."

"Where were they from?"

"All I know is if there was something to be known, I would know it."

"Here meaning where?"

"This street. The Go Down Boys."

Rowe hung out for a couple more minutes, then thanked them and left.

A block or so down, he stopped in a doorway to unwrap a stick of Doublemint and think a minute. This was not Kip Cubitt's neighborhood, either: the boy lived with his grandmother down in South Central next to the mission. A gust of wind picked up a torn newspaper and skittered it along until a weed growing from a crack caught it.

He heard sudden, purposeful footfalls. He stepped from the doorway.

From the direction opposite where the bar was, two people came up to him and stopped. Seeing that one was a woman, Rowe might have relaxed except for the looks on their faces.

The guy said, "You're not wanted 'round here, you know that?" He had been working on a crop of dreadlocks for quite a few years, it looked like; they flung around his face like stiff pasta. He was tall and excited.

"What's it to you?" said Rowe, holding the man's eyes with the central part of his gaze while his peripheral vision kept track of the man's hands. Quietly, he dropped the pack of gum. He held his hands low and ready at his sides.

"Quit asking stuff!" cried the woman.

Rowe glanced at her—she was a meaty white girl with dull eyes overlaid by hectic anger.

The man shoved him. "Go on, now." As Rowe regained his balance, the woman threw an overhand punch, which, awkward as it was, connected with his cheekbone.

Rowe dropped to a squat, momentarily baffling his attackers, then came up with a stiff-arm for each of them, intending to drive a gap between them through which he could escape.

He connected well, and the man spun easily, but the woman's body weight gave her some serious inertia; she barely swayed. She whaled him again, this time putting some leg-drive into a sidearm punch, and he felt the force of the blow in his ribcage.

The man was back in his face, but not punching. "Go on, now!" he screamed, spittle flying. "Go!"

The woman dropped her hands in preparation to kick, and Rowe seized her wrist and pulled her smoothly and forcefully, like you'd pull the starter cord of a lawnmower. She gained momentum, staggering in the direction Rowe wanted, toward the protruding brick corner of the doorway. She writhed away from the brick but collided with the metal door with a smart *thunk*.

She collapsed, moaning, not badly hurt, and Rowe was glad because he would have been reluctant to kick out one of her knee joints or smash her face, her being a woman. He was old-fashioned that way.

As most fights do, all this had taken just ten seconds or so. Rowe spent an instant considering whether to hurt the man or just get out of there. A discussion at this point didn't seem likely.

Rowe sidestepped the tall man and dashed away.

The hard soles of his shoes sounded like gunshots on the pavement.

He felt exhilarated.

He had made a mistake, but not a serious one; he was unhurt except for a sore cheek. He could have gotten inside the dreadlocked man and neutralized him with one or two blows to the body, in spite of the man's greater reach. Rowe ran into very few men who could outfight him. Most times they underestimated him.

But the fellow on the street had not actually thrown a punch, so he didn't warrant a flattening. Besides, experience told Rowe it might be useful to have been seen running from the neighborhood.

And beyond all that, it was worth a sore cheek to know that the boy Kip Cubitt was of great importance to someone.

That evening he put on his usual loungewear of shorts and T-shirt, this one a green Adidas he'd found in a bargain bin at the REI on Santa Monica. He slipped on his comfortable cherry-red flip-flops.

Sighing with hunger, he tore up and washed a head of romaine, dressed it with oil and salt and pepper, and cooked a large hamburger in a pan with a sliced onion. He ate at his kitchen table, listening to a Count Basie CD, then he cleaned up the dishes and went to the living room, where he usually had one or two whiteboards going. He made notes on a board with a green marker:

> *Beating intentional*
> *Drive-by maybe mistake?*
> *Kip en route?*
> *Attackers from?*
> *Local gang (Go Down Boys) not significant*
> *Bartender unleashed Dick and Jane?*

Next he settled down at his computer and shifted his mind back to dogs.

An avalanche of beagle information poured at him from the Internet: he waded through beagle-for-sale ads, beagle stud services, and he looked up beagle winners at dog shows. He learned that beagles came in two sizes, thirteen-inch and fifteen-inch, meaning their height at the shoulder. Ernest and Rondo, he found, were both fifteen-inchers.

Nicholas Polen, the Canadian breeder Markovich thought had

abducted Ernest, did indeed have a Montreal address. While his most successful stud, Rondo, was a multiple champion, the other sons of bitches Polen kept seemed to be subpar. As a breeder, Polen had been a one-hit wonder, with Rondo.

He searched for other areas of income for Polen and found none, not that that meant there were none. He searched property records in the international databases he paid hundreds of dollars per month for the right to access.

He looked at a picture of the man on the home page of his stud service Web site. Polen, smiling slightly, was helping Rondo pose, one hand cupped beneath the dog's throat, the fingers of the other lightly supporting the tail. Polen looked out proudly over Rondo's back. In spite of his silver hair and perfectly pressed tweed jacket, he looked like a round-headed fourth-grader doing show-and-tell with the family dog.

And yet—Rowe discerned a glint of something in the man's eye. Was it steel, or slickness? And, closer—was that a scar on his jaw? An unmistakable furrow ran impressively from his right ear to his chin.

Another photo showed Rondo at play, facing off against a large antique pull-toy beagle.

"Heartwarming," muttered Rowe. He picked up the telephone and reached a friend who taught veterinary medicine up at UC Davis.

"Susan," he said, "if somebody were trying to fence a hot beagle—pedigreed dog—how would they do it?"

"A hot . . . dog?"

"Yes, inevitable joke."

"Sell a stolen purebred?"

"Yeah. If somebody wanted top dollar for it."

"Well, I'm sure you know purebred dogs have papers. You couldn't sell a dog like that to an honest person without the certificate proving the pedigree. I suppose you could forge something, but you'd have to expect the rightful owner to report the theft. Word could get around fast, what with the Internet. Of course, a mature dog that's already been in shows is going to be recognizable in photographs from its markings."

"Yeah?" Rowe curled the phone cord around his finger.

"An experienced person could tell." Susan's voice was straightforward with an edge of Okie, from her roots around Salinas. A hammering-down on the *R*s. "Breeders these days get their dogs microchipped or tattooed. The AKC has guidelines. There's DNA tests too, especially if it's a stud that's been used multiple times."

"The owner mentioned that. How do you get a microchip in, and where would it be?"

"You inject it subcutaneously with a large-bore hypodermic needle, at the shoulder, it leaves no mark. Then a clinic or a shelter with a scanner can read it. The larger breeders, they have scanners too, to keep their dogs straight."

"Who decides what goes on the chip?"

"Oh, the chips are numbered, and all the owner does, once the vet implants the chip, is register the name of the dog with that number to the chip company. You send in a form. The chip company keeps track."

"I see. Can a chip be removed?"

"Oh, yes. Small matter to do that."

"What about those puppy mills?"

"Ugh. The Romanian orphanages of the pet world. An outstanding dog'd be wasted at one of those. Is the dog in question male or female?"

"Male."

"An unscrupulous breeder *could* use the dog as a stud in place of whatever stud or studs they have papers for—if it's a better dog, of course. If he's superdog, then the pups would be likely to have excellent characteristics, provided the bitch is good. Then the pups would bring a good price, and you could do a spay/neuter agreement with the buyer, thus negating their ever needing a DNA test."

"The owner made that same speculation."

"You could probably get away with slightly inferior bitches, if the male's blood is so good. That might give you *some* leverage as a breeder."

"Yeah, I see. How's Larry?"

"Oh, he's great. Fat and sassy. You seeing anybody?"

"Not really."

"Well, it's going to be your turn someday, George, you know that?"

Rowe thanked his friend, hung up, and gazed at the street from his window. His apartment overlooked a chicken shack and a billboard with an ad for a new movie about a nun who becomes a porn star, then gets into politics. He could also see the rear of a strip plaza where immigrant businesses took root and stayed: a Japanese teriyaki restaurant next to a Vietnamese nail salon next to a Honduran check-cashing place. Trees, lush eucalyptus and undulant palms, tossed a wreath of greenery over the neighborhood. Rowe liked unpretentious neighborhoods, and this was one.

Rowe loved all of California, and although his favorite city was San Francisco, he loved Los Angeles deeply. He loved how it strove to be all things to all people. And it damn near was.

In Los Angeles you can meet every kind of person, and every

single one of them is working on a dream. Shop teacher, taco slinger, shoeshine boy, film student. The thing is, L.A. can deliver.

Even if one day you realize your main dream can't come true—say you're an actor and you wake up fifty and fat, well then you work up a magic act and do parties. If you lose your job selling cars, you walk into a hotel and learn *that* business from the bottom. If you have no green card you wash dishes for cash and save until you find another angle.

The city gave you suffocating smog one day and kelpy ocean wind the next. It gave you drug-addled crazies, Brahms trios, Chinese weddings with those true-red dresses, the Pacific Coast Highway, Marilyn's crypt, rumba, bomba, soul, jazz, heart-stopping enchiladas, the sight of yachts leaving Del Mar basin in a freshening breeze. Tijuana just yonder, the Mojave just yonder, Yosemite just yonder, San Francisco a little farther yonder.

To release the residual tension of his day, Rowe went into the sound-curtained alcove occupied by his drum kit, and settled in to practice.

His snare drum wasn't overly crisp, he had loosened the snares so they buzzed a little longer, to make an almost imperceptibly softer attack and finish. He moved his sticks around the kit, playing jazz patterns between snare, bass, tom, and cymbals. He experimented with some new transitions he'd thought of.

He hummed "You'd Be So Nice to Come Home To," accompanying himself on the drums, and thought optimistically of Rita.

EIGHT

Daniel, my big happy actor friend, came by early on Saturday to pick up Petey. He and Gina drank orange juice while I got my boy ready for a ride in Daniel's silver Porsche and a day in the San Gabriels.

Had Daniel been straight, Gina would have been all over him. As it was, she quizzed him about his feelings for Petey in a veiled way. "So what do you *do* with Petey all day?"

"Us guys do masculine stuff together," he answered. "We like to go up to the woods and work up a sweat, generate some real BO." He smiled his stunning white smile.

Daniel was preparing for a role in a micro-budget film, where he was going to be an auto mechanic stuck in a mountain town who gets mistaken for a serial killer by the father of one of the real serial killer's victims. The grief-crazed dad chases the mechanic all over the high desert before the cops stop him, and it turns out his daughter isn't dead after all, and in the end she and the mechanic get married.

Since Daniel was going to do his own stunts, as a good B-movie leading man would, he needed to train.

And since Petey relished climbing and hiking with Daniel, today would be a perfect day. They loved each other, and Daniel was a lot closer to a masculine ideal than Petey's own dad.

"But why take a little boy along?" Gina asked. "Why not join a climbing club or something?"

"I do climb with grown-ups," Daniel said, "but here's the funny thing. Grown-ups look at a rock or a tree as an obstacle. Petey sees it as a possibility. He hasn't learned to second-guess yet. I show him how to be safe, he shows me how to react to the rock like a lizard. Gina, it's a perfect association."

The menfolk took off, Petey launching himself down the front steps, braking his descent by the friction of his hands on the iron banister, as Daniel had taught him.

My ex-husband had been a star athlete in high school, but he possessed the imagination of a termite, and by this point in his life, all the spontaneity seemed to have been drained out of him by his accounting job at a restaurant chain.

On weekends when he had Petey, he'd usually do things like wash his car, visit his bimboesque girlfriend (who, granted, had a pool and a dog), or shop for new cargo shorts for himself. He used to do fun stuff with the boy, but he seemed to be plunging toward his dotage at thirty-two.

"How come you even care where they're gonna be?" challenged Gina, as I carefully stowed the paper on which Daniel had mapped their day. "I thought you trusted Daniel implicitly."

"My God, Gina, I do, he's my best friend. But as a mother, I don't care *who's* taking my son out of my sight, I've got to know the details."

She looked hurt. "Aren't I your best friend?"

"You're beyond that. And because of our ineradicable blood bond, you're coming with me to serve lunch to the needy at the ABC Mission today."

Her eyes widened in alarm. "I have cramps. I've already called in sick to—"

"I have some Midol in the glove compartment. Come on."

NINE

I watched the line of street people breathe deeper as they approached the soup pot and its vegetable beef comfort fumes. My instructions were to dip one ladleful from the bottom and one from the top per bowl.

"They get anxious if they see the first one come from the top," Amaryllis explained. "We call the diners sir and ma'am in the food line."

Gina got the job of wiping tables and bringing out more hot biscuits to the serving line. She hustled pretty well, once she got into it.

Amaryllis darted everywhere, checking the food, greeting diners, answering questions from staff. Lunch was an event.

The clientele were a motley bunch, as you'd expect. With some of them, I found my feelings torn between pity and revulsion. Neither emotion felt appropriate.

South Central Los Angeles is a huge swath of city, thousands of small houses flung down for working people of one color or another from the beginning. City Hall decided that we're supposed to call it South Los Angeles, to try to sidestep the Crip-Blood connotations, but except for the obligingly PC media, everybody still calls it South Central.

"Man, oh man," was Gina's only comment as I drove us in past corner after corner full of watchful drug dealers—so young!—in their sports-logoed clothes, and hookers seeking shade under disintegrating awnings covering urine-stained doorways.

All the major gang wars happen here, and you'll see murals to slain teens airbrushed on garage doors and minivans.

Underlying it all are the working people, making a hopeful go of it. Barred windows next to pots of petunias.

Specifically, the ABC Mission was located just off Compton Avenue, in the former Pueblo Junior High School. The school got so run-down that it would cost more to fix than it was worth, so Amaryllis had raised the money to buy it from the city.

Piece by piece, she set up shelters for men and women, a separate space for the single moms and their kids, a free store, a food bank, and a dress-for-success closet. The large classrooms were useful for all this.

When Gina and I had arrived, Amaryllis met us and told me that Kip had regained consciousness. "He's talking, and the doctors say there's reason to hope. The swelling on his spinal cord is going down."

"Thank God," I said. Gina nodded solemnly. We're about the same size, but she got our dad's high cheekbones and whorly chestnut hair, while I got the blond-and-blue combo via Gramma Gladys, on our mother's side.

"Was he able to tell the police anything?" I asked.

Amaryllis looked at me. "He won't talk to them."

"What?"

"Believe that. He will not say a word to any police individual."

"Well, did he say anything to you?"

She shook her head.

A lanky brown man, smiling widely, came by and said without breaking his stride, "Luncheon must occur, praise Him."

"Let's get to it," said Amaryllis.

How to describe the army of the needy that crowded into the huge cafeteria? They all were alike in that they had failed—if only for today, if only for one hungry hour—to look after themselves. And different in every other way.

The diners ate at the long cafeteria tables, the sound of eating and a little talking muted under the urgency of getting food down.

Many had lugged in a bundle or four. This was allowed at the staff's discretion. Relatively few diners were dressed in tatters; most of the men wore plain cotton shirts, T-shirts, blue jeans, and the women dressed variously in pants or sweats or giveaway dresses.

"Some people," said a volunteer at my elbow, a guy named Albert who said his people were from Colombia, "will never leave the street, even for a meal, because they won't be separated from their stuff. Not even long enough to use an indoor toilet."

Lots of the needy find their way downtown to Skid Row, because that's where most of the services are. Too, that's where the begging is best, at the interface between the commercial districts and the slum.

But more and more, the worst of the hopeless were ending up

in South Central, near this last-ditch haven of the ABC. Addicts so far gone they sit in their own urine and feces, because nothing is worth any effort except getting drugs. You see addicted hookers with their children—the kids still soft and round, but the boys already with that swagger and fuck-you look, the girls heartbreakingly wise to what's most likely in store for them.

I spoke to the people who came through the line. "Hello, sir. Good soup here."

"Hello," most said politely. "Hello. Thank you."

The crazy ones either avoided eye contact or gave me a suspicious glare.

Some wore tattered gray bandages—say, on a hand—that were either protecting a wound, or had simply become a habit long after the wound had healed.

"What's with the wheelchair thing?" I asked Albert.

"You mean why so many in wheelchairs, why so many who don't look like they have bad legs?"

"Yeah."

"Well, their health is bad, their coordination is awful, and one reason or another a lot of them receive a wheelchair. You see the amputations from diabetes. But others—well, they get their chair, it's supposed to be temporary until they get well, but they hang on to it. They barter 'em, and they steal them from each other."

"How come?"

"When you've given up on your life, a wheelchair's an easy thing to sink into."

Eating with their small children on one side of the cafeteria was a group of mothers, chattering and laughing. Looking more closely, I saw there were actually two groups, sorted between Latina moms and African-American moms, speaking two languages. There had been morning classes in parenting and reading. The kids, all pretty tidy, mingled and ran around.

There are gang tattoos that women will have on their necks, which can be hidden or revealed. It's a striking moment when you see one and realize, oh God, she belongs to this gang. I noticed a few of those.

Another couple of women with kids came through the line. Said one to the other, "So this guy says to me, 'You speak well!' Like he's surprised."

"Stop, stop, let me guess," said her friend. "White man, right?"

"Yeah, my boss's boss. They're always shocked when you don't sound like a sharecropper. I patted him on the shoulder and said, 'You speak well too!' You should've seen his face!" She laughed triumphantly.

I smiled in horror. *Good God, how many white people must say stuff like that?*

The pregnant ones all had that irrational upbeat glow you know so well, if you've been pregnant too.

Amaryllis, who had relieved Albert serving up glasses of water and iced tea, murmured to me, "They don't have a pot to piss in, but they're pregnant and happy."

"What'll they do?"

"If they stick with us, they'll be able to get work. They'll qualify for low-income housing, and they're getting trained in how to look after each other's kids so they can all work. We put 'em in trios."

"And that works?"

"When it works it works. Some of them are gonna end up on the street no matter how much help they get, understand that. You can't worry about numbers or you'd quit. You can only serve for the sake of serving and hope for the best."

One man, holding his full tray, thanked Amaryllis with tears in his eyes. She looked him up and down and said, "You thank the *Lord* before you eat that, sir. He's the one to thank. Dessert today is peanut butter cookies."

Something in her matter-of-fact tone made me well up with emotion. I looked out at the diners, in their rags and delusions and dreams and rock-bottom neediness. "Amaryllis," I asked, "why?"

"Oh, sister, don't cry," she said, almost gently. "Jesus himself assured us the poor will always be with us. So much of this poverty comes from drug abuse. A rock of crack costs so little, a dose of meth—so little. Five dollars this week, three next week. Heroin's not much costlier. Funny," she paused, thinking, "how gambling's all but gone from here. Why put two dollars on a horse when you can get high? Hello, sir, have some ice tea."

I put my smile back on and kept ladling. "Hello. Hi, ma'am."

Then the staff, as multiethnic as the people they served, came in to eat, and the food line kept going. Some of the men on staff looked very high-mileage, as if they'd bested their demons only after a long, perilous struggle. Some women appeared that way too, but then there were others with that ex-nun look, mild around the eyes but with a tough-set mouth. The women of service you see everywhere.

Finally us line workers helped ourselves. Gina and I took our trays to a table.

Gina, inspecting her nail job after its exposure to the harsh bleach water, said, "Black people make me nervous. I'm not supposed to say that, right?"

"Well, that makes you one of the more honest white people in L.A."

"It's because I'm afraid they hate us."

"That's what they think about us, of course."

"Yeah."

"Black people used to make me nervous too," I confessed. "But then I realized it's poverty that makes me nervous. Black has nothing to do with it. My friend Sylvan says that, and he's right."

"Yeah. I'd like to get to know a black person really well."

"Well, L.A.'s your chance."

The smallest group of workers was the security team, only three in number today, quickly identifiable by their gray-and-red T-shirts. There was an outcasty aura about them, like the kids who smoked in the johns in middle school.

I turned my attention back to my soup, hungry from having skipped breakfast getting Petey ready for his day.

Gina nudged me. "Look."

"What?"

"Those two."

I saw the security guard Wichita and another one, a black guy with a lot of hair bundled under a knit cap, disappear through the swinging kitchen doors.

"What about them?"

Gina dabbed a piece of biscuit into some margarine and ate it. "These are almost as good as Gramma Gladys's. Those two went up to Amaryllis a minute ago and started talking to her. She started to look upset, like mad. Then she walked off, to the kitchen. They just followed her in. Was he the same one that showed us where the bathroom is?"

"I don't know, I didn't see his face either."

I watched the kitchen door for a minute. Everybody in the cafeteria was talking and eating.

I stood up and said, "I wonder if there are any cookies left back there." Gina started up too, but I signaled her to stay there.

I went to the serving line, which we'd cleared off fifteen minutes ago, looked around, then glanced in the kitchen door. I heard voices but saw no one, so I slipped in.

The three stood talking on the other side of a bank of storage shelves. I took one silent step forward and peeked through a gap between a carton of powdered milk and a stack of bagged rice.

"Nobody's asking for the world," Wichita was saying, sounding more animated than I'd have expected, from my initial dumb, furtive impression of her. "This is a win-win situation, Amaryllis, and we can't understand why you're fighting it."

"Yeah," said the guy, tall and deep-voiced. "You're acting like there's a downside, and there isn't."

They sounded like a couple of junior executives, except for the menacing mood. Their backs were to me. I could see Amaryllis's face, a study in tight resistance, lips compressed.

She shook her head as Wichita said, "Look, this place is so safe! For you, for everybody. The risk is so nothing!"

"That's right," added the guy. "The police haven't set foot in here since you opened the doors. What's more, the beta test is going great. You've really been great."

"Denny's right," said Wichita.

Amaryllis said, "Things are about to change. You know. I'm trying to tell you. I won't be able to—nor do I want to—"

"Hey," interrupted Wichita, "you know the real risk that's gonna come down unless—"

"Don't you tell that to me!" Amaryllis stared hatefully at Wichita. "You know who hurt my grandson! Just the same as—"

"I don't! I don't!"

"We don't," agreed Denny.

"You're lying dogs. I have no more to say to you!"

Denny said in a low tone, "Hey, let's all relax here, nobody wants bad feelings."

"Just think about it," urged Wichita in an attempt to sound friendly. "That's all."

Amaryllis looked hollow.

The two security staff went out together.

Amaryllis stood there a moment. I heard her breathing, short and angry, then longer and more regular as she got hold of herself.

She walked out, and I waited a minute before hurrying through the back passageway to the dishwashing station, where volunteers clanged and splattered. I picked up a brush and joined them.

Lunch was over. Clearly, I'd be in over my head if I tried to interfere with whatever was going on. Yet I wanted to know *what* was going on.

When I saw Amaryllis head for the garbage bins, I strode over to help her wheel the bins to the alley. At first the stench out there halted my breath in my nostrils, but then a breeze came up, clearing the air while it lasted. I started to say something, but suddenly Gina appeared at our heels, pushing the last can out.

"Oh, thank you," said Amaryllis.

Something moved stealthily in the weeds along the foot of the building.

"Oh, my God, there's a rat!" Gina screamed.

To be sure. The creature emerged, gray and supple, its cold black eyes expressing ownership of this alley. Gina, in an unimaginable feat of gymnastics, leaped to the top of the dumpster, where she perched on its steel lid like a panicked monkey.

The rat sauntered to an ant-covered apple core, chomped it,

then carried it in its mouth to a knee-high cluster of rags at the foot of a drainpipe, where it disappeared.

Amaryllis laughed so hard at Gina she almost fell over.

By force of will I'd kept myself under control, although the instant I saw the rat I wondered whether I could outrun it.

"Literally," Gina confessed from the dumpster lid, "I think I've only ever seen one on, like, National Geographic."

"Well, get down from there," said Amaryllis, "because rats can climb."

"And they're attracted by the smell of herbal hair conditioner," I added.

"Damn you," said Gina.

"Forgive the swearing," I said.

"Makes no never minds to me," said Amaryllis. "Do you know we served two hundred twenty-three lunches today? Goodness, but it is hot! The dog days are in full swing."

"What are the dog days, anyway?" I wondered.

Gina said, "It's when it's so hot."

I looked at her like, *duh*. "I meant, is there some, like folk belief about dogs, or—"

Amaryllis said, "It's about the dog star, Sirius. It comes up during August, and the ancient people blamed the heat on it."

Something else rustled, and Amaryllis set her knuckles on her hips and watched. Gina clung atop the dumpster. A man rose from the pile of rags the rat had disappeared into, shook himself, and shambled toward us, talking fast under his breath. His eyes were unfocused. "I didn't, I didn't, I didn't. The Cheerios man he ain't got nothing on me—nothing!—because when brains were handed out all he got was a circle. I got brains, but you never cared about my luck, and you never bought me that trombone."

The dirt on his face, neck, and hands was as worn in as if he'd grown it. He came closer. He stank unbearably; I could almost see the fleas. One wrist sported a filthy cloth bandage.

"Eric," said Amaryllis sternly, "go around front and get you a hygiene kit. Take it in the showers and use it. Then we'll be able to see who you are under all those layers of dirt."

He mumbled something.

"I predict you'll feel better if you do." She took his arm, actually making full skin-to-skin contact, guiding him toward the alley's mouth. He wandered away.

"That would be a dual diagnosis," mused Amaryllis.

"Dual diagnosis?" said Gina, clambering down.

"Addiction and mental illness together?" I guessed.

"Yes," said Amaryllis. She unlocked the dumpster lid and we flung it open. "You take someone in thinking they have a problem with addiction, then you realize they're crazy too."

"You keep peeling the onion," I said.

"You keep peeling the onion."

Gina piped up, as we lifted the cans and dumped them, "It's the government's fault."

"Yeah?" I said.

Amaryllis sighed.

"Yeah," said Gina, "they kicked everybody out of the mental institutions years ago, to save money. Mostly it was the Republicans."

"Jeff told me something like that once," I said. "But wasn't it a little more—"

"Complicated than that?" broke in Amaryllis. She snapped the dumpster's padlock shut. "In actuality, the Civil Liberties Union and the mental health advocates got together and decided that being crazy and free is better than being crazy and locked up against your will by the government."

"Oh," I said.

"That was the core of it. They got their way. It's not necessarily a bad thing. I understand," said Amaryllis, "how good it feels to lay blame. But the fact is, all the money in the world can't persuade a person to get help when they don't want it. You see this with Eric. My door is open to him, but he stays out." She wiped her hands on her apron. "And you know, some folks outside aren't ill or addicted. They just don't fit in. They choose the streets with as much purpose as you choose to go to work and live in a house."

The lean, smiling man who had called us to lunch duty stuck his head out and said, "Amaryllis, you're needed on the phone."

"This is the Reverend Bill Culpepper," said Amaryllis in quick introduction as we trooped back inside. "Reverend Bill, will you please escort these two ladies out?"

"Amen, I will."

I said, "I thought we could stay to help out with dinner."

Amaryllis glanced at me. "I don't think so. No, we're fine for help tonight."

The Reverend said, "But didn't we just lose Tony and Juanita from the Saturday night shift?"

"No, Bill, I said we're OK for tonight." A look passed between them. He shut up. Amaryllis nodded goodbye to us and took off.

Gina and I exchanged glances, then went with the Reverend Bill. He wore an all-black outfit, little preacher shirt and pants, with spongy white running shoes. His eyes, behind aviator glasses, looked tired. The glasses looked as if they'd been bent and straightened out a hundred times.

He led us back to the lobby, where before saying goodbye, we looked out to the clusters of street people hanging out by the gates.

I saw, past the homeless, a dog slinking along. Then I saw another one, and another, all lurking at the edges.

Perhaps ten in number, they moved sinuously, a smooth river of dogs, led by an alert-looking dark one—a Rottweiler, I guessed, or mostly Rottweiler. He was big, not the tallest—there was a Doberman among them, and other large mongrels—but he was clearly the leader, watched by the others for cues. His short coat was full of burrs and twigs. All the dogs were dark in color.

Calmly, the pack hugged the scraggly bushes just beyond the gates, nosing along, checking the leader every few seconds.

The street people moved away from them, except for the man Amaryllis had called Eric; he squatted and held out his hand to one of the smaller dogs. He appeared to be offering something edible. The dog, pied with mange, approached to within about ten feet, sniffed, barked, then rushed. Startled, Eric jerked his hand away. The dog snapped its jaws shut on the food and the homeless man's fingers, set his front legs, and tugged. Two other street guys ran over and pounded on the dog until it let go. It swallowed whatever piece of food Eric dropped. The leader barked once, and the dog ran to rejoin the pack.

The other street men gestured toward the mission, evidently urging Eric to go in and get help for his bleeding hand, but he moved away from them. As the Reverend Culpepper and Gina and I watched, he unwrapped the dirty bandage from around his right hand and transferred it to the left. The blood stopped dripping.

"Shouldn't we do something?" Gina said. "Like, you know, rabies or something?"

"Oh, sister," said the Reverend, and shrugged. "I know Eric. If he gets rabies, that'll probably *improve* his mental capacity."

It hit me: "Is that the pack? You know, that they talk about?"

"The notorious feral pack of South Central." Reverend Culpepper looked after the dogs. "Yes. That's them."

This pack of dogs has achieved legendary status in L.A. for consistently eluding the city's animal control officers, none of whom, as you can imagine, are pantywaists. Up until then, I'd never believed the stories.

"It's unusual to see them in the daytime," said the Reverend. "Mostly they move and feed at night. Did you notice the athletic fields?"

"What athletic fields?"

He laughed nonhumorously. "Yes, what athletic fields? When you leave, you'll notice around back what's become of them—gone first to weeds, then scrub, now there's real trees growing on the fifty-yard line. The pack roams there sometimes, up to twenty strong, I've counted. I find myself more fearful of them than the gangs."

"My God, I thought they were an urban myth. You know."

"Oh, no, sister. Well, you see them."

"I heard they live by the river."

"They do," he said. "They often take cover in the riverbed. From here they range to that rail yard"—he gestured easterly with a hand I saw to be mangled somehow—"then they find their way through the vacant lots and alleys to the river." He dropped his voice. "Nobody knows how much time they spend on this property, though. Such a good hideout for them."

I said, "I heard rumors that when a homeless person dies out there, unless somebody notices, the pack drags off the body."

The Reverend cleared his throat. "There is truth to that rumor."

"Oh, God," Gina and I said simultaneously.

He saw me checking out his hand.

"Have you always been a preacher?" I asked.

He held it up: instead of a thumb there was just a fused-looking stub. "Oh, me, I used to be a longshoreman, back in the day. This here got roped off just like a cowboy's—you toss a loop, and if the slack disappears and your thumb's in the way, goodbye thumb."

He watched the dogs. "If we could clear those athletic fields and restore them to the community, that might expose the pack and help the city capture them. Looks like they're headed east now, to the river."

I observed, "That five million dollars coming from Mr. Khani Emberton sure will help."

He peered at me carefully, kindly, through the smudged lenses of his glasses. "Amen, sister. And you have a blessed day."

TEN

I took a slow, yogic breath of the clean Sunday morning air, then squatted and dead-lifted the Sunday *L.A. Times* from the mat. A photo caught my eye right away. For some reason it caught my breath too. Caught it tight.

You know how you see something quickly, almost subliminally, and your mind blots it out until you pull yourself together to deal with it?

I carried the paper to the breakfast counter. Gina started some eggs and gave me a mug of coffee. I drank some.

Then I looked again.

OFFICER KILLED IN GUN BATTLE

An LAPD sergeant was shot to death while on patrol on Mateo Street yesterday afternoon, then her fleeing killer was shot and killed by her partner, authorities said last night. According to LAPD sources, Sgt. Annette Soames, 32, and her partner, Officer Leroy Dent, were ambushed by a single gunman, who stepped from a doorway as they sat in their patrol car, having stopped at the curb to talk to a neighborhood shopkeeper.

Wielding a semiautomatic handgun, the suspect shot Soames, who was at the wheel, twice in the chest at point-blank range, then fired at Dent as well but missed, police said. Dent returned fire and fatally shot the gunman, according to a high-ranking department source.

Soames and the gunman, identified as Jerrol Bays, 28, of Los Angeles, were pronounced dead at the scene.

Dent said, "It looked like his goal was to kill Sgt. Soames and that was it. He fired at me without looking. I had a clear shot as he turned to run away, and I took it."

I closed my eyes for a long moment. Then I was ready to digest the photograph.

The department portrait showed Sgt. Annette Soames in uniform, hat off, eyes full of purpose and promise.

"No," I said. "Oh, no."

"What?" Spatula in hand, Gina came to look over my shoulder. "Hmp. There's your doppelganger."

The slain officer was a narrow-shouldered white woman who wore a chin-length blond bob, whose face was wholesome and spritely, with a straight nose and a pixie chin. Arched eyebrows, no glasses.

Just like me.

And she'd been shot on north Mateo Street, possibly on the same block as the little grocery store.

Just like me.

"Oh," said Gina. "Oh."

"It could have been me," I murmured. "My God."

"No," said my sister, her voice hardening. "Whoever did it thought it *was* you."

We stared at each other. Her face was as bloodless as plaster.

GEORGE ROWE TRIED to block out the sound.

"Ump! Ump! Ump!" grunted the man running beside him. *"Ump! Ump! Ump!"*

The fellow was a pleasant sort, but he found it necessary to grunt like a pig with each footstep. This got on Rowe's nerves, plus the guy couldn't run faster than an eight-minute pace. They were headed south on Alvarado, approaching Olympic.

Once in a while Rowe joined a Sunday-morning running club for a good long workout. They met in MacArthur Park and ran into the city from there, covering eight to ten miles. The runners began in a group, but strung out as everyone asserted their own pace. They always picked some coffee shop as an end rendezvous point.

Rowe ran along, enjoying the city morning. He liked to be surprised by clumps of flowers growing in ugly places. He loved how hardy the California Golden Poppy was. The sight of one pushing its tough little stem through a crack in a curbstone delighted him. The orange of the petals hit his retinas with a special vibe he felt all the way through him. Growth is stronger than pavement. He liked the color orange.

Colonel Markovich had called last night, again, asking for a progress report.

"Nothing yet," Rowe had said bluntly.

"Well, I'm afraid I've been singing your praises to a few key people, so the expectations are mounting!" Markovich's voice was happy.

"I beg your pardon, Colonel?"

"Ernest's disappearance is big news in the canine community. The AKC has been in touch with me. They know you're on the case, as do several of the top beagle people. Odd—I sensed a little nervousness in them."

"You spoke of me by name to these people?"

"Yes—just a few."

Rowe's toes had dug into the decks of his cherry-red flip-flops. "I wish you hadn't done that."

"Ump! Ump! Ump!"

Rowe told his running companion, "Hey, I'll meet up with you at the doughnut place, OK? Is it the one on Sixth?"

"Ump-kay!"

Rowe peeled off and went his own way, heading east on Olympic, feeling his heart pumping harder as he accelerated. His legs felt good. He sped up until he hit a good equilibrium between heart and legs. He thought he'd go all the way to the river, then north to Elysian Park, then down again to inhale some carbs at the doughnut shop on Sixth. This shop was new-agey in that it served whole-wheat fried cakes.

He sucked in the Sunday morning air, smelling a cedar hedge as he ran past it, then an old man's cigar smoke, then hot ham grease from a diner. He thought about what to pack for a trip he was planning to make to Nicholas Polen's house and kennel in Canada.

Usually he carried toys on trips, because he liked them, and because they're useful for breaking tension with anyone, not just children.

He liked to fling a kite up while doing informal surveillance, because people saw the kite but not you. He liked wind-up toys that walked or rolled. He liked yo-yos and superballs. When he was a boy, his uncle had given him a rock-hard black sphere from his garage and said it was an original Super Ball. After playing with it for a few minutes, he figured out how to spin it into a wall to make it rebound to the floor and then accelerate back into the wall *by itself*. That ball was as close to a magic object as anything.

He hated batteries.

He liked toys made of metal—gyroscopes and jumping discs and wire puzzles. The older he got, the more he understood toys.

This trip was going to be a bit different, and he would need to do some shopping.

He reached the railroad tracks at the river and turned north, leaving what little traffic there was behind him. He slipped through a break in an Amtrak fence and pounded along on the gravel, watching two gulls fighting over a broken green melon on the opposite embankment.

Even this sluggish urban stream smelled—well, good. River water had an organic, fresh odor that reminded him of growing things. He skipped over the tracks and ran just above the channel's sloping concrete wall. No rain had fallen in weeks; the river still flowed, less than a foot deep, around the usual junk—tires and chicken buckets and shopping carts.

Oddly, he heard a vehicle gunning its engine directly behind him. He had left the roadway five minutes ago. The vehicle must have gotten into the rail yard from a level crossing somewhere behind. The engine came on quick and hard, tires bit into the gravel, and his ears told him he had time either to turn and see the vehicle before it struck him, or jump for it.

He flung himself into space.

Peripherally, he saw a clunker of a beige sedan flash past, motor screaming.

Knowing how to fall, he tucked his body, shut his eyes, and tumbled, trying for an angled descent. The vehicle's roar faded sharply as he rolled down the sloping concrete embankment. He felt the serial jolts of the fall as well as the ugly sensation of his bare arms and legs rolling over warm grit. His body came to a stop at the water's edge. One arm splashed into it.

He was OK except for feeling like somebody'd taken a sledgehammer to each of his joints.

"Ohh."

He heard a low snarl.

He opened his eyes.

There were twelve or fifteen of them, a few facing him in a line, the rest mixing behind. One near him was three-legged and looked to be mostly spaniel, a larger one was mottled, like an ash-bin Dalmatian, but its head was a shepherd's. The dog that had snarled was a sizable burnt-shit-colored Rottweiler with a faceful of scars. It snarled again.

Slowly, he sat up. His arms and legs were shining with sweat and stuck over with dirt and ants, but they worked all right. Both of his elbows and one knee were bloody, but that was just the skin. His head was OK.

He looked up to the top of the embankment. The car was gone. He would've needed only a glimpse of the license plate to remember it, but he hadn't gotten it. Well, well. A long time had passed since someone had tried to run him over, and in that case it was a spur-of-the-moment thing, involving a kicked-in motel-room door, a Polaroid, and a guy who was having sex with a stripper instead of working late.

But this was certainly different, quite different.

The Rottweiler advanced, braced his front legs, and growled, baring its teeth. The other dogs in the lineup began to growl in their throats. Those that were moving wove in smooth unison through the brush that had sprouted in the dirt bars along the river bottom.

Rowe had to get up. The leader would challenge him, but there was nothing else to do.

He moved into a crouch.

The blood dripped from his elbows and knee, and he knew they could smell it. He could not outrun the pack through the brush along the riverbed. He had to climb the concrete embankment, but they'd attack him as soon as he turned his back. The leader was showing aggression, and Rowe had heard of this feral pack.

The dogs looked as if they'd been whelped in eat-or-be-eaten Mexican junkyards. Their eyes were intent, their bodies lean, except for the heavy-bellied Rottweiler.

The breeze shifted, and then he smelled them, rank with musk and sharp with stink.

He swallowed.

If they attacked, he might be able to vanquish the leader and escape at the cost of a few chunks out of him. Or they might take him down. How hungry were they? How bored this morning? How unified as a pack?

He knew they'd defeated the efforts of the city to live-trap them. Wary of people and people-smell, they hid away except when they thought they could score something. And he had invaded their morning's lair.

He looked up again to the channel of blue sky. No one was around; the tracks stretched empty. Cars swooshed over the Main Street bridge in the distance.

Here in the middle of a city of four million people, he had plunged into the wildest, loneliest, most savage place he'd ever entered, including the exercise yard at Folsom.

He knew the pack did not force battles they couldn't win. Why hadn't some vigilante with a rifle come along and wiped them out? Well, what's the point, he thought, as soon as you dropped the leader, the rest would vanish, only to regroup later.

The Rottweiler snarled and inched closer, forelegs low, foam dripping from its jaws, its bulging black eyes locked on Rowe.

Rowe took a full breath and let it out. Then he did the only reasonable thing.

He attacked.

He let out a piercing scream and lunged, fists up. The dog sprang.

Rowe met it with his fists, and he concentrated only on the dog's jaws. He pounded its snout as fast and hard as he could, left-right-left-right, punching from his shoulders, driving with his legs. He could not allow the dog one shred of purchase on him, because once a Rottweiler latches on to you, you're toast. Once he had seen what a Rottweiler had done to a human leg. The inmate at Folsom who had sustained the injury, years back, took pride in his calf muscle that looked like a shark had eaten most of it.

Rowe did not try to protect his belly and groin from the dog's thrashing legs, he did not think about the other dogs who could circle behind him and snap through his hamstrings, because he knew he had to attack the lethal part of the emperor dog, and devil take the rest.

His knuckles tore open on the creature's teeth; the dog's lips showed blood too, and still it attacked. He knocked it off balance, and as it gathered itself to strike again, the Dalmatian-shepherd darted behind him. He screamed at it, and it cowered back, uncertain.

The lead dog leaped again, and this time Rowe took a bigger risk. He flexed his knees, raised his elbow, and aimed it to meet the dog's throat. If he miscalculated, the dog's fangs would be right in his face.

But he didn't miss. Against the full force of his body, the dog's neck felt as hard as a fencepost, but at the last millisecond it seemed to yield just a little.

The dog fell back with a yelp of pain.

"Yeah," grunted Rowe.

It stared at him as if trying to remember something. The other dogs watched in stunned silence.

Rowe stood, hands on hips, panting.

The dog turned, and the sight of its stinking bob-tailed butt running away from him was the prettiest thing Rowe had seen all morning.

I NO LONGER wanted breakfast.

It was time to consult Gramma Gladys.

I drove my Honda down to Santa Monica and headed west, the morning sun at my back, gold-washing every building and tree. Half-empty streets all the way to Beverly Hills. If you want a clear path to anywhere in L.A., pick early Sunday morning. Everybody's at church. Haha.

I pulled into the empty parking lot on the west side of Rodeo at Santa Monica. All the boutiques on Rodeo still slept. I parked overlooking the intersection.

I rolled down my window.

"Gramma?"

I waited.

After a minute a bus honked, and I began to feel the spirit of my dead but still wonderful grandmother, who'd clawed her way out of poverty, loved fancy clothes, and would have gone mad for Rodeo Drive had she ever seen it, which she hadn't, as her whole life long she never left central Wisconsin.

I loved her the more knowing she would have loved the spectacle of Rodeo as much as the shopping itself: the hordes of tourists dressed like toddlers in their shorts and sneakers taking pictures, so openly fascinated by the stores and the customers actually buying Dior and Hermès and Baccarat. You can see them trying with heartbreaking frankness to understand, to *grasp*, a fellow creature with the means to buy a pair of yellow leather pants with mauve insets at the hips and crotch for fourteen hundred dollars, and the will to do it.

Gramma Gladys, dead eleven years now, would have gone for Chanel and Halston if she'd had the dough, for sure.

It was inexplicable, this certainty of mine that she was there and had picked this place to commune with me. I'd first sensed it when I was facing the fact that I had to leave Jeff. I'd been so upset, so needing of advice and comfort, and I'd felt so alone, trying to hide a black eye with makeup and carrying on with it because I hadn't wanted to admit I'd made a terrible mistake.

The only good thing that came out of that marriage was Petey.

Gramma Gladys had listened and given me good advice then and ever since.

Now, this distressing Sunday morning, I began. "Gramma, there's this woman and her grandson. Someone's after them. This woman, Amaryllis, she helps poor people, and everybody loves her, except something's going on, something bad, and I don't understand what it is."

I sighed. The traffic fumes wafting from the intersection weren't overpowering at this hour. Faint car exhaust is baseline air in these parts. Eau de L.A.

Get to the point! I felt Gramma Gladys say. She'd never been the most patient person in the world.

The growl of an approaching airliner began to gather in the soundscape, a jet coming in to LAX from Austin or Paris or Louisville.

"I think that now—they're after me too. So what do I do? Fight? Run? If I stay, who do I fight? Gramma, I'm just a little white girl from Wisconsin, and these tribes in South Central— I'm not as tough as them."

They're just people, goddamn it! They're no tougher than you!

"Amaryllis gives so much to others that I wonder if she bothers to look out for herself. You know. Which can be dangerous, and which I certainly know something about." I realized I was on to something. "Everybody says they love her, Gramma. They love her like God—with plenty of fear mixed in! But I don't know if anybody really knows her."

The jet plane's roar pulsed in the atmosphere.

Go back! I felt Gramma Gladys say. *If you care so much, go there. Stand and fight. Never run!*

"But what do I do?"

Just go there. You'll see what to do.

"Just be myself, then?"

No! Don't be yourself!

"Gramma, what do you mean, don't be myself?"

But it never did any good asking her to clarify.

I felt her spirit recede.

" 'Bye, Gramma. Thanks."

ELEVEN

Deep inside George Rowe's sleeping brain a movie started up involving himself and Rita and a soft grassy field, her golden hair riffling in the wind, her small hand on his chest like a bird. He slept deeply, having worked for two days trying to figure out who had attempted to run him over at the Los Angeles River. He knew why.

His dream graduated to kissing, with Rita so lovely in that green blowing meadow.

Then a horrendous sound! And in his dream he thought something the size of the Kremlin must have crashed into Earth a few yards away, and he turned but there was only more soft meadow, but suddenly Rita was gone and something told him to run, and he ran himself awake.

He bolted upright. He smelled it, and he heard the shriek of the smoke alarm.

He grabbed his pants, already hearing muffled thuds in the apartments above and below. Dangerous acridity in his nose. From his living room came the gut-dropping sound of crackling flames. Dirty light from the street helped him see.

"Fire!" he shouted. "Fire in the building!" He crouched beneath the smoke and scuttled to the living room. He saw that something had crashed through his living-room window, and the thing had been full of burning gasoline. Holding his breath, he skirted the fire and seized his kitchen extinguisher. He grabbed a breath in the kitchen.

Flames leaped and boiled in the living room, the couch stuffing feeding them, his whiteboards moaning as the plastic buckled.

He pulled the pin and shot the white plume at the base of the flames, and the fire died back, but the canister quickly emptied. Fresh air blew in from the broken window, and the fire gathered itself like a hungry hyena and fed on it.

He ran into the corridor shouting and began pounding on doors. He found his cell phone in his pants and called 911. A tenant who worked as an EMT met him in the corridor, which was filling with smoke and panicked neighbors.

"Get the people downstairs out," he said.

"Don't go up! George!"

He sprinted to the stairwell—good air in there. He leaped up the stairs, gulped a big breath, touched the door, and opened it to the third and topmost corridor.

A gray haze chased people into the hallway. "Come on, come on," he urged, forcing calm into his voice. "It's OK this way. Go, go."

He knew all the renters by sight and mentally checked them off. There were only twelve apartments.

Sven, the widower, stood motionless in his doorway, deciding whether to make an effort.

Rowe yelled his name in his face.

Sven put up an arm to fend him off. Then his knees buckled. Rowe caught him, maneuvered him over his back, and stumped down to the street.

A siren screamed up, and the firefighters took over.

THE DOOR BUZZED at six thirty Wednesday morning and Gina opened it to reveal George.

He strode in wearing clothes that were too big for him.

"You might hear something on the news," he began.

Five minutes later I was throwing questions at him, thinking hard, trying not to freak out.

"You didn't put yourself in danger, did you?"

He shook his head and smiled that shy, heart-melting smile. "No heroics. Everybody got out. The place is a mess, though. I got out with my wallet and keys and my cell phone."

"Stay with us." The words were out before I knew it.

He smiled again. "No, thank you, Rita. I'm crashing with my friend Gonzalo, over in Los Feliz."

"Is that the trumpet player?" Gina asked from the kitchen.

"Yeah. He's a neurologist too."

"I didn't know that!" Her eyes lit up, and I could tell she was thinking *income*.

"Down, girl," I said.

I thought about those muzzle flashes coming out of that dark car at Kip and me. I said, "OK. You said you might just 'look around' after that drive-by occurred." I used the passive voice in case Petey came out.

"I did."

"What happened?"

"I got chased off." He took a seat on the sofa.

"Was this connected, then?"

"I don't know. I'm doing some other work too."

"What other work?"

"I can't discuss it."

I looked at him. His guyness filled up the room, the way he took up space with such ease. Gina turned on the TV and pulsed coffee beans in the grinder.

I swallowed. "You're in trouble because you tried to protect me, aren't you?"

"I don't know that for a fact. Someone's unhappy with my existence, though."

"Then you're a pair," said Gina.

"What?" he said, turning.

"Didn't you see the Sunday paper?" She scrambled through the recycle bin while he looked at me penetratingly. "Here!" She slapped down the story of Sgt. Annette Soames. "Law student look-alike slain in trigger-happy neighborhood!"

He looked at the picture and read the story carefully.

"George," I said, "what happened to your knuckles and elbows?"

"Little mishap," he murmured, reading.

"You look like you got in a fistfight with a pit bull or something."

He coughed.

I felt my gut tighten.

Gina handed him coffee. "You like sugar, don't you?"

"Yes. Thank you."

He folded the paper and looked up with an expression of total, extreme calm. "I think it might be good for you to leave town for a while."

Fear ignited my temper. "If L.A. isn't safe for me," I hissed in lieu of yelling, because of Petey, "it isn't safe for you!"

Gina said, "Aren't the police investigating everything?"

"The police don't know where to bear down yet," said George. "I mean it, Rita, you should get out of town."

"If you think for one instant that I'm going to run away from this trouble and let you face it alone! I'll be damned if I will. Farmers don't run!"

"You have to trust me," he said.

"You don't know me in the slightest."

"What about law school?" Gina said.

"The hell with law school, Gina," said George, "a law degree won't help any of you if they throw a firebomb in here next. No, all three of you should go. You could drive out to Colorado. I have a friend who runs a ranch there. He'd—"

"Why don't *you* get out of town, George?" I scream-whispered irrationally. "*You* go, OK? The women and children will stay and fight this!"

He smiled a little, amused. "I don't run, either. They find you in the end."

Gina said, "Look."

The television showed a night shot of George's apartment building in flames. A dazed-looking retiree said into the camera glare, "I don't know what happened. I fell down. My neighbor carried me out. He saved my life. George, my neighbor, he saved my life."

I turned to him. "No heroics."

He looked away.

" 'Trust me,' you say."

He sighed. "I'd prefer it if you went away until I figure this out."

I straightened to my full height. I felt galvanized by George's opposition. *"No."*

"I'm not going, either," said Gina stoutly.

He took my hand. "Then at least send Petey."

We exchanged a long silent look.

TWELVE

Petey jumped at the chance to go on an airplane trip with Daniel, whose time was flexible until his movie started shooting in two weeks. Daniel's job was to deliver Petey, that very night, to Aunt Sheila and Aunt Toots in Wisconsin, and do a recon on their living conditions before heading back to L.A. My aunts were joyful at the prospect of initiating Petey into the rural Wisconsin way of life.

I'd initially assumed Gina would take him, but she shook her head. "I'm somewhat on the outs with them."

"How come?"

She sighed as if we'd been over and over this. "Remember that old black car they had?"

"You mean their prized vintage Rambler? That they kept in perfect condition?"

"Um, yeah. Well, I borrowed it last spring, and—" She paused. "Mistakes were made."

"They let you use that car? I can't believe—"

"Well, I sort of pre-borrowed it before getting total permission. Because my car was in the shop, see, and I *needed*—"

"Gina. What happened to the Rambler?"

She gazed at the herb pots on the patio, and beyond them to the side courtyard between our building and the next.

"Gina," I said.

"It's at the bottom of the quarry."

"Oh, my God."

"They know where it is and everything! I mean, I didn't try to hide anything after the fact."

"Oh, my God!"

"Involving the Burris brothers and some other people and a case of Jack Daniel's and a really fun time, I mean, Rita, it's *such* a fun time with those guys. I kind of don't want to go into the exact betting situation that led to the car going off the edge—nobody was hurt!—but suffice it to say Sheila and Toots are almost certainly still mad at me."

"That's the kind of idiotic shit high school kids do! Gina, you're thirty-three years old!"

She suggested Daniel escort Petey. I said, "I thought you were suspicious of Daniel around Petey."

"Oh, gosh, no. I mean, I wondered there, at first, not being any more familiar with the gay lifestyle than Mr. Johnson in typing class with that toupee. But oh, Daniel's great."

So that was a bit of progress.

Jeff, who knew nothing of the drive-by or anything else, was only too pleased to have his weekends free for the time being. I started to tell him a made-up story about Petey's trip, but he didn't even care to hear it.

Daniel said little. "Something heavy's about to go down, right?"

"I hope so."

"Is George in it with you?"

"Yes," I answered.

"Then you'll be all right."

At the apartment's threshold I hugged and kissed Petey to the point of suffocation. He grabbed Daniel's hand and never looked back. After I closed the door I cried until Gina finally yelled at me.

AS AN OPENING move, I went to see Kip Cubitt in the hospital the next day, Thursday.

Kip's eyes were bright and black like his grandmother's and you could see the vigor deep inside.

He took my hand. "I don't like to be alone."

It was ten days now since he'd taken two bullets moments after getting the crap stomped out of him. He was propped up in bed.

The shooting had barely been reported on, due to some politician plunging his car off the PCH with a load of gay prostitutes in the backseat, which pushed all else into the shadows. So this was just another inner-city shooting. Both of our names had been withheld for safety anyway, so the public didn't know that one of the victims was the grandson of the Iron Angel of Los Angeles.

"Do you know who I am?" I asked.

He nodded slowly. "Thank you for helping me."

Now I could really see this young man. He was a little older than I'd thought, maybe seventeen or eighteen. His body was quiet, but those eyes were quick. Robust cheekbones, a fine chin, and I thought he was quite beautiful.

A white bandage clung to the side of his neck like a clamshell. I'd learned that the bullet had not touched his vertebrae, only the soft tissue in his neck. His voice was hoarse. I saw a shaved patch where they'd sewn up the flaplike wound on his skull.

"How're you doing, Kip?"

"I'm doing very well." He smiled. "I'm gonna be OK. See?" and he moved his body sinuously beneath the light blanket, like a careful tadpole.

"That's miraculous," I said.

"So says my grandma. But it was the doctors, you know. My guts are working almost right too."

I had almost forgotten about the wound in his side. "I'm so glad."

The usual paraphernalia of illness hung around the bed, but I noticed only one tube, snaking out from the covers. A nosegay of pink carnations decorated his bedside table. Kip said, "My grandma brought those first thing this morning."

"They smell sweet, don't they?"

I'd had to arrange for permission to see him, as, once out of intensive care, he'd been more or less hidden away in this unmarked private room, while the police investigated the shooting.

The room was nice and bright. We heard efficient voices on the PA system in the hall.

"I've been on my feet already, how do you like that?"

"That is excellent. Here." I gave him a football magazine, a basketball magazine, and a secondhand copy of *The Red Pony*.

"Hey!" he said when he saw the book.

I'd looked for something with a black kid in it, but saw this and remembered how good it was. "I read this when I was your age. John Steinbeck."

Ignoring the sports magazines, he said, "This is a good book. I read this oh, a couple summers ago."

I smiled. "Well, then maybe I'll take it back and get you something different."

"Oh, no." He clutched the novel, his long hands and wrists elegant against the hospital linens. "I want to read it again." He looked at the drawing on the cover, of the white boy and the red horse. "This happened in the West, right?"

"Yes."

"Here in California?" He tried to remember.

"I think so, yes."

"I hope I'll be able to start back to school on time."

"Senior year?"

"Yeah."

"I hope so too, Kip."

We sat for a while. Occasionally a gull or black crow would skim past the window, which otherwise was an exact square of blue. Wispy clouds today, up high.

I said, "Do you know that I'm not a police officer?"

"Yes."

"I understand you didn't want to talk to the police."

An agreeing grunt.

"Still don't want to talk to them?"

"That's right."

"You know we're in this together."

He looked at me questioningly.

I said, "They're after me because they think I saw who shot us.

I didn't, though. They tried for me again. I imagine they'll try again for you, too, don't you think?"

He shrugged, trying for the tough thing.

"And they're after your grandma, did you know that?"

His eyes darted to mine.

I went on, "I don't know if anybody's explained it to you like this yet. Your grandma's certainly not going to tell you. You might think that keeping quiet will get you out of this. Maybe you feel loyalty to someone. But it'll come at a cost, and the cost will be to Amaryllis. Because they're messing with her."

He heaved a sigh and looked away.

I had only the vaguest idea of what I was talking about. "And she would do it, Kip. She'd sell out for you, she'd die for you, you know that. But it wouldn't be right. And it wouldn't end there."

Kip murmured, "What do you do when something bad's got ahold of you? I didn't know what to do. I tried to get away. I was trying to get away that day."

"Tell me about it."

I'm sure you know teenage boys are not the most articulate species, nor the most introspective. I waited hopefully but realistically.

He closed his eyes, and a long shudder ran through his body. I watched the blue square of window. Then I watched the sunlight brighten on the speckled floor, as a bit of mist or smog blew over.

My young friend opened his eyes and reached for the bed control. He pressed a button without looking, and the head of the bed moved higher so his head was level with mine. He cleared his throat, wincing slightly.

Quietly, he began, "One day this dude comes up to me and he

says hey Kip, you want to make some money? I know what that means, so I say no. He says I'll give you five hundred to take one bag from this corner where we're at to a house in Brentwood. I say oh? He was, five hundred plus we do you a favor on top of it. You need some favor, we can do it. I say, I don't know your gang. He says we're not a gang, we're an organization. We go and go, and he hands me the five hundred. I say in my head I can put this to college. He says you got a car. I drive my grandma's car sometimes. I got my license." In spite of his hurt neck, Kip shook his head at himself. "I was a knucklehead like any of them. Why me and why five hundred, is what I don't ask him. I do it. He comes up to me next day and says what favor you want, and I say to have no more to do with you. Because I had thought about it, you know."

I felt a surge of dread listening to this story, combined with a swell of love for Kip's courage in telling me. "What was in the bag you delivered?" I spoke softly, as he had done.

"Drugs, ma'am. Half a kilo of coke, something. That's a lot, you know, but still five hundred was too much for the job. I didn't understand that either."

"When was this?"

"Oh. School was almost out."

"So a few months ago, like in May?"

"Yeah. Then this dude starts coming to the mission. I work there, I do the computers. People donate stuff, sometimes we can't use it but I sell it on eBay, and the money goes in the mission account. My grandma pays me ten dollars for every hundred I convert."

"Pretty good deal."

"Yeah. But I say I don't want to be a mule. Plenty of fools out there, you know what I'm saying? He asks me about the computers. He wants to know about the ABC's accounting, and the stuff I'm doing on eBay. I'm like, well, I don't know anything about any accounting. Then, ma'am, he says to me hey, we know your daddy's in jail. So what? So if you don't come with us, he's gonna get hurt. I just laughed."

"Did you know this guy?"

"I saw him around. He was older. Those kids that lived on Slauson's uncle? That big family. His name's Jerrol."

"Jerrol?" I leaned forward. "Jerrol what?"

"Uh, Bay? Bays?" He saw my face. "What, ma'am?"

"Ahh."

Jerrol Bays was the name of the gunman who murdered Sgt. Annette Soames. "Uh." I shook my head, motioning him to go on.

"Well, then next week my grandma says to me boy, your daddy's been cut." Kip's eyes narrowed at the memory, and he swallowed. "They cut my daddy, and it was my fault."

"Somebody stabbed your dad in prison?"

"Yeah. He didn't die, though."

It took me a minute to internally deal with this information. Carefully, I said, "So they reached into prison and carried out that threat they made to you?"

Kip nodded, and told me the next time Jerrol came around he agreed to work for him. "I thought just until Daddy's out. Maybe six months."

"Did your grandma know about it?"

"She didn't know why he got cut, and I certainly did not tell her I was running drugs!" He moaned. "Oh, that was a bad day."

He pulled himself together and went on. "I go to see my dad up at the Colony, I go with my grandma. He asks her to get me a

117

Dr Pepper and she goes out, and my daddy says, boy, get out of it. Go to your cousin's in Phoenix. Don't tell anybody when you go, and don't tell them where. I say what about you? He says I'll be OK. But if you stay, the both of us'll wind up here or dead. So I tried to go. I got mixed up trying to find the Greyhound."

"And they caught up with you?"

"Yeah." Tears welled in his huge soft eyes. "I helped my grandma. I was doing good, and one time I didn't listen to her. One time."

Kip Cubitt cried, and I reached for tissues and helped him wipe his eyes and his nose.

We sat together for perhaps an hour longer, speaking little.

THIRTEEN

Amaryllis shut the door and folded her noble, giraffelike thighs into the bare metal chair that served as her office throne and said, "Now what is on your mind, sister?" Her vibe was not friendly, and I sensed the same desperation beneath the surface, as if she had agreed to see me against her better judgment.

"I saw Kip yesterday," I said. Today was Friday, going on two weeks after the shooting.

"Did you now."

"I'll get to the point. Kip's in trouble—still. You're in trouble. And *I'm* in trouble, just because some caterer got behind on his payments to the roach control company."

"What?"

"Never mind. Look, the problem, whatever it is, won't go away by itself. I've heard you say that on the radio."

Amaryllis gazed at her knees, large knobs beneath the flimsy flowered dress she wore today.

I took it that this cluttered office was usually about as private as a dime store, what with people zooming in and out to drop off donations, pick up hygiene kits, cajole bus tokens, get on-the-fly advice. The shut door was keeping everybody at bay for a few minutes.

Some of the stuff people deemed worthy to donate to the ABC Mission were a stack of empty Easter baskets, four stacks of VCR movies (no porn, just crap movies nobody would have wanted in the first place, like *You've Got Mail, Waterworld, Smokey & the Bandit 3,* and *Can't Stop the Music*), dozens of bars of soap, a clear plastic football filled with hard candy, a rubber lizard, hardback novels—none of which I'd ever heard of—with dust jackets that must have seemed alluring in 1965 or whenever, assorted used Bibles, bottles of shampoo.

An obsolete-looking laptop was in use on Amaryllis's desk.

At last she said, "Some kind of trouble is worse than others."

"But," I pressed, "no matter what, you gotta attack it, right? You know Kip feels he let you down."

"Truth is, I let him down."

I waited, but she didn't elaborate. "Well, Amaryllis," I said, "it's redemption time. Because you and Kip could climb out of this mess and shine a light on it, and now's your chance. I'm here to help."

"Why?"

"Mostly to save my own neck. Or you could be passive and let this . . . evil overwhelm you and Kip and ruin everything you're doing."

Amaryllis almost smiled. "Sister, how can you help us? You're a little blond girl who doesn't know squat about the way things work down here. I repeat, you don't know squat!"

That got me mad: her scorn combined with her almost round-shouldered manner of defeat. Coldly, I said, "Yes, I do. I know that a bunch of thugs are trying to take over your operation. Right? They think they've got you over a barrel because they can hurt Nathan as long as he's in prison. They tried to get Kip and his principles out of the way. Why was that? Are you gonna be easier to push around than a kid?"

Amaryllis stared at me, and as she stared, I remembered Gramma Gladys telling me not to be myself when I went to the mission. And I puzzled over that again, because myself was doing OK at the moment.

"I might be a blonde but I'm not a dolt," I went on. "You're running what amounts to a safe house here. Some drug boss or somebody thinks this'll make a nice place to do business out of. Just talk to me, goddamn it! I can help you."

"How?"

"I have a brain, and I have resources, and I'm not scared." Only one lie out of three. "Come on, sister."

Amaryllis studied her knees again, her hands flat on her thighs, and I saw how similar Kip's hands were to hers, long and thin and graceful. Hers had endured a lot more wear and tear, certainly, the knuckles large, the skin wrinkled and scarred with decades of kitchen cuts and burns.

She cleared her throat and said, "I want to shuck corn."

"Amaryllis . . . ," I began wearily—

"Come along, sister." She unfolded herself from the chair. "There's half a pickup truck's worth out there. Corn on the cob for dinner tonight."

So we stood together in the shade of the building and shucked sweet corn from the rusted tailgate of a pickup that looked like the Joads had driven it in from Oklahoma. We tossed the clean ears into a gigantic food tub on casters, and the husks into one of the cavernous garbage bins.

Hands now busy, muscles engaged in food prep, Amaryllis seemed to smooth out. She began talking in a low voice.

"When my boy Nathan got sent up, he shared a cell with a man named Vargas, Dale Vargas, and I guess Nathan talked so much about the mission that the Whale started thinking."

"Dale Vargas is called the Whale?"

"Dale the Whale, yes."

"We had one of those in my neighborhood. Fat guy?"

"The Whale is larger than life in many ways. He's an organized man, and he's a bad-ass. Most bad-asses are half-assed, you know what I'm saying? But this one's smarter than most. Not a fortunate thing."

The raw corn smelled marvelous, refreshing as a long drink of well water. Good living food. We shucked in silence.

"It's late in the season for sweet corn," I remarked. The pearly texture of the naked ears, the feel of the clumpy silk—almost but not quite creepy—parting it with my index finger before making the first pull. "When I was little, I couldn't break the ends off."

Amaryllis smiled, her gold side tooth glinting. "You're from where?"

"Farm country, Wisconsin."

Her smile widened. "You're used to a shorter growing season, then." She went on shucking. "Dale Vargas figured out that I, the famous Amaryllis B. Cubitt, have got control of a fair amount of money and goods that come through here. He's out now. He's a drug dealer, what else? Standard street fare. He's got big ideas, frighteningly big ideas. You know what? He wants to be the drug supplier for the whole of Los Angeles, the movie stars, everybody. Trying to worm his way in here, and he's violent, not indiscriminately so, he's very careful how he uses violence. Well, he *has* wormed his way in here, to an extent. Keeps trying to get money from me, tried to get Kip to fence stolen things for him on eBay."

"I have an obvious question," I said.

"And I will answer. When I said you didn't know squat, I meant you don't know the code of the ghetto. Why don't I get the police involved? If I called, they would come, and they would take me seriously, because the mayor likes me, the chief of police likes me, everybody likes me because I do good and don't try to leverage favors. But see here, sister Rita Farmer: police are dangerous if you're working outside the regulations. If you have trouble, you can go to the police, but then they're gonna want to look into your business. If somebody's got something on you, they can turn the cops' eyes bright on you. So people tend to handle things their own way."

"In other words, nobody wants the cops' help with anything, because they all have their own secrets," I said. "Sometimes criminal secrets—their own addictions, their own motives."

"You stabbed me in the arm," said Amaryllis, "and now I'm gonna break your kid's legs. You stole my money, now I'm gonna tell Dale the Whale you've got it in a shoebox under your wife's side of the bed. Maybe you've got a warrant on you, you're not going to phone the police about somebody *else*. Even simpler than that. I cut hair but I'm not licensed, so I'm not going to report that all my equipment got ripped off. My cousin'll help me get it back."

We went on shucking. The crisp sounds of it somehow took away the darkness of what we were talking about.

I remembered being little when, at dinner time, my dad would come to the back door from the garden with an armful of sweet corn. I'd push my brothers away to be the one to help him shuck it. (Gina was not to be found around mundane food tasks in that stage of her life.) The summer air would be as heavy and hot as molten iron, but the corn would be cool in your hands. Daddy showed me how to chew the white end of a corn husk and suck the sugar juice from its fibers. Then the corn would go straight into the boiling pot. "Holy mister," Daddy would say, crunching into it.

"Holy mister," my brothers would echo.

"Holy mister!" I'd pipe, then be told that girls couldn't say holy mister.

"Well, shucks!"

Gramma Gladys would smile. "That kid makes 'shucks' sound like the dirtiest word you ever heard." She'd reach over and pat me approvingly.

It seemed Amaryllis was remembering happy days too. "The corn," she said. "Did you ever see it so big and fine?"

"Tell me more about the Whale," I prompted.

"I've never seen the Whale."

"What?"

"He swims below the surface. I know him and he knows me. We are quite close, in fact."

Amaryllis told me that Dale the Whale was a major networker in jail and out, but rarely did business in person. A perversion of guys like Lee Iacocca and Warren Buffett, he considered himself an important businessman who gets ahead using principles of commerce and economics. "But for him everything's twisted: he uses those principles to—to—" She paused delicately.

"Screw over other people?"

"Amen. He reads business books, those ones people are always trying to get me to read?"

"Like *Give Your Mice the Cheese They Need*?"

"Yes. Ridiculous book."

"Seven Pumpkin Seeds: The Zen Way to Grow a Company?"

"That one too."

"And he's got underlings to deliver drugs and money and messages?"

My companion nodded.

"Like Wichita and Denny?"

She stopped shucking and, once again, stared at me.

I said, "It's obvious."

"Oh, sister."

"Tell me more."

Amaryllis sighed, recommenced shucking, and went on talking. The Whale, she told me, is on the "1-2-3 System" from that book by the guy who brought International Acids back from the dead. "He needs capital, he needs location, and he needs manpower. That's his 1-2-3. On top of everything else, he wants to put money into the collection box, then get me to pay him for jobs he didn't do."

Something finally broke on me. "The Khani Emberton money."

"To make matters worse, yes," said Amaryllis. "The Whale too, has plans for brother Emberton's upcoming endowment. He wants that money for himself."

I laughed incredulously, but Amaryllis only nodded.

I asked, "Has he threatened you over it?"

"He has vowed to get a confederate to kill my Nathan in prison if I don't give him the money when I get it. Uh—" Her voice caught.

"But won't the money be, you know . . ."

She cleared her throat, holding back a thunderhead of emotion. "Be tied up in a legal trust? No. Khani knows me. He trusts me to invest the money wisely." Her voice was heavy with irony. "It's uncertain if we will even have a board of directors. If I wanted to, I could draw the money out and use it for any purpose. The Whale himself suspects how vulnerable that money will be. Another reason the police will be of no help: even though the Whale did time, that was a freak occurrence. I understand he never carries anything incriminating on him—no drugs, weapons, messages, nothing. He's a very clean person in that way."

"Amaryllis, we have to stop him." I shut up as the Reverend Bill Culpepper came out and stretched in the sunshine. He strolled over to us in the shade, which had narrowed as the sun moved west, bathing more of that side of the building in afternoon light.

"Sister Amaryllis, sister uh—"

"Rita," I said.

"Hello," he said. He stared at me, then at Amaryllis, then at me again with his habitually tired eyes.

Amaryllis said, "Would you excuse us for a minute, sister Rita?"

I walked off toward the scrub-covered athletic fields, then remembering the dog pack, veered behind the building near the alley where the dumpsters were. I sidled into it, realizing that Amaryllis's and Reverend Culpepper's voices were aimed directly into it. By a quirk of acoustics, I was able to catch what they said.

Bill Culpepper: "I was unable to clear that business you asked."

Amaryllis: "Try again, brother."

Culpepper: "I have tried again."

Amaryllis: "Then you try a different way, brother, you understand what I'm saying?"

Culpepper: "It could go bad for us."

Amaryllis: "I have faith in you. You're a reverend, aren't you?"

Culpepper: "You ask a lot."

He went away, and I stood thinking for a couple of minutes. *What if Amaryllis is the real Whale here? Well, she's got connections at all levels of L.A. society.*

And standing there, trying to decide how deep to go to help this enigmatic woman, is how I wound up slipping beneath the surface to the second level of justice, with all its dangers, and all its savage satisfactions.

FOURTEEN

George met me for breakfast at Good Mood the next morning, Saturday. He listened carefully to everything I told him about my visits with Kip and Amaryllis. "So," I concluded, "we've got to learn more, and the mission is obviously the place. It's like this vortex, with Amaryllis in the center."

He nodded, chewing his French toast. He swallowed. "Might be a good place to have a look around." The thick French toast was fragrant with cinnamon. My vegetable omelette was good too.

It put me off a bit that George hadn't troubled to shave this morning. I'd never known him to skip a day; he was so fastidious. He ate his food steadily.

"We ought to find this Whale," I said, "and, well . . . do something."

George smiled. "I'll look into him. Do you think he might hang out at the mission?"

"Yes, but Amaryllis said she's never seen him."

"That's hard to believe."

"Well, I believed her. I think we ought to, like, infiltrate the mission. Somehow."

George laughed. "Now you want to play spy?"

"Well—yeah. I mean, I can't think of anything better right now. Obviously somebody's gotta have a talk with Dale the Whale. If he's the one hurting all these people, putting a stop to him ought to solve everything."

"That's a big if."

"You mean—"

"I mean there could be a lot of people interested in the Khani Emberton fund."

At the next table a twentysomething couple was discussing getting wedding tattoos. "But if it's a Japanese character we can say it means whatever we want," said the guy. Both had very buff bodies.

"That's not the point," she muttered, looking glum.

He said, "The coffee here is excellent."

It certainly was.

"Rita," said George, "you're jumping the gun. Let me look into this Dale Vargas first. We won't know what we're dealing with until I do. You just sit tight."

"I want to go and talk to Amaryllis again."

"No."

"Yes."

He sighed. "Rita, you're inexperienced. If you ask more questions, she could get suspicious. She might be a truly innocent victim of circumstance. Or not."

I ate my omelette and thought about that.

"Look," he went on, "I've been an investigator for half my working life, and I've learned how to move around undercover."

My temper flared. "Maybe you could give me a few pointers, since I'm such a complete ignoramus."

"Rita, come on. I'm not putting you down, I'm being real." He looked out the window at a bicyclist fastening his wheels to a tree with a lock that looked like it could moor a barge. "That's the difference between men and women, you women get so personal about everything."

I got huffier, then realized he was right.

He continued, "Yeah, I could teach you some things about investigating. Mostly, you use a computer mouse."

"Really?"

"Well, no. Depending on the case, you do have to get out and look around. Talk to people."

"I bet all it is is common sense."

"Rita, all anything is is common sense. But you have to have know-how too. You use common sense to fly a helicopter, but you've got to know a few things about aviation first! Please." He drained his coffee. "It's so easy to make a false move, just a little lapse, and suddenly you go from being in control to big trouble. Or dead."

I said nothing.

"I'm not calling you dumb or weak, OK?" he said. "It's just that we don't have time for you to go all the way through detective school before we move on this. So please—I'm asking you: stay away from the mission for now. I've got to run up to Canada in a few days on that other case I mentioned. By then I know there'll be work for you to do here. I just want to keep you safe. OK?"

"OK."

He looked at me harder. "OK?"

"OK!"

DANIEL PHONED AROUND noon, as Gina and I were cleaning the apartment to Nancy Wilson singing "It Never Entered My Mind" on one of her blues collections.

"Where are you?" I asked.

"On the way home from LAX."

"How did it go?"

"Petey's going to be . . . fine with them." But he spoke without his usual cheerful conviction.

"What's the matter?"

"Well, your aunts are . . . uh . . . eccentric."

"Oh! Of course. They've both always been a little nuts. That's just the family."

He laughed. "Right. Well, it's obvious they love Petey, they're thrilled to have him. He seemed to take to them pretty well too. They paid total attention to him and made sure he was cozy. Nice room for him, with about a thousand pillows. Those girls are mad for shams, you know?"

"Yes."

"Neither one of them's a big talker."

I laughed.

He went on, "Sheila's always going around in these army boots, digging in the dirt outside. Petey liked that. She said she's going to make him harvest the pumpkins with her, if he stays long enough."

"Well, good exercise."

"Yeah! Their house is this incredible time capsule. Those mahogany moldings."

"Yup. Do they still have the inlaid tables and the cream pitchers?"

"Oh, yeah. Oh, yeah. Thousands of cream pitchers."

"How was Aunt Toots?"

"Uh, fine, I guess. She's really into crafts. I'd forgotten about crafts. Nobody in California does crafts, do they?"

"Not that I know of. What's her thing now?"

"Was she into the beer can thing when you last saw her?"

"No, that must be new, what's that?"

"Well, she rinses out her beer cans and then she uses tin snips to cut them into little models. She knows how to do a rocking chair and a little car, but the car takes two cans plus some of those brass things teachers used to stab papers together with."

"I see."

"She's got fourteen beer-can rocking chairs on a shelf, and sitting in each one is a dried-apple-face doll."

"Oh, God. Are any of those in Petey's room? They'll give him nightmares."

"No, no."

"What else?"

"I'm afraid they found his ScoreLad offensive."

"Oh."

"They acted pretty horrified of it."

"Hm."

"They seem to think he'll go blind if he plays with it too much."

132

"I think they're getting that mixed up with another thing that if a boy plays with it too much he'll go—"

"Rita!"

"Well, they're probably right. For all we know, all these little boys with ScoreLads'll be going around with white canes when they're twenty-five. I hate the damn thing too."

"Do you know their phone service goes in and out?"

"Yes. That's the rural life, you know."

"Well, anyway, I think Petey'll be OK. He discovered this old gazebo that's all grown over with vines, a fabulous hideout."

"I remember that gazebo, Gina and I used to plot against the boys in it. Good. Did he cry when you left?"

"No, you know, he didn't. He's learned to be a pretty tough little guy. I told him his job was to take care of these two nice aunties, and he said, 'Roger, I'm on it,' and he took off into the field to pull up a rutabaga for dinner."

"Wow."

"He was disappointed they didn't have a dog, in spite of your telling him they wouldn't."

"But Sheila and Toots seemed, you know, OK?"

"Oh, yeah. They're pretty vigorous—you should see Sheila's biceps from all that woodcutting."

"Well, they're only in their sixties."

"Neither of them ever married?"

"No, I don't think they ever found guys who could handle them. I remember Toots telling me once, 'Men are too much bother. If I wanted a man around here I'd buy a goat!'"

Gina, overhearing from the next room, laughed long and hard.

Daniel muttered, "Sometimes I feel the same way."

"Me too."

"Well, anyway," he said, "Petey will be safe with them, and I'm sure he's going to learn ten times more living with them than going to kindergarten in West Hollywood. They were very gracious to me."

"They put you up, right?"

"Yeah, for both nights. Nice little bed in the den. I just had to avoid making eye contact with the taxidermized boar's head in there."

"Oh yeah, him."

"Those tusks."

"Yeah, my uncle Fritz shot him in Texas, oh, thirty years ago."

"It's an eclectic item."

"That head is their most prized possession, believe it or not."

"Well, they've got it pretty well secured, I'd say. Which is good, because Petey was immediately fascinated by it."

"Daniel—"

"Yeah?"

"You won't tell anybody where he is, will you?"

"Of course not. Relax, Rita."

FIFTEEN

George Rowe fingered the wig. The sign on the plastic bin said ONLY $3. He gripped the copper-colored vortex of curls firmly, then clawed it all over. The curls loosened, then sprang into a psych-ward tangle.

"Hey!" said the thrift shop's proprietor.

"I'll buy it," said Rowe. "These shoes too, and the sweatshirt. These briefs too."

"I'm glad I didn't throw those out," said the proprietor.

Back at his friend Gonzalo's house in Los Feliz he dropped off his bundle in the bathroom, then went to the kitchen.

Gonzalo, the jazz-trumpet-playing neurologist, had gone surfing on this pretty Saturday afternoon because tasty swells were coming in from the south at Malibu.

Fending off the attentions of Tamiroff, Gonzalo's assertive

Russian wolfhound, Rowe opened the kitchen cupboards one by one. He collected a bottle of corn oil, two birthday candles, a glass baking dish, and a roll of paper towels. He found a few safety pins and a book of matches in a junk drawer. He went out to the back-yard, sidestepping piles of Tamiroff crap, picked up a few egg-sized stones from a decorative bed, and brought everything into the green-tiled bathroom.

He stripped and sighed into the mirror. "Ugly bastard," he said to his reflection. Proud of his strong physique, he was glad his face was rough. Broad forehead, round nose. Straight eyebrows. Jutting ears. Guys should be ugly, he felt, except when they smile.

He lighted one of the birthday candles and held it to the bot-tom of the baking dish, depositing a layer of soot all over it. When the candle burned down, he blew it out and set the dish aside.

Holding the wig over the sink, he combed corn oil through the scratchy curls with his fingers, then blotted the thing with a paper towel and set it aside.

He stepped into the pair of gray, ragged briefs from the bottom of the underwear bin at the thrift shop. He had sniffed them and shaken them out in case of roaches in the store; they were OK.

When he had stooped to pick up Sven in the apartment-building fire, he had split his pants. He took out those black pants now and repaired the split crudely with the safety pins, then put them on. He dropped the stones into the pockets, making the pants sag sloppily.

He slipped his bare feet into the thrift-shop shoes, a pair of beige vinyl boots.

The sweatshirt was gray and had a born-free type picture of a howling wolf on the front, with a spirit catcher emblem on the back. He rubbed some corn oil on his hands, then smeared them in the soot on the baking dish. He dirtied the sweatshirt with the resulting black goo, not overdoing it, paying special attention to the seams and underarms.

He made more black goo, then worked over his ankles, neck, face, and hands, and looked in the mirror. He moistened a paper towel and wiped off some of the black, leaving a greasy smooth dirtiness behind.

Next, he opened a plastic mouthguard case and took out a set of upper buck teeth and fitted them over his own teeth. These were not cheap plastic teeth from a costume shop; they were realistic chompers made for him by a theatrical dentist he had once done some work for. The once or twice he'd used them, they'd worked well, very well. Only the two front-most teeth were really bucked out. The look was arresting, but not overkill. He stroked his stubble.

It was unfortunate for buck-toothed people that their buck teeth gave the impression of stupidity, but that's the way it was. When Rowe wore these teeth, people looked at him with pitying condescension, then away.

Lastly, he eased the wig on. The oily tendrils hung into his eyes. He tucked the side curls behind his ears, creating a pathetic fast-lane kind of look. That was it.

He smiled at himself.

ROWE GOT OFF the number 53 bus ten blocks from the ABC Mission and ambled toward it, settling into a loser's gait, low footswing. Then he changed his mind and perked it up a bit. He wanted to be down on his luck but hopeful, perhaps ready to listen to somebody's gospel of change.

He stopped at a liquor store and paid for a pint of Richards Wild Irish Rose wine with two singles and change.

The only other white person in the store caught his eye: a skaggy pregnant woman buying a pint of bottom-shelf vodka.

Inwardly Rowe shook his head at the miserable series of choices the woman had to have made. She'd taken to the streets and gotten pregnant to boot, and still she was using; he could practically see the residue coming out of her pores—her skin had that unmistakable drugged-out slackness.

He left the store and walked along. Just before rounding the corner to the mission he unscrewed the wine cap and took a pull, momentarily forgetting his teeth and bumping them on the bottle's threaded mouth. He swished the poisonous-tasting stuff around his mouth, and stepped over to the curb ready to spit it out. But a couple of young guys turned from a doorway to watch him, so instead of spitting, which would have looked odd, he swallowed it. Jesus, how many unknown chemicals were in it, each trying to cancel out the bad flavor of another. He uncapped the bottle again and discreetly spilled a little on his sweatshirt.

A serious alcoholic he'd known had once explained to him, with great patience, how fortified wine gives you the most alcohol for the money, and all you have to do is get to know the pricing at your local booze shop to decide which brand to buy. This man had made a point of dressing as cleanly as possible so that he could occasionally treat himself to better wine by walking into the family-style Italian restaurants of Oakland, which is where he lived, and sitting down at a table just vacated by diners but not yet cleared. He'd slug down whatever few ounces of wine they'd left behind, usually in the woman's glass. He'd smell her lipstick on the rim as he drank, and he told Rowe to try it sometime, it was a turn-on. The friend was principled enough not to steal tips.

Rowe shook off that memory.

The foot traffic at night around the ABC Mission was fairly heavy; addicts find it hard to hold on to cars. The slow shuffle of the homeless sanded down their shoes as they formed pairs and trios to talk and smoke and scheme about where their next meal or high might come from. Lots of wheelchairs too, some powered, some piled high with possessions and pushed along by their owners.

He clumped up to the security person at the mission's gate. He was surprised to be looking into the face of the tall dreadlocked black guy who, with the white woman, had chased him away from the Eighth Street district where Rita and Kip had gotten shot.

Well, well.

The fellow seemed all right; that is, calm and intelligent.

Rowe didn't show his surprise; he kept his slovenly poise and said in a thick voice, "I'm hungry."

"Come in then, brother," said the man kindly.

A short time later Rowe was chowing down a bowl full of macaroni and cheese and some green beans, drinking hot tea at a long table with other men. Almost all the roughly two hundred diners tonight were men. Rowe noticed that among the few women was the pregnant addict from the liquor store. She ate slowly, her head lowered to her dish like a dog's.

All too typical, he thought. Spends what few dollars she's got on that pint of liquor, then comes here to eat free.

The woman wore a pair of pink sweatpants, the waistband

distended around her bulging belly. How far along was she, he wondered. Six, seven months? Her grimy feet sported a pair of parakeet-blue sandals. Her arms, sticking out from a tight Donald Duck T-shirt, were like broomsticks, and a dirty bandage covered probably some festering sore on an upper arm. She might have been pretty had she not let herself go; she looked to be about forty-five but was probably much younger.

He felt sorry for her and for the baby she was carrying. What a lousy start some kids get in life.

The sebaceous tendrils of the wig hung in his eyes.

Amaryllis B. Cubitt had gotten up in front to say a grace, then had taken off.

Rowe kept glancing around. He caught a look at a female security guard but didn't see her face very well. Her fireplug build was right.

It was dark out now, and many of the diners wandered into the night because it was clear and warm, perhaps still in the seventies. If you had some cardboard—or even a plentiful supply of newspapers—you could insulate yourself quite well to sleep. That's a fact he'd learned a long time ago.

He followed the rest down to the men's dormitory, lingering slower and slower in the corridor until he was alone. He slipped away.

The mission's business spilled into all the rooms of the former junior high. He wandered the halls, trying to get a feel for the place. He looked for doors with newer locksets. He found two, one at either end of an upstairs corridor.

The security staff were busy overseeing the bedding-down process, which was mostly handled by volunteers who were one of two types: mild-looking but very big sons of bitches, or little and ex-con-looking. As he moved, he kept hearing the same voices coming from the lobby and realized the custom of the security people must be to congregate in the front lobby whenever they didn't have something else to do. That way they could keep an eye on the courtyard and the street out front, and handle anybody coming in or going out. He wondered if anyone patrolled the outer reaches of the property after dark.

It was easy to elude the security staff. He counted five of them tonight, four men and the woman.

He thought about those two locked doors and decided to wait, maybe until midnight when the security detail might go down by a couple more.

He found a hiding place behind a pile of donated junk near an open stairwell. No sooner had he settled down to wait, however, than he heard a commotion.

"Leave me alone," a female voice rasped, over sounds of scuffling.

Rowe poked his head up.

The pregnant skag was being followed down the corridor toward him by a couple of bums he'd eaten dinner with. One said, "All I want's a kiss, that's all."

The other drooled, "You're so pretty."

They plucked at her like gulls testing a piece of garbage.

"Get away from me," she croaked, her voice practically shot, like the rest of her. Scared shitless.

Rowe sprang from his hiding place.

The two creeps and the woman were so startled they almost fell over each other.

"Leave her alone." Rowe's buck teeth helped him to remember to speak a little slurringly, as he had earlier in the evening.

"Easy, man," said the first creep, backing away like the coward he was.

The second simply grunted and strolled off down the corridor, flinging over his shoulder, "Ugly bitch anyway."

Rowe stared the two all the way down the corridor. The air in the corridor smelled of cardboard cartons.

He took the woman's thin arm. She turned her face up to his. Their eyes touched.

For seconds, neither could speak. Many, many seconds. Their faces were as blank, as stupefied as if they'd been smacked with a couple of frying pans.

At last Rowe choked, *"Rita."*

SIXTEEN

Seeing George's face coalesce from beneath those greasy curls was one of the great shocks of my life.

I was too stunned to even laugh.

Both of us stood stoically gazing at each other in our horrible ensembles, then George guided me down a quiet corridor.

"You're marvelous," he murmured.

"You look as convincing as I do," I said. He really did look atrocious. Further, I was impressed with how he'd changed his body language, ordinarily so strong, to that of an anxious loser: canted forward from the waist, his lower body lagging behind, as if he wasn't quite of one mind about where to walk, let alone anything else.

He said, "I wouldn't if I were trying to look pregnant. I told you to stay away from here."

"Yeah, well. Who did you?"

"Who did me?"

"You know: who did your wig and makeup and costume?"

He laughed silently. "I did."

"No way."

"Way."

"Awesome, George, awesome." I have to admit, my heart was fluttering with pleasure, having run into him so unexpectedly. Goddamn it. "Down to the dirty ankles. The safety pins up the butt seam are inspired."

He smiled with those horrible teeth. "I thought so too."

IT HAD TAKEN me *hours* to get ready. With personnel!

My friend Chino, a costumer, brought over the pregnancy vest, essentially a leotard with a twenty-four-week foam abdomen built in, and the obnoxious Donald Duck T-shirt, in children's large, which was just right for that my-tits-want-to-pop-out look. My slight build worked well here: the big belly made my arms and legs look spindly.

Gina supplied the pink sweatpants, having found them abandoned in the laundry room downstairs last week. She also furnished the blue jellies.

I told Chino I was planning to crash a party hosted by an ex-boyfriend and needed to blend in with the crowd.

"Some company," he said. "What are you gonna do there—sabotage?" He had a cute mustache and a barrel chest.

"No, just some eavesdropping."

"Oh." Another journeyman in Hollywood, he got his start doing blood and gore effects for low-budgets, and moved into costumes after losing a chunk of his forearm in an explosive-squib mishap.

He did a lot of costumes for Half Fast Pictures, of *Fingershredder* fame, and we'd worked together briefly when he dressed me as a young mother for a detergent ad. He didn't get much chance to design original costumes; mostly he combed the secondhand shops and went to estate sales.

Then my good friend Yvonne swept in, trailing her makeup trunk on wheels. She was wonderfully large and beautiful, wearing one of her signature flowing caftans, this one a Japanese-patterned silk in shades of gold and charcoal. Very cool.

Chino took off, with a thank-you bottle of wine from the interested hands of Gina.

I sat in a kitchen chair under the best light in the apartment, the bland fluorescent tubes over the middle of the kitchen. Yvonne supplemented with a small mechanic's lamp that she plugged in and hung on a cupboard handle.

She pushed her sleeves up to her elbows and fastened them in place with rubber bands. She stood before me, hands on hips. "Now, then. What do you need?"

"A couple of years on the streets," I said. "Drugs. Booze."

"You got it."

She was a freelance makeup artist, one of the best in Hollywood. She was an unapologetic fat chick who loved life.

As she worked, she murmured aloud. "I'm gonna use this new liquid latex, it's very thin." She stretched the skin on my left cheek and painted on the cold liquid with a brush. The latex dried almost immediately. She released the skin. "See, this thin stuff makes the finest of wrinkles, nothing too much. We use a thicker brand for aging. I'm just making you look shopworn."

"That's it," I encouraged. The smell of the liquid latex was sharp at first, then nothing as soon as it dried.

Yvonne did this over and over, in the right places on my face and neck, also my arms and hands.

"The hands and wrists have to show equal wear," she said.

Gina was fascinated. "What's that?"

Yvonne tossed an auburn tress from her eyes. "Mortician's wax." She molded a lump of it over the bridge of my nose. "I could give you a real honker, but I gather you're going to be in close proximity with the people you want to fool tonight, so we won't overdo it."

"That looks good," said Gina.

Yvonne dropped my chin with shadows and deepened my natural frown lines. "I'm adding tiredness lines here under your eyes, and the way I'm gonna do it will suggest bags. But I won't actually thicken up bags for you, because that too, can be detectable on close-up."

Yvonne used a fine brush to paint a line of red along my inner lower lids. "This stuff used to sting, but they've improved it," she said. I'd never had it on before. She used a coarse stippling sponge with two shades of foundation to make my face mottled and weary.

Next she picked up a small palette kit with five rich-colored pastes. "Now I'll use a little of this stuff—"

"What's that?" queried Gina again.

"This is a bruise-and-burn wheel. I'm going to apply just a little of the darkest maroon to suggest an almost-healed bruise under her left eye here." She dabbed it on and smoothed it with a foam-tip applicator. The applicators were like disposable plastic spoons, except with white foam tips about the size of a fingertip.

"I remember using makeup to *cover* a black eye," I said.

"Yeah, I can do that pretty well too," said Yvonne, and named a male film star. "I've covered him up on more than one occasion."

"Wait, what?" said Gina.

"Yeah, he's sort of a postmodern Montgomery Clift. Goes out to leather clubs in search of rough trade. They give it to him, all right."

Gina was dumbfounded. "You mean you've covered up bruises he got in *gay clubs*?"

"Yes."

"But he's such a stud! How could he . . ."

I said, "Man versus myth."

Yvonne shrugged and went on, "Bruises change with time, so this kit gives me everything I need to blend a bruise of any age. See, here's red, sick-yellow, olive-green . . ." She rummaged through another drawer in the trunk. "Now we've got to make you dirty. Here." She came up with two vials of soil-colored powder. "Let's see, shall it be Flagstaff Umber, or Cheyenne Russet?"

"Skid Row Black," I suggested.

"We call that 'Chimney Sweep.' "

"Ah."

Her laugh rang out like an opera diva's. I just loved Yvonne. She worked with the powder.

I'd already stripped off my nail polish and gnawed my nails short. Gina had mourned that, but I'd said, "For art, you gotta suffer." Yvonne forced some grime under what nails I had left and reddened my knuckles.

"What else have you got in there?" Gina wanted to know.

"Apart from all this? Blood, sweat, and tears, honey! Blood, sweat, and tears."

"Yeah?"

"I've got fresh scab, blood capsules—here's one I really like." She held up a flat plastic container of Contac-sized capsules. "This kind has red powder in it, not liquid blood. You tuck it back in your mouth and when you crush it in your teeth a little bit, the powder mixes with your saliva, and you can spit blood over the course of a fairly long scene."

"What if you swallowed one?" I asked.

"Oh, they're nontoxic. I mean, this month they're nontoxic. Everything's going to gang up and kill us someday, right?" She laughed again, her hands nimble and busy with tissues and puffs.

She painted some nicotine stains on my teeth with a tiny brush. "This stuff comes off with alcohol," she mentioned, "so if you drink tonight, be careful."

I sucked wind in and out through my teeth to dry them.

Even though hair wasn't her specialty, Yvonne helped me darken mine with some water-soluble dye. I studied myself in her hand mirror.

"That doesn't look right," said Gina.

Yvonne agreed. "Your haircut's too good. Even if we slicked it back, drowned-rat style, you'd still look too crisp."

"Get my scissors," I told Gina grimly.

"Wait!" cried Yvonne. She plunged her arms into the bottom of her trunk and came up with a dead poodle and a raccoon pelt—at least that's what they looked like.

"These got wrecked during a murder sequence in *Sumo IV*— remember when the sumo trainer attacks the wasabi merchant after the kid throws the match and the bad guys win their bet?" She paused. "You guys probably didn't see that one."

"No," Gina and I admitted.

"Well, anyway—"

"I like the raccoon one," I said. I tucked my hair into a wig stocking and put it on.

Gina said, "That's it. It's very you."

Yvonne held up the mirror and I had to agree. The jagged, short-fur pile made me look as if I'd tried to cut my own hair with a propane torch.

"Man," said Gina, "you look vile."

NOW, IN THE dim upper corridor of the ABC Mission, I whispered to George, "I thought you were going to start by looking into this Dale Vargas online."

"I did, after we ate breakfast. A man by that name exists. He did time for check fraud at the Men's Colony the same time Nathan Cubitt went in, they did overlap, so that part checks out."

"Where is he now?"

"I don't know. That's a project for me, all right—try to find this guy. But I think there's something of interest to us right here, tonight." He led me up the staircase. "You're going to be my lookout."

We ducked into a recessed classroom doorway. The door was solid oak.

"The other doors have windows," I observed.

"Yes, and they're not triple-locked. There's another one like this at the opposite end down there." He sized up the door.

"Is there a basement?"

"Yeah, there must be, for the boilers for the hot water." He drew a leatherette case about the size of a checkbook from his pocket.

"You going to pick the locks?"

He glanced upward at the old-fashioned transom with a swivel pane. "I should, but on second thought, let's save some time. Good old public-school architecture."

"Wait," I said, "that's like ten feet up there. You're not going over it."

"No."

"Good, because—"

"You are."

Well, I hadn't come here to sit around and eat bonbons. I stifled my fear, and all I can say is, I'm glad I'm little, and flexible from my yoga.

"Can you take off that—fetus?" George asked.

"God, no, if we get caught—"

"Yeah, OK."

I climbed his thighs and he boosted me to his shoulders. The transom window was about two feet by three—perfect classical ratio. I was able to push the pane in at the top, then pull it out fully at the bottom. Balancing on George's shoulders, I clambered in, first my left leg, then my pregnant belly, then my right leg, then the rest of me. I had to hang on to the edge and drop down, about five feet. I could see just well enough to judge the drop. I landed OK.

I unbolted the locks and George came in.

Watery shadows danced on the ceiling from the traffic skimming by one story below.

The desks and American flag were long gone, though the chalkboards remained, even the trays holding pieces of chalk. The boards were empty of writing, however. The room smelled musty, and I thought I detected a machine-oil odor as well.

The room was unoccupied except for three black things that looked like overbuilt refrigerators. They said BROWNING in nice lettering across the fronts.

"Gun safes," said George.

A chill gripped the back of my neck.

"This would be the glory hole, then," I said.

"Maybe." He sucked his hillbilly teeth.

"Can you break into them?" I asked.

"Not without a welding torch. Let's move on."

We went to the door. "How are we going to throw the deadbolts from the outside?" I asked. "I can't climb out the way I came in."

He again pulled out his leatherette case.

"You can pick a lock *shut*?"

"I can, yes."

George fiddled with his picks as I watched the still-empty corridor. Glancing back at him, I remembered encountering Vince Devereaux begging on the street last year at Gramma Gladys's parking lot; he'd been in homeless-guy costume and character, preparing for a role, and famous as he was, I didn't recognize him until he said his name. People's assumptions really work with you when you're trying to fool them.

"There," said George.

We walked down the corridor, flanked by the rows of lockers, all without locks—doubtless too much trouble to tear them out. "What could be stored in these?" I wondered.

George said, "I doubt anything of interest to us. These hallways are in use during the day for counseling and group meetings and so on. Some of the offices are up here too. No need to hide bodies in the lockers."

We stopped at the other triple-locked door, which was recessed like the first.

George set himself back on his heels, thighs out, and I gripped his hands and began climbing him to the transom, when we heard a man's voice.

"Hey, who's there?"

George had half lifted me. He straightened his legs so that I more or less fell into his arms. He looked at me with a gleam, and began madly kissing me.

He grunted like a bear rooting for grubs, and I whined with pleasure like one of my neighbors did at night with her sleazy boyfriend. He couldn't kiss me properly with those buck teeth, and his breath smelled of the awful wine he'd bought, but all that plus his corn-oil dirt couldn't cover up what a virile damn stud he was. I dug my fingers into his strong shoulders like a white-trash cat and kissed him back in spite of myself. My pregnant belly got in the way somewhat. He gave me a tiny shake, as if to say, "So there!" He fumbled with his zipper. My pulse raced double-time.

A security guard in his gray T-shirt stomped at us. "Now why'd you two come up here?" He was a thick-boned Latino guy with blackwork tattoos on his forearms.

Slowly, we disengaged ourselves, grinning stupidly.

"Why do you think?" George said lewdly. I giggled.

"Well, get the hell away from here. Go outside in the bushes if you want to do that." He shooed us down the staircase. "You, sir, are disgusting!" he said to George. "Can't you see she's expecting?"

"I like 'em that way," he slurred.

We moseyed along. To our surprise, the guard didn't march us all the way back to our respective dormitories, on either end of the main corridor, but peeled off to patrol another corridor.

I led us to Amaryllis's office, which was also locked, but with only the regular type of doorknob lock. George took a Safeway card from his back pocket and slipped it easily.

"I don't know if this is even worth it," I said, "but—"

"We're here, let's make the most of it."

"What are we looking for?"

"Anything unusual."

"Everything in here's unusual."

Among the piled-high donations were half a dozen boxes of coconut cookies, four infant bathtubs, nested, a horse's-head ashtray, a Parcheesi game from about fifty years ago, fat orange hanks of extension cords, and a tall pile of used Bibles.

George rifled through her desk drawers. "I'd like to find an address book. A phone list."

I flipped open her laptop and powered it up. At the sound of its welcoming *dwing-dwong!* we caught our breaths, but realized the sound would have been barely audible out in the corridor. I clicked around, but without her password I couldn't get into any of her files. I guessed she kept her address book with her, or on the laptop.

"Ah, here's a locked one," said George. He got out his leatherette kit again and in a second the drawer came open.

In it lay a thick brown envelope, with a string closure and a number scrawled on it in black marker.

"That's tomorrow's date," I realized. I unwound the string and handed the envelope to George. "You look."

153

"It's cash, all right," he said, drawing out a stack of hundred-dollar bills. Ben Franklin never looked so calm and neutral. *You're at the center of so many things, buddy, aren't you?* George quickly counted it. "Ten thousand."

"We could buy a lot of fortified wine with that," I remarked.

He put it back and handed the envelope to me to retie. I started to wind the string around the paper circle, when he touched my hand.

"No," he said, "the string was wound counterclockwise."

"Whoa," I said.

"These are the kinds of things you have to pay attention to. We could rearrange all this crap lying around here and I bet she wouldn't even notice, but if she goes to untie this envelope again, she'll realize it wasn't like she left it."

I wound the string counterclockwise.

"There was about an inch and a half left out," he added.

He walked me to the women's dormitory. "Do you suppose she'll be here in the morning?" George murmured as we went along.

"Maybe, they have chapel every Sunday morning in the gym. I'd think she'd want to be here for that."

"Let's try to watch for her, OK?"

"OK."

Wichita, the security guard, was hanging around, talking to a volunteer who was handing out towels.

"Oh," said George when he saw Wichita. He stopped walking.

"What?" We weren't quite within earshot of them.

"Nothing. Rita?"

"Yes?"

He looked into my eyes with such warmth. "You know I care for you."

"Yes, George."

He paused. "Good night, then."

"Good night."

In the women's dormitory everyone was getting ready for bed. There were maybe twenty of us. A volunteer had put out a last-minute snack of taco chips, poured from a giant bag just past its sell date, donated by a grocery store.

Earlier, I'd stashed my vodka between the sheets of the cot I'd been assigned. The toothless black lady who'd taken the cot next to me watched me check for it.

"I could have helped myself to that," she said.

"Uh," I said, "well, want a slug?"

She smiled and reached for it. "It's against the rules," she whispered, "but we'll be real quiet-like." She wiped her mouth carefully on her sleeve before and after swallowing a third of the bottle. She handed it to me and I took a sip.

I said, "I'm DeeDee."

"My name's Pearl."

"So, uh, do you come here often?" I asked like a complete total moron nitwit.

Pearl smiled, and it looked like even her gums were decayed. Her face was as seamed as a Texas ranch wife's, and her long gray hair had been wild when I first saw her, at dinner. She'd just bathed, though, and wrapped up her hair in her towel, which gave her a queenly look. She seemed to feel it, holding her head to me in profile.

"Way too often," she answered. "But this is the nicest shelter I've ever been in, and that's saying a lot."

"What brings you here tonight?"

"Oh, I only come in when I run out of drugs."

Well, that was frank.

"I like crack," I ventured.

"Me too. You don't happen to—"

"No. Wish I did." I laughed world-wearily.

"I like to rock it myself. When I have the means."

"Uh, yeah, me too." Whatever the hell that meant. "I like heroin too," I added.

"For going to sleep I like pills."

"Like what?"

"Ox."

"Uh . . ."

"You know. Downers. Oxycotton." Pearl hugged herself. "Mm."

"Oh, you mean OxyContin?"

"Whatever. You know, I don't usually talk to white girls."

I smiled. "Well, we're all in it together, you know?"

"Mm."

"So do you know the folks here, like the guards and stuff?"

"Not the guards so much. But Amaryllis, I know her from forever."

"Oh, yeah?"

Pearl recalled one of the old jazz clubs on Central Avenue, now defunct. "We all liked to go listen of a Friday night, Saturday night. People seemed to have more time in those days. Amaryllis always made friends. She was older than my crowd, but I did see her there, listening to Squire B. Jones, Gloria Rivers, artists like that would come through."

"She's made a lot of her life in this neighborhood, hasn't she?" I suggested.

"She's done a lot more than people know."

"Good stuff or bad stuff?"

"Well, good, to my way of thinking."

"Like what?"

Pearl tucked her chin and lowered her voice. "Like she helped a lot of girls. When they got in trouble, you know what I'm saying?"

"In trouble, like . . . ?"

She stared pointedly at my pregnant belly.

"Oh, you mean she helped them get abortions." I offered the bottle again.

"Thank you." She drank. "Mmm. I mean she did it herself. Long time ago she did that. People in the old hood called her Nursey. She was a real nurse, went around in a white cap? She did abortions on the side, because of course it was illegal then. She'd do for all kinds of people, you'd be surprised. 'Nursey, I'm in trouble,' they'd say."

"How do you know?"

"Because she gave me one! Then she kicked my ass for being so stupid. And she said, 'You only get one. No more ever.' That was her rule. I straightened out for a while. There's others that did better. And worse."

She looked at me. Somewhere in her fucked-up depths, there still existed a weak glow of wisdom.

I laid down. Through that whole evening at the ABC, so many emotions coursed through me: the excitement of sneaking around, the fear of getting found out, the utter satisfaction of acting my way through every difficulty. I felt the way I'd felt when, in an insanely tough improvisation clinic in acting school, I'd drawn the short straw of Amanda Wingfield (the delusional mother in *The Glass*

Menagerie) transplanted to a kibbutz on the outskirts of Tel Aviv. I mean really.

I knew nothing of Jewishness, let alone Tel Avivian culture, so I just plunged in and made Amanda get all spiritual in a generically middle-aged way. It worked. Seeing the faces of my classmates and teacher—well, not exactly seeing them, you don't make eye contact out of your frame, but you're damn well aware of their vibe.

I remember warbling, "One does wonder how the creator knew—how he *knew!*—that a simple desert plant like this, this *cactus!*—would come to symbolize hope! For so many!"

Feeling their credulity, my heart soared. *It's working! They're buying it!* I learned that you can fling total bullshit out there, but if you do it with every nerve in your body, they will buy it.

That's the magic of acting.

And that's how I felt that night at the ABC Mission.

SEVENTEEN

In the morning I followed Amaryllis's voice to the cafeteria. Boldly, I strode through the food line. I'd slept carefully and avoided all but minimal washing, so my makeup was still good.

Actually, to say I slept is a slight overstatement. When the supervisor turned out the lights, I listened to the shifting and turning and cot-hinge-creaking, then I started to question what the hell I was doing. I did that for a long time; I'm so good at it. Then I thought about Gramma Gladys and told myself to shape up, for Christ's sake, then I thought about Petey and sent him happy vibes. It felt appropriate to say a silent Our Father, so I did that. I'm sure I drifted off a few times, but those women snored like locomotives.

The Iron Angel herself slapped a whopping ladle of oatmeal into my bowl, saying, "You need extra, ma'am, being expecting.

Get you some milk to go on this, OK? And you eat it all. Good Sunday to you."

I dared flick my eyes directly into hers.

She didn't know me.

I found a seat and ate heartily. George was at breakfast too. About half of the guys had slunk off at dawn, but I still had to really look to pick him out of the multitude of human wrecks there. We avoided each other.

I finished quickly and kept my eye on Amaryllis. When she left the serving line, I got up to follow her. However, with a hellish shriek, the toothless pillhead from last night collapsed into some kind of convulsive state right in front of me.

Pearl's eyes locked on to mine as she writhed on the floor, then they rolled back. I knelt to her. Her head started ramming rhythmically into the tiles, so I balled up a cleaning rag a volunteer had left on the table and put it under her head. I heard someone shout for help.

I thought I should put something between her teeth, which I seemed to remember you're supposed to do, but her jaws were clenched tight.

I held her hand as it tried to flutter off her arm, and said, "It's OK, it's OK," over and over. In a few minutes, a volunteer and Wichita came up and took over.

Wichita flipped open a walkie-talkie. "We got one down in the cafeteria." Pause. "I dunno, old." Pause. "I dunno, maybe a OD." She shut the device, lowered herself, hands on knees, and studied the woman with silent interest.

The guests of any shelter have medical troubles like you wouldn't believe. TB, hepatitis, open sores, asthma, diabetes, cancer, schizophrenia. I'd known all this going in, and tried to keep away from germs, but you never know. Last night I'd felt that sharing the vodka with Pearl had been OK because alcohol kills germs.

A volunteer showed up with some first-aid skills, so I took off, but Amaryllis was gone. George too. Volunteers were moving everybody toward chapel, in the gym.

I hurried to Amaryllis's office, thinking maybe she'd stop there before going on to chapel.

The office was unlocked and unoccupied. For the hell of it I tried the desk drawer that had been locked last night, and somehow I was not surprised when it rolled open. The fat brown envelope was gone.

I glanced out the window and saw Amaryllis, the envelope wedged beneath her arm, walking to a car in the narrow front parking area. A volunteer flagged her down, perhaps to talk about the medical situation unfolding in the cafeteria. Amaryllis stopped and listened, leaning against the car, a plum-colored Taurus with a clouded-over back window.

I dashed into the corridor, almost colliding with George.

"She's leaving with the envelope!" I said excitedly. "Let's go!"

"I don't have a car!"

"Mine's on the next block!"

"You brought your *car* down here?"

"It's in a driveway down the first side street." I pointed. "Meet me there."

We separated, dashing for different exits. I had not simply Left My Car On The Street, but had approached a Latina grandma with penciled-in eyebrows sitting on her porch and paid her five dollars for the privilege of parking it in her driveway overnight. Which was no guarantee of safety, but a thief would have to be scraping pretty low to bother with my liver-spotted Honda anyway.

We arrived panting at the car at the same moment. Rapidly, George said, "I respect you as a woman and as a driver, but give me the keys."

I tossed them to him and got in to ride shotgun.

It was lucky the volunteer had kept Amaryllis talking for a minute, because she'd just peeled out onto Compton when we came up. An ambulance zoomed the other way toward the mission.

"Looks like that rear windshield got busted out," George remarked, "then replaced but they did a bad job."

"It'll make her easier to keep in sight," I observed.

"More important, it cuts down on her rear view."

Amaryllis headed north on Compton, then turned left on Vernon.

"Gotta stay well back, but I gotta make every light she does," my companion grunted. I settled in for the ride.

It's funny how you'll be rolling along through the butt-ugly utilitarianness of South Central, when you'll just see this gout of red bougainvillea spilling breathtakingly over a fence. Talk about gated communities, there's a hell of a lot of fences in South Central.

Amaryllis turned out to be an aggressive driver. She beat lights like a NASCAR wannabe and jumped lanes at the slightest impediment. Shockingly, she leaned on her horn when a delivery van slowed down to get safely around a bicyclist.

"Jeez!" I exclaimed.

George laughed, his fake teeth glinting in the morning sunshine. There we were, a pair of scuzzes motoring along in my weather-beaten old Honda. At one point when we did stop for a light behind Amaryllis, a nicely dressed couple idling next to us looked over, then pursed their mouths in disgust.

I smiled widely and gave them a wave, and they snapped their eyes forward.

"I can't wait to take a hot shower," George said.

"At least you're not wearing latex," I said. "If I don't get this stuff off of me soon, my skin's gonna rot." I rolled down the window to breathe the fresh morning air.

"It's funny about you," he said, looking at me sidelong.

"What's funny?"

"You're beautiful no matter what."

"Shut up and drive."

Amaryllis turned onto the 110 north and we all cruised through the city in easy traffic. "Ideally," George said, "we'd have a couple of cars and take turns being the near car. Three or four's even better. But we've got pretty good cover now, with the traffic. If she exits quickly we could miss her, though."

We followed her through the tunnels and the long single-file lane to the 5 north, and on northward from there.

The I-5 up from L.A. is broad, bright, and hot. Through the San Fernando Valley the pocked pavement had been repaired with mustardy-looking patch material. I rolled up my window and flipped on the air-conditioning.

The parched mountains and dust devils make for a moonscape near where Route 14 comes in. This is Koyaanisqatsi country, where giant power-line towers march down the canyons, part of the mammoth transmission corridor that electrifies Los Angeles.

I wondered how Petey was doing in Wisconsin, with its soft fields and woods.

As the highway opened out into longer and longer straightaways, George allowed Amaryllis's car to become a speck in the distance.

He said, "Two of her so-called guards are the pair that chased me out of the hood where you and Kip Cubitt were shot."

"Really?"

"Yes, the white gal and that tall black dude with the dreads."

"Is his name Denny? Deep voice? He had his hair under his cap when I saw him."

"Deep voice, yeah. I didn't get his name. He had a brown leather wristband?"

"That's him," I said. "I'm starting to think Amaryllis's story about Dale Vargas being the big villain is bullshit. She's inside her own crime ring, George! She's got to be. I mean, she might have some connection with this guy, but—"

"You gotta wonder who's the real Whale. What the hell's this money about? I don't think she's on her way to invest in mutual funds."

"Yeah," I said, suddenly reluctant. Because I still wanted to believe in her.

We entered the Grapevine, that towering pass you must climb to get to the Central Valley. Millions of years of geology fly by as the road cuts through layer after layer of canted-up rock. The Honda's engine strained; better-powered cars chugged past us. "Come on, baby," George urged. I flicked off the AC to take that load off the engine. The air here was cooler than back in Burbank.

We passed a car on fire in the breakdown lane of southbound, its engine burnt out on the task of making the miles-long grade. A cop stood at a safe distance with the morose family, watching the flames.

"I can still see her," I said.

"Where the hell's she going?"

"We're eating up the miles, all right."

I'm always struck by seeing actual tumbleweeds once you get to the valley, yes, there they are, beach-ball-like plants skeletonized by the wind, pulled from their roots to bump and skitter until they huddle against barbed-wire cow fences. Ravens, vultures, and hawks soar on the thermals rising from the valley floor.

The threatening mood ebbs as you roll deeper into the Central Valley. Multicolored oleander flourishes in the freeway median. Prehistoric-looking pump jacks suck up the last of the oil from beneath fields that have been cultivated around them. Onion fields, almond groves, grape fields, and it seems the world has gone forever flat.

"She going all the way to San Francisco?" George checked the gas hopefully. I knew how much he enjoyed that town.

But no, Amaryllis exited to a county road south of Bakersfield and headed east.

There was no traffic at this point, so we either had to follow her openly or let her go. "Hell with it," said George, "I really don't think she's aware of us." He stayed back maybe half a mile.

The purple Taurus kicked up a spume of dust and set off down a farm road. In the distance I saw a two-story house on the right.

"This dust is great cover," George said.

Amaryllis turned in at the farmhouse. A light blue sedan, an old one, was parked in the yard.

"Memorize what's on the mailbox," said George. "We'll just cruise by."

"Seventeen Thistle Route. No name. She making a drug buy, you figure?"

"Maybe."

I looked back at the house. Surely it was once quite nice, a little Victorian with gingerbread; now its angles lacked squareness.

This was a countryside of small farms and ranches—at least small by California standards, perhaps a couple of hundred acres apiece. Agribusiness hadn't taken over everything. Some of the fields lay fallow, others grew knee-high greenery, I guessed spinach or peppers.

George stopped the car on a rise and we got out to view the house from a distance. To our surprise, the Taurus was already on its way back to the county road.

"That was quick," I said.

"It was a money drop," said George. "I don't think she was on that property for thirty seconds."

"Shall we try to catch up to her?"

"No, she's done whatever business it was."

Godforsaken was the word that popped into my mind when we looked at that house, sitting next to the dirt road that cut indifferently through the land. The pretty, tended green fields that lay in the distance made the house, surrounded by its dry patch, look all the lonelier.

By the time we went through the Grapevine again, all that remained of the burned car, the family, and the trooper, was a fire scar on the pavement and some white dust. Misfortune gets cleared away quickly in these parts.

EIGHTEEN

I called Aunt Sheila and Aunt Toots early the next morning, missing my boy. Toots answered.

"How's Petey?" I asked.

"Fine," she said in a guarded tone, which was more or less her usual voice.

"You're so good to take him in for a while."

"The law after you?"

I paused. "Of a kind."

"Well, you just stick it to 'em, kid."

I could have said, *Yes, I robbed three banks last week, and a minute ago I shot a G-man, so I can't talk long,* and she would have said, *Well, you skedaddle, then. You can always hide out here, you know.*

Total family loyalty, coupled with a healthy strain of incuriosity.

"OK," I said. "May I talk to him, please?"

Not bothering to muffle the phone against her bosom, she hollered, "Petey! C'mere!"

He grunted into the phone.

"Honey, how *are* you?"

"Lousy. They beat me."

"Honey!"

Toots grabbed the phone back. "Goddamn it, Sheila told him to say that. Here, kid, tell her what's really bugging you."

Petey said, "They took my ScoreLad."

Toots cackled and grabbed the phone. "That thing's a brain-rotting piece of shit!"

"Toots, can you try to tone down the swearing just a little? For Pete's sake?"

"We gave him a pot holder weaving kit instead." She laughed. "Now he can do something productive with his time indoors! Hah!"

"I see."

"I hate it!" Petey cried from her side.

"Here, put your head by mine," said Toots.

I said, "Petey, honey, just give it a try, OK? Hey, what did you do this morning?"

"Ate ham. I drove the tractor! We went outside and did stuff."

Toots told me, "Ham and eggs and hash browns, the real kind. Manly food, the kind we eat every day! Ha! Yeah, he pretended to let Sheila drive the tractor, but it was really Petey doing all the driving, right, boy?"

"Right!" he shouted ecstatically.

That was life with Shelia and Toots.

George called later to tell me he'd spent half of last night looking up stuff online. "Then this morning I went downtown and did some digging in records and the library."

"But Bakersfield isn't in Los Angeles County, is it?"

"Right, but listen." Whenever I heard his deep-water voice, something way down inside me relaxed. "The house is owned by Mrs. Diane Keever, age seventy-eight. Her late husband, Bruce Keever, bought the place about forty years ago. He died last year at the age of eighty-one. Right up until he died, he worked as an attorney in Bakersfield."

"Yeah?"

"For decades he worked as an ordinary town lawyer. Seems the wife never worked outside the home. Doesn't that sound like a dull existence?"

"Some people prefer a quiet life."

"But OK, before they bought that farmhouse, Keever was a district court judge in Los Angeles, one of the youngest ever appointed. Barely thirty, I think. A federal judge! That's a prestigious position, a lot of power. Three years after getting that appointment, he resigned his seat with no warning, no reason—at least no reason given publicly—and moved his wife up to Bakersfield."

"Hm."

"Why did he abruptly do that, and start doing wills and divorces for the carrot farmers?"

"Yeah. And what connection does this Diane Keever have with Amaryllis?"

"The fact that the Keevers used to live in L.A. might be the thing."

"But that was forty years ago."

"I know," he said.

"Does she live there alone?"

"I don't know. She might not live there at all, she could be renting it out."

"Maybe to some gangster."

"What gangster would want to hang out in that place?"

"Any children?"

"None were listed in Keever's death notice."

"How did you learn all this?"

"Oh, property records are mostly online for free, and if you do the legwork, the bureau of records in any county is a treasure trove. I mean, some stuff isn't online, you've got to physically go there and look it up. Sometimes even if I can find things online, I go in person just to get that extra feel. I hate hauling out to do it, but once I get in there, with all that musty old paper and ink, I like it. I can sort of feel the, the—*life* in those documents, you know?"

I smiled.

"And the libraries," he went on. "You can get a lot from old phone books, and of course, newspapers. Keever's resignation from the bench made the papers back then, not big but it was in there."

"Why don't we just go up to the house and knock on the door?"

He laughed. "You really should join my firm."

"YOU LOOK GREAT," I told Kip Cubitt when I dropped in to see him at the rehab facility, a friendly place in the dauntingly huge L.A. County General Hospital complex.

He smiled and took my hand.

Places like this, you always notice if they smell clean. This one did.

170

My young friend had gotten stronger, though he still looked too thin. Wearing a royal blue track suit and blinding white gym socks, he sat carefully on the edge of his bed. He gestured for me to sit next to him. His eyes were quick and clear. I gave him a careful hug and handed him a paperback copy of Richard Wright's *Black Boy.*

"I thought this was an amazing book," I said. "Maybe you've already—"

"No, I haven't." He studied the picture on the front—a painful abstract—and read the back cover.

I said, "A young man who doesn't fit in. Different time, different place, but some things stay true, you know?"

"Yeah, I'll read this one," he said.

I asked, "Why do you think Vargas's guys haven't hunted you down here?"

He made a sound of rueful amusement and set the novel on his bedside table. "They saw I'm not ratting. I haven't ratted on anyone and I never will, you know what I'm saying?"

"I'm glad you talked to me."

"You're different." He ran his palm up and down his thigh. He squeezed his thigh muscle as Amaryllis might test a cantaloupe. "Plus, how would they know? I see it now that the Whale's nothing but a bully, and he thinks he gave me a warning. They ought to kill me. But now he knows if they finish me off, my grandma will get more dangerous to them than the whole LAPD."

I thought about that.

He eased himself to his feet, arms out for balance. He shuffled slowly to the window. We were on the sixth floor. He seemed to drag his left foot, and when he got to the window he cradled his left arm in his right and looked out at the world.

"You're walking beautifully," I said, remembering him lying in the street bleeding.

"Not bad," he acknowledged. "They say I'll be running before long. The bullets took a lucky path through me. You know my mama named me after Kip Keino?"

"He was a famous runner, wasn't he?"

"Yeah, he was one of the first to come from Africa and kick it in the Olympics." He sighed. "I'm kinda tired now. Had me three hours of therapy already today. Mondays they hit you hard. You know, I never used to be tired. Grown-ups would say they're tired, and I didn't know what they were talking about. Now I know."

"I guess you're grown up."

"Yeah."

That was a somber thing.

I asked, "What connection might your grandma have with a house in Bakersfield?"

He turned in surprise. "How do you know about that?"

"I'm trying to help you and your grandma, and that seems to be where it's going."

He turned back to the window and gazed at the high-rise medical building across the way, its glittering windows shielding all the little boxes of lives and deaths, then he looked down at the scrum of street traffic. A faint honk came up.

"That was one of the things I was sorry about. I used to go to Bakersfield for her every month. My dad did it before me. She counted on me to do it."

"Yeah?"

"It's money, you know, right?"

"Yes. What's it for?"

"Ma'am, I don't know."

"Ever see the people in the house?"

"No, I never did. They're in there, all right."

"How do you know?"

He turned from the window. "'Cause every time I dropped that envelope through the mail slot—every single time—I heard it hit the floor and then somebody go *Ruh!* Like that. Like they just won something."

"A man or a woman?"

"It's a lady, I think. A mean one, judging by her voice."

"Did the money belong to your grandma?"

"She always handed me the envelope."

"What do you think was going on?"

He was silent, his soft deer eyes focused in the middle distance. At last he said, "You know my grandma."

"Yes."

"Then you know that look of hers. There's things you don't ask questions, you don't even *wonder*."

"IT'S JUST ABOUT the nicest prison in California," George told me as we cruised up the 101 to San Luis Obispo. "Low and medium security, education programs, rehab, team sports. Would you pass me my fries, please?"

It was now Tuesday, noonish. We'd driven through an In-N-Out next to the highway in Woodland Hills and thus were participating in that great American practice of eating hamburgers while driving. Plus we were doing it in California, on the Ventura Highway. In the sunshine.

"What a glorious day," I remarked.

"Yes," agreed George. "It's always a glorious day with you."

"You just can't leave it alone, can you?"

He smiled apologetically.

To me there's always a carefree, teen feel to sipping Coke from a waxed cup while the world flashes past your window. Yet for all the fabulousness, for all the privilege, our minds bore the burden of the faceless presence of Dale the Whale Vargas. It occurred to me that less than two weeks from now, Khani Emberton would sign over his five million dollars to Amaryllis.

George was a neat eater, no spills, which was nice, because he was wearing a beautiful pair of brown slacks with a first-rate weave. Little blue flecks in a chocolate-brown summer worsted, I thought. He told me he'd gotten them at a thrift shop and I was shocked.

"You can get great clothes at those places," he said, embarrassed by my reaction. "Much better quality than some of the new stuff."

"You just don't seem the thrift shop type, that's all."

"Well, you know, I'm starting from scratch since the fire."

"Yeah. That's such a shame. Have you filed with your renter's insurance?"

"No, I don't have any."

"George, really?"

"I like to—handle things myself. I have some savings."

He didn't really believe in insurance, he told me, in spite of having worked as an insurance investigator and knowing the ins and outs. He didn't like to go crying to anybody about anything, and that's what it was when you filed a claim.

"Your drum kit!"

"Oh, everything, my files, everything. Fortunately I upload all my important computer files, so they're safe. You know, when I was growing up, the other kids took advantage of the free paper and pencils the school district provided, but I always brought my own. They made fun of me, but then the coolest teacher in the school said, 'I respect a man brings his own paper.' I carry car insurance because I have to. I pay my dentist in cash, and the last time I needed a doctor was when I was thirteen, for a wrestling team physical."

He'd warned me not to wear anything blue to the prison today, no jeans either blue or black, no sweats. No forest green or tan (guard colors), no blue chambray. "And one other thing," he said, awkwardly. "No, ah, underwire bra."

"Really?"

"You can't have any metal on you at all. They will find it. It'd be best for you to wear long slacks and a plain blouse. No jewelry, of course."

"OK."

Now, as the Ventura unspooled before us, I said, "I understand why Nathan would have been sent there after his drunk-driving bust, but it seems like they would have sent Vargas to someplace tougher."

He wiped his mouth with his napkin. "Remember what he went in for: check fraud. The guy's violent, but he's never had a real rap. No assault, no robbery, no possession. He slipped up just one time with a stolen ID and a checkbook. Only ninety days in the Men's Colony—that's a sterling record for the likes of him. Are you cool enough?"

"Yes, I'm fine." The air-conditioning worked well in his yellow Beetle. Everybody's air-conditioning was on today, even this close to the coast. It was probably ninety-five in L.A. now, at noon.

George said, "You got word to Nathan who we are?"

"Yes, I got Kip to call him."

"And he really insisted on meeting you?"

"He did, George. And dammit, I'm part of this thing, you know? I want to see Nathan myself, I want to see what kind of guy he is."

"He might open up more to me alone."

"Well, I can leave the room or something." But I didn't intend to.

I found myself studying his pants too much. I kept glancing at them, admiring his strong legs beneath that fine fabric, his trim hips, his wonderful, sensitive stomach. My heart had skipped when he said the word *bra*, can you believe it? *Do not, do not, do not think about it,* I told myself.

Forcing my mind away from—well, sex, I said, "Did Vargas, like, invent himself, or did he come up from somewhere?"

"Rita. Good question. He's from Tucson originally—started small there. Unlike most small-time dealers, however, I don't think he ever used.

"Eventually he got big in Tucson dealing crystal meth first, then cocaine and heroin. He's a comer, all right. Police heat got too much for him in Tucson, so he left and turned up in L.A. a couple of years ago, as far as my friends in the police can figure. L.A.'s still a big coke town, but the best customers aren't to be found at street level."

"What do you mean?"

"If you're a dealer, the customers you want are the upscale ones, the lawyers and entertainment people—they like their deals quiet, and if they're addicts, they're regulars, and they pay. If he doesn't want to move into bulk sales, they're the customers that'll do him the most good."

"How did he get to the top in Tucson?"

"I think our exit's coming up."

NATHAN CUBITT HAD once, clearly, been a cheerful person. I don't know how I knew that, but I did: remnants of a light manner were evident, but the man seemed to have been gnawed pretty hard around the edges.

The three of us met in a teacher's-lounge-like room with vinyl furniture and a coffeemaker. Nathan, wearing his prison blues stamped CMC, had been brought in fairly casually by a guard.

"Laid-back place," I'd remarked to George as we watched prisoners crisscrossing one of the peaceful courtyards, like college kids between classes. The grounds were very neat.

"It's not," he said. "That fence alone'll kill you."

"Why, it looks like an ordinary mesh fence with innocent-seeming razor wire on top!"

He'd smiled. "Plus eight thousand volts. And believe me, we're being watched. My CO days don't seem so far behind me right now. Corrections officer," he preempted my question.

Now Nathan said, "Nice to have visitors in the middle of the week."

"You mean this isn't ordinary?" I asked.

"No," said he and George together.

"Well," I said, "your son sends his love."

Nathan smiled eagerly, sadly. "How is he?" I saw where Kip got his slenderness and good face bones. Father and son's lips were firm.

"Doing great. He and I have gotten to be friends. He's walking, doing his therapy, being active. He's reading. He'll be home with his grandma soon."

"We want to talk about Vargas," George said.

Nathan said, "First, I want to speak to this lady. May I take your hand?"

I extended it without hesitation.

He engulfed my hand in his pink-brown mitt. His palm was rough. He looked into my eyes. "I know what you did."

I said nothing, but made an open gesture with my other hand.

In a very soft voice, he said, "Thank you for my son."

"Well . . . you're welcome. Let's hope he stays healthy. We're here to try to ensure that, you know. Your mama too."

"Yes."

"About Vargas," said George.

Nathan nodded, releasing my hand. "He was my cellmate for five weeks and two days."

Seeing my puzzled smile, he said, "You keep exact track of time when you're in prison. And with the Whale, I counted the days especially so."

"As bad as all that?" George asked.

"And then some. He's very smart, he puts himself up very high and people believe it. He left some books behind for me. They're good books, but I can't say I got into them."

"Like what?" I prompted.

"About people telling each other stories, then they make a lot of money. They work together and they think outside the box and then—somehow—they make a lot of money. I haven't figured out how the money comes. Stories about people agreeing. Making agreements. Sinajizing."

"What?" I said.

Nathan tried to think of the right word. "Sinajizing," he repeated.

George suggested, "Synergizing?"

"Yeah!"

"You mean like running a business?" I said.

"Yeah. Somehow." Nathan Cubitt's tilted head indicated the perplexity of an uncomplicated mind trying to grasp the hyped-up metaphors of business self-help.

"I understand," said George.

Nathan said, "The Whale's a smart brother. I didn't like him one bit, not one bit. He had a lot of followers in here."

"Yeah?" said George.

"Yeah, they all can't wait to get out and go to work for him."

"The officers here tell me Vargas got a guy to knife you after he was out. And they say a guy named Masters was killed in the shower on Vargas's orders."

"Ooh, yeah, that was a bad lockdown." Nathan wiped his face on his sleeve. " 'Course nobody told it was the Whale, but yeah, like I say. The motherfucker's good at getting people to owe him, excuse me, ma'am."

I said, "What did Masters do to him?"

"Oh, nothing!" Nathan glanced at George like, *Innocent lady!*

"It was a control killing?" suggested George.

"Yeah, he called it, um, human resources management. He needed to show what he could do if he wanted to. I didn't know there was so much blood in a body."

"You saw it?"

"If you're an old CO," Nathan told George, "you know nobody sees anything in the joint." He set his chin in his hand. "So much blood."

George said, "The guy or guys who did it—did they owe Vargas some money or drugs, and he called in the debt by making them kill this guy?"

"That was it." Nathan gazed at Rowe. "Seems like you know him too."

"I heard about Tucson," said George.

"The whole world knows about Tucson."

I said, "What the hell happened in Tucson?"

Nathan gave George a look I wasn't supposed to see, coupled with a microscopic head shake.

"Come on," I said.

George sighed. "Vargas made his rep in Tucson by committing a very stylish murder." Nathan looked away.

"A stylish murder? What does that mean?"

"I have to tell her," said George. "Don't worry, Nathan."

George looked at me for the first time as if I were another guy. No softness in his expression, no politeness.

He said, "Vargas picked four witnesses—gangbangers—to watch him kill his boss, the top drug lord in Tucson. Which he did by— uh." He took out his handkerchief and wiped his upper lip and neck. "It was a torture killing, Rita."

"Go ahead and tell me."

"Well, all you really need to know is the first step. After tying the guy to a chair, he sliced away his eyelids so he couldn't miss anything that happened next."

I said nothing.

180

"He sent out for pizza for the witnesses, since he took about six hours to kill the guy." He stopped.

"Then what?" I said.

"He let the witnesses loose in the city for a day, where naturally they told their buds what they'd seen. Then, over the course of the next week, they disappeared, one by one."

"Oh, my God."

Nathan put in, "After that he owned Tucson."

"But like I say," George added, "the police started to get too close. Nobody knew he was in L.A. until that check bust. I don't know why he got so dumb that one time. Just an old bad habit, maybe. The LAPD wants this guy bad, as you can imagine, as does the FBI. Things are going well for him in L.A., though. He's building up business here; he had contacts in the city already, of course, and he's got them in Mexico."

"Meat and Bones," said Nathan.

"Yes, that's the name of the cartel, or importation gang, he deals with."

"Guys are so witty," I remarked.

Both men shrugged.

Nathan said, "Furthermore, he bragged to me about taking out two guys that he said tried to threaten him about Tucson—they'd seen something, or *said* they had, which if that's all it was, was stupid, because it just got 'em murdered. 'Nobody's gonna find *them*,' he said."

"Supposedly he did that in L.A.?" asked George.

"Yeah, my impression was he got somebody do it for him, and it was in L.A. somewhere."

George found that interesting. Then he said, "Did you talk to him about Bakersfield?"

Nathan clamped his teeth down on his lower lip.

George said, "We know it's Bakersfield and we know how much."

"All right, then. Yeah, I talked to him about it. But it was before I got him pegged. He got me pegged first! I sure didn't say *much,* but he kept at me. Once you say something about money to the Whale, he won't let you alone. You get so you'll tell him anything to—see, he figured out who my mama is. Cubitt's not an everyday name. And he got to thinking, and he thinks, oh, this lady runs the biggest business in all the hood, I got to hook up with her.

"If you go bragging to the Whale about anything, it's gonna come back and bite you hard. You let him do you a favor, your ass is like oh no, now you owe him. All I said was, I act as a courier, I have handled large amounts of money. I say this to let him know I'm nobody's fool. My own man, you know. That's all I wanted to say, that's all I *intended* to say, but he kept at me and at me, and at me and *at me!* until I told him—way more than I should have." He bounced his heel on the floor.

"What's the ten thousand for?"

"I don't know, faith, I don't know. Mama just said one day, oh, last year some time, she said, you take this envelope and you drive it away out of town. She drew me a map with the exit on it and everything. I had done it maybe five times, second Sunday of the month, then my situation happens and I come in here, and I understand Kip took over handling it. Uh . . ." He paused.

George made an encouraging palm-up gesture.

Nathan said, "She did say one thing about it. She called it her reverse welfare payment."

George and I looked at each other. Nathan shrugged.

I asked, "If Vargas knew about this ten grand going out every month, why didn't he just take it? Follow Kip when he left the mission and rob him?"

"Now you sound like me." Nathan looked at me sympathetically, as if recognizing another feeble-minded individual. "Einstein I ain't, you know? But I have learned this, and I learned it from the Whale: The first principle of success is, when you see golden eggs, you don't go after the eggs. You go after the goose."

NINETEEN

George Rowe had never been to Canada; his impressions of it were: maple syrup, the Edmonton Oilers, curling, voyageurs, Indians pushed around, and French priests. A few Eskimos up top. These days, Canada was a nation of friendly underachievers. As a boy, Rowe had read a book about the fur-trading voyageurs and had briefly planned to become one. Then he had read a book about a falconer, then one about a race car driver, and the voyageur thing had receded, except he still thought about how tough those bastards had been.

As the bilingual airliner banked over the forests of Quebec there was the broad St. Lawrence winding its silver way to the sea, and Rowe considered the white men who'd first seen these things. Misfits, criminals, fucked-up guys looking for a new start, men who wanted to test themselves, men who found farming or running a grog shop just not enough. Men who found a wife and kids too much.

And he wondered the thing every postmodern man wonders: Would I have measured up? Tramping in wooden snowshoes through dick-deep snow checking traplines, shooting a cougar coming at you mad because you disturbed its fresh kill, knocking your own tooth out with a rock if the pain got bad enough because you were three hundred miles by water from the nearest trading post, where they'd only lend you pliers anyway. If you shot the cougar, you'd have to kill it instantly, since otherwise the time it'd take you to reload your musket would be your last half minute on earth.

Rowe valued decency. As soon as he stepped off the plane, he sensed decency coursing through all of Canadian culture. No one thing, simply a general feeling. The way people talked and looked: calm, reasonable. Little arrogance in Canada, little reason for it.

When he hit the air outside the terminal, the air smelled north. It smelled like it smelled when you got off the plane in Seattle— you can inhale the miles-away forests, even though the shuttle buses and cop cars are slithering everywhere. He could smell the coolness of the river. It was August here too, and quite warm, but the river smell made it OK.

He rented a little white car of some kind and, following a map, drove to Nicholas Polen's address in Baie-d'Urfé, in the part of the city called West Island.

This was Wednesday, not quite noon, not quite a day since he had sat talking with Nathan Cubitt. Compared with the pictures he'd seen of the city center, which looked quite European, here it looked American; all the outlying neighborhoods seemed to. In well-heeled Baie-d'Urfé, the houses ran the gamut from glass cube to faux-chateau.

Rowe stood on the doorstep noting how similar Polen's house was to Markovich's. Baie-d'Urfé was the Hancock Park of Montreal, and like Markovich, Polen lived in a mansion with lots of stonework, a walled lot, and a heavy oak front door with a fist-sized knocker. Markovich's knocker had been a wolf's head, while Polen's was a massive bronze fleur-de-lis. Rowe lifted the old heraldic symbol and let it go.

Kunnk!

"I'm Simon Westfield," he told the man who answered the door. He flexed his knees very slightly, as he did when talking to a man shorter than himself.

"Yes, come in," said Nicholas Polen, who had fought a duel with a knife.

The men shook hands. Polen seemed to have to remember to shake firmly.

"Let's talk in the kitchen, my favorite room," he said. "Would you like a glass of wine? I'm going to have one."

What is it with these dog people and their midday alcohol?

The house was in flux. Furniture was draped or absent—bright, nonfaded areas of the carpets told that a shutting-down was going on. Rowe saw empty display cases, empty shelves with odd patterns of dust on them. *Yes,* he thought. *I was right about one thing, anyway.*

In the kitchen Polen took down two plain glasses, then opened another cupboard. In a furtive move, he filled the glasses from a large jug of Gallo red, trying to shield the cheapness with his body.

This house probably had a wine cellar in the basement, Rowe thought, which must be stone-floor empty. The kitchen featured expensive built-ins and finishes, but the table was a wobbly thing that looked fresh from a junk shop. Rowe noticed two marred places on the maple floor where the former table, a heavy trestle one, perhaps stone-topped, had sat for a long time.

Before it was sold.

No sign of a wife.

All right, then.

Polen settled them down to business right away. "I understand you're only in town for the day," he said in a somewhat pint-sized voice, which matched his small stature. "You say you're interested in purchasing Rondo?"

"Yes. Interested." Rowe took a swallow of the slimy, warm wine. At least it wasn't Richards Wild Irish Rose. He set his glass down respectfully.

"Anyone who acquires Rondo would acquire a dynasty."

"Yes."

"Mr. Westfield, I don't know your name. Have you been in the business long?"

"I'm a spaniel man."

"Oh! Fine dogs." Polen spoke with a bare trace of a European accent.

"Cocker," added Rowe. "All varieties."

"Ah! Ambitious. You have had some success, or . . . ?"

"Moderate. I don't like to boast about it."

"You're then different from most dog people!"

Rowe smiled. "My mother is crazy about beagles, she's owned one or two as pets, but now she's retiring, and my dad's dead, and she wants to go into beagles seriously. I'm lucky enough to have the means to help her."

"She'd be starting at the top with Rondo."

"That's what I'm here to determine. I told my mother she ought to start small, just acquire one or two fine puppies, get some show experience under her belt, then build a kennel from there."

"Good advice. But she's impatient."

"She is," agreed Rowe.

"Women!" said Polen, with the air of a lifelong loser.

Rowe studied him. Polen wore khakis and a blue shirt with a fanciful bow tie. He ought to be a suspenders man, with that tie. He wore a belt, though, with a too-shiny gold buckle.

Markovich had said Polen had fallen on hard times. Rowe had expected to meet a confident man, a man of substance. Even bad financial trouble shouldn't diminish a truly confident man. But Polen struck him as uncertain.

Rowe saw the furrow on the man's jaw he'd noticed in the picture online, and wondered.

But for that, Polen looked like a professor of English—Canadian English.

"Been in this country long?" asked Rowe.

"Twenty-two years. I came over to work with some North American trainers and fell in love with the New World." Along with that trace of European, Polen's vowels were Canadian—those unbent vowels. *I keem over.*

Rowe suddenly grasped the man's essence. He was someone who, his whole life long, had been worried about what other men thought of him, like a perpetual adolescent. And he'd acted accordingly. If Markovich's tale of the duel was true, Polen had made his challenge not out of pride but fear.

Rowe had known other men of Polish blood, and they'd all been blacksmith-bellows-tough. Women too, for that matter. A timid Pole. This was a new species as far as Rowe was concerned.

He said, "Rumor has it Rondo is sick."

Polen's smile was too quick. "Where did you hear that?"

"The beagle world is a small one."

"Have you been talking to Markovich?"

Rowe was ready. "What do you mean?"

Polen stood up quickly, not like a man but like a teenage girl about to flounce out. "I'm not sure I want to do business with you after all."

If Rowe had been a dog, he'd have bitten him. He rose to go. "Too bad." His feeling had been right: Polen was an overgrown child, not even a terribly bright one.

Then Rowe paused, took something from his pocket, and placed it on the table.

Polen stared at it as if he couldn't believe his eyes.

He burst into excited laughter. "It's—it's a Strügen Cycle Beagle!"

Rowe picked up the friction-powered toy. He revved it on the tabletop and the little tin dog, perched on a tin penny-farthing bicycle with a tiny outrigger, whirled its bitty legs madly and shot across the wood, straight for the edge. Polen cried out in alarm, but Rowe darted to the other side and caught it just in time.

It was an absurd little thing, but sublimely made, as all the best toys are. Rowe had paid a cantankerous woman in New Jersey almost three thousand dollars for it. When he spoke to her on the telephone, she hadn't wanted to sell it at any price. The Strügen company of Bonn had only made a few hundred of these, before World War II, and they had delighted little Nazi children all through that horrible time. This was the only perfect specimen known in the world, presumably having been originally owned by an anal-retentive child now collecting Krugerrands, perhaps.

But Rowe had reluctantly let slip that he worked for the IRS, and that got the New Jersey toy maven to dealing. Unfortunate but convenient that so many private dealers try to fly under the tax collector's radar.

Polen, his mood now joyful, said, "How did you know I collect—collected"—rueful change of tense—"beagle-themed toys?"

"Your Web site."

"But I don't say anything about—"

"The picture of Rondo with the pull toy."

"Oh!"

"I made an assumption."

"Ha! How did you find this?"

Rowe saw that Polen had broken into a full-body sweat at the sight of this toy. "Did some research online. Found this woman in New Jersey, and—"

"I know her! I know her! The witch! This is the one thing I could never get!" Polen took out a folded tissue and blotted his upper lip, then his forehead, then he blew his nose. Rowe did not particularly respect men who used facial tissues, although it was better than fingers and the ground. Polen said, ogling the toy, "Everybody wants the Strügen Cycle Beagle. This truly is the Holy Grail. This is the Holy Grail."

Rowe was pleased with himself. Everybody has his sacred object of desire.

Rowe was lucky that his was Rita.

Polen's was this stamped-metal trinket.

Polen said, "I guess you noticed all the empty shelving? I had to sell my whole collection. It'll keep me going for a while, until I sell this place. Too big for me anyway."

"What's the matter financially?"

"I've had some debts. You don't really want to buy Rondo, do you?"

"No."

"What do you want?"

"I want to meet Rondo and see the rest of your dogs."

"Why?"

"Ernest is missing."

"You're working for him!" Polen slapped the table. "You're working for Markovich, aren't you! He wants Rondo! He's wanted Rondo for years! That's because Ernest isn't worth a damn. That dog couldn't carry a show—couldn't carry a *breed*!—if you—if you—I don't know what! Shot him full of moon juice!"

"What's moon juice?"

"I don't know, I'm just saying."

"Right. Well, Ernest was a champion in his day."

"Tuh!" Spitless exclamation. "Ernest is not missing, I tell you. Oh, I've seen the notices on the club sites. But you've got to be an idiot to think somebody deliberately took that dog. Let alone me!"

"Why so?"

"Ernest is past his prime, he's finished. Nobody cares about that dog!" Polen's face was fiercely red. "They'd want my dog! They'd want Rondo! He's not for sale to the likes of Markovich, however."

"I haven't said I'm working for him."

"Well, you can meet Rondo and a few other dogs, but my current show team is en route to California."

"What!"

"Yes, for the Pan Pacific Canine Exposition." Polen said this with a note of smugness.

"In Los Angeles?"

"Yes."

Rowe chuffed with exasperation. "I thought you'd agreed not to show in America."

"I had. I had. But Markovich is out of the business, he's retired. End of agreement, as I see it. Neither Markovich nor I are young fellows. Once you pass seventy, all bets ought to be off."

"Shit," said Rowe. "Well, if Rondo's so great, why isn't he going to L.A.?"

Defensively, Polen said, "He's got nothing left to prove. And OK, he's a little slower than he used to be. You would be too, if you'd accomplished what he's done."

Rowe hooked his thumbs into his belt.

Polen said, "Well, you might as well come along."

Rowe followed Polen outside, where four beagles were sleeping in the deep shade of an oak tree. Polen whistled and the dogs roused. Without barking, they ran across the grass to him, who mumbled endearments.

"This is Rondo."

Rowe squatted to meet the dog. He'd studied his picture and was gratified to actually recognize him.

Rondo moved a bit slower than the other dogs, but even Rowe could tell the dog had been a champion: he carried himself like a retired head of state. Rowe offered his hands and the dog sniffed them calmly. He looked closely at the dog's coat.

Polen was assertive enough with the dogs, guiding one firmly aside with a slight movement of his leg. Polen was their leader. They could never snicker at his bow ties.

When Rowe felt Rondo was comfortable with him, he rubbed his muzzle vigorously, then his back. Nothing came off on his hands, no dye, nothing. Markovich had thought Polen would try to pass Ernest off as Rondo. This was just not the case. The other dogs, Rowe saw, were females.

"I've heard he's sick," Rowe said again.

"Well, you see him. I wouldn't entertain offers for a sick animal. It'd be unethical."

This pathetic guy would tell any lie to get an edge, Rowe thought. But his gut didn't feel he'd taken Ernest.

Rowe asked again, "What's your financial trouble about?"

Polen considered for a moment, then went ahead. "You must know, Mr. Westfield, that nobody makes serious money in the dog business. If you don't treat it as a passion, you'll be sorry."

Rowe listened.

"Some of us," continued Polen, "have contrived other ways to get ahead. Unfortunately, it doesn't always work out."

"What are you talking about? Gambling?"

Polen smiled in shame.

"For God's sake," said Rowe, "you're losing your house because of gambling debts? Betting on your own dogs to win shows?"

Polen turned his back and went to the house. Rowe followed him in.

Polen poured more wine for himself and said, "I'm going to win the Pan Pacific."

"How do you know?"

"I just know. One of my dogs will earn best in show. Beagles are being taken much more seriously in the top shows these days."

"No more for me," said Rowe, when Polen looked at him questioningly. "Is the story of the duel true?"

Polen shut the cupboard and looked at Rowe. "Yes. What do you know of it?"

"He got you in the chest."

"That's so."

"And you survived because you'd hidden a medical unit nearby."

Polen said nothing.

Rowe said, "You challenged him to a duel over a woman, but you behaved like a sneak."

"I'd have instructed them to help him if he'd lost."

"Where did you get that scar on your face?"

"Another duel."

"My ass."

Polen belonged to a category of non-handkerchief-carrying men who were too plentiful in the world, Rowe thought. Never meaning harm, but their fear leads them into slyness.

"One more thing," he asked. "Who's going to handle your dogs at the Pan Pacific?"

"Oh, my longtime man, his name is Gold. He's gotten into breeding rough collies now—doing well, very well." He gave an oddball, inappropriately hilarious laugh. "I think he could take breed at the Pan Pacific. Go ahead and look him up, he'll show you my Copernicus Jumper and Mary Lullaby."

"Won't you be there?"

"Oh, of course, I'm flying in on Friday. But I'll be in the stands; I get too nervous to be anywhere near the dogs on show day."

"I see. Thank you, Mr. Polen. I'll be going now."

Rowe turned to the kitchen table and looked at the Strügen Cycle Beagle. Polen did not deserve to have this prize toy, but Rowe left it anyway, out of pity.

He walked out, shook himself, and returned to the airport.

TWENTY

I felt slightly forsaken by George when he went out of town on whatever other case he was working on. "The bad guys," I whined on the phone, "right here in L.A. are trying to annihilate you. Us. Why do you have to go?"

"Besides that it's business, I've committed to this particular client, and he's paying me? I'm starting to tunnel on this Vargas-Cubitt situation. I'll get a message to the Whale, but before I do, I want to be away from it for a day or two. You said you wanted to do more. Well, I've got an assignment for you, and I think you can guess what it is."

"Bakersfield."

"I think it's safe enough for you to stick your head in there, so long as you're cautious. Don't reveal yourself, you understand what I'm saying?"

"Yes. And then I'm going to poke around the ABC Mission again, because I've just *got* to learn—"

"Rita, no. Don't go near there without me."

"But—"

"I'm asking you. Please."

"But—"

"Look, isn't Bakersfield enough for now? See how it goes. But promise me—just for now!—you won't go to the mission."

"Well, OK."

He'd gotten on his red-eye going "somewhere in North America"—so discreet!—and the next morning, Wednesday, I drove up to Bakersfield.

I passed the exit to the farmhouse and went on into town. I found the main senior citizens' rec center and picked up a bunch of literature, including the business card of the activities director.

Then I asked directions to a pharmacy, where I bought a jar of Digest-All, a bottle of Vitamax Silver, a pair of support hose (medium), a seven-day plastic pillbox, a tube of hand cream, a tube of face cream, a thing of gel sanitizer, a bar of olive oil soap, a packet of rose hip tea, and a mug with a picture of a barefoot farm boy asleep on a haystack. All for only $18.78.

At the open trunk of my car I arranged the stuff in a wicker basket I'd been using for bathroom towels. I tied a yellow grosgrain bow on it and headed out to the farmhouse. It was eleven o'clock.

Typical dog-day weather in the San Joaquin Valley: ovenlike heat. The land lay flat as if the sun had hammered it that way. The tumbleweeds blew, and the long irrigation channels flowed siltily.

In the distance the worn gray house, a couple of hundred feet back from the road, stuck up from its weedy patch like a tombstone. My pulse quickened at once again taking a matter into my own hands. I pulled all the way up to the house.

The whole way there, the whole morning, the weight of this errand had grown. It's one thing to imagine yourself walking into what might turn out to be a scorpion jar, and another to actually do it.

But long before all this began, I'd gone hunting for a dark place inside myself. I'd found it, used it, and now I knew where it was. As an actress, I had a leg up when it came to pretending not to be afraid. And I knew that the key thing, when the chips go down, is to get fierce, stay fierce, and fight with everything you've got.

Nothing stirred in the house as I mounted the board steps, though as soon as I'd stepped out of the car, I'd sensed a sudden alertness behind the weathered walls. The sky-blue sedan was parked there as before. It was a dusty Impala.

Red-winged blackbirds trilled from the swaying tips of willows growing in the drainage ditch across the road.

I felt a flash of anger at Harper Lee for making me think of Boo Radley at this moment.

I saw the mail slot in the door, although of course there was the rural mailbox on a post at the road.

From a distance 17 Thistle Route looked merely forlorn; up close it was almost malevolently decrepit, its sun-baked planks showing only the ghost of a paint job. Where I'm from, when a house begins to decay, the paint starts to flake, then it blisters off in the summer humidity. At this house it appeared that the paint had simply desiccated in place and fallen away in granules. A piece of board trim veered away from the doorway at the top, its rusted nailheads extruded by decades of slamming.

I rapped, and after a full minute, I heard someone approach

stealthily. The door creaked inward, and a stout Asian woman stood staring at me, hands on hips.

Smiling blandly, my purse dangling beneath the brimming basket, I exclaimed, "Good morning! I'm Sharon Pressley from the senior center!" I held out my card. "Somebody's got a birthday this month! May I bring this in?"

The woman's face did not change one molecule, but her posture softened just perceptibly. She wore a blue service dress, black leather sneakers, and a silver crucifix the size of a pair of scissors around her neck. Crow-black bun hairdo, with two tendrils hanging down from the temples. This part gave her a slightly Spanish look. The Philippines, then.

"Wait," she said, and shut the door firmly in my face.

"Great!" I responded.

I heard muffled voices, then a minute later she returned and reached for the basket.

"I take it."

"Oh, but no!" I got in her face like a jolly fistful of firecrackers. "It's my *job* to deliver this Friends of Bakersfield assortment personally. They'll have my *head* if I don't report that I actually came in and personally—"

"OK, OK."

She stepped backward and I went in, my shoes all but sliding out from under me on the slick board floor. It was lusterless, just worn smooth from years of cleaning.

A bone-thin woman sat in the front room, her hands gripping the padded arms of a wheelchair.

"Diane!" I exclaimed, striding to her, in one smooth move setting the basket within her reach on a low table and drawing a straight chair near. "Happy birthday. Look. Presents!" George had advised me to tumble right in, no hesitation. Although Diane Keever's natural impulse was to recoil—hell, anybody's would be—the force of my do-gooderism overcame her. She smiled suspiciously.

I went on, "It's so wonderful to meet you. I'm Sharon Pressley, from the senior center."

"How do you do?" said Diane Keever. "What is all this?"

Blue Dress watched.

"We have a new director," I explained, toning down my volume and pace, segueing into pure warmth and sympathy, channeling a relentlessly compassionate Greer Garson or Florence Henderson or some such. "Do you know Kevin John Wilson? He's the new director, and he made a decree! A decree went out from him that the BSC would locate every citizen over—well, let's between us girls say *a certain age!*—and check the public census records for birthdays. 'No homebound senior is going to celebrate their birthday without some senior cheer, not while I'm in the driver's seat!' That's what Kevin John Wilson said."

"Neneng invited you in?"

"You need this things," said Neneng, poking in the basket.

Her boss said, "My birthday is in March."

"Oh! Oh! Oh, my goodness." I sat there helpless. "Oh, my goodness."

Mrs. Keever took the opportunity to be magnanimous. "It's all right, dear."

"Well, mistakes do happen, don't they?" I trembled on the verge of embarrassed tears. "I'm so sorry to have barged in here like this—what must you be thinking? My goodness. Well, I know one thing: the basket stays!"

"It's all right," she repeated. Then, as if from an unused portion

199

of her brain, a hospitality reflex awakened. "Well, ah . . . would you like some tea, before you go, Mrs. Pressley? Some iced tea?"

"Oh, yes, please!" I fanned myself delicately. "I'd love to visit with you for just a minute or two, Mrs. Keever." I decided to switch to that after having used her first name just once, to achieve initial disarmament.

"Neneng, bring us some tea and cookies. The good ones."

I was tremendously pleased that the old delivery trick had worked.

The house wasn't as bad on the inside as out: once fine, now frayed, but clean and tidy nevertheless. Basic cleaning, I realized, can go a long way. The furniture, the wallpaper, which was a charming old pattern of green vines against a rosy beige ground, all were holding up more or less OK. The Keevers had had good taste.

Mrs. Keever was well turned out for the day. Her pure-white hair was nicely waved and combed back from her large ears, she wore a peach silk (or perhaps easy-care polyester) blouse and a soft knit skirt. Her skinny legs were encased in white-person's-flesh-color support hose, and she wore Minnetonka-type little shoes. A battered aluminum walker was stationed near the hall.

One gnarled hand sported a fairly whopping diamond. Silver button earrings. She cared about the way she looked, and in fact, her face was quite fine; she even wore a little lipstick. This was a woman who carried on the routine.

She sat straight and studied me with wary clarity. She was plainly thirsty for company, yet there was an antisocial vibe about her.

I oriented my chair so as not to face her directly, more like side-by-side. But I kept myself in front of her so she wouldn't get the feeling that any part of me was out of view. A subliminal thing. "Someone at the center said your late husband was a lawyer in town." I made my body language open, nothing crossed, open re-laxed hands, slightly forward-leaning posture. "I do remember the name."

"Yes," she said.

I showed her everything I'd brought, with narration. "And the lavender in this lotion makes it double as cologne!"

When George and I had talked this over, we'd tried to think of a foolproof pretext for me, but it was hard.

"Well," he'd said at last, "you'll just have to figure something out."

"What am I supposed to do once I get inside?"

"Observe. And if it feels OK, mention Amaryllis and see what happens."

Of course, Mrs. Keever might not be living there, but we also felt it was a pretty good bet, especially as George could find no al-ternate address for her.

So right now, step one was good. Either Mrs. Keever or this Neneng was receiving the ten thousand a month from Amaryllis.

It was very hot inside that house, but a few windows were open, allowing a stifling breeze to push through the screens. Like all old people, Diane Keever barely sweated.

What was the money for, what was it for? Did Neneng take it to the bank for her mistress? Was there a gigantically fat mattress upstairs? Did the envelope go from here to somewhere else?

Well, my goal was to simply make friends. As I talked about the lotions and so forth, I glanced about the room carefully for ev-idence. Of something, anything. Bricks of heroin, slave manacles? It was an ordinary living room, not very big.

Diane Keever was suspicious, and Neneng was a cold-eyed one. My impression was she lived in. Neneng looked late-fortyish, maybe as old as fifty. Realistically, Mrs. Keever was no drug dealer. But Neneng was a person to figure out.

"You haven't been over to the senior center yet, have you?" I asked my hostess.

She paused. "I still don't think of myself as 'senior.' Isn't that funny?"

"Not at all! We're all just kids, really. All our lives."

"You're very young."

There was no television in the room. A baby grand piano had been wedged into a corner. Mrs. Keever saw me look at it, then at her crabbed hands.

"I don't play much anymore," she said.

A book, *Grieg Lyric Pieces,* perched on the music stand.

Heavy on her feet, Neneng carried in a wide silver tray with the tea and cookies. She seemed respectful enough of Mrs. Keever.

As she served us, I gestured to Mrs. Keever's wheelchair. "Is it arthritis?"

"Yes. Just osteo, but it's really got me, as you can see." She said it tight-mouthed and bitter. Perhaps a drop of self-pity in there too. But I wondered: If her mind is sharp and she's got this evidently faithful servant, doesn't she at least get out a little?

Neneng said, "It rheumatoid."

"These aren't the good cookies," Mrs. Keever said.

Neneng said, "More in oven."

Mrs. Keever's hands did seem to have that tight redness of rheumatoid, just like Gramma Gladys's. Her knees too.

"I used to play, quite a lot," she said. "Now Neneng plays, don't you, Neneng?"

I found that hard to believe; Neneng seemed as musical as a crocodile.

"Shit itch me," said Neneng.

She teach me.

There was a pause.

"Well," I said, "I brought all this information on the wonderful activities we do at the center."

"I should have volunteered there, when I was younger," Mrs. Keever mused.

"Well, we'd love to see you now." I shuffled through the flyers.

She said, "I don't . . . interact . . . much."

"I would think an intelligent, attractive woman like you would have lots of friends!"

"Oh," she said, brushing away the compliment. "No."

"I it," said Neneng.

"Neneng takes care of me. I couldn't do without her."

Neneng nodded possessively. "I drive." She left the room.

The tea was good. The shortbread-type cookies tasted rancid.

"They are terrible," said Mrs. Keever, grimly amused at my attempt to hide my reaction. "I've never gotten used to them. She puts duck fat or something in the dough."

"Plus oregano," I guessed. "How long have you lived in Bakersfield?"

"Oh, a long time," she said vaguely.

I took her hand gently and said quietly, "Please consider me a new friend." She squeezed my hand rigidly and stared at the floor.

Then I got her vibe. It wasn't antisocial, it was angry. Beneath that fine-lady façade was a crust of anger and resentment.

Why?

"You know," I ventured, "senior activities today aren't what they used to be. In the old days it was cutting paper dolls and watching television, but now we've got dance classes—even for wheelchair folks!—we've got ice cream Thursdays, and sometimes Harold does Elvis. Our handyman."

"Oh."

Neneng returned to check our glasses.

"Neneng, please play something," asked Mrs. Keever.

The sullen Filipina said, "I have to?"

"No," said her boss. "No, of course not. But I'd like to hear some of the Grieg. Just a little something. You pick."

Neneng looked at me hatefully, heaved a bone-rattling sigh, and stomped over to the piano. She yanked the heavy tufted bench; it made a hideous screech on the wooden floor.

Neneng laid her buttocks over the bench. The blue fabric of her dress smoothed and strained against her back as she opened the keyboard and reached to turn pages in the Grieg book.

She touched a few chords to warm up, then, peering at the complicated-looking music, began to play.

BALDWIN, said the logo above the keyboard. The instrument, of polished walnut, gave forth several pure notes.

The room instantly became lighter, brighter, cooler.

At first Neneng played a small melody, high on the keyboard. Then the sound deepened into full, ringing chords.

The air came alive. God stepped in.

Mrs. Keever tipped her head back, to open her ears to the wider room—the sound came to us from every direction as it poured from the piano and swelled against ceiling, walls, floor.

I'm not a classical musician, but I felt Neneng's playing was extraordinary.

The music lightened and returned to the original melody, only this time the melody was prettier—somehow—I don't know.

Then it diminished to a few wistful droplets.

Silence.

Neneng dropped her hands into her lap and bowed her head for two seconds. Then abruptly she rose, the bench screeching out from under her.

Mrs. Keever came back from wherever she'd been transported to. "Thank you, Neneng. That was very good."

I could only stare, smiling.

Neneng, stone-faced, stood at the piano. "Tuner man come yesterday." As if that explained it.

I made a sound of amused bafflement.

Neneng returned my gaze. "I have knack," she muttered.

"I don't know what I'd do without her," said Mrs. Keever. "She comes from a terrible place in the Philippines. A lot of family depend on her."

"What was the name of that piece you played?" I asked.

In a blunt voice, Neneng answered, " 'To Spring.' "

"How beautiful."

Now I could understand how Mrs. Keever could stand to isolate herself in this wasteland of a home. With music like that, I could exist happily in Hell itself.

Neneng stalked out, and we heard cookie sheets sliding from the oven. The smell that wafted in was no better than the taste of the first batch.

While listening to Neneng, I'd noticed framed photographs lined up on the piano.

One was of a young, fine-boned woman. The shot was professional; it looked, in fact, like a film studio starlet shot: burgundy drape, professional hair and makeup, jewels, a silk strapless gown that looked like pouring milk, perfect lighting, and I realized it was Mrs. Keever in her twenties. What a shot. She gazed frankly into the camera, an amused smile on her lips. Everything about her was hot except for that cool smile. What a hell of a shot.

I saw a picture of a man I took to be Mr. Keever, receiving a plaque from a local-looking politician.

Then there were pictures of another beautiful girl, ranging from toddlerhood through first day of school, on up to her teens. A few were snapshots—astride a new tricycle at Christmas, stepping off a balance beam with a determined grin—then a series of school portraits with missing teeth, then long burnished hair like a pony's coat, then new breasts and a spark of adolescent defiance, then—no more. No college picture, no wedding picture. No womanhood picture.

I wondered.

Through this whole visit I'd tried to *feel* what was going on. I almost started to wonder if George and I had imagined Amaryllis's whole errand here.

I'd observed Mrs. Keever closely, Neneng too. The two women were tied in an unusual relationship, what with their isolation, mitigated by the beautiful piano music. Very tough to read. Was Neneng a conduit for money going overseas?

I needed to pop a question or two, but I wanted to be ready to make for the door at any moment. I asked to use the bathroom.

When I came out, Neneng had taken the tea tray away, perhaps to replenish the cookies—some family recipe from her village in the wilderness of Mindanao? Mrs. Keever sat waiting for me with a sourer expression than she'd had before.

I picked up my purse. "I have to be going. You know, my sister lives in Los Angeles, and sometimes I go down to visit her. Sometimes I take our seniors on little junkets down there, to a ball game, you know, or to a show, or to the races at Santa Anita. Because I realize lots of people have connections in L.A., from past times." I paused. "Do you?"

"No." She dropped the word like a brick.

"Ah."

She stirred uneasily, shifting her wasted thighs in the slinglike seat of her wheelchair.

"So many nice people in L.A.," I commented. "I have a friend who works down there—his name is Dale Vargas."

Mrs. Keever looked blank. She wondered what my angle was. Man, she was a jawbreaker.

I said, "There's another friend of mine—Amaryllis B. Cubitt. When I'm in L.A., sometimes I stop in and volunteer at her—"

Mrs. Keever made a startled, incoherent sound. "Guhh?"

Neneng appeared from the kitchen as if shot from a popgun. She was holding some kind of pronged knife, not in attack mode but not *not* in attack mode.

"What is it?" I said. "What's wrong?"

"Why did you come here?" said Mrs. Keever angrily. Instead of Boo Radley, I'd gotten Mrs. Dubose.

"I—I—to deliver your basket!"

"Don't give me that."

I followed her eyes to my purse. Shit! I'd left it on the entry table. They could have looked at my ID while I was in the bathroom, and seen that I was not Sharon Pressley.

Both of them were enraged, and scared shitless, even Neneng with her shining knife.

I didn't know what to say.

Neneng demanded, "Who send you?"

Finally I said, "No one sent me. I'm trying to help Amaryllis."

"Hah!" said Mrs. Keever. "In that case, go!"

Neneng chimed, "Go!" She kept tight hold of her shank.

I went, escorted out by Neneng, who gave me a haughty shove at the doorstep for good measure. I waited to feel the knife plunge between my shoulder blades, but it didn't.

TWENTY-ONE

My adventure in Bakersfield was still reverberating in me when I called my aunts the next morning, Thursday, to check on Petey.

Sheila answered and told me my boy had adapted to the pot holder kit with a vengeance. "He's made twenty-seven of them and counting. Toots is cutting new loops as fast as she can. Pretty soon she'll have to go out and buy some."

"Dear God. What do you cut loops from?"

"Old socks, you cut them crosswise. We're running out of even new ones, though. She thinks she's gonna sell all these pot holders on the computer. We don't even have a computer." Like Toots's voice, hers was as demure as a wolverine's. "Hey, you know that old rotten shed we used to use as a corn crib? Me and Pete are gonna tear it down today!"

"Oh! Cool."

"We're gonna rig it with chains and pull it down with the tractor."

"He'll love that."

"Yeah, then I think we might burn it."

"You can do that?"

"This ain't California, honey, you can damn well set fire to your own shed if you want to."

"Why not just burn it in place?"

"I want to save the copper from the eaves, there's this copper sheeting. I can sell it. We're gonna tear those off once the roof's down. Pete's gonna help me, right, Pete?"

I heard him laughing in demonic anticipation.

Sheila went on, "On Saturday we're going to the church carnival."

Petey seized the phone. "I'm getting a dog!" he shouted.

"What!"

Sheila grabbed the receiver back. "A *corn dog*. We told him we'd buy him a corn dog at the carnival. Pete, it's a food you eat, not a real dog. We told you that already."

"Whatever became of Reeve?" I asked, remembering their dauntless little terrier.

"Oh, old age. He couldn't walk anymore."

"I'm sorry. Had to put him down?"

"Yeah, I shot him last year. Buried him next to Mashy. More or less on top of Mashy, actually. You don't have to get a dog down as deep as you do a horse. Haven't gotten another dog yet."

"I see." I should have known Sheila wouldn't have given the job to a fancy-pants veterinarian with a hypodermic. Mashy used to pull their pumpkin cart before they got the tractor.

THAT AFTERNOON, GEORGE called from some airport hotel where he'd gotten stranded overnight. I told him all about Diane Keever and Neneng.

"Good work," he said in his steady baritone voice.

"Really?" I stood watching Gina fuss over the herb pots on our patio. Peppermint runs rampant if you let it, we were learning. Golden streamers of sunlight were spilling into the apartment. Some kid in the alley was throwing a glider in the air over and over, just the glider swooping in an arc above the back wall.

"Everything helps," said George. "We now know she's got some kind of personal connection with Amaryllis."

"Yeah. I'm still digesting what I took in."

"Good."

"I have a question. How hard would it be to find out Diane Keever's last name before she got married?"

"I can try it right now online."

"Can I just do it myself?"

"I've got subscriptions to certain databases, so let me look it up for you. I'm logging in right now, I've got my laptop."

"Oh, you bought a new one?"

"Yeah. It's a—"

"Don't bore me with the details."

He laughed. Faint sounds of keystrokes. I heard him breathing, patiently and evenly, and fancied I could feel his warm exhalations on my cheek through the phone. "It's amazing how much work these databases save. I'll have to search by county. Are we assuming they got married in Los Angeles County?"

"Yeah, I think that's reasonable. Didn't Bruce Keever's death notice say he was born in L.A.?"

"That's right, it did. Why do you want to know her maiden name?" His voice was so rich, so intimate to me.

Down, girl.

I said, "That picture of her, that semi cheesecake shot I told you about? I just wonder if she was in the studio system when she was young. That picture is important enough for her to see every day."

"So what if she was an actress back then? It's interesting, but how can it help our—"

"I just want to know. I think it might help me figure out her deal. Somehow. George, one thing I've realized that's different between you and me is that I can size up a woman pretty quickly. I *get* her, you know? But I'm not that astute about men."

"I think you're pretty astute about me." I heard the smile.

Not easily diverted from my point, I said, "I mean in general. Oh, I can figure men out, but it takes me a while. You, on the other hand, decipher men as quickly as I do women. You're always so insightful with guys."

"Hm. Here it is. Her name was Diane Ratkinson," and he spelled it. "They were married on February 4, 1950."

"OK. Thanks. Now about Amaryllis."

"Need some records on her?"

"No. It's just that I want to confront Amaryllis with what we know, or some of it. Tell her we know a few things. I want to do it today."

I heard him blow a breath away from the phone. "Don't."

My adrenaline surged defiantly. "I will."

"Dammit, Rita."

"You can't command me, George."

"Command, hell. As far as I can tell, you've always done exactly as you please. But you're being stupid, Rita. Forgive me, but you're being stupid."

"Why is that?"

"Because you're not listening."

"OK. What? I'm listening now."

He gathered his temper, I could almost hear this little whoosh. I really can be a brat sometimes. Calmly, he said, "I'm trying to tell you it's more dangerous over there than I thought. I won't tell you not to go. But if you do, be as careful as you possibly can. If you mention Diane Keever, don't say too much."

"How come?"

"I can just feel it. Remember, you can always reveal knowledge to a subject, but you can never un-reveal it. It's so much better to listen than to tell."

Gina began to sing "Stormy Weather," low and slow.

"What haven't you told me about Amaryllis?" I asked.

He sighed again. "Here's the whole warning. Remember that Sunday morning when we were over there? When that woman had her seizure or whatever, I considered it a good distraction, and I took off for the basement. I'd already found a door to it, and other than that second locked classroom, it was the only part of the building I hadn't gotten into yet, so I went down there while the security people were calling the ambulance and so forth. They all sort of herded toward the cafeteria to see if somebody was going to die, I think."

"And?"

"It's not a nice place. There's a little room-within-a-room made of gypsum board down there." He paused, expecting me to get it, I guess.

"Well, what's in it?"

"Nothing. They used two-by-fours to create an air space between the drywall and the concrete block wall. Walls and ceiling. There's a heavy rug on the floor."

"Yeah?"

"And there's a steel ring bolted into one wall."

"Explain it to me in baby talk."

"The room is totally soundproof. You could scream until your throat burst."

"Oh, my God."

"It's brand-new."

"How do you know?"

"Because the walls are perfectly clean. Not a stain, not a smudge."

"Oh, God."

"Yet."

"God, God."

"So now I've told you. They've got plans. I'm beginning to wonder if Vargas came up against somebody even more vicious than him: Amaryllis. Do you hear what I'm telling you?"

"Yeah. I think—I just might, ah, wait a little."

"That's my girl."

"I'm not your girl."

"I know, I know."

TWENTY-TWO

Rowe got back to Los Feliz and did his laundry, then he put on his bum disguise in Gonzalo's bathroom. He'd have time to find a new apartment as soon as he got these two cases resolved.

Gonzalo happened to be home this afternoon, reading a neurology journal in his den. The weather had clouded over, and he was feeling like cozying up in anticipation of cooler fall times. Tamiroff, the ninety-five-pound wolfhound, sat in the backyard quietly chewing the picnic table.

Rowe said nothing to his friend before going into the bathroom with his stuff. When he came out as the buck-toothed lowlife, he sneaked into the den. Gonzalo, absorbed in his reading, didn't notice. Rowe made a sudden move, as if to spring.

Gonzalo saw him, screamed, and reached for the five-shot

revolver he carried in an ankle holster. Rowe knocked it out of his hand, laughing.

When he heard Rowe's laugh, Gonzalo stared hard, then sank into his chair grasping his heart, too weak from the ebbing of adrenaline to get up and take a swing at him. "You about fucking killed me, buddy."

Rowe was pleased.

He took the bus to the ABC Mission and went in, but said he didn't need a bed.

This was, now, the fourth time he'd been to the mission. After the first night, he'd stopped in every day, just to be seen by the guards, especially Wichita and Denny. He'd gradually cleaned himself up, and would just stand looking at the bulletin board for a while before wandering out again. He'd missed only two days when he went to Canada.

Today he'd made himself look even less derelict, though Gonzalo's reaction had told him that between the wig and the buckteeth he still didn't look like George Rowe. Cleaner hands and face—he'd shaved—and better pants. He'd omitted the Richards Wild Irish Rose gargle.

After wandering here and there, he found Wichita in an empty classroom playing with an Etch A Sketch someone must have donated for the kids.

He had looked up Wichita's criminal record thanks to the fact that Wichita was her real first name and that Internet databases let you search using first or last. She'd done fourteen months at Chowchilla for carjacking. For Denny, he could find nothing without a last name.

Rowe waited until she noticed him.

"May I talk to you, ma'am?"

She looked up from the teacher's desk. "What you want?" She had been drawing a robot with what looked like a flower coming out of its head.

Quietly but clearly, he said, "Do you know where I can get some clean smack?"

After a moment, with a little smile, she said, "Why do you ask me? I'm just a security guard."

He smiled back, self-consciously and unsuccessfully trying to keep his upper lip pulled over his long teeth. "'Cause you look like you're nobody's fool around here."

She smiled wider. "I've seen you around."

"When I say clean, I mean really clean."

"You don't look like you use."

He laughed uncomfortably. "Guess you know a wino when you see one." He eased himself onto a student desk, feet on the seat. "But look, I've straightened up my act. Pretty much. Thing is, I used to deal, but I'm out of it. Doing other things."

She stared at him, and he watched the gears start to clank in her mind. Her forehead was high and rounded, lending her a belugalike appearance.

"What's up?" asked Denny, striding into the room, dreadlocked and dark-skinned, the locks up in a yellow Rasta hat.

Wichita gave him an irritated look. She turned back to Rowe and repeated, "We're just the security force."

"If you want to buy," said Denny, "you can hit the street." He had a gap between his front teeth that made him look more innocent than he was.

Rowe maintained eye contact with him. "I don't want street

quality, it's not dependable. I hear things. I know there's better quality coming from somewhere around here. I want to buy before the cut. If possible."

Denny asked, "What's your name?"

"James."

"I'm Denny, then."

"Wichita."

"I was telling this lady that I'm working on my own self, I'm pretty straight now."

Wichita said, "Who you need clean smack for?"

"Friend."

"He used to deal," she said to Denny, meaningfully.

"But no more." Rowe held his hand out as if stopping a bus. "Too dangerous, too much risk for a single operator. Never, ever again will I deal, even as a soldier—there's no source, no organization in the city that's safe."

"How much did you used to do?" asked Denny.

"Why do you want to know?"

"No reason. Fuck off, then."

"I just want three goddamn grams! I'm trying to be a goddamn customer!" Rowe wiped his face. "About fifteen thousand a week, if you're so interested. Mostly coke."

"That's not so big," said Denny.

"No, it's not," Rowe agreed. "I was comfortable. Worked in stolen guns on the side."

"Yeah?" said Denny. He wanted to ask a question, but second-thought it.

In spite of the Etch A Sketch, the classroom appeared to be used for adult reading. The teacher had posted a grown-up's alphabet on a bulletin board using cut-out magazine pictures:

A is for Avalanche (National Geographic)
B is for Brooklyn Bridge (Time)
C is for Condom (Playboy)

And so on.

The room smelled of something sweet and faint—the teacher's cologne? Rowe pictured her: very young, very idealistic, like some of the women who came and taught school in the prisons. If she were one of the old ones whose idealism was hardbitten, she wouldn't wear so much cologne. None at all, probably.

"I was an uptown boy," Rowe added. "Had a few clients in Beverly Hills, Hollywood, Bel Air."

"What happened?" Wichita looked him up and down with the frank interest of a child.

"Well, I made one bad friend, if you know what I mean."

"No, I don't," said Denny suspiciously. "What exactly do you mean?"

Rowe shook his head at himself. "I sank almost all my money into my house, in the Valley. Art, rugs, coins, you know. It's what you do instead of a bank, you know what I'm talking about. This guy, he thought I cheated him on a deal, and he torched my house. I couldn't claim insurance, the same reason I couldn't put my money on a tax return."

"Yeah, I see," said Denny. "Too bad."

"So I decided to get out of dealing. I could develop lots of my clients again, of course, since there's so much turnover in this business," he laughed, "but those days are behind me. I was in bad shape for a while, I owed some debts besides, after the fire. I fell into the gutter, but I met a good woman while I was down there, believe it or not."

"That's who the H is for," said Wichita, pleased with herself. A child who wore wet-looking red lipstick.

"You're a good guesser, ma'am. I'd been there before, but I never met anybody like her."

Bit by bit, Rowe revealed himself, pressing their credulity just enough, giving them just enough to stay interested. "My friend Gonzalo, over in Los Feliz, he's gonna let me work construction for him. That's where I'm living as of, uh, yesterday, to tell you the truth. Finally convinced him to not write me off anymore. I can make good money with him."

"Good enough to support your old lady's habit?" Denny demanded.

"Well, I'm not gonna quite, you know. . . . I mean, there's always stuff that fell off a truck, so to speak. Little of this, little of that. Anyhow—"

"You sure you're through with dealing?" asked Wichita.

Firmly, he answered, "Dead sure. I've gotta look after my girl. I'll buy for her, but I won't deal. I can't afford another narcotics rap. Damn bitchin' policewoman nailed me when I wasn't even carrying."

Wichita and Denny shared a meaningful glance. Denny tightened his mouth.

"What if, James," said Wichita, "there *was* a way you could deal again—in safety?"

"No such way exists."

"Oh, yeah? Well, let me tell you something!"

Denny grabbed her arm. "Wichita, I gotta say. I gotta say."

"Ow! The Whale needs another white guy! Goddamn it!"

"Let's not go too fast here, OK?"

She snatched her arm away. Rowe noticed the traces of deep

bruises on it, from his own hands, where he had grabbed her and slammed her into the door on Mateo Street. She didn't recognize him at all. He almost smiled.

"We're supposed to be *recruiting!*" she hissed. "This guy's got experience! I haven't had a bonus in forever!"

Denny looked like he'd like to bash her mouth shut, but clearly her status was greater than his. He restrained himself and had to simply plead. "Come on, Witch."

Rowe said, "You guys—I've heard of Dale the Whale, OK? Half the city has."

"We're not called 'guys,' " said Wichita with hot dignity. "We're all vice presidents. Denny and I are *executive* vice presidents. I respect the man. He thinks new. He don't just go, oh, look at me, I'm at the top of the pile, all you all a bunch of dirt—no. You treat him with respect, he treats you with respect."

She was white—didn't even look like she tanned easily—yet she'd adopted a style of talking that she must have considered street-black.

"You don't have to go on and on," warned Denny.

"I been around drug dealing for a long time. Long time," said Wichita, who looked to be around twenty-five years old, "and never I've seen something like what he does. He's got a whole master plan, but he carries it all up here." She tapped her temple, and Rowe was certain she'd seen the Whale do just that. She settled her hips more comfortably in the teacher's chair.

"Can't be anything new," Rowe said contemptuously.

"Hah! James! Just listen! The bad boys in the old hoods—they all go strictly by territory. They go, oh, this is my corner, you get the hell outta here or I'm gonna shoot choo inna ass. *No.* The Whale, he goes by days of the week, you understand that?"

"Witch—"

"Get out of here, Denny!" she shrieked. "I'm talking to this man, goddamn it! Just go, get your ass outta here!"

He did, his back hard and angry.

"Each dealer," she resumed eagerly, after a little goodbye eye-roll, "rotates through common territories. It's a *rotation,* you see?" She pronounced the word carefully and strongly, as if a host of meaning lay within it, as if she were explaining a scientific principle. "So you got five days on, two days off, which you *must take,* except for if a regular customer can't wait. So no one gets burned out. Because of course you're on call twenty-four/seven when you're on your five days on. We are not like any other organization out there. We are innovative. We do sinajizing."

This time Rowe nodded in comprehension. "But don't the customers get confused who to call? Which day it is?"

"Regulars who got your number, they're different. All this prevents turf wars. He's trying to bring every gang in L.A. into this. Scheduling's the main challenge. The Whale is first and foremost a peacemaker. What do you think of that?"

The Whale must have a whole lot of charisma to make anyone think his rotation system made sense, but slowly Rowe said, "Well, that sounds new."

"He takes care of his people. You get arrested, he gets you out."

"That's impossible."

Wichita paused uncertainly. "Well, he can explain it to you. Don't you think you might want to get back into it, just a little, you know? Maybe"—she realized she could go further—"*if* we give you clean shit for your old lady, then you'd do a little for us? I need a bonus so bad!"

Rowe pinched his lip. "So you won't give me shit before the cut unless I agree to deal? Not just pay?"

"OK, I'm not the Whale, I can't make the final say. I'll talk to him and see what I can do. You think about it, James, OK?"

"OK." He turned to go.

She looked after him.

He turned back. "Say, is Amaryllis B. Cubitt the Mrs. Whale?"

Quickly, "What you want to know for?"

"A man has eyes and ears, and he wonders things. She seems like a nice lady."

"Well," said Wichita, "if you want to keep your eyes and your ears *on you,* you keep 'em shut."

"OK."

"I'm saying?"

"OK."

TWENTY-THREE

I wondered and wondered about Diane Keever. What the hell was going on in that house? I thought about the disquieting Neneng, her rancid cookies, her mastery of Grieg, her pronged carving knife.

Today was Friday, and I lingered over my first cup of coffee at the breakfast bar while Gina showered. I guiltily reveled in my vacation from Petey, or his from me. I missed his assertive little spirit, his tiny quandaries and victories, yet life was so easy and peaceful without him. No worry about a nutritious breakfast; Gina and I could eat leftover popcorn or nothing if we wanted to. Certainly I didn't miss that damn ScoreLad.

But oh, the feeling of his soft-bud mouth kissing my cheek at bedtime! How fleeting it all is! When he was a newborn, Jeff would lie on the bed shirtless and place Petey bellydown on his bare chest, and Petey, no bigger than a puppy, would relax into that feeling of total security, riding gently up and down on his daddy's breath.

Those days were so gone.

When I weaned him I felt a physical change, a hollowness that had never been there, beneath my sternum, before. I felt the relief of not having the responsibility of suckling him and yet! He needed me less! Never again would I nourish him so directly and so completely. Weaning, I realized, was not merely an act of rejection on my part, it was the act of training him to reject me. When my milk dried up, I'd wondered, well, maybe that's it. No more babies for me?

Shit, if I thought about these things too much I'd bust out cryin'.

I went back to brooding about the Keever house.

The piano? The instrument itself could not possibly be a place to hide contraband, nothing so crude—it sounded beautiful, full and resonant, no bundles of drugs taped inside it. Microdots, perhaps.

The photographs atop the piano intrigued me. I tried not to give them a whole lot of weight—I mean, any idiot could focus on family pictures. I really should be looking into Neneng. But how? Who was she? I didn't even know her last name. Maybe that was her last name. I typed "Neneng" into a telephone search and didn't come up with anything.

When I'd mentioned Dale the Whale, Diane Keever made no reaction. Amaryllis's name had triggered the angry reaction. Mrs. Keever had made a questioning sound in her throat, as in, Why would you bring up *her*? Or was it—Why would *you* bring up her? She emoted anger, but why anger, unless it was solely directed at me? Amaryllis was dropping off ten grand in cash to her house each month. How could you be angry at someone who was doing that?

I remembered Nathan saying his mom called the money her "reverse welfare" payment. Why? Because she was black and Mrs. Keever was white? Because she felt sorry for Mrs. Keever for some reason?

I should look beyond the goddamn pictures on the piano, but they were all I had. The young girl—I'd noticed a resemblance between her and Diane, a straightness of the mouth, sort of a similarly set line. But that could be my imagination wanting to glom on to something. Maybe not a daughter, but a doted-on niece, or a foster child? Did Bruce Keever find himself taking on the result of some client's ulterior relationship?

Had the girl turned into an ungrateful, drug-using bitch teen who ran off to Thailand and had then been disowned? What the fuck, what the fuck.

Then I dwelled on the luscious photo of what appeared to be a young Diane Keever. I'd been struck so hard by the expertness of the picture, her beauty, her self-possessed expression, and by the questions it raised.

Gina came out wearing my newest top, a grasshopper-green scoopneck jersey. She looked terrific in it, and she knew it.

"I love this top!"

"Hey, I didn't give you permission to—"

"But doesn't it fit me better than it fits you? You're a little shorter-waisted than I am. Don't you think?"

"Oh, just wear it. Where are you going?"

"I can eat something with you, I don't have to be there until eleven. Equinox, a few people are getting together." Equinox was that new organic, low-emissions chain of espresso bars. "I'm so in love with that place, the one on Highland. The guy making the drinks told me if somebody comes to work wearing Nike shoes, they get fired on the spot!"

"The people who make the drinks are called baristas. And he was joking, for goodness' sake."

"No, no, he was serious."

"So what's going on at Equinox? A meeting for that environmental thing? What's it called again?"

"It's not a thing, it's a movement." She shook out her hair and felt it for dryness. "The longer it gets, the more it takes forever to dry. It's called EP."

"What's it stand for?"

"Rita, you don't know? My God, I thought you were so hip. Earth Puppets." She looked at me for a reaction. "Earth Puppets," she repeated.

I burst out laughing.

"That's the point," she said. "They started out as actual puppeteers, doing environmental marionette shows in schools? And then they just grew into a movement. People hear the name and laugh, but they're dead serious. They fly under the radar of the authorities."

"Earth Puppets," I said, marveling. "That's what they should have called the demonstrators in *The Canary Syndrome*."

"It's going to change the world, that picture. I'm so proud you're a part of it."

I just laughed.

She went on, "Well, a few of us are getting together this morning to—"

"Us?"

"I'm thinking of getting involved. I mean, they're a coalition, you know, not like a party or anything. They've got much higher goals than that, they're more like individual cells that form and carry out education, and . . ." She trailed off.

"And?"

"Like go on missions."

"What kind of missions?"

"To save the earth in—various ways."

"That's what they told you?"

"Rita, the earth is in desperate need of saving! In case you haven't noticed. Look, they're not a terrorist group, OK? They just try to get people fired up about the environment. They hold rallies and stuff, OK?"

"OK, OK. But hon, you know we've got quite a mission right here."

"You haven't asked me for much help yet. It's just been you and George."

"Just wait. I'm going to need you soon. Hey, is Toby involved in the Earth Puppets?" She'd been regaling me with tales of the wondrous Toby, her brand-new boyfriend.

"No, he's not interested yet. But I'm working on him. Oh, God, he's so wonderful. I want to bring him over. *Not* a bartender, *not* a musician, but a regular guy with a day job and a driver's license and seemingly no ex-wives."

"What's so attractive about him?"

"He lets me talk. And he's a boxer guy. You should see his butt, it's like a Michelangelo sculpture. I like boxer guys, briefs guys creep me out."

"Me too. Wait a minute, have you slept with him already?"

"No, not quite exactly yet, I forgot my diaphragm the other night."

"Oh."

"Is George a boxer guy?"

"No comment. Bring Toby home soon."

"You'll love him. He's *sweet*. He's *kind*. He looks like a little boy when he smiles!"

"Does he pick up the tabs?"

"Oh, yes, he's quite the gentleman."

He'd wandered into the record store the other week and started up a conversation, she told me, and they'd hit it off. He'd taken her on a couple of jaunts out of L.A.: down the coast to San Diego, up the coast to Santa Barbara where Gina had seen her first sea otter. "It was so CUTE, Rita! He just revolved in the water and floated on his back, looking at me. He was so CUTE!"

"I know, otters are very cute."

"No! They are not 'cute.' They're CUUUTE!"

"Yes."

"It's like I want one, you know?"

"Typical first reaction."

"You are so unromantic, you know that? No wonder George is having such a hard time with you, poor guy."

"Shut up."

"No, you shut up."

"No, you shut up."

"Anyway, Toby's really opening my eyes up about a lot of things, both social and—"

"What does he do, anyway? And what's his last name? Toby what?"

"Toby Phillips. He's a consultant."

"Oh?"

"Yeah, he works with, uh, various organizations."

"To help them do what?"

"Maximize their potential."

"Huh, sounds like Dale the Whale. All this business bullshit."

"You can belittle just about anything I do, can't you? Just about anything I like."

"I'm sorry, I wasn't really being serious."

"Toby is very romantic. I've told him about you, and he didn't say anything snide about *you*."

"Once again, I apologize."

"In fact, he'd like to meet you."

"Oh?"

"He *asked* about you. Because he's interested in *me*. In *my* life. He wants to get to know me better, and you're family, so."

"Have you met his family yet, or any of his friends?"

"Uh, no, but it's only been two weeks."

"Has he lived in L.A. long?" I continued our customary third degree about boyfriends. Sisters can wring blood from any turnip of a topic.

"Yeah. Yeah, I think so. He doesn't talk much about his family."

"Well, do bring him. How about tomorrow night?"

"I don't know. His work schedule is kind of unpredictable."

"OK, whatever. I feel I know him now just about as well as you do."

"Oh, no!" she laughed. "I haven't told you the best part." She looked at me expectantly.

"Well, what?"

"He's *black*!" She looked victorious.

I understood.

I said, "Well, hey, you did it. You made friends with a black person."

230

"Not just *friends*. But I'm not using him, Rita."

"Well, you're pretty proud of yourself. Hey, I'll see you later, I gotta go over to campus."

"What for?"

"To look for a ghost."

IN A SURGE of ecological feeling I took the bus across town to UCLA. The bus sort of sucks, because you have to expend personal energy guarding against the assorted dirt and weird behavior and cell phone conversations. The main good thing about it is the virtuous feeling you get.

As you'd expect, the UCLA arts library, housed in claustrophobic quarters in the Public Policy Building, has a huge collection of books on the art and business of making films. I searched on the computer, didn't find a title that looked right, so I plunged into the stacks, looking for some kind of reference book on starlets from the old days of the studio system. I picked up a few tell-alls from the era and checked the indices for the names Keever and Ratkinson, no good.

I trudged to the reference desk and waited until the veteran-looking librarian was free. A nattily dressed guy near retirement age with a really good manicure and the snowcap of a Montblanc pen peeking up from his shirt pocket—I thought if anybody could help me, he could.

"I want to find out if a certain person was ever an actress with one of the studios back in, oh, the late 1940s, I'd guess. I know her name, but I'm sure she would have used a screen name."

He thought for a second, finger on cheek. "You say you have her birth name?"

"Yes."

"None of these books is going to help you."

"Oh."

He peered at me over a pair of reading glasses with sun-yellow frames and said, "Mario Salvio."

"Who's that?"

"Mario Salvio"—he said the name as if presenting me with a platinum ingot—"wrote for *The Hollywood Reporter* from 1932 to 1962. He was a compulsive list-keeper. He sort of became the archivist of the studio system."

"Oh, yeah?"

"He made friends with every secretary in Hollywood—that's what administrative assistants were called back then, you know, secretaries—and he collected data from them. He actually photostatted every contract anybody signed with MGM, Paramount, Fox, RKO, and Warner Brothers. Probably a lot from Columbia and Universal as well, though they were smaller, and not really into the studio system per se, where the product's controlled from conception to distribution."

"How did he get away with that?"

"They say he was a *most* charming fellow. He left his papers to the university."

"I see. Well, how do I—"

"They're in the archives. Not in this building. Not open to the public without an appointment."

"Oh." I summoned forth the spirit of a young Shelley Winters, that disappointed softness she did so well. "Oh, gosh."

He exhaled stressfully and looked at his watch. "I'm on lunch as of . . . *now*. Follow me."

He was the perfect blend of prissiness and alacrity: *My job is essentially beneath me, but I'm glad in spite of myself to have an unusual request where I can show off my own personal arcane warehouse of knowledge, the full scope of which you will never grasp.*

We walked across sunny Dickson Court to the Schoenberg Music Building.

"Wait here." He indicated the benches in the stark lobby.

"I can't come too?"

"Since you didn't make an appointment, it'll be quicker if I just do it for you."

"Oh, OK."

He took out his Montblanc and an index card. "What's the name?"

I spelled it for him, and he disappeared into the bowels of the building.

The windows had just been washed and I had nothing to do but watch the students walk by, in their denim and earphones and all those T-shirts of semihorrible UCLA blue. I'm sorry, it is just the weirdest blue.

Fifteen minutes later my librarian returned, looking as if he'd hiked across the Mojave: his tie was crooked, his wispy locks mussed, his eyes bright. He handed me back the index card.

Beneath Diane Ratkinson's name he had printed, PARAMOUNT, 1948–1950. VERA LUXON.

"Standard contract," he said. "She either washed out or got pregnant. Now you can search that name elsewhere to find out if she was ever in a picture or what."

"Thank you," I said fervently, squeezing his arm in gratitude. "That must have been quite the ordeal, you were gone for so long."

He withdrew his arm. "No, not really."

I looked at him in surprise.

"My boyfriend works down there." He winked and strolled away.

TWENTY-FOUR

George Rowe was so used to sizing up guards and security systems that, like a career burglar, he did it almost subconsciously. He smiled at that thought.

The security at the Pan Pacific Canine Exposition was haphazard—everybody who had business there was supposed to have an ID badge on a neck string, but no guards were stationed at the chutes to the arena floor. The guards, wearing blue blazers with whatever company's crest on the pocket, randomly patrolled about with good posture. Usually, private security people are easily outwitted, but he'd noticed a sharp eye or two among this bunch.

He bought a program. The beagles would begin in the ring in a few minutes. This was an invitation-only competition, like the Masters or presidential fund-raising dinners, featuring only the cream of the litter from all over the world. Still, more than two thousand dogs were entered, and brother, that's a lot of dogs. The vast arena floor was sectioned, by thigh-high playpen type fencing, into thirty or so small rings, where all the breed competitions were held.

Nice that the dogs were so beautifully clean—of course they would be—and unsmelly. Rowe had a sensitive nose.

He saw the logistical challenges of moving all those dogs and their handlers in and out of their competitive rings on time, giving them space to wash and groom, space to wait, well-isolated space to relieve themselves, which in this milieu was known by the euphemism "exercising."

He took all this in.

Not that he was planning anything except talking to Orlando Gold, handler of Nick Polen's dogs, and looking at the dogs, but it was wise to have options.

He had never seen so many calm dogs in his life. Rowe knew how perceptive most dogs were—they picked up vibes people didn't even know they were giving. To make it all the way here, handler and dog must have proved themselves many times elsewhere. Every single dog he saw was lovely—clear-eyed, smoothly brushed, beautifully proportioned—and eager to compete.

He walked through one of the exhibit halls. He saw, for sale, a nearly life-size raccoon made of soft plastic that squeaked in pain when chomped; a DVD called *Rescue Dog! True Tales of Heroism in the Andes*; dog treats shaped like slippers, a thousand books about puppies, a portable dog therapeutic Jacuzzi that cost $678.95, and a cleaning kit for same ($16.95 extra). He stopped looking at merchandise.

He settled down in the stands near ring 22 and watched the day's judging for thirteen-inch beagles. He could hear the ring coordinator call for the dogs. The judge was a pudgy woman in a pantsuit. He checked his program against the numbers on the handlers' arm bands and focused on Orlando Gold, number 8, a white man with a bronze tan and blond-tipped hair. He was, Rowe perceived, an elegant fellow in the pejorative sense of the word: tall and thin, wearing a form-fitting suit of a light-absorbing fabric, black velvet or velour. White shirt, straight black tie with a gold stripe—he looked like a backup singer for Elton John. He didn't make excessive gestures, it was just that what gestures he did make were carried one-tenth of an inch too far.

When Gold trotted down and back to show the judge the dog's gait—it was one of Polen's, a female—he was graceful on his feet, matching his stride to the dog's natural movement.

The judge inspected the beagles, opening their mouths, running her hands over their shoulders and rumps.

Polen's bitch came in first, and, smiling professionally, Gold grasped the blue rosette ribbon and put it in his pocket.

Rowe followed him from the arena but lost him in the crowded exhibit hall en route to one of the grooming areas. Polen had mentioned that Gold bred and showed his own collies, so he roamed around until he found that grooming zone.

It was a maze of cubicles, assigned one per handler or owner.

"Do you know where I can find Orlando Gold?" he asked a woman who was currying a zonked-out-looking Pomeranian.

"Down at the end," she said shortly, intent on her dog. She murmured to it as she worked.

Rowe thanked her and walked on toward the last cubicle.

Hearing a sound inside, he paused, stood on tiptoe, and peeked over the high partition. A very large, exceedingly gorgeous collie stood on a grooming platform, its neck leashed to the safety post.

It was the Lassie-type collie, deep-chested and proud. The head was fine, the expression calm. Odd to call such a silky-looking dog a rough collie, but Rowe knew the white-and-sable outer coat was coarse to the touch. The undercoats of these dogs were thick and soft as sheep's wool. The coat was a big part of the collie's appeal.

A beautiful woman with a strangely excited expression had just plugged in a large set of electric shears and was advancing on the dog.

Although Rowe was very close, both dog and woman were unaware of him. She was a dark-skinned black woman with a trim waist and pretty calves.

The dog looked at the woman quizzically, but held still. Its legs trembled.

She parted the collie's coat at its withers and switched on the shears. The dog twitched at the hornetlike sound.

"Oh, now, you know me," she crooned. She wore a striking black-and-white dress, like a life-sized yin-and-yang symbol, that fitted her perfectly.

Rowe stepped into the cubicle.

The woman sprang back and shut off the shears. "Who are you?" The hand holding the shears, he noticed, was quivering.

He smiled and said, "You're not supposed to be here, are you?"

Before she could answer, a blazered security guard came in, one of the sharp-eyed ones.

"Where's your badges, please?"

Rowe slapped his chest and looked down. "Damn," he said, then smiled and extended his hand. "I'm Dr. Garner, veterinary staff." The guard, a mustachioed older dude, hesitated, then reached out to shake.

"Sorry about the badge, I must have left it at the clinic." Rowe stepped to the collie, cocked his head and squinted at it, then ran his hands over the patient dog as he had seen the judges do. He felt the dog's strong chest and shoulder muscles. "This guy here's fine. Mrs. Robertson, let's move on. What about your bitch over in Hall G?"

The woman looked at him in mute gratitude.

"Yes," she said.

"Let's go check that ear discharge," he said. "I'm sure I can get to the bottom of it."

Lightly, he took her elbow and guided her to the nearest deserted spot, a crapping zone used by the miniatures.

Well, Rowe reasoned to himself, she was a beautiful woman caught in an ambiguous situation, and his instinct was to get the both of them out of there. It was what good PIs in the movies did, all of them, and invariably it worked out for the best.

The woman turned to him. She certainly was a dish, with a perfect complexion, a graceful neck, and not much age on her. She looked faintly familiar. Rowe noted that her panic had been replaced by relief.

"Thank you," she said, breathing, meaning it.

"What's your name?" he asked.

"I'm Cici Emberton."

How very interesting. He paused, thinking.

She said, "Oh, you recognize me?"

"You're Khani Emberton's wife?"

"Yes"—she tossed her head with irony—"I'm Mrs. Khani Emberton, big-shot wife of the biggest self-made nigra in L.A."

He nodded neutrally. "My name is George Rowe. I'm thinking of doing some business with Orlando Gold."

"You're not going to buy a dog, are you?" She looked genuinely alarmed.

"I don't know. You might as well tell me what you were doing."

"You're not an actual vet."

"No."

"I was—I was—" She stopped, deciding whether to lie.

"You were going to ruin that dog's coat. How come?"

Someone had spilled a bit of kibble on the concrete floor; she nudged the dry bits with the toe of her black-and-white shoe and said, "I suppose if I said it's a secret, you'd threaten to go to Orlando and make up some story about me."

"You wanted to play a trick on him?"

She looked him in the eye. "Not a trick. I want justice." She glanced around. At the far end of the crap zone a handler set down a toy poodle, which squatted to make its deposit. "This isn't a nice place to talk."

"It is awkward," Rowe agreed. "Look, if you convince me that you're really after justice, maybe I can help you out. Maybe you can help me too."

She smiled slightly, looking at him. Where had Emberton met her? She sure didn't have much of South Central clinging to her.

Rowe guided them to a storage room he'd spotted earlier.

The room, really a large closet, was crammed with bales of cleaning rags and drums of antiseptic. He flipped on the light, and they sat on the bulging bales. The bales were soft, and Rowe, propping himself on an elbow in a nonthreatening posture, felt like a Bedouin in a tent.

She noticed, and, as if to call him on it, said, "I know you have the upper hand."

He did, but perceived she could be quite a cat if pushed into a corner.

"Yes, I was trying to ruin that dog's coat," said Cici Emberton. She wasn't afraid of being alone in this little room with him. There was, Rowe now heard, a hint of street in her speech—"trying" sounded like "trahn." It stood out, given how polished she looked, and how nearly perfect her grammar was. "If I shaved a nice big X in Conqueror's fur, he wouldn't be able to show him for a year. Wouldn't hurt the dog, only Orlando."

"I see," said Rowe.

She folded one neat leg beneath her, smoothing her skirt. The air smelled of clean cotton. "He thinks this is Conqueror's year. It might be, I mean did you see that dog?"

"Yes."

"He's very vain about that dog. And I do believe he has some money riding on him."

"Oh, really?"

"Well, I won't allow it."

"What did Gold do to you?"

"Took me for a fool. And I was. I was a fool," she mused, her voice quieting. "But you don't mess with Cici. My last name has nothing to do with the fact that you don't mess with me. I know what I am: I'm a child of Watts, OK? Look me up on the Internet"—grimness took over her tone—"you find *that* out first thing."

Rowe smiled, liking her.

"Don't give me too much of that," she said, tipping her head back and looking at him through half-lidded eyes. "You're a white man. You're not going to understand."

"Maybe not. You don't know me, either. You don't know I won't try to screw you over."

"I appreciate that. No, I'd like you to understand. Some-goddamn-body to understand." She patted her foot on a rag bale. "Ragpicker at least would have been a trade my daddy could've done," she mused softly. "Well, at least he gave a damn, thank the Lord."

Cici Emberton's voice strengthened, and now Rowe could hear, beneath the street, the sweet inflections of the West Indies.

"Khani and I met at a school dance. He's a star. He loved me at first sight."

He nodded. "Is this where you're going to tell me how you learned right from wrong?"

She glared at him. "You really don't understand, do you? Mr. Rowe, it's been *hard* for me to come out from the hood!" She said it deep and blue, from her gut. "I mean, everybody wants out from the hood, right, but the hood's your comfort zone too, you see? When I became his wife and he got so successful, I had to change. We got a big house—houses! Martinique! We had staff." Her voice accelerated. "Suddenly I'm going to opening night at the opera and eating foy grass with chopsticks or some *damn* thing, trying to talk to these people. What do you talk about? You don't talk about the rhinestone tips you're gonna get on your fingernails, because that's not classy. I found that out.

"I don't *ski*. We don't have kids yet. I don't speak Swiss or some language. The men can always talk business. Nobody thinks less of Khani because he came from the streets. But somehow, they think less of me." Her eyes softened with hurt. "OK, I said to myself, I'll fit in. I worked at it. Nobody knows how I've worked at it."

"Vocal coach?" intuited Rowe.

"Yes!"

"Fashion—uh?" he gestured, taking a further risk.

"My tasteful outfit! Yes! Haha! You can spend a lot and still look like hell. There's people who'll help you with that."

In the cocoonlike atmosphere of the closet, Cici Emberton opened up, and he listened. He learned that she had observed other multimillionaire wives talking about their horses and dogs. She was afraid of horses, but she decided to get a dog that she could dote on and talk about. It had to be a special dog. One of the women had introduced her to Orlando Gold.

Collies were making a comeback, she'd learned. "Nobody in that bunch has pit bulls, *nobody*."

Orlando Gold had made her think she was latching on to him, while all the time he was latching on to her. He'd charmed her, being refined, graceful, and white—"but easygoing, you know, an easygoing white man"—and she'd learned about dogs from him, and she'd bought a dog from him.

"He wanted me to sleep with him, but I stopped short of that, thank the Lord!" She laughed bitterly. "That's one thing I kept! The integrity in this ring!" She held up her rich gold band. "Orlando wanted me to invest in other dogs, show dogs, so he could win more. I said no to that too. Some of the other women, they invested, yeah, he was quite the stud. I paid him ten thousand dollars for a collie dog he said was a champion. I took the dog home and before the week is out, the thing poops on our bed. Khani was so mad! I thought the dog had a nervous problem. Poor Shasta. I take her to the vet, and the vet says, 'This dog ain't sick, she's dying of old age! She's going into organ failure, and she's got arthritis too.'"

Gold, Cici Emberton went on, had pumped the dog full of amphetamines. "He gave me pills to give her, vitamins. Well, they weren't vitamins, they were speed. Soon as they ran out, she crashed. I confronted him, and he denied it. But I could tell he was lying. Tried to hand me more pills!"

"How did you know the pills were speed?"

"The vet told me. Should have figured it out myself. That poor thing had to be put down."

Of course Cici had been furious, but Gold had weasled, and wouldn't give her any of her money back.

"I don't understand," said Rowe, "why he played such a rank trick on you. Did he think you wouldn't ever figure out the dog was old and worn out? Why not sell you a good dog?"

Cici said, "He took me for a dumb nigra. That's the simple why. If he saw me at this show, he'd die. He thinks I'm too embarrassed to act on him. That old dog was no good to him, so he fixed her up and unloaded her on me. Do not mistake me, the ten K is not the point."

"Yes," said Rowe. "Why don't you just sue the guy? I'd think your husband would be glad to—"

"Oh, he offered! But I said no, I want to handle this myself. I made the mistake."

Rowe really liked this woman's spirit. "Where's Gold staying?" he asked.

"Oh, he lives over in Glendale, so he's not at a hotel. But the in crowd hangs out at June's, that bar across from here? I heard he's on the prowl every night."

"OK. Tell you what. Meet me in this closet again tomorrow morning. Say ten o'clock."

"The herding group goes out at eleven."

"Plenty of time."

"COLLIES ARE THE new ocelots," Orlando Gold said earnestly, then took a sip of a pink drink from a champagne flute. Rowe watched and listened from a few feet away in the crowded bar.

"The new what?" The well-dressed woman was drinking a similar cocktail. Her silver hair was pulled back smooth and held by a pearl fastener. She wore more pearls around her neck, as well as gold bracelets and rings.

"Remember how women in the sixties used to walk up Fifth Avenue with an ocelot on a gold chain? Diamond collar?"

She laughed. "Are you old enough to remember that?"

"Well, I read about it, I've seen photographs. Oh, they were gorgeous!"

Rowe saw Gold's manner—ingratiating, affable—and he heard his oily tone. Beneath that, he saw the pridefulness in his eyes, and the opportunism. Gold was the kind of person who considered every new acquaintance a potential mark. If he hadn't been good-looking, with that thin, refined face and long upper lip, his shtick would have been much harder to pull off.

People were talking dogs everywhere.

Gold wore the exact same hairstyle Rowe had noticed on certain other male dog handlers—nipped short and pushed up in front, stiffened with goo, the frost-tipped hair being like a little tiara.

Rowe could not understand this hairstyle. He sipped his beer.

The woman tittered faintly in Gold's face. He was ladling the shit, all right. He called, "Two more Kir Royales here!"

Rowe edged closer and heard, ". . . and I'm telling you, the opportunities that open up when you invest in show dogs—well, I'm talking international opportunities. Ever been to the St. Petersburg Winter Carnival?"

"No!"

"Well, they put on an amazing dog show there, you know, as part of the week. And the festival itself—it's just beyond words. The people, all the big society people of Europe, go every year. They fall all over you when they learn you're a member of the AKC. Ever watched the aurora borealis from a hot tub for two?" He chortled subtly, and the woman dropped her eyes in discomfort.

Rowe waited until the woman went to the powder room. He approached Gold and introduced himself, using the name Simon Westfield.

Gold said, "Oh, you're that guy Nick told me about." He looked Rowe up and down with distaste, pursing his mouth at Rowe's plain pants and shoes. "I'm a little preoccupied right now," he said in an uptight voice, sipping his drink.

"Yes," said Rowe. Guys like this couldn't make a muscle if their lives depended on it. He talked to Gold about Markovich.

Gold knew who Markovich was, of course, and he was aware of Ernest's disappearance. "What about it?"

Rowe said, "Markovich thinks Polen took the dog, or arranged for it to be taken."

Gold laughed a genuine, unforced laugh. "Ernest the beagle is retired from the ring, but you can bet Markovich's put up hundreds of units of his semen. A champion sire's lifespan is almost irrelevant these days."

"He doesn't seem concerned about that part of it. He misses Ernest's companionship."

"I'm sorry. Shit happens."

As they talked, Gold kept one eye out for the woman. Rowe had noticed, however, that she'd slipped her purse and wrap off the back of the bar stool before going off.

His feeling had been growing that Polen, whatever else he was up to, was innocent of dognapping Ernest. And this Gold had other rackets going; he was running all over the dog show handling other owners' dogs, Polen's two among them, and he had his own prized collies to look after. He had, it appeared, investors to keep happy, and he had sub-par dogs to barter to people who didn't know any better.

"You seem to have a way with the ladies," Rowe remarked.

"Oh . . ." Gold waved his hand.

"I bet some of them are—fringe benefits, in your line of work."

"Ha!" Gold warmed up now, helped by the next Kir Royale. The one at the woman's place sat giving up its bubbles. "Well, it's a pretty good position to be in, I have to admit. It's amazing what these rich women'll do just to have some fun." Rowe snickered encouragingly. Gold went on, "It's amazing how far a few good manners will get you. And clothes, you have to look good, rich broads notice. If you look nondescript, they won't even see you."

"I see," agreed Rowe.

There was a certain charisma about Gold; you had to have something going for you to relate well to dogs—yet there was an overwhelming slyness about him, as well as something stunted. Rowe supposed Gold and Polen got along splendidly. As far as Rowe knew, Gold hadn't killed anybody, he hadn't beaten up a woman, he hadn't gotten drunk and crashed his car into a pre-school; he was just a sleaze. "I bet a lot of these folks," Rowe said, "while they'd like to have a show dog for bragging rights, probably aren't going to actually show them."

"That's right." Gold smirked.

"I saw that your collie, Conqueror, won breed today. Congratulations."

"Thank you. He'll wipe the floor with the herding group tomorrow morning."

"And tomorrow night?" Rowe asked.

Gold just smiled.

Rowe said, "Polen let slip that he gambles on his dogs."

"What's wrong with that?"

"It didn't seem to work out for him."

"Hey." Suddenly Gold was force-nine huffy. Rowe almost winced at how easy this was.

He said, "Polen trusted you. He's trusting you now. And you've got reverse money on his dogs."

Gold made a move as if to jump to his feet, then, really noticing Rowe's sloping shoulders, thought better of it. He jutted his chin and said, "Hey, buddy, I have just one thing to say to you—"

"Who carries the bets? How does it work?"

"*Fuck you!*"

TWENTY-FIVE

That Saturday afternoon, Gina went to work at the record store, which needed all hands on deck as it prepared to release Quint Watkins's long-awaited next album. They were doing some kind of bait-and-switch giveaway of the original Shenanigans—remember them, they had that TV show where they drove this bus around, fighting crime with music? Weird band.

I took the opportunity to do a day spa for myself, starting with a bubble bath. I lounged in the suds with my clay skin-tightening mask on, thinking about Amaryllis and Mrs. Keever.

The phone rang, and I let the machine get it. But in two seconds I was slushing from the tub, running for it without even grabbing my towel, because Aunt Toots's voice had a life-and-death pitch to it.

"I'm here! Aunt Toots!" My clay mask fractured around my mouth.

"Rita, is that you? God damn it!"

"Yes, yes! What is it?"

"Petey's on the roof!"

"Oh, my God! Can't he get down?"

"Hell yes he can get down, but he won't!"

I breathed. "OK, what's the matter?" I stood naked, dripping suds.

"He says he's busy!"

"Doing what?"

"Exploring. He says he's being Chet Glaston."

"Oh."

"Who the hell's Chet Glaston?"

"He's a famous mountain climber." I brushed bits of clay from my face, trying to make them fall on a coaster.

"Oh. Well, he's crawling all over the chimney using just his fingers and toes. I'm having a heart attack."

I pictured their stone chimney. "Oh, he's bouldering. Our friend Daniel taught him that."

"God damn it!"

"How did he get up there?"

"First he climbed the maple tree and then he swung onto the roof from the branches!"

"Really? Wow."

"None of you kids ever did that."

"The tree wasn't as big then."

"You don't seem very upset!"

"Well—"

"I want to call the fire department but Sheila says no, let him stay up there until he cries to come down. I said I'd ask you what to do."

Maybe because it was impossible for me to deal directly with the situation, I felt calm. "Are you prepared to send up sandwiches and candles? Because for all I know—"

"God damn it, Rita, we need help here!"

I'd spent all five years of Petey's life worrying about him, and the past year and a half—as he grew out of toddlerhood—absolutely freaking out if I thought he was in the slightest bit of danger. That's typical, I guess. But now I felt almost elatedly calm. Petey had spent so much time climbing and roughhousing with Daniel, that for the first time, I felt confident that he was OK.

"Oh, Toots, I'm sorry he's being such a pain in the ass." I thought for a moment. "You know, the psychology you should *not* use is Gramma Gladys's Old You're Gonna Fall And Crack Your Head Wide Open. That's totally useless on him. What you've got to do is lure him down with something even more dangerous than climbing on the roof."

"Ah!"

"Like, I'm trying to think of—"

She interrupted, "Hey, I'll tell him we're gonna dynamite that stump in the pumpkin field."

"That's excellent, Toots. Uh, do you guys actually have dynamite?"

I wondered if Gina and I would someday wind up like Aunt Sheila and Aunt Toots. Then I wondered whether that would be a good thing or a bad thing.

"Oh, yeah," said Toots, "we use it on stumps all the time. One time Sheila moved a boulder with it, but it didn't go in the direction she wanted. Hah! A fella brings it around to us."

251

"Really."

"It's so useful. Sheila said if she got stuck on a desert island with only two tools, she'd want her Sawzall and a crate of dynamite."

"Really. Well—OK, I guess you know what to do now."

"Thanks, Rita."

"OK."

"I'm glad I never had kids."

"But you love Petey, don't you?"

"This is not the best time to ask me that."

I laughed.

She growled, "Of course I love the little shit! We both do."

When I was pregnant with Petey, I couldn't remember what it was like to not be pregnant. Then, half an hour after he was born, I couldn't imagine life without him. I could barely *remember* life without him.

I climbed back into my womblike bathtub. I lay back, smelling the pretty lavender oil I'd poured in, and I thought about childbirth and how small Petey had been—barely five pounds, barely there. Holding him, I felt the dark mystery of the place he'd been before he pushed his way out of me. I could not imagine him not existing.

I dozed.

I bolted upright. "Oh!" I said out loud.

After I finished my bath, I put on my kimono and went to my computer. I got online and searched on "California abortion law."

GEORGE ROWE PASSED a photographer's booth where a woman and two dachsunds had composed themselves in front of a woodsy backdrop. The jolly photographer had rigged a fishing pole with six feet of line and baited it with a foxtail; he jerked it to and fro, and the dogs' eyes followed it eagerly. The woman smiled. He squeezed his shutter.

It was now Sunday, the final day of the Pan Pacific Canine Exposition. Rowe watched Orlando Gold enter the arena with yet another client's dog, this one a Bedlington terrier, which had made it to the terrier finals. The detailed printed program, plus a quick Internet search of Saturday's winners, had made it easy for Rowe to figure out Gold's logistics for the day. Gold walked tall with the curly silver terrier, his stride steady in spite of all those Kir Royales last night. He and the Bedlington were early for the finals and would wait on the sidelines.

Rowe knew that Gold's prize collie, Ch. Conqueror Whitehill Face the Music, would be relaxing in his crate in cubicle 729, along with Polen's two beagles, one of which would be competing in the hound finals this afternoon.

Rowe met Cici Emberton at the storage closet. Her eyes shone with excitement. Today she had on a peach-colored outfit with a towering matching hat—very attractive, and clever besides: people would notice the hat and not so much her face. She carried the electric shears in a flowered tote bag.

Most of the cubicles were empty, as most of the losers in breed had gone home last night.

Yesterday Rowe, from ringside, had watched Polen's male beagle, handled by Gold, come in third in the fifteen-inch category. He had compared the dog's profile with a picture of Ernest and immediately seen that the slope of the dog's forehead was slightly different, and the muzzle just a tad shorter. A beautiful dog, but not Ernest.

The woman with the Pomeranian was in her cube fluffing its amber fur. Rowe noted that the name strip on her cube said MRS. LAURIE FURTADO. The dog reared, and the woman said, "No. Four on the floor. Good girrrrl."

When Rowe and Cici passed by, she lifted her head and stared at them. Then she set down her comb.

Gold's dogs stirred in their crates. "Hello, kids," said Cici.

Rowe turned to the doorway, intending to block any possible view in. He almost bumped chests with Laurie Furtado, who said, "Excuse me," in an on-the-muscle tone.

"Yes?" he said calmly. He heard Cici behind him talking to the dogs in a voice intended to sound casual.

"Ah," said the Pomeranian-owning Laurie Furtado, whose lustrous bangs and small eyes lent support to the cliché of people looking like their dogs, "what is your business here?"

Rowe never minded monkey wrenches of this kind.

"I'm Dr. Garner, veterinary staff, Mrs. Furtado. May I help you?"

The woman only stared hard at him. Rowe watched her brain register something. Slowly, she said, "There is no veterinary staff at this show. The show vet is off-site. I know him: Dr. Baer."

Rowe smiled. "Well, I can assure you, I've been hired. The committee made the decision to add me as a floating doc, so to speak, just Thursday. There's a virus going around Southern California that they were a little nervous about."

"Well, d'you have your badge?"

"I'm very bad about that sort of thing."

"Who's she?"

"Ma'am, may I ask what your interest is? You understand."

"Oh! Well, Orlando"—here she sighed ever so slightly, ever so fondly—"asked me to keep an eye on his dogs while he's doing terriers. So that's what I'm doing."

Rowe threw back his head and laughed deeply.

Startled, the woman added, "I mean, Orlando's got all his hopes riding on this collie, he told me so."

"And a good bit more," muttered Cici under her breath, behind Rowe. He laughed louder to cover it.

"Haha!" Rowe caught his breath. "How narrowly we escaped a misunderstanding, Mrs. Furtado!"

She looked at him beadily.

"Mr. Gold stopped me in the concourse," he said, "on his way with the Bedlington and he asked me to do a quick check on Conqueror here. Mrs. Robertson, I wonder if—ah, thank you!"

Cici released the dog from its crate and as it leaped gracefully to the grooming platform, she bit back a smile.

"My assistant," he explained professionally, as Laurie Furtado took in Cici's outfit with a flat expression. "Now then, let's see."

Now convinced, Mrs. Furtado said worriedly, "I hope he's OK."

Cici piped up, "I believe Mr. Gold mentioned a rectal problem, doctor."

"So he did, so he did," said Rowe, cutting her an evil look. "Hm. Well, without gloves, I'll only be able to do a visual examina—"

"I have disposable latex gloves!" exclaimed Mrs. Furtado. "I use them to shampoo Ginger." She ran down to her cube and stampeded back before Rowe and Cici had time to exchange more than a look.

Suddenly sweating, Rowe drew on the gloves, as Cici guided

Conqueror's head into the safety leash. "Yes, OK," he asserted, amping himself for the task.

Mrs. Furtado watched, quite concerned.

He cleared his throat. "Tail, please, Mrs. Robertson." Cici lifted Conqueror's tail, and Rowe had no choice but to steady the dog's hips and peer at its butthole. "Rectal area looks normal," he observed.

Next, he looked skyward as casually as he possibly could, and took a deep breath. He parted the dog's hair and gently inserted his right index finger into Conqueror's anus. The dog flinched, but Cici held his head confidently and murmured, "Good boy, good boy. It'll be over soon."

Not fucking soon enough.

The dog's sphincter closed tightly around Rowe's finger and he felt the animal's warmth through the thin glove, disgustingly reminiscent of intercourse. He felt inside the dog's rectum. "Uh, prostate appears OK. Hm. Hm." He withdrew his finger and stripped off the gloves without looking at them, tossing them into the wastebasket.

"I don't know," he remarked, "if diarrhea is the problem, or not. I'll have to speak to Mr. Gold again, and perhaps get this big guy into my office for further testing after the show." He smiled jocularly. "That OK with you, Mrs. Furtado?"

"Oh, yes," she said. "Sorry to have bothered you. But—you know. I heard one time somebody drugged somebody else's dog so it couldn't compete."

"I've heard those stories too," said Rowe. "Well, no bother! You were just being a good neighbor."

Mrs. Furtado went away.

"Quick," muttered Rowe.

Cici was already plugging in the shears.

Rowe knew the dog would not be hurt, but he couldn't bear to watch. He stood at the doorway. He knew that in the nearly deserted area, the angry sound of the shears would prick up Laurie Furtado's ears; indeed, she was on alert, her face squinched in puzzlement, when Rowe and Cici swept past on their way out.

Three minutes later they were striding along Twelfth Street in the sunny morning, talking. Cici's happiness was complete: she had achieved her goal, and she was grateful to her new friend. Rowe felt sorry for the dog but not at all for Orlando Gold, so it balanced out.

They walked fast for a few blocks.

"Yes," said Rowe, "you owe the hell out of me for that rectal thing."

"It was all I could think of at the moment. Listen, you said yesterday you thought maybe I could help you in return. I haven't forgotten." She gave him a look that was half arch, half tough.

"Let's duck in somewhere and I'll tell you."

They were in L.A.'s fashion district, where wholesalers used the cheap spaces of run-down warehouses and old mercantile exchanges to sell everything from handbags to jeans to perfume. Rowe had gone running through the area many times.

Cici snorted at the jeans displays: oddly, all the butts of the mannequins faced the street.

"You know why that is," Cici said scornfully.

"No, but I like the custom."

"Males own these stores, you know. And guys like to see what *they* like to see, which is women's asses. Women want to see jeans from the front, like they're looking into a mirror."

"Ah," said Rowe.

They went into a café and sat on high stools and ordered coffees. Cici ordered a bagel too, saying, "I'm hungry, but I'm too jazzed to really eat." Rowe knew his appetite would return after the memory of Conqueror's rectal exam had faded.

"You and I," he began, "we have a friend in common. Amaryllis B. Cubitt."

Cici smiled quizzically.

He said, "She once helped someone dear to me, and now I have an interest in her."

"Yes?"

"That big donation your husband's making will take the mission to a whole new level."

Cici's face clouded. Her peach-fuzz suit jacket and the black soft blouse she wore beneath formed a kind of cup, like a cup made of petals, for her breasts. He saw how well-fitted clothes make a woman not just more attractive, but more secure in herself. Yes, that was it. He thought of how Rita looked in those short-sleeved sweaters she liked to wear. He sighed.

"Do you know Amaryllis well?" he asked.

"Not as well as I'd have expected to by now. I mean, she's like my foster mother-in-law, but . . ."

"Yeah?"

Cici hesitated. Rowe prompted, "Is she a little hard to get friendly with?"

She nodded to him. "You got it. Actually, that's an understatement, you know? *Hard* is the word for her. She's the Iron Angel, OK, she helps people, but if there's a soft side to her, I haven't seen it. It's like, I do good things, so I have license to be a bitch. Let me tell you, one-on-one, she's rugged."

"So you haven't spent a whole lot of time with her?"

258

"No, not really. Khani sees her pretty often." She nibbled her bagel, which had been sliced, toasted, and buttered. Rowe smelled the good hot bread.

He said, "You seemed a little—I don't know . . . something—when I mentioned the five million."

His companion said nothing.

"Do you know if anything unusual is going on with Amaryllis?"

Cici's gaze sharpened. "Why?"

"I'm concerned there may be some illegal activity surrounding her. Something trying to get at her."

Cici sighed.

"About the five million," Rowe said. "Do you know how the fund will be set up—you know, how the money will be controlled?"

"You're concerned about someone stealing it? Or you want to get in on it?"

"I don't want to get in on anything. I just want to protect Amaryllis."

Cici Emberton swirled her coffee, then looked up. "Well, Khani's been worried about her too."

"Yeah?"

"Mind you, I don't wish the woman ill. In no way. I'm not sure I should tell you this, since it isn't public information yet."

"If you don't know by now that you can trust my discretion, I'll just point out that you owe me big-time, Cici."

She smiled into her coffee. "Yeah, I know."

"Does it have to do with Khani's gift?"

"He came home last night and said Amaryllis told him to call off the gift. Just call off the five million!" Cici smacked her palms.

"Really," said Rowe.

"I know, I know," said Cici. "Khani asked her what's wrong, and she wouldn't say. He says are you sick? Do you need a doctor? Did some doctor tell you you have cancer? Is that why? You ain't gonna leave us now, are you? He was quite upset. She wouldn't say anything. He says, is there trouble? She wouldn't say. Next he asks her if she needs the police, and that got a reaction out of her. No way, she says. He's got private security, you know, so he offers that to her. But she says no."

Rowe asked, "What does Khani think is going on?"

"He told me he got the feeling she was ashamed of something. And afraid of something too."

TWENTY-SIX

George called me Monday afternoon and told me to meet him in my derelict persona that night.

"It's time to meet the Whale. Ten o'clock."

"Yeah?"

"I let them know I might want to deal drugs for them, and I just got word he wants to see me. He wants to meet you too, my heroin-addicted girlfriend."

"Why would he want you to deal drugs for him?"

"He thinks my skin color can help his organization. So our objective tonight is to make friends with that human cesspool. This time, make yourself look a little cleaner, like we're living under a nonleaking roof."

"OK."

We managed to talk about different things, then I asked, "How's your other investigation going?"

"Interestingly, it's beginning to dovetail with this one."

"Really?"

"I'm finding out that L.A.'s a smaller town than I thought."

GINA HELPED ME suit up; I knew I'd need her for that if I ever returned to the ABC in my bum disguise. Yvonne had, at my request, left some tubes of latex and scrapings from her bruise wheels, saying, "Sure, you guys can re-create this. It'll take you longer, and it won't look as good, but you'll achieve your basic effect if you don't get too ambitious. I mean, everybody takes a course in makeup in acting school, right?"

"I did."

"Wear long sleeves next time so you won't have to do your arms, those are hard. Plus, intravenous drug users, if that's what you're going for—they wear a lot of long sleeves anyway, so you'll be consistent."

Chino had said it was OK for me to keep the pregnancy vest for a while, so I was good there.

I made sure to lighten my face a bit, and I omitted the dirt. I filed the chew marks off my nails.

George and I rendezvoused at MacArthur Park and bused it from there. I almost laughed to see him wearing an extremely wrinkled but clean white shirt, and a striped silk tie, warped from improper cleaning. He seemed much less loser-esque, having cleaned himself up, combing his wig and washing his hands. The wig was still fairly oily and excellent, but the reddish curls now swept back farther from his face, making his lips over the buck teeth appear more protruding than ever. He looked like he could actually hold down a job.

We got off the last bus and headed down Compton on foot. "You're waddling very well this evening," George complimented me.

We passed beneath a billboard for Megaton Pictures, the studio making *The Canary Syndrome*. It was a funny name for a small, upstart studio, I thought. But in Hollywood, it's go big or go home, you know?

He said, "I learned something interesting today about the Keever family."

"Yeah?"

"They had a daughter."

I knew it, I just knew it! "Where is she?" I asked.

"She died shortly before her father quit being a judge. She was fifteen. I checked her birth certificate too, she was definitely their daughter."

I took that in. "How did you find that out?"

"I looked up Bruce Keever's interment information because it wasn't in the death notice. I wondered if there was any significance to that. Found that there's a family plot at Forest Lawn. The first grave is occupied by Deborah Keever, died 1965. Bruce Keever was brought down here and buried next to her."

"So her birth year was—"

"Nineteen-fifty."

The year Diane Keever left the studio system. "Yeah," I said slowly. "Of course."

We arrived at the mission's front gate.

He peered into my skag face with concern.

I said, "George, something's dawning on me, and I—I need to think. I might have something, but I still don't understand how it fits into—"

A deep, melodious voice called, "Hey, hey, James!" and a man came to the gate. When he flung it open, it rattled like Satan's teeth.

"Come on, DeeDee," George said. "This here's Denny."

"Hi."

There was an air of expectancy about the mission that night. Everybody seemed quieter—waiting for something.

Denny ushered us, in true French-courtier fashion, to a room upstairs to wait for Dale the Whale. The room was the one George and I had been interrupted breaking into: the second of the two with fortified locks, the first having been the strange room that was empty except for the gun safes.

Wichita met us at the door with a smile for George and a sudden look of disgust for me, like a medieval fishwife finding a rotten carp among the trout.

"I'll get him," Denny said. Wichita waited with us silently. This room was in the back of the school, overlooking the dark, ruined playing fields. I thought about the feral dog pack and wondered where they were tonight.

All the windows were open. The Los Angeles night air whispered in, flavored with traffic noise and the random shout. The windows were the pull-in kind, along the whole length of the room, just like at schools all over America, just like at Rutherford B. Hayes Junior High back in Wisconsin. This had been a science room—there were lab tables with sinks and gas valves, a ceramic eye wash fountain, and a periodic chart way above the blackboard. A side door led to what must have been shared teachers' offices between this classroom and the next. I could almost smell the spilled acetic acid and hear the clink of the pipettes. I liked science.

This was definitely a hideout now, streety grunge with Cheetos wrappers and old newspapers in the corners, as if the wind had blown them there. Someone had dragged in a tattered black leather sofa and a few motley chairs. A half-acre-wide coffee table had been made from a mahogany dining room table, its legs amputated above the knee.

There were two gun safes in this room too.

I sensed something, and turned from the windows. As Dale the Whale Vargas glided into the room, the air before him seemed to compress in concentric waves, as water would before a massive sea creature.

"Hello. Hello," he said in a soft voice, like a priest's.

The Whale was fastidiously groomed—clean-shaven, perfect manicure.

"Hello, I'm James," said George, extending his hand. But the Whale wouldn't shake it. He didn't explain, just ignored it with a smile.

You don't shake hands with a deity.

The Whale cruised the room lazily, pausing before each of us. I didn't expect him to acknowledge me, but he did. "Hello, ma'am. How are you this evening?"

"That's DeeDee," said George.

"Hello," I mumbled.

Vargas's movements were deliberate and fluid, and I saw his way—by being so soft, his viciousness, when it came, bit more horrifyingly still.

Wichita and Denny remained standing. The straight butt of a

pistol stuck out of Wichita's waistband, the bulge of it crammed into her pants. Over his SECURITY T-shirt, Denny wore a loose sport shirt that flapped around his middle, so I couldn't tell if he was armed.

The Whale was a sizer, all right. Maybe three hundred pounds, and only five-foot-four or so, about my height. Even his knees were fat, straining the fabric of his Dockers-type pants. I foresaw diabetes in his future. He wore a thick silver chain around his neck that looked like an anchor chain. I realized it was probably platinum. Matching baby-anchor bracelet.

He wore some kind of minty aftershave, but when he passed me, I detected an undercurrent of perspiration, and I swear to God, his very sweat smelled mean.

Behind Vargas, three more men came in, all dressed in the gray security guard T-shirts. They were wearing their jewelry tonight, typical ghetto bling, the pavé diamonds spelling out nicknames: SPUD, JAKE3, RUMY. It looked fake but was probably real. I wondered which level of vice president they'd attained. One was black, one Latino, one white, or whitish, anyway. I saw the flat meanness of the street in their faces, with an undercurrent of fear of their boss—little strain lines around their eyes. Their eyes wanted to see something happen.

"Phones on vibrate, people," said the Whale, still moving. "This place is a pigsty. Crud in the corners. Did your mothers develop you individuals this way? Looks like a meth shack."

The vice presidents scurried to clean it up, a five-minute flurry involving brooms and a garbage bag produced from somewhere.

Vargas turned to George. "OK, so what have you got for me? I can give you fifteen minutes. Go ahead and sit, people, sit, sit."

George took a chair at a right angle to the sofa, which he must have perceived to be the power throne. The sofa looked greasy. The Whale remained standing.

"I need clean heroin for DeeDee," said George, "and—and if the only way I can get it is to sell a little bit for you, then OK."

"Why not get it from somewhere else?"

George hesitated. "I understand you've got a never-before system."

The Whale laughed.

George's body language was great—a little round-shouldered, yet with head high, trying to break out with some confidence.

I hung at the edges.

"Is she the main reason?" The Whale made a soft gesture in my direction.

"She's the only reason."

"Isn't money another, naturally? Honestly, now."

"Maybe so."

I rasped nastily, "He'll be dealing full time before you know it."

George gave me a deadly look, as planned.

The Whale laughed. "Ambition! He admits it. Nothing wrong with a little healthy greed as well, time to time."

George just smiled fleetingly.

"Where do you come from, Jim?" George was taller than him, but lighter by many pounds. Then the Whale said, "Jimmer," and seemed to like how that sounded. The nickname was a definite ranking thing. "Jimmer," he repeated. "You kind of came out of the blue."

"Does it matter?" George said.

"What else you do?"

"Got some honest work now, construction."

"What are you going to do if you don't like it?"

"Go back to busting warehouses, I guess."

Vargas laughed again. "What you steal?"

"Electronics, you know. Get a guy to resell the TVs."

The Whale said, "Everybody wants to work with us, but we don't take just anybody. You've been almost vetted."

George looked like he was about to say, "I'm honored," but changed his mind because of that *almost*.

The Whale didn't sit, just kept slowly moving through the pools of light around the room, cast by a few mangled lamps. He was keeping his overhead low, that's for sure.

His face was childlike, and he wore a little smile. Button nose, his cheeks packed tight with meat, like that kid with the funny voice who did all those sneaker commercials. Pale skin, his hair Hitler-straight and combed slick. He was dressed like a yuppie on casual Friday.

Like the Whale, I kept moving, acting shifty and weak. I tried to skirt the brightest of the light. I went over to look at a bulletin board with that wild-hair picture of Albert Einstein thumbtacked to it.

A couple of the others took seats, finally, but nobody sat on the sofa, except Wichita perched herself on its broad arm. She watched the Whale adoringly, and at one point when he passed her, he reached out to touch her brittle-looking hair. *Yeah, I see.*

The sofa seemed massive and alive.

I had the sense something was going to give.

"I have to say, your ideas intrigue me," said George.

"I'm the guy to be with?" Vargas sounded very assimilated—I caught a tiny bit of barrio inflection, that was all.

"Seems like you're taking out some of the competition. What I hear."

"Oh, no, no," said the Whale, troubled. "Competition, that's not my thing." He paused and put up one foot on the coffee table and leaned on his knee, town-meeting style. "Let me ask you. What made America great? Not competition. What was it?"

"The cotton gin?"

"No."

"Unions!" declared George firmly.

"Hell, no," still in his baby-blanket voice. "Guess again."

"Surround sound?"

"No! *Cooperation* is what made America great. Not competition. Competition never did anything for anybody. Have you ever read a book?"

George looked at him attentively.

"Did you read about the railroads? The railroad companies were starting to compete, making their own size tracks, so that only their own trains could run on them. They tried to shut each other out that way. But then somebody said, hey, if we all make the same size track, we can all run anywhere! Everybody made more money, and that's what made America great. You try to think creative. I plow my profits back in. I'm gonna write a book."

The Whale was an interesting guy, I had to admit. I was almost starting to like him, his charisma was that ingratiating. His feeble-minded followers were like a creepy little cult, hanging on his words, deferring to him.

George pulled a clipping from his back pocket. "Do you want to know what impresses me the most about you? This." He laid the clipping before Vargas. "I admire a man who can bring off a cop killing this well." With slow vitriol, he said, "Sgt. Annette Soames."

The Whale smiled, amazed. "Haha," he laughed softly, "you give me too much credit. I was nowhere near that extermination."

"Well," said George, "I knew this particular one. She busted me for a moving violation, then planted shit on me to jack up her numbers. She wanted to be like the guys. I always thought I'd get her someday, but then I saw this."

The picture of pixie-faced, blond-bobbed Sergeant Soames lay there, its edges tattered from George's pocket. The Whale looked at it approvingly.

"Word gets around," said George, "so I just want to say I admire the way you handle things. I can't tell you how happy I am this Sergeant Soames is in her grave."

The Whale just smiled, thinking. Then he said, "Denny," and pointed to the middle of the table. "H."

Denny went to one of the gun safes and punched in a code. He brought a Baggie to the table and set it in the exact center. The Baggie contained a fist-sized amount of white powder.

I let my eyes light up. I stopped moving and everybody watched me breathe.

George said, "She got some bad shit 'n' almost died. I can't have that again. If I can get her on clean shit, at least, you know. I don't have any illusions about getting her off of it, even before the baby comes."

"I," said the Whale, "am all about clean shit. And unity. People say no, unity's not possible, you can't do that. But I can, and I do."

"He does," said Wichita. This evening she wore a necklace with BEEATCH spelled out in the same pavé bling as the guys. Plus yellow eye shadow, and that stupid T-shirt.

Well, I thought, *he's certainly got a diverse team here,* quite unusual in South Central, where hatred between the Latino-Americans and the African-Americans is a staple.

Vargas asked George, "Do you use?"

"No."

"Good business. Then you won't mind getting tested."

"Huh?"

"None of us use, a matter of professional conduct. None of us are *supposed* to use," he corrected himself. "We're about to initiate random drug tests for our staff, vice presidents on down. Anybody who won't get tested doesn't work for me."

George coughed to hide incredulous laughter, and I simply turned my eyes down to keep my composure. Drug testing for drug dealers. Yep, this guy's the bellwether, all right.

"Wouldn't bother me," said George cheerfully. "Pee-type test, like parole?"

Every now and then, one of the vice presidents would pull his cell phone out of his pocket and check the display. Occasionally he'd leave the room through the teacher's door, then come back a few minutes later, looking antsy.

"We got business to do," one complained carefully.

"This is business," said the Whale. "You guys need to learn how to handle recruitment. You don't think creative enough."

They looked at their knuckles.

"I saw a rat by my car," said the Whale. "Too many damn rats in this neighborhood."

"There's rats everywhere," said Denny.

"Well, I better never see one in here. That's why you're supposed to sweep up after yourself. You leave garbage around, you're gonna get rats." He kept smiling, really a nice smile, and the vice presidents responded, smiling slightly through their cultivated toughness.

I saw that this bunch was a cut above the boneheads selling on the street corners, but just barely. That's the kind of staff the

Whale was after—smarter than the average thug, smart enough to be charmed by his manipulative shtick, but not intelligent enough to see through it.

"Pretty good place to do business, though," remarked George. "You got creative."

The Whale laughed. "I did, I got creative! Hahaha!"

Someone knocked, and Denny went to the door. The Latino guard who'd interrupted George and me from breaking into this very room came tottering in, almost hidden by a stack of huge white cardboard food boxes. A wonderful smell wafted along.

"Let's see," said the Whale.

"Hey, I only bring the good stuff," said the guard, opening them.

Half of the boxes were full of saucer-sized quiches, others contained sliced cheeses and fresh fruit, and others were crammed with chicken skewers.

Wichita brought the two biggest boxes of food to the Whale. Rolls of paper towels appeared.

He arranged the food on either side of him, spread paper towels across his lap, and began to eat, slowly, with both hands. Wichita hovered over him, making sure he had everything he needed.

Someone handed around Blue Bolts, the teenage caffeine drink in those phallic bottles.

"Any ice cream tonight?" asked Wichita. No one answered. She sighed, "I love Tülky's, I just love it. It's that new brand from Denmark, it's the best."

"Do you know," asked the Whale, "they're a subsidiary of Frito-Lay, and they make the shit in Pennsylvania?"

Wichita sulked. "I don't care, I'd kill for some Tülky's right now. Their cocoa-peanut swirl? *Mmm!*"

George took a quiche on a paper towel to be polite. "DeeDee, have some food."

I shook my head, craving heroin.

"You need to eat."

Glassily, I took an orange quarter and sucked it indifferently. I ogled the heroin in the center of the table, which was in the center of the room, which had become the center of the universe.

As the Whale ate, he cleaned his hands constantly with paper towels, rubbing them so vigorously in his palms that they shredded.

"The premoistened towelettes," he said at one point, and Wichita jumped up and retrieved a fistful from one of the lab cabinets. Vargas opened each foil envelope with fingertip delicacy. I thought about the Tucson drug boss whose eyelids he'd sliced away before killing him inch by unspeakable inch.

And I remembered what I'd read about murderers often being obsessed with cleanliness, and I remembered what Amaryllis had said about the Whale never actually carrying drugs or weapons. Yeah, I thought, just surround yourself with people who do, and maybe you'll be OK. Unless one of them turns on you.

"You guys order in good stuff," George remarked.

"Oh, this is free!" said Wichita, gulping grapes. She reached over and popped one into the Whale's mouth. She couldn't do enough for him; he was like this big delicate baby she wanted to take care of. "It's wedding food. The caterers bring it by sometimes if they got a lot left over."

One of the guards, ebullient over the food, said, "They think they're feeding the homeless!"

Vargas remarked, "These are inappropriate dishes for the homeless. Too rich, make them throw up." Everyone nodded. "We do enough for them," he added. "And bigger plans."

"Yeah?" said George.

The Whale addressed me. "You like heroin, don't you?"

"Very much," I said in a hoarse whisper.

"Check her, Witch," said he.

Wichita, who had been en route for more food, lunged at me and seized my arm. Roughly, she pushed up my sleeve and inspected my inner arm. "Nothing!" she barked over her shoulder. I was glad Gina and I had applied some patchy latex on my arms anyway, just in case.

I shrank from Wichita, Bambi-like. "I use my feet," I whispered.

"Let's see."

Just before I'd walked out the door, Gina had said, "Wait. You need tracks."

"Oh my God, yeah."

"I was watching that doctor show, the one in Amsterdam, where the needle exchange clinic is this floating barge and—"

"Right, what'll we—"

"On the show it just looked like red dots along the vein. They showed a closeup. Really red little dots. And on this show the person's veins in their arms were no good, so they used their feet."

So now I lifted my foot in its zap-blue jelly sandal. "Here."

Wichita said, "You are such a compost heap," and turned away, muttering, ". . . while yo' pregnant, unbelievable, talk about *trash*!"

None of the men seemed to give a damn about that. Denny came up and said, "Let me look." He knelt and took my foot in his hands and looked it over carefully. I began to sweat, but maintained good breathing. "Well, you haven't wrecked these veins yet," he remarked, looking me directly in the eye. The veins on my feet happen to be quite prominent. Denny looked at the Whale and nodded.

"How do I know your shit's as good as you say?" George asked Vargas.

Every pair of eyes in the room turned toward me.

Of course.

They expected me to shoot up.

My guts went into panic mode, but outwardly I kept calm, thinking rapidly.

"I don't have my works," I rasped.

"I've got 'em," said George.

I cannot describe my shock at that. I couldn't have spit if my life depended on it.

"Help yourself," said the Whale.

Denny brought out a small digital scale and set it on the table. George knelt before this little shrine to happiness and death. Had he planned this? What the flying freaking fuck was he doing?

I pasted an anticipatory smile on my face, feeling desperate yet playing along; George had an improv going, and I had to support it.

"What percent is it?" he asked.

"My standard's fifty," said the Whale, "but this here's seventy-five."

"That's good," said George, gratefully. "That's real good."

He used his jackknife blade to scoop a bit of the heroin onto the scale. The heroin was quite fluffy, easily spoonable. The read-out pulsed, and he scooped a tiny bit more. He drew a syringe from his shirt pocket. The bastard. And a metal teaspoon. *Bastard!* And a rubber ligature!

I retreated to the shadows beyond the lab tables and sweated harder.

"That's a nice knife," said Vargas.

"You like it?" George folded it. "Here, it's yours."

The Whale's mouth dropped open.

"What's the matter?" George proffered the knife, a large folding hunter like my brothers carried. The handle was especially beautiful, a rich zebra-striped wood. "The pawn shop hasn't gotten it yet, good thing!"

"Nobody gives me anything," said the Whale, and I almost thought he was going to cry. "Everybody asks *me* for stuff."

"Well, this is just a token. A courtesy to you."

Vargas reached for the knife and turned it over in his hands. He opened and closed it. He hefted it in his palm, then he opened it again.

So fast that I almost doubted I'd seen it, he raised his arm and, with a perfect movement, flicked his wrist. I heard a *thock!* and turned to see the knife sticking into the bulletin board, smack in the center of Albert Einstein's throat.

Wichita laughed delightedly.

Denny clapped and said, "Good shot, boss!"

The other vice presidents concurred. "Yeah."

"Thank you," said the Whale feelingly. "I was actually aiming for his left eye. It's a good miss, though." All the vice presidents looked jealous of George. I could see them wondering what they could give to their boss.

"You take that knife back, Jimmer. I ought not to carry a blade. But I sure do appreciate the looks of that knife. Good balance too."

George pulled the knife from Einstein and put it in his back pocket. He returned to the table, tipped the heroin into the spoon, and came to me, cupping the dose in his hand. He winked at me.

And with that wink, I breathed. Everything would be all right.

In a second I saw the trick: he set the spoon down and brought an old-style metal lighter from his pocket. Carefully he opened it, and I saw he had a second bit of powder hidden in the lid of that lighter.

I felt like grinning. Home free.

But then he fumbled.

I saw it in slow motion: a thread from his pants pocket had caught in the lighter's hinge, and in almost dropping it, the hidden dose spilled out and dissipated in the air like Disney dust.

He breathed, "Shit." He licked his lips and then met my eyes. *Gotta do it now.*

"So," he flung over his shoulder, "I won't need lemon?"

"Nah, nah," said Vargas, lazily.

I wondered what the hell that meant.

"What's the other twenty-five, then?" George asked.

"Standard mannitol," came the answer.

George turned on the tap at the nearest lab sink, and once he saw it was working, he screwed down the flow and added a few drops of water to the heroin.

He sparked his Zippo. The mighty flame was enough to illuminate half of a biker bar, and he held it resignedly beneath the bowl of the spoon.

I took the ligature and began to tie it around my left calf.

"Nah, honey, let's just skin-pop you tonight, since this is better than the shit you're used to."

He said it so earnestly that the Whale laughed in his soft way. "What's so special about her to you?"

George looked over at him flatly. "Her mind."

The Whale laughed again, slightly uneasily.

The whole time, George and I were behaving as if we did this two or three times a day. We communicated with our eyes.

Trust me, said his, *I know what I'm doing.*

I could kill you, said mine.

You'll be all right.

Take care of me.

I will.

There's always been, of course, much over-the-top hysteria about street drugs. Before we had Petey, I'd smoked pot with Jeff a few times and felt ho-hum about it. That was the sum total of my experience with illegal substances.

At the moment, what scared me more than the heroin itself was that my alertness was about to be compromised while in the company of these lowlifes.

And I realized why George had wanted me here: I was, in effect, his job reference.

I held the teaspoon as he shifted the lighter. He murmured, "We can just use your arm, since we don't need a vein."

Bizarrely, I recognized the spoon as an Oneida pattern like the one my best friend's mom had back in Wisconsin. Maybe from his friend Gonzalo's kitchen—then I realized: Gonzalo the neurologist and jazz trumpet player, that's where he must have gotten this pristine syringe—it even had a plastic cap—probably the doctor had even given him whatever harmless powder he'd intended to substitute for the heroin, and showed him how to inject it.

We crouched there, and the heroin and water melted into a skim-milk-like potion. A small, salty smell rose up.

"*Act,*" breathed George.

And with that, I snapped into feeling like the most depraved person in the whole world. I felt so horrible for what I was about to do to my poor little unborn foam fetus, I almost cried. I rubbed my foam and mourned my lack of integrity. I grieved for the shitty, shitty birthright I was handing to my child.

But I wanted that heroin. Too bad, tyke, Mama's got to fix.

"Hey," said Wichita, "whatchoo doin', knittin' a sweater over there?"

George jacked the insignificant-looking puddle into the syringe. I suddenly understood the intimacy of shooting up. I actually kind of got into it: it's like taking a sacrament, a powerful, devilish sacrament, and you want to hide, and you want to fully experience it. And I understood then how depraved you have to be to do it on the street in broad, unfiltered daylight.

George shielded me with his body as he grasped my left arm, stretched my skin with his thumb, and with a quick motion, thrust the needle beneath my skin.

He began to hum something, and I realized it was "I've Got You Under My Skin," Cole Porter's night-rhythm song of—well, addiction. Suddenly I was deeply scared.

George injected only a little, then withdrew the needle, squirting the rest invisibly down my arm; I smeared it off as if some blood had escaped. I put my finger over the hole and he replaced the equipment in his pockets. We returned to the group.

"Let the lady have a seat," said Denny.

I felt the drug hit about one minute after I sat down: a warm glow started somewhere in my middle and grew outward from there.

Suddenly my fear and manufactured self-loathing were gone, and I felt nothing but serenity and acceptance. And I felt beautiful. Everything was beautiful. I looked down and my skaggy hands were beautiful. My needle-tracked feet were beautiful.

"How is it, DeeDee?" asked George.

"Mmmm." I hugged myself like a happy platypus.

Everyone in the room looked so nice and attractive—their

jewelry sparkled so—and there was no trouble. Deep down, of course, I knew everything was fucked up, same as when I walked in, but the difference was *I didn't care.*

The nearest I'd come to such a feeling was when I'd gotten a shot of morphine after I hurt my back once—I knew the pain was there, but suddenly I was totally indifferent to it.

I smiled lovingly at everybody.

One of the guards looked wistful, and I could tell he wanted some. *Yeah, it's only a matter of time, buddy, before you give in to this again.*

Satisfied that we were for real, the Whale welcomed George into his organization.

"From now on you don't have to worry about her. Get him a bag, Witch. Take yourself a couple of ounces, Jimmer. Gonna start you small. Keep an eye on you."

As I drifted on my cloud, I heard quite clearly George and the Whale talk terms and conditions.

One by one, the vice presidents drifted out, but the Whale evidently found something resonant in George—who had been, of course, outthinking him, trying to be as resonant as possible. Wichita hung around.

"I don't want to get in too deep," George said. "Wichita told me your organization's safe. But how can it be?"

"This type of business—the street level business—is just a paving stone for me," he said. "I have a vision for Los Angeles. The people, they need their drugs. One day, and I'm thinking ahead here—*all* drugs will be legal. Look around, you know it's true. The signs are there: high prices for American pharmaceuticals, low standards of living in the countries that produce marijuana and dope, growing tax burdens for new immigrants. I'm not saying you can't go out and get busted. It happens. Wichita was really talking about the future, and I'd say she misspoke."

Wichita scowled. "I still get my bonus, you promised."

"So," Vargas went on, "drugs will be legal. And whose network will already be in place? Who will already have revolutionized drug sales? Who will have been the peacemaker of Los Angeles, because gang wars are so last week? Our children will have that legacy."

"I see," said George.

"What I'm after is unity. You, Jimmer, I dress you up, say an outfit like mine, nice polo shirt—lose that crazy white shirt and sorry-ass tie, nice try, though—you could drive a BMW through Bel Air making deliveries. Nobody looks twice: clean white man in a BMW. The people up there say they're not racist, but they are, they prefer a white dealer. Through my rotation system, I can build unity throughout this city—no arguments over turf! I implement strict schedules, good management, cooperation—it all fits, you see how it all fits? It synergizes! It's like a movie!"

I listened vaguely. It was hard for me to grasp how the Whale's rotation system was supposed to work.

George nodded. Solemnly, he said, "You're a cross between Che Guevara and Bill Gates."

The Whale startled him with his shout. "My Lord! My Lord! You get me! You get me, brother!"

"Every great man's hands have to get a little dirty," said George.

"But you want to know a secret?" said the Whale.

Respectfully, but with great anticipation, George said, "Yes." The Whale was about to reveal something big.

Possibly something that could really nail his ass.

"I guess I'm like a lot of people, who do one thing but deep in their hearts, they wish to do a truly magical thing."

"Yes?"

The Whale leaned in. "Eventually, what I really want to do is direct."

TWENTY-SEVEN

George took me home, where I slept like a sow until ten in the morning. Before she left for work, Gina fixed me some coffee and I took a bath.

George called around noon. "How do you feel?"

"When I first got up, I had a fierce headache, but now I feel normal."

"That's good."

"Except I want more heroin."

I heard him swallow.

"Just kidding," I said.

"Goddamn it, Rita."

"You have *no* right to swear at me! You should be crawling on your knees over broken glass begging my for—"

"Listen, I didn't want to talk it over with you in advance, because I thought you might freak out."

"You know me so well."

"I brought the kit along as a contingency. Gonzalo helped me."

"I thought so."

"I wasn't sure they'd suggest that you fix, I just thought it was a possibility to be prepared for. Didn't you expect it?"

"No."

"Your naïveté is showing, Rita."

"Well, I'm not naïve!" I cried, deeply insulted. "I've smoked dope! Several times! I'm not little Baby Darla here, I've hung out with hoods."

"Yeah? Who?"

"Well—my ex-husband."

He laughed. "OK, OK."

"What was the lemon thing? You asked the Whale something about lemons."

"Oh, if you've got heroin that's poorly refined, you need a little acetic acid to get it to melt, and you can get that from lemon juice or vinegar."

"Oh."

"It probably wasn't necessary for me to ask that, but it added to my credibility. I really *was* hoping that stuff was good. But I called to tell you something. Remember I found out about Deborah Keever, the dead daughter?"

"Yes!"

"And I told you I checked her birth certificate?"

"Yes?"

"Well, this morning I got my hands on her death certificate as well."

284

"Yeah? I've got a very funny feeling about what you're going to say."

He was surprised. "What do you mean?"

"Did she die under suspicious circumstances?"

"Absolutely not."

"Oh."

"As far as the attending physician was concerned."

"Oh?"

"It just says under cause of death, 'cardiac arrest.' Only that. No reference to a police report, either, for example. Nothing."

"Cardiac arrest? What does that mean, exactly?"

"I guess it means your heart stops beating."

"That's a pretty general term, isn't it? I mean, if that's all it means, then everybody who dies, dies of cardiac arrest. You're dead when your heart stops beating."

"Well, it struck me as odd too. Fifteen-year-old girl. I know sometimes kids die suddenly of heart disease, but you'd think in that case they'd do an autopsy. But they didn't."

"Where did she die?"

"St. Irene's Hospital, in Westwood."

"I've never heard of it. I've never even heard of St. Irene."

"It's been a nursing home since the eighties. It was a small private hospital to begin with."

"A loony bin?"

"No, a regular hospital."

"Hm."

"Rita, you're on to something, but you're not telling me."

"I—I can't even bring myself to verbalize it, yet. Even to myself."

"Well, what would you say if I found a financial oddity? Because I did go deeper."

A smile broke over my face. "Ah." Good old competent, smart George.

"You're smiling," he said.

I fought with my face. "No, I'm not."

"Yes you are, I can hear it. Anyway, get this: Bruce Keever paid sixty thousand dollars to the doctor who signed that death certificate."

"Oh, my God."

"The day before he signed it."

"Oh, my *God*. The day *before*?"

"Do you think Keever could have had his daughter quote-unquote murdered by this doctor? I'm trying like hell to—but the daughter's death might be totally unrelated to this Amaryllis thing—"

"Oh, no. It's not unrelated."

"Rita, tell me!"

"I just can't. I *can't* right now, George. Give me—just a day. I have to think. How the hell did you find that out, anyway?"

"Well, I've learned that financial records can yield exceptional information, if you can get your hands on them. I started with Piedmont Commerce Bank, because in the 1960s half the professional people in L.A. had accounts there. I've got a contact in Piedmont's morgue—their old paper records. Both Keever and the doctor had accounts there."

I said, "Keever being a judge and all, you'd figure the family was a real pillar-of-the-community type."

"Oh, yes. The wife served on the symphony board, and he was active in two or three charities himself."

"Reputations, then."

"Yeah." He waited. "Now you're quiet all of a sudden." I kept thinking. In my continued silence, he went on, "Did the mother or father kill the child—maybe accidentally—and then bribe the doctor to cover it up? But why postdate the death certificate? I don't get it at all."

"George, I think we're holding it in our hands."

He said, "Another possibility is that the payment had nothing to do with the child's death, it could be just coincidental, the settlement of a personal debt."

Except that I had one piece of information he didn't have. And as a woman, I had to check it out myself before I even spoke it to another soul.

"NO, SISTER, AMARYLLIS is meeting with the scout troops this afternoon. There's no interrupting her when she's with the children. Then she's got her Tuesday radio program to do."

"Oh." I shifted the phone to my other ear.

"Tomorrow," said the Reverend Culpepper, "she'll be in, business as usual. Ah, is it something important?"

"No, no."

"Well, you have a blessed day." His signature tagline.

I wanted badly to talk with Amaryllis, because it was time, it was time. I was dismayed to have to wait, but then I remembered that I'd promised Gina I'd cook tonight. She was bringing her new boyfriend Toby home.

I vacuumed the apartment in a thinky, fuguelike state.

Gramma Gladys was on my mind. Before picking up some groceries, I dropped in at the parking lot at Rodeo and Santa Monica, to commune with her spirit more for courage than for guidance.

I called her down through the smog as the drone of L.A. life surged around us. She counseled patience, and warned me to take nothing for granted.

Just when you think you've got it sewed up, that's when everything goes to hell! I felt her say in her bitterly wise way.

"Yeah," I said.

At home I prepared Gramma Gladys's baked pork chops, a homey dish guys love.

Gina came home from work and hustled through the shower and into a pretty outfit she'd scored at Madwoman in the Attic, my favorite resale shop. It'd been tough to get her to save money, but as soon as I mentioned that I'd spotted Calypso Henderson there browsing the vintage bowling shirts last month, she was into it. Calypso's latest movie, where she plays a nurse's aide trying to infiltrate a terrorist network but it turns out to be the Pentagon all along, was a hit at Cannes, and she'd signed a whopping contract for her next film.

A word Gina had gotten into lately was *cachet,* which of course usually comes with a really high price tag. People chase all over L.A. for cachet, they go broke trying to trap it and own it. Sometimes cachet is, I admit, worth the price, but once in a while you can get it for cheap, like at Madwoman. Gina had scored a two-piece Rhonda Tripley ensemble—you know, with the hand-done geometric lace—which she'd accessorized with a copper lunch box as a purse. She looked as chic as they come.

I put some Art Pepper on the stereo and felt lonely for Petey. I wondered how the dynamiting had gone.

My sister swept into the living room, trailing a beautiful fragrance. "Is that the dregs of my last free sample of Chanel No. 5?" I asked, knowing full well.

"I love Chanel No. 5," she said, "it makes me feel so *adult*. Do you really like my hair?"

"It's just so different."

"I used Gramma Gladys's secret weapon: Dippity-Do."

"They still make that?"

At Halloween time when we were little, we'd build a spook house in the basement for the neighborhood kids, featuring a feel-the-corpse-in-the-dark exhibit. We'd mix Dippity-Do with a handful of rubber bands (his guts), and we'd have cold fruit cocktail (brains), and there were other things too, as we thought of them and could score the ingredients. I remembered the excellently slimy Dippity-Do well. We thought it was hilarious. Gramma Gladys's hair would stay put in a typhoon.

"But my real question," I said, "is why?"

Gina tossed her stiff tendrils. "Toby's got dreads, and I was just feeling like looking a little less smooth, myself." She sighed. "He's so wonderful! He knows all the words to 'Squirrel on the Barbie.'"

"That's quite a credential." In case you've been in a coma for six months, "Squirrel on the Barbie" is that allegorical Aussie pop song about global warming.

The door buzzed and she flung it open to welcome Toby.

"Hiya, honey!" she trilled.

"Hey," he said, stepping in.

She pulled him by the hand to meet me, and it was good that it went so fast, *TobymeetRitaRitaTobyHaha!* because the guy who walked into my apartment, kissed my sister, and shook my hand was Denny.

It was absolutely him, his dreadlocks long and loose, his smile ready, his hand large and warm as he shook mine.

One time I played a poker dealer in a TV ad for some Indian casino near Palm Springs, and I had to keep a neutral expression while a guy at the table laid down a thousand-dollar bet on what turns out to be a bluff. I was glad for that experience, as well as the many insane concepts Petey had put to me as he came along as a human, because now I drew on that skill to keep my face friendly and open.

"So good to meet you," he said, and it was Denny's deep, bluesman voice, this fucking guy was Denny, phony guard at the ABC Mission, sidekick to Dale the Whale Vargas. The guy who, with Wichita, had tried to intimidate Amaryllis as I'd listened behind the bags of rice, the guy who, last night, had held my foot and inspected my fake needle tracks while I prayed to God for survival.

My heart surged into my mouth and I said brightly, "Hi, Toby. I've heard so much about you."

"Don't believe half of it," he responded, smiling.

I withdrew to the kitchen.

What the hell was going on? I'd seen no recognition in his eyes, no calculation. He was totally this guy named Toby. He was wearing a pressed sport shirt with a red-and-yellow Kente type weave and a pair of Levis. No sign of the homeboy gold chains. He'd politely slipped out of his loafers at the door.

What the hell, what the hell, what the hell, I thought as I poured smoked almonds into a dish. The guy had two identities: Toby the consultant, and drug-den criminal Denny. What for? Was it just coincidence that he'd walked into the record store and struck up a conversation with Gina?

At a furious pace, I reviewed the time Gina and I had gone to the mission to serve lunch. He'd been there, he'd been there! I hadn't really seen his face. How had that gone down, again? Gina had seen Wichita and him hassling Amaryllis, then I'd followed the three of them into the kitchen. I'd eavesdropped from behind the rice, but I hadn't seen his face! I'd looked up as their backs were disappearing into the kitchen, I'd heard his voice and followed, but had not seen his face.

Had he seen mine? Gina's? Gina had not, to my memory, gotten a good look at him that day either. He and Wichita were all the way across the cafeteria, at least sixty feet away, when Gina had noticed them arguing with Amaryllis. Maybe she hadn't seen his full face at all, with those dreadlocks flying around.

But maybe he'd seen her. Fallen for her at first sight, or what? And decided to make it his business to find out who she was. And where she worked. And who her sister is.

What the hell, what the hell, what the hell.

This guy carried out orders from the most dangerous drug boss in Los Angeles. When I really interacted with him—just last night!—I'd been, of course, DeeDee the pregnant skag. If I'd have let him, he probably would've skin-popped me himself. Mainlined me, for that matter.

What else had he done for the Whale as one of his top thugs—oh, 'scuse me, executives? How many people had he gotten hooked on drugs? Had he committed murder? I remembered him smirking as George and the Whale gloated over the slaughtered Sgt. Annette Soames. Had he carried out that execution, been in that car? Had he blasted the bullets that drilled into Kip and me? Had he beaten and kicked Kip, before I blundered into the scene?

Then it hit me: *twins!* Oh, my God, maybe he's a *they!* Yes! Identical twins! My whole body relaxed at the possibility. I'd seen all the twist-of-the-twin movies, and even watched Daniel's pirated reruns of *The Patty Duke Show*, so I knew how hideously twins can diverge.

Yet as I opened the oven to check on the savory pork chops—I'd thrown in a few sprigs of fresh thyme—yum—I also realized what a far-fetched, desperate idea that was.

I went back to the day of Kip's beating. One assailant had been short and fat-assed, the other taller and thin—Wichita and Denny? I'd been thinking that for some time, even though at first I'd thought both attackers were guys. A malevolent bitch like Wichita could've swung that piece of lumber. Then I remembered George talking about Wichita and Denny driving him out of the same neighborhood a few days later.

OK: my sister was going around with a dope peddler, this thug, this criminal-mastermind wannabe. My God—was she using? How could I tell? You don't start injecting right away, do you? Plus I'd heard how wily drug users are, at first, before the drug really takes hold and starts to show. What kind of danger had she just let in through that door?

Dinner, for me, was a bit of a strain.

During salad, Toby referred to his dad having been in the army. "You're an only child?" I asked, taking a flyer.

"Yes, how did you guess?"

Damn it to hell, that destroys the twin theory. "Oh, I don't know. Something about your confidence level, maybe. I've found that only children have a certain—confidence."

"Hm," he said, relentlessly smiling.

"Toby, what do you do, exactly?" I asked, cupping my chin attentively. I wanted to hear about his "consulting work."

He swallowed—my food, my wine, at my table!—and said, "I help companies manage their inventory and personnel."

"Ah. Like . . ."

"Like helping them design ways to anticipate customer needs, and then stock or restock accordingly. These potatoes are delicious."

"Thank you! Gina and I have had our troubles working for bosses, haven't we? Do you get along well with your boss?"

"Oh yeah, he's—you know, he's a regular guy. We get along real well."

"So if a client has a problem with an employee, what do you advise?"

"Well, it all depends on the situation."

You know, acting can get pretty emotionally heavy; even in a doughnut commercial you can be called on to summon both agony and ecstasy, not to mention what you have to draw forth to do *Streetcar* or *Lear*. You let your emotions surge, and you feed off the emotions of your comrades. Actors and actresses talk about "working dangerously," which means taking risks that you're not sure you can pull off—throwing in a physical bit on the spur of the moment, or asking for something new from another player.

But never, while speaking memorized lines and pretending to be somebody else, had I felt anything remotely like the danger I was facing now.

I hadn't been terribly afraid of Denny while at the mission, because George had been there.

But now, with the son of a bitch sitting in my apartment acting like a charm boy, I was beside myself with fear. As the dinner went on, however, I remembered how great it is to transform your fear into cunning. I realized: *If he really doesn't know who I am, then I have an advantage.*

"Let's say," I said, "somebody's not performing up to snuff. Not doing their job with enough—alacrity."

"Well," Toby responded, "first of all you have to make sure they fully understand their job, you know, maybe you have to do some, uh, retraining. You try to bring them up. You try to think creative."

Jesus H. Christ, one of the Whale's favorite sayings. "What if," I wanted to know, "they don't come up?"

"After a point, you gotta, you gotta make a change. You gotta terminate 'em."

"Or if they get caught stealing from the company?"

"Termination for sure."

"No second chances, is that your motto?"

He sat back comfortably in his chair. "Not so much a motto as a necessity. What're you going to give a thief a second chance to do—steal again?"

"Right."

"Isn't he cute?" said Gina. "He's got so much cachet. You and George and us ought to go on a double date, you know? What do you think?"

"Who's George?" asked Toby immediately, smiling.

"I've got strawberries for dessert," I said.

TWENTY-EIGHT

Meal tonight—dig it, sister!—going to be jambalaya." Amaryllis beamed like a lighthouse. Before her lay an unbelievably huge pile of raw shrimp, heads on, blind black eyes, netted so recently from the sea that they made the sharp-edged, institutional kitchen smell as salty and cool as the wharves up in San Francisco.

"We got fifty pounds to clean here, so let's get at it. This is just some of what we got today, the rest is in the walk-in. Three hundred pounds we got this morning."

"Wow," I said. The shrimp curled onto themselves, heads touching their tails, their undersea feelers tapered to delicate points. "Where did it come from, so fresh? Do they have a shrimp fleet out of L.A.?"

She shook her head. "All I know is a man drove up in a freezer truck and said, I need to not have this load anymore. It ain't spoiled. The Reverend Bill Culpepper told him, OK, we'll help you unload."

"That would seem a little suspicious, don't you think?"

She just smiled to herself. "One thing I have learned after all these years: when it comes to carrying out your mission, don't tempt fate. Jesus did not advise us to ask every last question that comes into our mind."

"I guess he didn't."

"Faith, he didn't."

"Well, I have a few questions to ask you," I said with a smile, "and I don't give a flying crap about Jesus this morning, frankly."

She gazed at me, hands on hips. "Get an apron, then, and work with me. We can talk. Steve, Katy?" She dismissed her two helpers, who took off, casting uneasy glances back at me. They were civilians, they were OK.

Knowing that at this hour—two o'clock, lunch all done and cleaned up—she'd probably be prepping food for dinner, I'd sneaked into the kitchen via the back passageway and the alley. All I wanted was not to be spotted today by Denny, twin or no twin. Amaryllis had been surprised to see me walk in from that direction.

I'd intercepted Gina last night before she left to go out clubbing with Toby, but just as I'd pulled her aside in the kitchen, he came in, looking for something to wipe up coffee he'd spilled. I shut my mouth and tried to use telepathy to warn Gina, but she misunderstood, thinking I didn't like Toby. "See ya," she said curtly, and although she did catch my final, desperate vibe, she'd already committed, and was gone. I'd thought too late of feigning a cerebral hemorrhage or something.

Thank God she'd returned safely, barging in at three in the

morning, and falling into her usual deep slumber. We were going to have a long talk before she went out with Toby again.

I watched Amaryllis gather herself to begin working on the shrimp. Food was therapy for her; I would be patient. I wrapped a heavyweight apron around myself and tied the strings. Amaryllis handed me a short knife, and we set to work. I stood across from her, the fifty pounds of shellfish on the worktable between us looming about two feet high, a pink mountain of protein.

If you've cleaned shrimp, you know how fussy the work is.

To clean a shrimp for cooking, you twist off its head, grasp the first ring or two of shell, rip those away, then pull the body from the rest of the shell by the tail. Then you take your knife and make a delicate slit along the gut line and try to strip out the icky thing in one piece. If you love the sweet ocean taste of the critters, you knuckle down to the work with a minimum of bitching.

"Yeah," said Amaryllis, reading my mind, "when I went back to visit my Cajun side, the boys would tote in their mess of shrimp or crawdaddies and all we'd do was tear the heads off and drop them into some spiced boiling water. We'd throw the lot onto a table—you strow it with newspapers first, bottle of Tabasco on the side? Everybody dives in and peels for themselves. Now that's good eating. If we did that here, a food fight would break out, I'd stake my life on it! Haha!"

These shrimp were the kind that are rosy, not pearl-gray, when raw, their bodies as long as Amaryllis's sizable thumb. Her fingers moved rapidly, throwing tender pink body after tender pink body into an ice-filled tub. "Got to keep them fresh, like they were still alive," she muttered.

"How's Kip?" I asked, preliminarily.

"Better and better. After this job is done, I'll go and spend some time with him. Going to bring him home next week, no later, the doctor says. He's been reading those books you brought. Over and over, he's been reading them. But you didn't come to talk about Kip." She made eye contact only with the little shrimp.

"My friend," I began, "I was reading too, the other day. History. You know I'm a law student, well, I was reading some legal history of the state of California. Had to do with abortion law."

Amaryllis worked silently.

"Before 1967," I went on, "abortion was illegal in this state. Between 1967 and '69, a panel of doctors could recommend abortion in special cases. Then in 1969 the state supreme court entirely liberalized abortion laws."

Amaryllis said, "I'm going to cut up some sausages too, once we're finished with this. Got to have hot sausages in jambalaya, I feel."

"I'm most interested in something that happened in 1965," I went on, "when girls and women in L.A. didn't have much choice when it came to terminating an unwanted pregnancy. I learned that some women, especially if they had medical training, helped others by providing secret abortions. The local abortionist was often an RN, a woman who knew a lot about medicine and who might have assisted in abortions, or seen one too many young girls with a coathanger wire up her vagina, bleeding to death."

Amaryllis swallowed. "My secret ingredient is dill pickle juice. I use also bay leaf, and plenty of salt and pepper, of course. The key to a jambalaya is the slow simmer, you know, because that brings out the flavor."

We continued to rip the heads off the shrimp, strip off their protective shells, and slice into their bodies.

"There are," I said, "lots of women walking around L.A. today, silently grateful that they didn't become mothers when they were in junior high or high school. Women of position and achievement. Mothers today, many of them, and grandmothers, who had children at the right time: when they could provide for them. They're not going to go on TV and shout about it, and I'm sure they wouldn't rush to be a character witness if their back-alley abortionist winds up in court for some reason."

Amaryllis just kept listening.

"It was sheer luck I didn't get pregnant when I was a teenager. I had hormones and about half an ounce of horse sense. It was luck, Amaryllis. But by my day, abortion was legal. Would I have gone through with a pregnancy, or would I have killed my own flesh and blood? I'm glad I didn't have to find out."

Amaryllis was skipping ahead in her mind, wondering how much I knew, and how much I'd say.

"One morning a fifteen-year-old girl woke up vomiting, and she'd missed her period, and she went *oh shit*. Well, that happens all the time, doesn't it? Except this girl was the daughter of a federal judge, and her parents had high expectations. By the look of her, she had high expectations of herself too—I've seen the determination in her eyes, the set jaw. She was a gymnast. She went to a good school, bound for college, I'm sure. She was horrified to be pregnant."

"Properly, you should have ham in a jambalaya as well," commented Amaryllis. "*Jambon,* you know, that's ham in French. But I've got no ham right now." She paused. "Even if I did have ten or fifteen pounds, I think I'd reserve it for breakfasts. Then you've got the great tomato debate: in or out? Cajuns say out, Creoles say in. I'm one-fourth Cajun but I do like tomatoes, so in they'll go." She surveyed the mountain of shrimp.

I resumed, "Somehow this girl found her way to you. I bet her mother was instrumental in this, having given up a film career when she became pregnant at age nineteen. But I don't understand something. With the judge's position, you'd think the parents could've gotten a doctor to do it. A white doctor uptown. Why did this girl come to you?"

Amaryllis said, "You can call her Debbie, for that was her name." Her fingers still flew over the shrimp. The mound was still dauntingly large. Amaryllis's face was like a carved version of itself, solid and hard.

"Deborah Keever, yes," I said. "She came to you, but something terrible happened, and she didn't survive. Judge Keever was able to cover it up, but nobody—not them, not you—was ever the same. And you've been paying for it from that day to this."

Amaryllis bowed her head as she had when, weeks ago, I'd delivered Kip's message of apology. Then she lifted it, at last meeting my eyes. "You got quite a bit of it, and I am surprised and sorely dismayed. You don't have all of it, though. Nobody does."

"Are you feeling any relief?"

"Not yet. I expect I will. I'm surprised at you. The main facts have been floating around out there forever. But nobody's figured it out before—nobody's cared to, I guess."

"It seems like a few different kinds of trouble are converging on you right now."

"Yes," was all she said. Tired, tired voice.

"I'd like to help you."

A melancholy smile skewed her lips, but she was tougher than to cry. Her hands continued their work on tonight's dinner, but slowly now. The shrimp bodies plopped softly.

"Amaryllis, tell me what I don't know. Then we can work out what to do. You realize we're in this together, don't you?"

She sighed heavily. "Federal judge doesn't mean they had it made, you know. He didn't want to be in any white doctor's debt for giving Debbie an abortion. No, he went to the colored part of town to find somebody he could pay and be done with it. Somebody who wouldn't even know who the family was. I had a good reputation; he found me through a black man he'd done a favor. Anyhow, everybody knew me."

"They called you Nursey."

Her widely spaced eyes flicked to mine. "Where did you hear that?"

"A wise old junkie told me. You helped her out one time too."

"Oh, my. Well." She chewed her lower lip. "Bruce Keever knew me as Nursey, and I knew him as Mr. B. Didn't know who they were until—later. I did the procedure for the girl; she wasn't the only white child I'd helped, for sure. It went fine, no problems."

"It did?"

"Healthy girl, no problems. I made my field as sterile as possible, every time, and I boiled all of my instruments. Funny— Mr. B., he paid in advance, you know, and he expected me to charge him a high amount of money because he wore a nice suit, but I said no, my regular fee is all I want."

"How much was that?"

"One hundred dollars, for someone who could pay it. Back then a bill went a long way, you know. The mother brought the girl." She leaned to the pile of shrimp and raked five or so pounds closer to her. Our aproned bellies were turning damply pink. I glanced into the waste bin, where hundreds of severed shrimp heads stared back at me with their peppercorn eyes.

"Afterward, I counseled her," said the Iron Angel of L.A. "I asked if she was done playing dangerous, having sex with no protection. I love him! she says. She barely knew what sex was. You got to insist he wears a rubber, I told her. I told all the girls that, of course. And like all of them, she was shook up, especially after. It's not nothing, undergoing a D&C on the kitchen table of a black lady in South Central without anesthetic."

I listened.

"She says yes, yes, of course, I will. I will. Nobody promises as heartfelt as a scared young girl. Her eyes were like pie pans. I said that's it, honey. Remember you only get one."

I listened, staring at the pink curled shrimp in my hand.

"But then her daddy, Mr. B., came around again, four or five months later."

"Oh."

"Yes, she'd gone and conceived again, oh, it was springtime then. I said, 'No, sir, only one to a customer.' It was partly to protect myself, you understand. Repeat business can get dangerous. It was not a job I liked to do. It was a job I felt it necessary to do. I saw too *much*. Too much womanly misery, and too much misery of the children no one wanted." She sighed heavily. "But the man insisted. He didn't want to find somebody else. Trusted me, he said. I said no. Then he offered me ten thousand dollars."

"Oh."

"A queenly sum!"

"I'll say."

"The man bought me, sister Rita, he bought me. Ten thousand to me then, in 1965? It was like a million. I did the abortion.

Again, the mother brought her. But this time . . . *uhrr.*" She cleared her throat. "The girl panicked partway through. She was pretty stoic the first time, but this time the pain got to her, and the trauma. Also, she was a little farther along this time, twelve weeks or so. She struggled to get off the table, and before I'd got her calmed down, she'd been perforated. I knew exactly what had happened. She began bleeding more, and all of a sudden it was chaos, the girl was bleeding, I couldn't control it, the mother was cursing me *and* her daughter, and I was trying to save the girl's life. She needed surgery, of course. I told the mother she's bleeding internally, more than what you see, we have to get her to the emergency, and the mother said yes, yes. I got her loaded into the backseat of that car—big black Lincoln, I can still see it, like a fair hearse itself. I started to get in too, to go with her, you know, but the mother stepped on it before I could."

"Oh, my God." I stared at six boxes of Morton's salt on a shelf behind her. One was out of line, and I felt an impulse to walk over and tap it into place.

Amaryllis said, "I waited all night for the police to come."

"But they didn't?"

"Instead, later, I received a package with another ten thousand dollars in it, and I knew what that meant. This was one week later. I knew the girl was dead."

She wiped her hands on her apron, finger by finger. "When I saw a picture of the judge in the paper telling he was quitting being a judge, then I knew who they were. Later on, I learned the mother had taken Debbie home, didn't take her to the hospital immediately. Hoping she'd get better overnight. No way was that going to happen, the girl needed emergency surgery. By the time she got to the hospital—I don't know how many hours, maybe even the next morning—it was too late. She did actually hang on for another day or two. I'm not sure how they eventually lost her, but I suppose sepsis played a role, as well. I learned all this later, many years later."

"From Mrs. Keever?"

"Yes, from her."

"The Keevers preserved their reputation."

"They managed that, yes, at the cost of their daughter's life."

"It wasn't your fault, Amaryllis."

"Oh, yes, it was. I made several mistakes, sister. Shouldn't have done the second on Debbie. Shouldn't have begun until she was mentally ready. I don't think she wanted to go through it again, I actually think she might have wanted that baby. And when she got agitated, I should have withdrawn my curette instantly. It was stupid of me to leave it in while I tried to settle her. I made a very bad error. The memory of that girl writhing on my kitchen table hangs over my head to this day."

Amaryllis went on to tell me that she stopped being Nursey, she stopped doing abortions, and she used the money from Bruce Keever to found the ABC Mission, beginning with a soup kitchen.

"I've tried to atone," she said. "There never is any atoning, though. It's just my life."

She heard nothing more from the Keevers. "I understood their hearts were broken. Nothing could bring back their daughter, and they didn't want to see my face or hear my name. That's the way it was for all those years."

"Did things change when the judge died?"

"Right, when he died, about a year ago? Mrs. Keever came after me. The woman has been angry—and righteous so—and messed up, and obsessed. Been a recluse for most of her life since they moved to Bakersfield. I believe the judge protected her from the world."

"And the world from her," I added.

"That's one way of thinking of it." Aimlessly, she picked up a shrimp and muttered, "Yeah, I got to work." She cleaned it, then another, then I joined in again. My fingers were sore from the sharp shells.

"The woman is very nearly a physical shambles," said Amaryllis, "but I've never met a more calculating individual."

"You haven't met the Whale?"

"Not yet," she said wryly, glancing over at me. "He comes and goes at night, you know. I've got the place in the daytime, he's got it at night. It's like we rotate through here. Of course, he's got more than that, he's got my integrity under his thumb. I don't care to meet him in the flesh."

"You've acquiesced to his demands, some of them, because of his threats to Nathan."

"Yes, that's right."

"And so now Diane Keever has been extorting money from you?"

"She knows that without help in her old age, she's likely to have to go into a nursing home. The good ones are very costly, you know. That sidekick of hers is costly."

"Neneng."

"Yes, that one, I wonder if she sends a lot of money away somewhere. She's got some kind of hold over Mrs. Keever, I don't know what. The judge, once he went up to Bakersfield, he never made very much money. I think if somebody couldn't pay, he'd say oh well, catch me next round, you know? I think he was trying to atone too, in his way. Never saved up much, from what I understand. Now the widow wants money, she thinks it's her due, and there's nobody stopping her. She knew I had access to money, everybody knows it."

"But you couldn't give her a huge lump of money."

"That's right, not all at once. I'm embezzling money from my own mission to pay her the ten thousand a month, ten thousand being what I got for killing her little girl. Ten thousand twice, actually. I'm repaying it over and over, in order to avoid being shown up for what I was: a brand X abortionist. If she makes trouble for me in public, I won't have the spiritual gall to deny it. Me, the Iron Angel. What would that do to my mission, do you think?"

"So you're paying her money that was donated or raised by other people?"

"I do consider it reparations, and I will go on paying it as long as the woman asks. Of course, someday I'll have to pay it back to my mission; I've kept all my own books. Don't really know how I'll do that, sister Rita Farmer. It's not a pretty picture, to be solving extortion with a new dishonesty. I rationalize by saying I am needed here. The mission must go on no matter what."

We talked about Dale the Whale Vargas, and his feeling that he needs the ABC Mission as a safe, unspotted base of operations. "You know he wants his hands on the Emberton money," she said.

"Yes."

"And you want to know the kicker?"

I realized it: "So does the widow Keever."

Amaryllis spanked her palms together and laughed bitterly. "She read a news story about this upcoming gift, and she sent this Neneng to tell me that money must be hers. She's a sinister one."

"Uh-huh."

"Neneng had better watch out, all I have to say."

"Neneng? What do you mean?"

Amaryllis looked to the pantry shelving, and I could see her mind had turned away. "Rice," she said, "is always tricky when you're feeding so many, but you've got to have rice in jambalaya. I'll have to time it exactly right so it doesn't get gummy."

I remarked, "I bet most of your guests won't notice if the rice is a little gummy, or care."

She gave me a shocked look. "Sister, everybody deserves rice cooked right!"

Then she slumped in exhaustion, elbows on the worktable, head down. "I told Khani not to give me that money after all. It cuts my heart to refuse it. But I wouldn't want the Whale to force it away from me, holding Nathan's life over my head."

I moved to her side of the table and touched her shoulder. Her shoulders began to shake, but she made no sound. After a long time, she stopped trembling.

She looked up and murmured, "I think I'm losing my mind."

TWENTY-NINE

Well, that's a disappointment," said Colonel Markovich, in his no-nonsense, old-guy voice.

"Yes," agreed George Rowe, shifting his cell phone to his other ear while lifting a bowl of dog food from Gonzalo's kitchen counter. "I think Polen's troubles are pretty far-reaching, beyond the dog business. That doesn't help you, though." Gonzalo's dog, Tamiroff, had been shoving his muzzle at Rowe's waist from the instant the dog heard him open the bin of dry food in the kitchen closet. The Russian wolfhound's bowl was a mighty steel vessel now brimming with a pound of food to which Rowe had added some warm water to make juice. The smell excited the dog and made Rowe want to hurl.

"Easy, boy," he said, lowering the dish.

"Do you have company?" asked Markovich.

Rowe ignored that. "One reason I think so: Polen's not all that bright, you follow what I'm saying?"

Markovich liked that. "He always did try to get by on charm, rather than brains. I don't say he didn't work hard."

"Yes, he seems a fairly well-organized guy. But based on meeting him, looking over the dogs at his house, and the ones this Orlando Gold showed for him, I don't think he's harboring Ernest, and frankly, I don't think he had anything to do with Ernest's disappearance."

"And why is that?"

"Look, against my advice, you put the word out that you'll give a huge reward for Ernest's return, right?"

"Yes, but you yourself put up those flyers that said 'reward.' "

"But I didn't specify how much."

"What's that got to do with it?"

"Anybody who's connected to the professional dog scene— certainly among the beagle people—knows you'll give fifty grand for Ernest's return. That's like offering a ransom, no questions asked."

"So?"

"So if you're the thief, after you forged your documents, you'd have to sell a hell of a lot of puppies from him, or shots of his semen to make it worth it, or why not just return him anonymously and take your fifty K? And if there was a conspiracy, you'd think one of the plotters would have turned for that money by now. I now realize that your public offer of the reward was a good move."

"What are you saying? He could have been taken out of the country and resold before I got the word out."

"Well, conceivably, but—"

"The Chinese have all the money these days."

Rowe paused. "Look, the chances—"

"I think you should go to China. I'll pay, of course."

"Colonel—"

"The circuit over there is small, but incredibly lucrative." Markovich's voice got energized. "Moreover, they're starting to breed dogs, good show dogs, and bringing them over here to compete. Hm. Know what? We should go together, I could help you."

"Wait, I'm not so sure—"

"Yes," said Colonel Markovich briskly, "let's do it. China's got to be the place. Got to be. Time for me to get involved. Makes me feel young to be around you, Rowe, you know that? Let's get over there and hunt down those beagle rustlers, what do you say? Your passport up-to-date?"

"Oh, God," muttered Rowe involuntarily. He was annoyed with himself for not having found this one stupid dog yet, and he was irritated by Markovich's desperate theories of intrigue, and he wished to just back out of this case and focus on Dale the Whale Vargas.

That, however, would be admitting defeat.

He'd never thrown over a client before. The controlled pleading in Markovich's voice—the man's thirst for the chase not to end—moved him. Steadfast persistence paid off, Rowe had learned this. He liked Markovich, and shit, maybe he was right, maybe Ernest was this very minute peeing against the side of some Ming temple.

He took a nice slow breath and felt better. "Look, Colonel, if Ernest is actually in China—or who knows what overseas country—"

"China. It's China. Stands to reason, the more I think about it, the more I realize—"

"OK, China. If he's there now, he'll be there next week. Let me look into things a little bit from here first, before you go buying tickets to Beijing."

"A *week*?"

"A few days, then, OK? Just let me work on this new angle, OK?"

"All right," said Markovich, satisfied. Then, "Oh!" he muttered.

"What's the matter?"

"I just remembered a doctor's appointment I have in an hour. I should get moving."

"Anything wrong?"

"Just a checkup. Blood work."

"OK. I'll be in touch."

Rowe could not be upset with Markovich. It was because of the quest for Ernest that Rowe had met up with Cici Emberton, and learned the crucial fact of Amaryllis's reluctance to accept Khani's huge donation.

Tamiroff had licked his dish and gnawed on it for good measure. Rowe washed it and then went outside to pick up the shockingly large dried feces with which Tamiroff had mined the backyard. It was a disgusting chore, but he did it for Gonzalo as a way of thanking him for his hospitality. Rowe also did some cooking, though Gonzalo was a fancier cook. He used vermouth in things.

No wonder dogs get arrogant, Rowe thought: humans seem obsessed by their crap. As he scooped up a newer, moister piece of shit near the back board fence, he stopped and looked at the fence.

Built of heavy cedar planks, it had been chewed by Tamiroff in places.

"Oh, you idiot," he said to himself.

As soon as he was finished, he washed up and drove over to Hancock Park. He checked his watch and parked around the corner from Markovich's house.

He strolled up to the white board fence between Markovich's house and the next one, to the broken place through which Ernest had disappeared. The brown plywood patch was still there, having been nailed from the inside.

He squatted and looked closely. He carefully fingered the splintered edges of the hole.

He heard a skateboard in the distance, and waited until the kid passed, his wheels thunking over the seams in the pavement.

Swiftly, he leaped, grabbed the top of the fence, and scrambled over, scissoring his legs to avoid the pointed finials. He dropped to the lawn. The house was quiet; Markovich had gone to his appointment.

He went to the garden shed, found a hoe, and went back to the fence. He pried off the plywood and squatted again. Touching a knee to the ground, he realized that chicken wire had been installed on the ground bordering the fence, to prevent the dog digging out, and the grass had grown through it.

The fence had been chewed from the inside, not sawn, not kicked in. The fibers of the wood had been forced outward, and the hole was just big enough for a beagle to get his chest through.

Why would Ernest escape? Restless spirit. Why do dogs go on the run? To see new things.

Rowe looked around. The yard was like the grounds of a high-class mental institution, everything soft and fine and clipped and just so.

Hell, who wouldn't want to get away from this? Who wouldn't want to walk on the wild side, before you're too old to waddle after the mailman?

A man suddenly appeared from the other side of the house, hedge shears in hand. He was a grim-faced Japanese guy, wiry and unafraid. He stared at Rowe, then approached.

Rowe smiled and asked, "You the gardener?"

The man nodded, looking at the fence. A smirk crept over his face. "You here to fix fence?"

"Yeah, the dog got out. Dogs are a lot of trouble."

"Better dog gone," said the gardener quietly.

"He used to dig up your plants."

The gardener nodded.

"Did you see him get out?" Rowe asked.

Another nod.

"Didn't you tell the boss?"

The gardener looked down at his work shoes.

Rowe smiled promptingly. "The dog chewed all that wood away?"

"I—I help a little."

WHEN GINA CAME home from work that evening, I waited for her to change into her knockaround skort and sweatshirt and get some ginger ale. I'd put a tuna casserole in the oven.

"Toby thinks it's cute that I like ginger ale," she said after taking a gulp. "You know what's cutest about him? He—"

"Gina, we have to talk."

Her guard went up instantly. "Now what?"

"About Toby, actually. Why don't you sit down with me?"

She remained at the breakfast bar, hands on hips, looking at me as I sat cross-legged on the sofa.

I said, "I'm really concerned about you seeing him." I talked fast, because I could see that already she'd made up her mind that she didn't want to hear it. "I think he's involved in—"

"*What?* What is he involved in?"

Flatly, "I think he's a criminal."

It's unfair that between the two of us, I'm the one with the reputation for a quick temper, because Gina's can flare just as fast. Maybe not as high, but just as fast.

"Oh, right, Rita, right." She shoved her glass. "Toby: a criminal. He's as much of a criminal as I am! What's gotten into you?"

"Gina, listen to me for just a—"

"You've never liked any of my boyfriends!"

"That's not true!"

She took the boyfriend ball and ran with it. "You don't like Toby because he's black! You're *scared* of him because he's black! Admit it!"

"Gina, I don't give a damn what color he is!" I bounced to my feet. "The fact is, I think he's heavily involved in drugs! Because—"

"The fact is, you are a racist! You, Rita Farmer, are a racist! Listen to me saying it, I am finally saying it!"

"*Finally?* Gina, I'm not! I—"

"That's what all racists say!" she yelled. "Hah! He's black, so he must be a drug dealer, because all black people are druggies! Plus you're jealous because he's such a stud!" She was working herself up into a real thoroughbred lather.

314

We stood toe-to-toe in the living room.

"Gina, for God's sake—"

"Finally I make friends with a black person, and you can't handle it!" Her spit flew like mad.

"You are so full of shit!" I screamed in her face. "If you'd just shut up a minute and listen to—"

"*You*? Listen to you? *You're* the one who's full of shit!"

"His name—"

"He's a good man, I can tell! I know men, believe me! All you—"

"Gina, please!"

"All you want is a chance to slander a good man!"

She grabbed her purse and stormed out, still yelling, ears firmly shut.

I slumped against the door. I suppose if I'd played a video of Toby committing an axe murder, she'd say the images were doctored.

I wiped up the ginger ale she'd spilled and did yogic breathing to compose myself. I'd blown it, I'd put her on the defensive, and I'd let her get me off track.

The phone rang and I grabbed it, hoping it was her on her cell.

It was Petey, sounding desperate.

"Petey! Sweetheart."

"Mommy!" he screamed. "Aunt Sheila's gonna kill me! Aunt Toots won't hide me!"

"Honey, calm down, Mommy's here."

"She's really gonna kill me, she guarantees it this time!"

"Oh, Petey, what did you—"

Toots grabbed the phone. "He traded our boar's head to some kid for a *puppy*!" She spat the word *puppy* like a glob of rotten food.

I pictured the boar's head, wild-bristled and fierce, mounted on a walnut board, high on their den wall.

"The boar's head," Toots repeated, "that Uncle Fritz killed just before he had to, you know"—she dropped her voice—"go away."

"Oh, gosh—"

"It's the last good memory we have of him!"

A long time ago, Uncle Fritz had burned down the barn then beaten up the sheriff. A doctor had said he was mentally ill, and he went to Mendota, the state mental hospital down in Madison where, I believe, he still was.

"A puppy?"

"Yeah, he made friends with a kid over on the Rawson place, and they made a trade. Just a little mongrel, cute as shit, but we can't keep him."

"Why not?"

"Because we want the head back!"

Petey wailed in the background. "Oh, relax, Pete," growled Toots, "get manly here. I don't know exactly what Sheila's gonna do to you, but you'll have to take it like a man. Haven't we taught you anything?"

He stifled his wailing, and I heard frenzied yipping. Petey's little voice piped, "She's white and her name's Whitey!"

Toots told me, "Sheila's beside herself. She's putting her boots on to play Elvira Gulch over here. Gonna get that head back if it's the last thing—"

"Toots," I interrupted, fascinated, "how did he get his hands on it?"

"Well, he was goddamn clever, I have to admit. He climbed the wainscoting and on up the shelving, then he hung from a rope he hooked to the crown molding. He made a block and tackle with some parts from that old wringer washing machine out back. He really wanted that head."

I muttered, "He really wanted that puppy."

THIRTY

It took an intervention from Khani Emberton to get Amaryllis's butt into my ugly old car and ride with me up to Bakersfield.

"I want to emphasize that I'm not doing this for myself," she said, smoothing her skirt as I peeled onto Compton.

"I don't give a damn," I said. "I'm just glad Khani was able to ram some sense into your head."

"It wasn't sense I was lacking, sister," she said humbly. "It was courage."

I smiled.

This was Friday. George and I had visited Khani at his mansion in Baldwin Hills last night, the meeting arranged by Cici, who had brought home George's message to her husband: Amaryllis is in crisis and considering giving up.

People call Baldwin Hills the black Beverly Hills because so many affluent African-Americans live there. It's not far from South Central, and it's literally uphill from it, so there you go: movin' on up. The houses are really nice, plus you can get a view.

Khani quickly grasped the whole picture when George and I laid out what was going on at the mission: that Amaryllis was totally under the thumb of drug boss Dale the Whale Vargas, who was using her safe haven as a base of ever-widening illegal operations.

Unconsciously showing his street savvy, Emberton didn't ask why we hadn't involved the police. All George mentioned was, "The guy's too clean for the police to get him on anything good."

"We can help her, but she's not ready to let us," I told our host. "We figure a kick from you might convince her."

Khani's eyes were intent. "How can you help her?"

George answered, "In your position, the less you know, the better."

Emberton looked at his wife. Cici said firmly, "They would not be in our home if they were not trustable."

"I feel that," Khani said.

I thought Cici looked tense, but never having met her, I didn't know her normal state. A look passed from her to George—anxious? conspiratorial?—which he answered with a calm nod of reassurance. After that, she seemed to feel better. A surprisingly sharp jolt of jealousy galvanized my skin. I took a breath and let it go.

"All right," said Khani, "how do I approach this?"

I advised, "First of all, you can't treat her like your surrogate mama anymore. She's not in control of anything right now. She's scared and practically paralyzed. You can't be nice to her. You can't even talk about the five million. You have to shame her into taking back control."

Our host nodded. "I can guilt-trip her, yes, I do believe it. Do you know I haven't canceled that endowment ceremony for Sunday?"

"Oh, my God, I thought you had," I said. "*Sunday?* That doesn't give us much—"

"Keeping my hope alive," he interjected, "though I despaired of convincing her."

Until we talked through the situation, I hadn't fully realized how many threads were entwined around Dale the Whale Vargas: the Whale as parasite on the Cubitt family, the Whale as enemy of civilized life in Los Angeles, the Whale versus Sgt. Annette Soames, the Whale versus George, the Whale versus me. All that was enough; we left out the stuff about Amaryllis's abortionist background, and the grief-fueled predations of Diane Keever, which formed, essentially, the root from which the whole sick grapevine grew.

The Emberton house was a whopping Colonial, somewhat like Graceland without the vulgarity, all bright carpeting and yellow furniture, all of it coolly retro. I looked around for servants, but I guess they were in the background. Cici had put out some almonds and olives, and Khani handed around glasses of iced tea.

"The Iron Angel simply needs to know," I emphasized, "that if she'll trust us, George and I can help her stare down the devil."

"I think I can couch it in those terms," Khani said with a smile. "May I threaten her with my disappointment, as well?"

"Great idea," George and I chorused together.

"For she's the one who gave me courage, truly," Khani went on. "If she's faltering now, she's giving in because Satan seems so

320

strong. But his is false strength, I learned that." He sat back in his chair, his eyes on a distant memory. "It's my duty to honor Amaryllis B. Cubitt by kicking her ass, just like she kicked mine."

NOW, IN THE car, Amaryllis's eyes were wet remembering Khani's surprise visit that morning before breakfast. She didn't need to tell me what he'd said. She was struggling, there in that front bucket seat. She was scared shitless. It was about eleven now.

"I don't know why you're so nervous," I said. "I mean, you've met Diane Keever since—the terrible night."

"Oh, no, sister, I haven't. Neneng was her proxy at all times. I've never been inside that house, only up on the porch. Never wanted to."

We swept through the hot countryside on the downslope from the engine-shearing mountain pass, and into that valley of tumbleweeds, vineyards, carrots, and oil pumps.

"How do you know she'll be there?" Amaryllis objected uneasily.

"You know as well as I do that she'll be there."

I drove on, keeping a lid on my own unease. This meeting, this job, was mine, George and I had agreed. It made sense: I knew these women, and moreover, I knew how women behaved in company. I really could have used some chocolate right then.

The farmhouse was as desolate as ever, with its ghostly peeling paint and sagging porch.

Neneng pulled open the coffin-lid door. "Remember me?" I said, stepping in before she could slam it.

The meeting was surreal and to the point. No introductions were needed.

"I've been expecting you," said Diane Keever from her wheel-chair in its spot across from the piano. She was no less fierce today.

"You have?" I was surprised.

Neneng shot hate-rays at me.

Mrs. Keever said, "They've been here."

Amaryllis and I glanced at each other. "Who?" I said, helping myself to a seat. Amaryllis did so as well. Neneng remained standing.

Mrs. Keever addressed Amaryllis, "The two from your gang."

"What?" I said.

The tension in the room was enough to bend steel.

"Oh, my God," I realized, "Wichita and Denny! Was it a short fat white girl and a thin black guy?"

Mrs. Keever said, "They didn't leave their cards."

I said, "They wanted to know about the money?"

"They talked about drugs. It's the same as money, these days, I guess."

"Where were you?" I asked Neneng.

She looked at the threadbare rug. "I hide." She fingered the daggerlike silver crucifix around her neck.

Diane Keever said, "They kept asking, 'What are you about? What are you about?' They said something about a golden goose, and the eggs rolling downhill, as if I was supposed to understand something. They said, 'What's your racket?' The girl, she said something like, 'We have to think outside of the coop.' I had no idea what she was—"

"The Whale's getting impatient," I said.

"Who's the Whale?"

"This guy we need to bring down together. Together," I repeated. "Those two he sent? They'll come back soon to do worse than frighten you." I thought for a minute, then said, "His name is

Dale Vargas, I believe I mentioned him when I was here before. Dale the Whale. Actually, I see he's becoming more like an octopus, reaching into everybody's world. None of us, individually, have been able to defeat him."

"Who is he, exactly?" Mrs. Keever insisted.

I answered, "Somebody's little boy who grew into a monster. He murdered at least five people in Tucson few years ago, and he arranged for other murders here in California. He tried to kill Kip Cubitt, Amaryllis's grandson. I was nearby that day, and he almost got me too. His big idea is to unify all of Los Angeles via the distribution and consumption of street drugs. While he was in prison with Nathan Cubitt, Amaryllis's son, he found out about the hush money she's been paying you."

"Your son Nathan was the first messenger?" Diane asked.

Amaryllis nodded.

"And now," I went on, "the Whale's got his hands around Amaryllis's throat. He's taken over the ABC Mission by night, running his drugs and weapons and dealers through it. He wants the five million Khani Emberton has pledged to the mission. And now it looks like his soldiers are trying to find out what's behind Amaryllis's monthly payments to you."

Amaryllis sat in stony humility, staring at the photographs of young Deborah Keever on the piano.

Mrs. Keever was like a bag of radioactive bones, danger-poison forever. Neneng paced slowly, her hands twitching. When she passed the piano, she reached out and, with one finger, struck one key. *Binnng!* The note crystallized the air in the room.

The blood rushed through my body, pounded up through my neck and into my head so hard that I thought I was going to have a stroke.

If someone had walked in with a machine gun and started shooting, I'd have welcomed the change in mood.

Finally, Amaryllis spoke.

"Diane Keever, I asked you a long time ago for forgiveness. I didn't expect it, and you didn't give it." Her eyes softened as she used all the courage in her body to look straight at her. "That's all right. But I do ask you again: Forgive me, please, for causing Debbie's death."

The old lady was waiting for it.

"No." She savored that one short word like a spoonful of buttercream.

Amaryllis nodded and looked at her knees, knobby through the cloth of her flower-print skirt.

"Now that that's settled," I said, "we need to be utilitarian here."

"You can go back to hating me later," said Amaryllis to Mrs. Keever. "I predict I will endure your hatred and unforgiveness as long as I live. That is my life."

"Mrs. Keever." I leaned forward, glancing at the studio photo of her on the piano. "I want to know why you left Paramount."

Mrs. Keever opened her mouth. "Ah?" She stopped, stunned, trying to figure out why I was asking.

"Under the name Vera Luxon," I added.

She sighed. "I'm sure you've guessed why." She turned her gaze out the window to the flat, hardworking land. I could see her remembering. "It was a great life," she said after a few minutes. "The studio did everything. They put gorgeous clothes on me, they worked with my skin and hair, they even helped me learn to act. All they asked was that I show up on time, don't take drugs, and don't get pregnant."

"Two out of three, right?"

"Right. Bruce and I got married immediately, but I'd broken a rule that only the stars got away with breaking. I thought I could go back to Paramount after I had Debbie, but they didn't want me. I'd lost my opportunity."

"Did you like acting?"

"Ohh," she breathed, suddenly animated, "I loved it. I *loved* it. They had plans for me, you know. Mr. DeMille—*Mr. DeMille!*—noticed me one day walking across the lot, and he asked my name, and he said to his assistant: 'Watch that one. She's got it!'"

Amaryllis broke in, "Let her sign your autograph album, sister Rita, and let's move on. What are we gonna do?"

But I hadn't finished listening to our hostess. "Go on Diane," I urged.

"I poured everything into Debbie." Diane Keever clasped her bony hands. "If I couldn't succeed at the thing I loved the most, I was bound and determined she'd have the chance to."

"And that's why it was so important to end her pregnancies," I suggested.

"I'm not ashamed of that. I paid for my role in it." She brought herself to look at Amaryllis fully. "It makes me sick to see you."

No one spoke for a minute.

Then Diane Keever said, "I hoped that maybe Debbie would go into acting. I know it's wrong to expect your children to live out your own unfulfilled dreams. But sometimes—you can't help it."

What a sad waste. *Note to self: Don't be a stage mother.* I felt a short, intense gush of gladness that Petey was male: never to have periods, never to see your archenemy in the exact same prom dress as you, never to get pregnant and feel the pull of that insatiable little barbarian growing in your belly.

"Were you in any pictures?" I wanted to know.

"Oh, yes, I played little bits, waitresses and people's younger sister, but I never starred in anything. My biggest role was in *Silver Wings Over Okinawa*, the war picture with Jack St. Hodge? I played a USO barmaid, and I remember I had twelve lines in that film, more than I'd ever had before. But I was already pregnant, and I just made it through shooting before I started to show."

And then something sensational happened. Diane Keever sat up straight in her wheelchair, shoulders back, and said, "Major Diggs, if the enemy captures you, remember that Mary Ann will wait for you, no matter how long it takes. She told me to tell you that." Her eyes focused tenderly on the invisible face before her.

Then, from the side of her mouth, she muttered in a rough voice, "Oh now, honey, no Japs are gonna get their hands on me!"

She gazed up into the Major's eyes, her body yielding just perceptibly. She whispered, "Good luck, Mike."

Her glance followed the invisible officer across the room and out the door. She lowered her eyes and sighed, clearly in love with Major Diggs herself, but too noble to move in on her friend's man.

She lifted her head, and she was the elderly Diane Keever again.

"Wow," said Amaryllis.

"I can't believe it," I murmured. I could practically hear the shells exploding in the distance. I stared straight ahead, thinking. An idea crept into my brain. *Wait, no way. Well, maybe. Maybe yeah, maybe this is it.*

Amaryllis said, "The Whale's reign of ruination has got to stop."

Like Khani Emberton, Mrs. Keever did not ask about getting the police involved. Little wonder, the homespun extortionist.

She did say to Amaryllis, "But this Whale—he's just a criminal. He doesn't deserve your money, he's just trying to horn in."

326

"So you'll work with us?"

The widow nodded. "I want to protect my income."

She was talking about the ten thousand a month from the coffers of the ABC Mission! *Damn you,* I thought. Amaryllis looked wretched.

I took a deep breath. "Can you two commit to tomorrow night?" I asked.

"If we don't take the son of a bitch out before Sunday," said Amaryllis firmly, "I'm backing out of that endowment ceremony. What's your plan, sister Rita?"

"It's not coherent yet, but now that both of you are in, I'm getting ideas every minute."

GINA HAD NOT spoken to me in two days. That wasn't terribly unusual for Gina, actually; she always had to stew after an argument, and I'd really put her on the defensive about "Toby." I was worried about her, but there was no way she was going to listen to me until she was ready. Besides, I knew hell was going to break loose soon at the mission, and Toby/Denny would be out of the picture one way or another.

So I'd kept quiet, knowing they weren't supposed to go out again until Saturday night.

When I got home from Bakersfield, I made coffee, got out a yellow pad and a pencil, and set to work. I thought about the picture of Albert Einstein with the knife sticking in his throat, and I thought about how clean the Whale liked to keep his hands, and I thought about Diane Keever talking to her Major Diggs.

After a while, pieces of plan began to coalesce in my head. My whole being was focused on the end goal of seeing Dale the Whale sitting in the back of a police car with a stunned expression on his face.

At seven o'clock, Gina came home, looked surprised that I hadn't started dinner, then flung herself on the sofa in a melodramatic swoon. "Ohhhh," she moaned.

I sat swiveling to and fro on my bar stool at the breakfast counter, deep into my planning, biting my knuckle, oblivious, writing. Yes, yes, a plan was jelling.

She sighed heavily a few times. She sat up and finally broke her silence. "Rita!"

"I—I'm thinking, hon. Uh."

"Rita, I need to talk to you."

I looked up. "What about?"

"Toby."

Aha. "What about Toby?"

"I don't think he's exactly who he says he is," she blurted.

"Yeah?"

She hauled herself up and joined me at the counter. "He's not a 'business consultant.'"

"That's what I was trying to tell you!"

"He's involved in some kind of secret *thing*."

"Yes. What happened?"

"We were out walking, just down on Melrose, and we passed by this couple of cops, and I swear one of them recognized him. There was like this *I know you!* in his face, you know? Toby turned away and ducked us down an alley. He is smooth, very smooth, you know."

"Yes."

"He just laughed it off, but suddenly he was sweating. I said, that cop looked like he knew you, and he said oh, he'd had a run-in

328

with him one time, he was a son of a bitching cop. I go what kind of a run-in?, but he wouldn't say. I got this *feeling* all of a sudden."

"Gina, he works for Dale the Whale Vargas. He's an enforcer."

She stared at me, mouth open, one of her slow gasps beginning.

I said, "That cop probably knew him from some drug bust or assault charge or something. He's this 'Denny' I've been mentioning, at the ABC Mission."

She completed her gasp. "Of Wichita and Denny? Oh, my God. Why didn't you *tell* me?"

I could only laugh incredulously.

"Oh, my God!" she said. "I am so *creeped*! Look at my hands, they're shaking!"

"Well, hon, now that you know, you're going to help us nail the Whale. Calm down, now. This is complicated, and I'm trying to figure—"

"Oh, my God, I'm remembering, oh my God, all these little *moments* when something wasn't quite right, you know, some little glitch that I couldn't figure out, but now it all falls into place. He never likes to go out in the daytime. Like a vampire! He didn't even want to walk around on Melrose, I sort of dragged him. He's been mighty curious about you and George. Oh, my God! That's why he wanted to date me! He didn't even care about *me*!"

I said, "He saw us at the mission that day we helped at lunch, I realize. But as it happened, neither of us saw him very well. I really didn't get a look at his face at all. Now, maybe it was a pure coincidence that he walked into the record shop and asked you out. Or, he might have zeroed in on us somehow."

"What do you mean?"

"Gotten suspicious of us, somehow. Maybe we looked too . . . focused."

"I think we should just talk to the police," said Gina. "Get them involved."

I threw down my pencil. "Maybe we could convince them to raid the ABC Mission. Then what? They'd find some drugs and guns, and Amaryllis would get in trouble, and maybe they'd make a few more arrests. But as far as putting a stop to the Whale—nailing him for murder, and attempted murder, and conspiracy? I'm sorry, honey, but that won't do it. He's got more buffers than the Godfather. His hands are clean, incredibly clean. Might as well try to nail Petey for bank robbery." I stopped, horrified.

Gina commented, "Suddenly you've got that thousand-yard stare."

"Yeah." Because I could all too easily envision my little boy as a bored, alienated teenager dropping down from the ceiling and making off with a sack of cash before the wide-eyed tellers could react. *Oh, God, please let that not be my future. Note to self: Lesson for Petey: We don't steal.*

I came back to reality. "OK, shut up for a minute while I get George over here. We've all got to get together on this."

"You shut up," she said reflexively.

"Because until that murderous asshole is locked up, we can't ever feel safe. I can't bring Petey back. Can't have my life back."

I picked up the phone. "Plus I gotta call Sylvan and ask for a favor," I remembered.

"The animal wrangler guy?"

"Yeah, and Chino again, and Yvonne. Yeah, that ought to do it."

George said he'd come right over. Then I reached Sylvan. "Doing anything tomorrow night?" I asked.

"Want to catch a show?" he suggested.

"I want to catch something else," I began.

THIRTY-ONE

I need ten minutes of your time," George Rowe told Dale the Whale, "but I have a select feeling it'll be a good ten minutes."

Vargas, pleased to see him, indicated one of the chairs in the science room. "What do you have for me, Jimmer?"

It was past midnight now, on Friday night, and Rowe and Rita had finished working out their master plan. She was getting some sleep.

A couple of male vice presidents, stripped to the waist, were busy at a lab table, weighing mannitol and heroin on digital lab balances, and mixing the powders together in stainless steel bowls, like you'd mix flour and sugar to make a cake. It was a warm night.

"First of all, I sold the two ounces and I have your money."

"That was quick. But I don't handle funds directly, you know.

Put it in that drawer there and I'll have my account man take it in the morning."

"OK. Second, most important, this: you know I like weapons, and you know I can bust into places. Your organization already has firepower, but if you want to get bigger, you don't want any heavier of an arsenal lying around than what you absolutely need."

"That's right!"

"I propose firepower on a just-in-time basis. You don't want to over-inventory. Just like the heroin. You do just-in-time with that, mostly, right?"

"That's right, too risky otherwise."

"An opportunity came my way yesterday. So I put my brain to work on synergizing. And I came up with a plan for more guns, exactly when you need them, all hinging on *reliable resupply*."

"What's your plan?"

"Let me just say these three words: U.S. Olympic Shooting Team Training Camp."

"Ahh." The Whale sounded as though he'd just gulped a cold beer after five sets of tennis. "You think like I do, Jimmer."

"I can come in tomorrow night, no earlier, and tell you all about it."

"Why not right now? I'm not tired."

Rowe said, "I needed to hear the interest in your voice. Now that I have, I'll go ahead and procure a sample for you, to prove what I said."

"Little Jimmer."

"Yeah?"

"What is your goal?"

"To move up."

"No, I mean your *ultimate* goal."

"To be honest? You're too smart not to know, Dale. Sure, I want your job someday."

"Hahaha! That's the honesty I would expect from a person like you! Come on in tomorrow night. Midnight sharp."

Rowe let out a long breath. The most important point was established.

"WHAT ABOUT MY boy?" Amaryllis wanted to know, her voice metallic with anxiety as she swept the mission's long kitchen floor. "My Nathan behind bars, at the mercy of those thugs that do for the Whale."

"George got word to him to commit some infraction that would get him put in isolation for a few days," I explained, straightening a stack of clean towels. "He's done it, and now George knows he's safe. We can proceed."

"What did he do?"

"I don't know, he spit on the warden's shoes! What difference does it make? Now, listen. Your first job is to make Wichita disappear tonight. Ideally for the whole evening, but she's gotta be out of there no later than eleven thirty. I know you own the day and the Whale owns the night, but you've got to work late tonight, you've got to require her help on some critical errand."

Amaryllis's broom had a wooden handle and bright purple straws. I'd never seen such a broom. "What about the rest of the guards?" she asked. "I can't get rid of them all."

"I know, I just want to reduce their numbers."

"Well, Saturday night, most of them are going to be out making deliveries anyway."

"OK. But see what you can do specifically about Wichita, she's the loosest cannon among them."

"Amen to that."

"GINA, YOU'RE GOING to make sure Denny's busy all night." I talked to my sister as she chopped parsley for some tabouli she'd decided to make for lunch. Saturday now. The day of The Night. We were expecting a few friends. "Take a drive somewhere, then stop for dinner." The fresh green herb smelled good in the kitchen.

"What do I do if he wants to bail early?"

"Well, you guys have been sleeping together, right?"

"I am not going to sleep with that creep tonight or ever again. I'm only doing this for you. I never want to see him again after tonight. My God."

"You don't have to. But you've got to keep him away from the mission at least through one a.m., and that's cutting it close. Do whatever you have to do, just keep him with you."

"OK."

By late afternoon, everything was set:

Gina had scored tickets to tonight's exclusive Earth Puppets benefit concert up in Ventura, featuring Sock Baines, Denny's favorite jazz saxophonist. At the proper time, Amaryllis was going to send Wichita out with the ABC van to pick up five gallons of Tülky's ice cream for the mission, which I'd remembered was Wichita's favorite brand, which was going to be left over from a private party hosted by Khani Emberton, who was going to make sure she got pleasantly delayed in the process.

My friends Yvonne and Chino showed up, and after we ate Gina's tabouli, they helped me get ready.

BY SIX O'CLOCK I was alone in the apartment. I drank some water and stood on the patio, going over tonight's sequence in my head. I listened to the sounds of North Curson Street, my little street in West Hollywood—cars whooshing by, sparrows chittering in the trees, a siren way off in the distance somewhere, a kid laughing out by the curb.

And as the lemon light of this Los Angeles late-summer day disintegrated into evening, my feelings arranged themselves in layers, like one of the big sandwiches at Canter's or someplace: excitement laid over fear, laid over wondering, laid over feverish thinking to make sure I get everything right, plus mustard.

I waited, and the lights came up in the city around me. I thought about my fellow humans here in Los Angeles. Night in L.A.: everybody with their dreams, everybody with their heart's desires. The sky deepens into that blue-vein color and you evaluate your day, what you've done and—you can't help it, you relax because the earth is relaxing, even if you can only allow yourself a little relaxation, because you have much to do yet. Because everybody knows night here in Los Angeles is unlike night anywhere else.

You look out for excitement when it's nighttime. Excitement could be coming straight at you—in the form of an out-of-control druggie driving a carjacked Porsche at 110 mph—or in the form of a handsome stranger in the candy line at the movies who turns to you with a smile and a funny question.

Movies, movies, movies. You'll be driving at night and you'll gain altitude on an overpass and you'll see searchlights sweeping the sky at a premiere, and your impulse is to follow those swinging cones of energy to their roots. Something new is happening there, something is happening that has never happened before.

GEORGE, AS JIMMER, picked up me, as DeeDee, at ten o'clock, and we drove to MacArthur Park where I would catch a bus to South Central right away. He would get moving half an hour later.

On the way, to break the tension, I asked George how it was going living at Gonzalo's.

"Oh, fine," he said. "I was looking online at apartments the other day."

"If all my stuff had gotten wrecked in a fire, I'd be so lost. What's been the hardest?" I asked, thinking I could surprise him with something, buy him a little something.

"You know," he said, "I had stuff, and I liked some of it quite a lot, but I just don't bond tightly with property. You can replace just about—" He stopped.

"What is it?"

"I do miss one thing." He shook his head at himself. "Funny. A little blue china bowl I had. Just a little blue bowl from when I was little. My mother gave me soup in it when I was sick." He smiled inwardly.

My heart turned for him. It was getting harder and harder to keep my emotional distance.

"Boy, it's been hot," he said, changing the subject.

"Yeah, the dog days. I want to see Sirius."

"The Dog Star—in Canis Major. You'll have to stay up pretty late to get a glimpse of it, I think."

Then he got quiet. "You know," he warned, "once I get in there with him, it could go very fast."

"Yes. We'll all be ready."

He shook his head. "This plan's got way too many moving parts for my taste." Then he brightened. "Well, nothing's fail-safe, is it?"

AT ELEVEN THIRTY, I tiptoed up to the ABC Mission through the back alley, as I had the last time. Now, at this hour, the exterior door to the kitchen corridor was locked.

This time, however, I had a key.

And I was glad for that, because of the feral dog pack; I heard them baying along the edges of the grown-over athletic fields out back.

I slipped inside, toting a duffel bag containing clothing and a few supplies. I didn't intend to meet up with anyone, but I'd gone to the trouble of becoming DeeDee just in case. If someone accosted me, I could be searching, confused, for the dormitory or a bathroom.

Amaryllis had suggested I hide in the small kitchen office, but I saw a light under the door—perhaps a volunteer working late— and kept moving silently on my ugly rubber shoes. I didn't want to have to talk my way out of anything. All I needed was a place to change identities and wait until I was needed. My heart was pounding, and I realized I was beginning to like the feeling of adrenaline.

I skirted the dormitory area, hearing the homeless guys snoring and coughing like a thousand grampas with TB. The women were quieter, but not by a whole lot, I have to tell you.

I kept going, away from any activity. At a place where two corridors joined, I heard a couple of guards chatting, coming my way, and I quickly slipped through an unlocked door. Which turned out to be the stairwell to the basement.

I had seen—and auditioned for—enough teen-scream flicks to know *Don't go down the basement,* but I had little choice at the moment.

The institutional-cleanliness smell of the mission gave way to that verging-on-turpentine smell of mold in a dry climate. In California, you rarely smell the typical dull mold reek in dark places; here it's a thinner, old-dirt type of smell.

I descended the concrete steps, the metal railing cold under my hand. The lights, a series of caged bulbs, were on. Hm. The stairwell emptied into a concrete-block corridor, which led ahead to the main boiler room or whatever it was. Now I was hidden and I knew I didn't have to be here long.

I felt calmer.

Until I saw a bright red spatter on the concrete floor.

And another one.

Just as I had done when, seeing Kip Cubitt being beaten, I rushed into the street without even stopping to go *Oh, God,* I quickened my pace, following the blood trail, so hideously fresh, glistening wet, so very totally red.

And I realized that the blood was not exactly in droplets; it had been tracked along, smeared from the soles of someone's shoes.

The boiler room was a tight mishmash of pipes and ducts, rusted tanks and rivets and gauges. There were five-gallon buckets here and there, drizzled with the institutional gray paint they'd held, and in one place it seemed a few of them had been arranged in a little meeting circle.

The blood trail disappeared beneath a steel door that was held shut by a sliding bolt the size of my arm.

I put my ear to the door. Nothing.

I slid back the bolt.

A scuffing sound as I opened the heavy door, and a soft moan.

As the door swung open, I saw it had been lined inside with thick drywall, with an air space about two inches wide between the drywall and the inner surface of the door. The doorway was gasketed with weather stripping.

Someone was cringing on the floor in there. It was a woman, her back against the bright white drywall, beneath a dangling light-bulb, bleeding from the face. The walls of this soundproof chamber were no longer pristine, as George had seen them; one awful smear of blood traced an arc away from the woman, as if her assailant had brushed a hand against the wall upon leaving her.

The woman's hands were cupped at her face. Her legs stuck out in front of her like doll legs, black shoes pointing straight up, and she wore a blue service dress, and her black hair was done in a bun, with two tendrils coming down from the temples. She shrank from me. I reached and tilted the bulb to see her better.

"Neneng?"

She mumbled something through her blood-wet hands. Her forearms were bloody up to the elbows, and her wrists, I saw, were cuffed with a plastic zip tie. Blood had dripped from the tips of her elbows into her lap. I saw, also, that her ankles had been bound with a zip tie.

Above her head was the steel ring, bolted into the wall, that

339

George had mentioned. My feet sank a little as I stepped in: an incongruous plush rug, in corporate-office beige—another sound muffler, just as George had said. Neneng hadn't been fixed to the ring, but the simple sight of it made my flesh creep.

I realized she didn't know me in my DeeDee makeup. "I'm Rita," I said. "I came to see you and Mrs. Keever."

She grunted in comprehension.

I squatted and tried to see where her wound was. She was bleeding from the center of her face. For a moment I thought, oh, somebody punched her in the nose, but then I saw that she had no nose.

It was simply gone, sliced off.

My stomach dropped, and I rocked backward from the impact of the sight.

She was breathing mostly through her mouth, but now and then some air escaped from the hole in her face, bubbling blood as it went.

"Oh, God, oh, God," I murmured, my whole body cold with horror.

"Help me," she gurgled around her hands.

I got out a small towel from my duffel and folded it into a pad. She pressed it to her face as I rummaged again in my bag, wildly, listening for anyone coming. In a few seconds I grabbed the fingernail clippers I knew to be in the bottom, the only cutting tool I had.

I set to work on the zip tie around her wrists. It was tight, and the blood made things slippery. There wasn't the amount of blood you'd expect at a slaughterhouse, but it was in the way, and I wondered whether this woman could simply bleed out right here, direct pressure or no direct pressure.

Her shoes scraped anxiously against each other as I worked. I heard my own breathing in my ears, and I smelled the wet dankness of her blood.

"What happened?" I asked. It was slow work using the nail clipper, its tiny jaws gnawing away the tough plastic bit by bit.

"They surprise me. They take me."

"They who?"

She shook her head. "They ask me—uhhhh—my people in the Philippines. I tell them of my family. They ask about drugs—they think I send drugs. I no send—guh"—she gulped, swallowing blood—"I no send. They say I a drug dealer, they ask who, who, where, where send money. I say no, no. The fat man cut me. I no understand."

"Oh, my God."

"He say you sit, you think. I come back."

"Oh, Neneng." I worked the tiny clippers as hard as I could.

"It OK."

"What?"

"He no cut my fingers. Help me leave here before he come back."

I hurried.

THIRTY-TWO

George Rowe knew everything was set. He had taken care of this final preparation many hours earlier, at dawn, when he had quietly entered the mission to meet someone and do a bit of prep work. He allowed himself the hopeful thought that when all this was over, maybe he and Rita and Petey could take a little vacation, maybe a camping trip. They all enjoyed the outdoors.

For good measure and the hell of it, he'd told the Whale, "I'd like this meeting to be private, just this once. I trust you a hundred and twenty percent, but you understand I can't run risks, what with vice presidents I don't know very well yet."

Vargas had said, "All right."

"Ah, good. I was afraid you'd say, 'I trust these individuals with my life, so if—' "

"Oh, no," interrupted the Whale. "Actually, I don't trust them equally myself."

The shirtless vice presidents, whom Rowe realized were shirtless to make it harder for them to steal heroin as they cut it, had listened without comment.

Now, nearing midnight at the ABC Mission, Rowe stepped into the chemistry room and greeted Dale Vargas, who was sitting on the sofa reading a book in the dim light.

The Whale smiled. "I love a man who's early!"

The clock said 11:55. The Whale was alone.

Shiny blackness pressed in from the bare windows. The room smelled foody and stale, as if someone had eaten a bacon pizza here recently. Vargas did not rise, but closed his book. The boldly lettered title: *Leadership Is Only Gut-Deep*.

This time, Rowe did not extend his hand to shake. Vargas noted it. "You're learning my customs."

"I'm a quick study," Rowe boasted quietly.

"I see you looking at my book. This is a good book, you know this gentleman, Irving Sessions? He invented the Hydro-Cooker, and then all those choppers that women buy, one for every kind of food. He's a multimillionaire, and he wrote this."

"Ah," said Rowe.

"He has an empire."

"I should say."

"You know how I got my start reading?" Vargas's hands holding the book were so pink and chubby they looked like baby hands, except for the scale of them—along the lines of moon gloves. Rowe noticed what looked like a smudge of blood on the heel of one hand, where you might miss washing if you're in a hurry.

"How?" asked Rowe.

"From my great-aunt Lois. She started me on the newspaper, then she stole some books out of the library for me and said, Now you read these! Yours to keep, not every boy gets books to keep!" Vargas laughed. "*The Little Red Hen*. I'll do it myself, said the Little Red Hen. Now that's a lesson I've never forgot. *I'll do it myself*. My aunty taught me that books can make you powerful and smart. Maybe she had a different path for me in mind when she started this little guy on reading, but I learned that *any* path can come easier by reading." Vargas's eyes danced. "You hear what I'm telling you?"

"I do," said Rowe. He glanced at the bulletin board with the picture of Einstein with the slit in his throat.

NENENG GOT A jolt of energy when her hands came free. It took me another few minutes to unbind her ankles, at which point she jumped to her feet.

I told her, "I can get you out of here, but I have to stay and capture the fat man. That's what I came for."

She nodded. "OK, which way out? I wait outside."

"No, don't wait! You have to get to a doctor as fast as possible. Get on the bus uptown and go to the medical center, or flag down a cop. Ask anybody to point the way."

I could not interrupt tonight's enterprise for any reason, because I had no way to get a message to George. He was going to launch the whole thing, and he needed me, otherwise he'd very possibly die at the hands of the Whale. I had to get going; my time was getting short.

"Bleeding is less," noted Neneng, her voice hoarse but strong. She was one tough broad, I'll tell you.

"Where—where *is* your nose?" I thought I could wrap it up for her.

"Thin man, he kick it out the door."

"What thin man? What was his name?"

She shrugged. We searched the bloody floor outside the little room among the buckets and junk, but did not find her nose. I pawed around, noticing the opened package of zip ties on the floor.

"Never mind," said Neneng. "I go."

"Up the stairs, then turn right." I told her how to get out to the street via the gym, which wasn't used at night.

"I hide outside," she said. "If a policeman see me, they come in here. First, you kill the fat man. Then I go to doctor. Police can come then."

She staggered off and I heard her clumping rapidly up the stairwell.

I checked my watch—*shit!*—12:02. I was supposed to be in position by now, and I still had to change clothes and get upstairs to that chemistry room. I washed my blood-slick hands in a nearby scrub sink and dumped out my duffel.

As fast as I could, I scrubbed off my latex and makeup, pulled off my raccoon-pelt wig, brushed my hair, and changed my clothes. As I worked, I wondered who Neneng's "thin man" was. It couldn't be Denny; he and Gina were probably just starting back from the concert in Ventura, sixty miles up the coast. I turned to race upstairs, then froze in my tracks as I heard someone rapidly descending the stairwell. The steel-and-concrete staircase gave off one low *bong* per step.

I leaped to a hiding place behind a tanklike turbine thing. The person's tread quickened and didn't sound heavy enough to be the Whale's.

From the shadows, I peeped out.

A man came in, a thin one, and he didn't have dreadlocks. He was black and he wore black clothing, and I could see a rim of white at the back of his neck. Oh, no way.

Perceiving the door to the little room to be wide open, the Reverend Bill Culpepper spun around with a loud *"Huuuh?"* Yes, it was the one-thumbed former stevedore who pestered Amaryllis about various chores and said "amen" a lot.

I almost made a sound of startlement; I almost popped out to say hello.

"Oh, shit," he panted. "Shit. Shittin' Jesus, shittin' Jesus." He stepped to the little room's threshold, not wanting to look, looking, then staggering back a few steps. His eyes were stark as they scanned the suddenly menacing jumble of pipes and junk, rife with hiding places.

He stood in a pool of murky light for at least a full minute, breathing audibly, trying to calm himself. My pulse pounded as the seconds raced by. *I have to get moving.*

I watched him get hold of himself. He moistened his lips and swallowed. He spoke again, this time with malevolent self-assurance. "OK, where are ya, bitch? Where are ya?"

I watched him reach a lean hand to the top of a metal cabinet and feel around. He drew out a slim knife about a foot long, like a kitchen fillet knife. He looked relieved, as if he'd expected it too, to be gone.

Now armed, he squared his shoulders and decided to prowl

the boiler room. In the dim light, I saw the ropiness of his neck muscles.

I stepped from the shadows.

ROWE THOUGHT ABOUT how often he'd successfully used toys to distract, charm, or divert. Vargas was immune to toys in the typical sense, but Rowe knew that Vargas considered weapons to be the ultimate toys. Which is, of course, the way of it with men prone to violence.

Vargas went on, "Reading a book just opens up your entire mental capacity."

Rowe nodded.

"You're looking neater, Jimmer."

"I realize grooming is important."

"But if you're going to be working Beverly Hills and beyond—Hollywood Hills and the like—I do foresee that in your future, you've got to step it up a notch higher."

In fact, Rowe's clothes tonight were almost as nice as the Whale's, and he had shaved. He still wore the ridiculous reddish curly wig and buck teeth, but he had washed the wig and combed it nicely. He looked, he thought, like a high school class president.

"FREEZE! DROP IT!" I commanded in the deepest, toughest voice from my inner universe.

Culpepper stared me all the way from the peak of my LAPD hat to the bright oval shield on my chest, down to my thick-soled black tactical shoes.

The shock to his system was so great, I don't think he could've moved if he wanted to.

Given the fact that my gun was fake, I had no choice but to make this work. "Drop it!" I barked again, and the two seconds it took him to decide to do it felt like a week.

The knife hit the floor point first, *doinng,* and clittered to the corner.

Covering the Reverend with one hand, I hit the fake transmit button on my fake radio and barked, "Got him! Send the guys down!"

When I'd received my two hours of coaching for my work as a police extra in *The Canary Syndrome,* they'd shown us how to take down a suspect and apply handcuffs, which some of us were supposed to do with the protesters.

"I didn't do anything—" Culpepper began in a high voice.

I over-yelled him, "Get down! Down, down down!" as if I were so excited I might pull the trigger without knowing it. "Facedown, spread your legs, goddamn it!"

He was the Whale's money man, I realized, which is why he'd been part of the interrogation of Neneng.

The gypsum powder clinging to the raw wallboard absorbed and pinkened her blood that had been smeared on it.

Once you've ordered your suspect down, you kneel on his back and grab up his wrists one at a time. In the case of the Reverend Bill Culpepper, I used a handy zip tie from the package on the floor, reserving the steel cuffs on my belt for my work upstairs—if I got there in time. I talked loudly, harshly, and cursingly.

He talked back. "Oho, now, what you want to do this for? I've done nothing, praise God." He'd blipped right back into his phony preacher persona. Who ever gets fooled by that stuff? Well, I had been, for a while.

"There's been a little mix-up, sister officer, is all. I just came down here to check on—these machines, you know . . ." He actually put a cajoling smile into his voice, even as he grunted with my knee in his back.

I worked as fast as I could, fumbling for a moment with the stiff zip tie.

It was then he decided to struggle: I felt his leg slide sideways, as if to gain leverage to flip me off.

My anger flared so strong I almost saw it, like a bright-gold curtain billowing in my face for a second.

I bashed his face into the floor with my elbow.

He really wasn't expecting that.

"Oooh!" A primal, unnerving squeal. His body flexed enough for me to finish cuffing him. "Oooh!"

"Pile of scum." I zipped the plastic strip tight against his wristbones and half kicked, half rolled him into the little white soundproof room.

My heart was going like a string of firecrackers. "Scream as loud as you want, you goddamn coward! You're all cowards."

I used a second tie to attach his wrists to the heavy steel ring. This took some doing, as I didn't want to face him and have to reach around him, but it's amazing how pliant even a strong person's body is when they're discombobulated from pain and fear. I was able to yank him into position and lock that second tie.

"The Whale upstairs," I told him, stepping back, "just let slip that you were the one that took care of those two guys."

"H'h," he spat. He knew enough not to say anything incriminating. But he didn't say, "Which two guys?" like an innocent person would. He knew which two guys, all right: the sorry dead sons of bitches Nathan Cubitt had referred to, the ones who'd tried to threaten the Whale about what had happened in Tucson.

He writhed, damning me to hell.

I didn't take the time to glance at him as I headed for the door, although just before I slammed it, I said, "And you have a blessed day!"

"I KNOW YOU don't have all night," said Rowe, one thigh up on a lab counter.

The Whale rose laboriously from his seat, went over to the next lab counter, turned on the faucet, and bent to drink from it. He kissed the back of his hand. "So?"

Rowe began, "Self-defense is what we're mostly about."

Vargas loved that. "It *all* boils down to self-defense, doesn't it?"

"I mean," Rowe went on, "even the demise of Sgt. Annette Soames was self-defense in a way, wasn't it? In a proactive way?"

The Whale laughed, and Rowe joined him, his lips retracting from the fake buck teeth.

"You really hated her!" observed Vargas appreciatively, still not saying anything incriminating. He studied Rowe, standing now only a few feet from him. "You know, I'd like to spot you some dental work at some point, some point soon. Your spirit feels wrong for that mouth of teeth. No offense, as I know a man can't help the way he's born. Yeah," he mused, looking at Rowe closely, "the teeth don't fit you, somehow. They don't seem right, somehow." He approached Rowe, his belly rolling from side to side, his nose lifted slightly, as if detecting a new odor.

Instantly, Rowe pulled a large semiautomatic pistol from beneath his shirt. With a smile he held the muzzle up, finger on the guard. The Whale's attention snapped to the gun. "Ever seen one of these?" Rowe asked with enthusiasm. "It's a Siegfried Series B, forty-five caliber. It'll stop a grizzly bear, not to mention the chump on the street. The fishing guides up in Alaska actually use these for backup. I put some hollowpoints in." He dropped the magazine, showing that it was full, then rammed it back home.

It was a beautifully made gun: polished stainless steel, sharply checkered walnut grips.

"Four-and-a-half-inch barrel," said Rowe, "enough to aim, but not so much to get in the way of concealed carry."

The Whale admired the gun. "I thought you said U.S. Olympic team."

"That's right."

"I thought they used small caliber. Rifles, twenty-twos, I've watched it on TV."

"Oh, yeah, that's mostly, but they've added a large-bore division. Because more and more combat shooters are starting to compete. So, given your plans for expansion and eventually being legal, you need weapons that, if they're traced, won't lead back to you or your people in any way."

Vargas nodded.

"Here," and Rowe passed the gun, butt-first, to Vargas. "The safety's off."

The fat man took it comfortably, and, like everyone who grasps a new gun, he wrapped it in his palm and looked at its profile.

Rowe coughed loudly.

The lines of the gun were smooth, the machining perfect, and the satin finish made the steel glow.

A scuttling sound occurred near the front blackboard, near the door to the teacher's office—the sickening, unmistakable movement of a large rodent.

The Whale turned alertly toward the sound, shifting the gun in his hand.

A large gray alley rat nosed along the wall. It moved steadily, as if on a mission somewhere.

"Kill it, Dale!" shouted Rowe.

As reflexively as he had flicked the knife at Albert Einstein, Dale Vargas extended his arm and, leading the moving rat by just a hair, squeezed the trigger.

The rat leaped straight into the air, came down on four feet, and rushed for cover under the nearest cabinet.

The report concussed Rowe's ears, and after a moment the wafting gun smoke opened up his sinuses.

"Hell!" cried the Whale. Then he laughed at the splintered hole in the baseboard where he'd missed. "Hahaha!"

Rowe took back the gun and replaced it in his waistband. "You almost got him."

"I hate rats so much." The Whale was still laughing. "Get that broom, will you, Jimmer? See if we can poke him out of there."

Rowe stood watching Vargas.

Vargas said, "You've got to be hard on a rat, or else in three days you're gonna have his kids dropping down into your cereal. Ha!"

Rowe coughed again, loudly, in the direction of the teacher's door between this classroom and the next.

That door opened, and Diane Keever appeared, sitting expectantly in her wheelchair, which was pushed forward by Amaryllis.

Mrs. Keever looked at the men. "Where's the bingo?" she asked querulously. She twisted around to Amaryllis. "You said there was bingo." Her hands plucked at a checkered wool lap robe.

"Wrong room, I guess," said Amaryllis. She let go of the chair and stepped to the side. The Whale was too surprised to speak.

Rowe set himself, aimed the Siegfried Series B at the old woman, and fired.

The report was, again, earsplitting. The frail Mrs. Keever rammed backward in her seat, and a gout of blood and tissue burst from her chest. Her head, having whipped back, now wobbled forward, as if she were trying to see her wound, but suddenly her eyes went blind. Blood seeped from the corners of her mouth.

Dale the Whale stood speechless, eyes bulging. His jaws worked silently.

"*Ufff!*" he grunted at last.

Amaryllis stood impassively as Mrs. Keever took one last ragged breath. Her head tipped sideways, and her eyes rolled back. She stopped breathing.

Amaryllis turned the wheelchair sideways as if to leave the way they had come in.

"Wait," said Rowe.

"What the *fuck,*" shouted the Whale, "did you do that for?"

"I hate being interrupted," Rowe said.

"Little Jimmer, Jesus Christ, she's just an old lady! What— what—wait a minute, isn't she the one—the one from—goddamn it! Goddamn it, what the motherfuck is going on?"

Rowe strode to the main classroom door and flung it open.

GEORGE GAVE ME a wink as soon as he opened the door, to signify so far so good. I'd barely made it, sprinting all the way from the basement, my heart in my mouth as I heard the shots. Others in the building hadn't reacted yet.

Still catching my breath, I swaggered in, took a wide stance, and told Vargas authoritatively, "You're under arrest! On the floor, facedown."

George said, "Oh, hello, Sgt. Annette Soames! Hello, hello!"

Seeing me, seeing the policewoman back from the dead, stunned the Whale into incoherence.

"Ahhh, waugha!" he cried.

With his bulging eyes and stopped-open jaw, he looked like the guy that mistakenly eats the radioactive potato chips in *Up For Down,* that French existentialist sci-fi movie that was so big last year.

"I survived," I said, "thanks to my body armor. The department put out my obit anyway, thinking it'd make you feel more relaxed. You tried to have me killed. I take that personally, you know? And now I'm busting your ass, and it's a true pleasure."

He managed to blubber, "What for?"

"For the murder," said George, "of Mrs. Diane Keever here."

"What! But *you* shot that old lady!"

"Get down! On the floor facedown, down, down!" I shouted, flexing my crotch and aiming my gun with both hands, like cops are taught. By now I felt like an old pro.

Vargas stood perfectly still, beginning to come out of his shock—I could see his mind regaining function. I honestly believe his brain had been so overwhelmed that he hadn't even heard me command him to drop. He had no volition, yet, over his body. I was afraid he'd lose control of his bowels, he was that gut-level astonished. And with a guy his size—well, you don't want to think about it.

"Your fingerprints are on the gun," said George, "and powder marks are on your hand."

I glanced over to the inert figure of Mrs. Keever. Blood dripped from the seat of her wheelchair. I thought I saw one of her fingers twitch, but I couldn't be sure. Amaryllis stood there stolidly.

"What—," gasped Vargas, still standing there flat-footed, "what about *your* prints?"

George edged nearer to him but kept a body's-length distance. "Here, can you see this?" He held out his right hand, showing the clear, flexible tape, courtesy of Yvonne, he'd placed on his fingers and palm. She used it, she said, for temporary face-lifts because it was elastic, like real skin. "My prints," George said, "aren't on the gun. Only yours. Powder marks on me, then, are irrelevant. You're cooked, my friend." He spat out his buck teeth.

"I knew it! I knew it!" cried the Whale.

"You knew my ass," said George. "Now get on the floor and take the cuffs, or Sergeant Soames will have the pleasure of shooting you as you try to run."

SYLVAN BURRELL LURKED in the bushes, close to the mission's ground-floor windows. He enjoyed his occupation as an animal wrangler, which, since the day he started nine years ago with one well-trained dog, never stayed the same from one hour to the next. He had wrapped up his work with the police dogs on *The Canary Syndrome,* then he had done the TV gig with the hundred mice. Fortunately, this time he hadn't needed to train the mice to attack humans. Not that it was difficult to do, it was just too weird: the best technique he'd found was to release the mice into an open, coffin-sized packing case, strip to his Speedo, smear his body with peanut butter, then lie down in there with them. They'd swarm him and nibble the peanut butter. So long as he stayed mellow, they never bit. You do that a few times, then the next time you release them, they rush for the nearest human, looking for peanut butter. Sylvan felt that he should be able to find somebody who liked the kinkiness of that situation enough to do the job for him for free. He hadn't, though.

But tonight was different still than anything he'd done before. He had been told by George Rowe not to panic when he heard shots, although he was prepared to lose Norway 433. "It should be OK, but we might get unlucky," Rowe had said, as they worked together in the early dawn hours to create a rathole and a PVC tunnel into the chemistry lab, using a tangle of vines beneath the window as cover. "The guy's a pretty good shot, but the gun'll be new to him and he won't have had any practice with it."

"OK," Sylvan had said, "though I prefer my animals to die from natural causes."

The night had cooled off significantly, and he felt comfortable waiting. He smelled the greenness of the shrubs that had taken over the football field, and he was glad to be part of something exciting, although neither Rita nor her friend George Rowe had told him quite what it was. Rita had asked him for this special favor, and he had done it because he liked her. He thought she was a good actress and felt a little baffled as to why she was going to law school.

On and off, he heard dogs barking, mostly in concert as a pack—that is, he didn't hear fight sounds. So there was a group out there, with a strong leader. He knew about the feral pack of South Central, but had never seen it.

He had released the rat on George's cue cough, which he'd

clearly heard through the open pipe as planned. He'd baited the tunnel's mouth at the classroom, so the rat headed straight up.

He'd heard the shooting. He knew that the sound of gunfire wasn't terribly unusual in South Central. You heard it, you perceived whether it was near or far, then you either ignored it or took cover. Simple instinct.

Now, as he waited, decked out in his black SWAT-looking outfit with his equipment—flashlight, a belt pack with rat treats in it (yogurt candy drops), his cell phone, a loop of light rope, work gloves, and the holstered black canister of pepper spray he always carried if he had to go into South Central—a woman hurried along the side of the building, almost bumping into him.

This was, quite oddly, the second person he'd encountered out here; just a few minutes earlier he'd caught sight of another woman, wearing a dress that looked wet in front—it was hard to see in the dark, with only traces of light coming into these shadows from the street. She'd been hunched over, holding her face as if she were crying, but he'd heard no sound. She'd moved silently away and disappeared around the corner.

The second woman was a short, big-butted white girl. She stopped and looked him over.

"Who are you?"

"My name's Sylvan," he answered cheerfully enough.

She said, "The goddamn van broke down on Vernon and I had to walk back. I got *ice cream* to pick up! Do you have jumper cables?"

"No, I'm sorry."

"Hey," she said, peering again at his equipment and so on, "what you doing here, anyway?"

"I'm a wrangler," he answered.

357

Wichita pushed out her chest. "A wrangler? You mean like a bounty hunter?"

He didn't get what she meant. He tried to make it plainer, because she must be a little slow: "There's a rat upstairs, and I'm here to make sure he doesn't get hurt."

"A rat?" Wichita exploded. "Who's the rat? That bucktooth guy? He's up there with Dale! Goddamn it, I knew that son of a bitch was a rat from the beginning!"

She took off running.

THIRTY-THREE

The Whale, coherent now, on the tile floor now, amped into bitter anger as he struggled against the cuffs. "So you're the rat," he sputtered at George. "What did you do—get caught with that shit on you and turn on me? I want my lawyer!"

"You don't get what's happening," said George. He thrust his knee deeper into Vargas's back and I latched the cuffs on the man whose wrists were almost too stout for them.

"I was a bigger fish than you all along," George explained. "I was just pretending to suck up to you, so I could take over. I've engineered everything, as you can see." He left the Whale beached on the floor for the moment.

Vargas understood. "You guys couldn't get me by the rules, so now you're setting me up for murder." He twisted his head to glare at me. "You're a crooked bitching cop, you're in his pocket."

"Exactly," I said. "Quite a profit center it is too! And I've got Culpepper down in that little room, and he's just given you up."

George looked at me sharply. I gave him a look that said, *Yeah, I'm gonna improvise here.* As he realized that I'd really handled something down there—he still didn't know what—comprehension took over, then delight.

The Whale flopped onto his side, to better interact with us. "What happened, did he let her get away? Son of a motherfucker!"

I went on, "Yeah, we've got him on kidnapping and assault, of course you know that since you were in there too, using the knife on that poor woman, and he's gonna yell his ass off about you. He's already babbling about those two bodies from last year, the guys who were gonna cut a deal with us on what you pulled in Tucson. He called it 'Thinking *Inside* the Box.' Pretty funny. I'm sure you invented that term, right?"

The Whale's panic rose in his eyes like blood, but at the same time I saw him begin to calculate. With blinding swiftness, he got a grip and started to deal.

"Culpepper's got nothing on me that won't pull him down too!" he said rapidly. "I'm the one that can get *him*! You want the CEO? I just promoted him! He's the one that knows which dock down there that barrel went off of. Man, that thing sank like a tombstone." He stopped, almost smirking. "I won't say more right now, but just you talk to him about that. Just say, 'Hey Reverend! Which dock? Which dock again?'"

I remembered the one-thumbed Culpepper telling me he'd been a stevedore. Of course: docks, docks plural, down there, well, the Port of Long Beach?

I took a risk. "Before or after the strike?" I asked, the side of my face feeling George's surprise.

"Hah! During! I never had my hands on anything in that barrel!"

Now we knew that by checking the wharf schedules and zeroing in on the docks most isolated, and likeliest to be deserted during last year's much-publicized labor strike, at least two of the Whale's victims should be found.

That right there was huge, huge for us. Frame him for murder, get his guard down, then move in to pry some real information from him—information on a capital offense we could give to the police.

The horror of Neneng and the extra advantage that Culpepper gave us were unexpected, but I'd seen a way to use them. And it worked, dammit, it worked.

In a confidential tone—he even managed a sly look—the Whale offered, "I'll give you Culpepper *and* fifty grand, cash, apiece, *and* my whole operation if you let me go now. I was thinking of moving to Seattle, anyway. Let me go, I swear I'll give you everything."

I was happy. And I have to say, he was so invitingly conspiratorial, I almost wanted to take the deal.

Suddenly I remembered what Gramma Gladys had communicated to me: *Don't be yourself!* Well, I certainly had not been myself, I'd taken on the aspect of a pregnant junkie, then a dead police officer. I suppose if I'd thought it worthwhile to impersonate a one-eyed Laplander, I'd have done that too.

Yes, I was happy, and naturally I thought we were home free.

But I'd forgotten the other thing Gramma Gladys emphasized to me, something about *just when you think . . .*

The process of Everything Going To Hell started with a crash at the door. I turned.

Wichita, all tight T-shirt and stomper boots, tore into the room like a mad buffalo.

"Hold it!" she commanded, and my heart went cold to hear her crazed tone and just the whole damn *oh, shit* of it. She waved her pistol, which looked insanely big—like it could hold about fifty bullets. George had told me she carried a 9mm Conti-Boch, which meant nothing to me, except that it sounded aggressive.

I glanced at Amaryllis, whose nostrils were flaring at Wichita's unexpected, disastrous return. She remained near Diane Keever's crumpled body. And because of the bedlam that happened next, that was the last I noticed of her, until later.

My fake gun was holstered, and I knew that the only thing left in George's were blanks. Nevertheless, Wichita couldn't cover us all at once, and she couldn't shoot us all at once, and there were a few of us to shoot.

Her face froze as she realized that very thing. All she'd wanted to do was save her boss—her boyfriend, sugar daddy, whatever.

George was already reacting, moving subtly out of Wichita's central vision. As she glared at me, trying to decide what to do, he dropped behind the longest lab counter and crab-walked in a second to the other end, only a few feet from her.

He looked back at me and his eyes said, *Do something now!*

I drew my gun, wound up, and hurled it at her as fast and hard as I could. It struck her shoulder, even though she saw it coming. She also saw George leap from behind the black-topped lab counter.

She knew, probably, just about as much about gunfighting as I did, but she knew how to pull the trigger, and boy, that's what she did. He grabbed for the gun but she was fast, and with those massive haunches, she had a low, stable center of gravity. Her gun spat fire as he lunged for her wrist.

I rushed forward, but something like a well-padded locomotive slammed me from behind, and I went down headlong, skidding on the floor. The Whale was up, and after plowing me out of his way, he belly-flopped onto the George-Wichita pile, handcuffs and all.

Bullets flew around the room like popcorn as Wichita's gun snapped this way and that.

George, I perceived, would have gotten Wichita in hand in another instant, but the thrashing bulk of the Whale threw everything into question.

I couldn't believe we'd been in total control just a few seconds ago, and now were fighting for our lives. What should I do, lie there and wait for the shooting to stop? No, no.

I scrambled to my feet and hurled myself into the fight for Wichita's gun, attaching myself to the Whale's back and circling his throat with my arm. I pulled my forearm into his windpipe as hard as I could. I wanted to kill him, and next I wanted to kill that fucking Wichita.

Her gun kept going off.

The Whale's skin was slippery, he was sweating and so was I. The whole world was pouring sweat.

A bullet zinged past my ear with a terrifying whine.

I'd been expecting the volunteers down in the dormitories, if not whichever few guards were on duty, to have stampeded in here by now. But of course, all they'd heard were gunshots, and I guess it's like when you suspect a fire behind a door—you feel for heat, and if you detect it, you don't open it. What idiot would?

All the more surprising, then, when so much more hell broke loose. The door banged, and this time I heard a voice I really did not want to hear. It was Denny's, and here he came through the door pointing a big-ass gun, and he wasn't alone.

This was a very bad thing.

And it was an impossible thing: I was *counting* on Gina to keep this guy away! Where was my sister? A horrible image of her lying somewhere with her throat slit by this criminal asshole flashed through my mind as I kept struggling to strangle the Whale.

At first all I heard was yelling, lots of it, guys' voices shouting syllables that didn't register on me at the moment; I heard Wichita beneath it all, screaming and flapping like a chicken because George had probably busted her arm getting the gun away, which he had done just as Denny came; and when the shouting coalesced into words, I heard, "Police! Police! Drop it, drop it, get down, get down!"

"Huh?" I said.

It was the real deal: these guys behind Denny, to my astonishment, were the actual LAPD, they had guns and SWAT armor, and they poured into the room, five or six of them, and it was extremely chaotic for about thirty seconds until everybody stopped, and Wichita's gun scuttled to the floor and we all obeyed the order to get down on the goddamn floor and shut up.

The few seconds of gunshot-free silence that followed were so beautiful to me I cannot tell you.

Then, from my facedown position, with a cop's requisite knee in the small of my back, I heard George, totally inexplicably, laughing quietly.

"Shut up," said a cop.

Denny said, "It's OK, Ang, let him up. Let her up too. No, not her—the little one."

The knee lifted away, and I scrambled upright.

My mind worked ferociously to try to figure out what was going on. And what had been going on.

Denny—a cop?

He was in plain clothes, the others were in uniform.

If he was a cop tonight, he'd been a cop all along.

The whole fucking time! While he was hanging out with Vargas and Wichita and his family of thugs, while he sat at my dinner table and told that shit about his so-called job, everything.

I stared at him, and he smiled slightly in my direction as he handled the action in concert with an LAPD lieutenant, who was calling out Miranda rights.

Behind me, I heard someone crying.

Denny knew exactly what had happened, he knew exactly who everybody was, and he knew who he wanted to take into custody and who he didn't.

"You son of a bitch," George told him good-naturedly as he brushed himself off, "you sneaky son of a bitch." He stretched himself and moved his neck from side to side. Wichita whimpered in her shackles. I wanted to kick her in the head, the murderous wench.

Slowly, Amaryllis rose from where she was—essentially she had draped herself over the slumped form of Diane Keever, covering her head and torso, like a human blanket. She unfolded herself and stood upright, looking down at the old widow, panting as if she'd just outrun the hounds of hell.

Mrs. Keever was crying.

Amaryllis asked, "Are you all right?"

"Yes," said Mrs. Keever, "help me up."

Amaryllis extended her sturdy brown arm, and the parchment-pale hand fitted itself on it, and slowly, dripping blood, sweat, and tears, Diane Keever rose to her feet.

"Get the medics over here," said an officer.

"No," I said, "it's fake blood, she's OK. All she needs is a towel."

Yes. Diane Keever had just acted the role of her life. And she'd done it beautifully, triggering the compressed-air squib with her hand under the lap robe at the exact instant George fired the blank at her chest. I hadn't seen it, but I knew it looked fantastic (George confirmed this later), especially since Chino had added, inside the condom full of fake blood, bits of pink sponge that blew out along with the blood. Just great. We had scored Diane's white blouse with a razor blade over where Chino had taped the squib, to make sure the explosion looked good, and I sure wished I'd seen it.

And now Diane Keever was crying. She spat out Yvonne's now-spent blood capsule and clutched the wad of paper towels I handed her. Too overcome even to wipe her face, she took a tottering half step and threw herself into Amaryllis's arms.

"You covered me," she sobbed, her body wracking so hard I feared she'd disintegrate. "They were shooting real bullets, and you covered me."

Amaryllis held her, and looked over her head, her eyes a mile away. "I didn't have time to think about it."

I contradicted, "Yes, you did."

"You made the choice," sobbed Mrs. Keever.

"Stop crying now," Amaryllis scolded, and I could see that all the years of guilt were gone, vanished. Banished. Her face was clear and exhausted, and until that moment, I hadn't realized how much of her had been held tight by the past.

As for Diane Keever, she wept with the release of decades of hatred and anger. Amaryllis had, with her single act of self-sacrifice, plucked her out of the hell she'd built for herself for so many years.

"Oh, my God!" I shouted, "Neneng!"

Denny stopped me. "You mean the woman—"

"Yes!"

"She's OK, we found her outside. She's on the way to the hospital now."

"Minus her nose!"

"What?" said George.

Denny said, "She said, 'Doctor make new.' She's a tough little lady. What's her name again?"

"Neneng."

"We also collected the guy in the priest outfit—Culpepper. It was you who zip-tied him down there, right?"

I admitted it.

"What?" repeated George.

"I'll tell you later."

Denny said, "We'd have been in here sooner except for Ms. Neneng, she kept pointing towards the basement, so we thought the surveillance guys were wrong when they told us the first shot came from up here."

"With Culpepper's and Neneng's statements," I suggested hopefully, "you've got Vargas on kidnapping and maybe even attempted murder."

"That's right," Denny said.

George added, "And you'll want to check the Port for a couple of bodies in a barrel."

Denny asked the LAPD officers to go ahead and take Vargas and Wichita to booking. You never saw such a pair of stupefied faces in your life.

The Korean-descent officer named Ang stood back from me and said in amazement, "You're a dead ringer for Annette, I can hardly believe you're not her."

Still, I couldn't smile. I was well aware that I'd been impersonating a police officer, on purpose this time, which is a crime by definition. True, I was doing it to try to nail a bad guy, but they had me dead to rights.

Then Detective Herrera, the guy who'd questioned me as the ER doctor sewed up my arm, sauntered in, and the circle, for me, was complete.

"Just like you to show up," Denny told him, "well after the last ricochet."

Herrera said nothing, he just looked me up and down as if trying to decide whether to be angry or turned on.

Denny told George, "I've been working on bringing down Dale Vargas since Tucson."

"You're FBI, then?" asked George.

"That's right. Special Agent Milton Fairbarn." We all shook hands, and he smiled a good guy's smile, wide and relaxed, so different from the calculating smiles he'd given at my dinner table, and from the scowls he'd thrown around the mission. "I had no idea what you guys were doing."

He told us he'd infiltrated the Whale's organization by getting hired as one of the few civilian guards at the ABC Mission. Eventually, he met Vargas and became a vice president.

I interjected, "It was Wichita and that Jerrol Bays guy, wasn't it, who beat up Kip Cubitt, then came back shooting?"

"That's right, they were a little team. When Jerrol bought it after murdering Annette, I stepped into his place as Wichita's sidekick."

"Yeah," I said. "Yeah."

That got him a lot of face time with Vargas, plus he was able to

368

limit some of the damage Wichita was bent on doing. "Not all," and that gave him pause, "but some."

He'd checked George and me out, and started watching us. "We realized you guys were after the Whale too—and we knew you were a PI and you"—he pointed at me—"were *not* a drug addict!—and I was about to call you off when we thought we might as well see how you were going to do it."

I took that at face value, but George said, "Bullshit, Agent Fairbarn, you wouldn't have left us alone out of pure curiosity. You were coming up too empty for too long."

"Don't push it, Rowe." Then he laughed, sweeping his dreadlocks out of his face. "I must admit, I'm impressed. You got him before we did, you surely did."

I realized I wasn't going to get counter-busted. This time.

Agent Fairbarn told us they certainly could have gotten Vargas and all the vice presidents on possession and assorted assault charges long ago, but they wanted Vargas for murder—or at the very least, conspiracy—and it looked good now. Other agents were, this very night, rounding up the rest of the vice presidents.

"I have to ask," I said, "how you knew I wasn't a real drug addict?"

Denny said, "The needle tracks on your feet were wrong for heroin."

"They were?"

"Yeah, they were consistent for intravenous cocaine, but not heroin, so I knew something was wrong. With coke, you get the tiny red dots inside pale skin, but with heroin the marks are usually darker—browner, you know—and wider, like a piece of brown worm along your vein. You must have looked at the wrong picture on the Internet. I realized you were faking it, and that made me even more curious about you two. I'd already begun to date Gina, thinking she was the one mainly looking into things—having seen you two nosing around the mission that day—but then I realized it was you, and you really confirmed it that night with the needle tracks."

"So my pregnant-addict disguise didn't fool you."

"Oh, it did, at first, you were very good. It was only your muscle tone that tipped me off, your body wasn't slack enough when I held your leg. Then I looked closer at your tracks. Really, you're an excellent actress, do you know that?"

George offered Denny the Siegfried. "Want to shoot a real corpse with it and pin it on Vargas?"

Another laugh. "A bit of an end run, perhaps!" He shook himself—*"Uffuh!"* He had to come down from his adrenaline high too. "Nah, we'll just dredge up however many poor bastards are underwater at the Port. And we'll do some bargaining. That ought to be enough to put him away for a long time."

At Fairbarn's prompting, George explained how he'd placed one live round in the chamber of the Siegfried, then filled the magazine with blanks. "I had to have a hole in the rat or a hole in the floor to make him think the gun was real, so when I shot Mrs. Keever he really bought it."

"Were you guys going to let him go once you'd scared the shit out of him?"

"Oh, no; I was going to call the LAPD with the information and hope this citizen's arrest would hold up. Rita here was going to just disappear, so we wouldn't have the cop-impersonating problem, and those two ladies would go away as well. It'd be just me and the Whale, his word against mine. I didn't know how much, if any, information he'd spew, but I knew he'd be one scared little boy. I'm glad we got him to mention the Port."

"Which," said the agent, "I bet's going to hold up." He told us he'd been en route to Ventura with Gina when he'd gotten a text message from surveillance that something was up at the ABC, so he'd turned back, stuck close in to L.A., keeping the protesting Gina with him. Upon receiving a second message fifteen minutes ago, he'd ditched her at a bar downtown and raced here to join the SWAT guys who'd been called in. "I'll make it up to her," he promised brightly.

"That'll take some doing," I muttered.

THIRTY-FOUR

George Rowe walked into the Los Angeles night exhausted but happy. The breeze felt good on his face and dried the sweat under his arms as he and Sylvan walked to Sylvan's '80s-vintage Buick Riviera out front, talking. Sylvan was carrying Norway 433 in the crook of one arm and getting his keys out.

The lights of Los Angeles pushed back the black night sky. Sirius had not yet risen in the southeast. The heat wave was broken, and the star would continue to edge lower in the sky, and the ghosts of the ancient Romans were no doubt happier.

Rowe and Sylvan picked their way through the zombie-army flow of street people, some in wheelchairs, some pushing shopping carts crammed with plastic bags of God knew what—all of them feeling unsettled by the recent police activity at the ABC Mission.

Rita had accepted a ride from Agent Fairbarn to rendezvous

with Gina and get home. Before going, she had kissed Rowe on the cheek, and that had added to his happiness. Simply the touch of her lips on his cheek.

"Don't take this the wrong way," she had warned.

"Never!"

She gave him one of her looks.

Now, as Sylvan was about to unlock his car, he stepped back to let a man aimlessly piloting his power wheelchair go by. A black dog sat alertly in his lap, and as they cruised abreast, Rowe got a nervous feeling about the dog, but it was too late.

With an eager snarl, the dog sprang, startling Sylvan. It chomped Norway 433 right out of his grasp.

"Hey!" Sylvan shouted.

The rat was too heavy for the dog to really run with; it simply gave it a hard shake and dropped it on the pavement, then stood over it, ready to kill it again if it moved.

Rowe grabbed the dog by the collar and Sylvan picked up his rat.

The wheelchair guy said, "Oops!"

Rowe held the dog back.

"Hey, leave my dog alone! Give him to me!" The skinny guy and the dog both smelled pretty pungent.

"Fuck you," muttered Sylvan, squatting.

In the distance, they suddenly heard the feral pack set up a baying. Rowe judged they were roaming the brush directly behind the mission.

Sylvan held the limp body of Norway 433 in his large hand. "I spent a lot of time training this one," he remarked sadly.

The baying increased. Rowe pictured a scruffy jackrabbit leading them flat-out.

"Your rat dodged a bullet tonight," Rowe said, "only to have this damn dog—"

He stopped.

The dog's collar, he realized, felt substantial in his hand. It felt like good leather. Very dirty, but good. There was no tag dangling from it, only a ring from which a tag might have been torn, or pried.

He inspected the medium-sized black dog. It was a male.

"Give me back my dog!" demanded the wheelchair guy, his eyes glassy, his meager body slack in the chair. "Here, Whizzer!"

The dog ignored him. Rowe said, "Sylvan, this dog looks like a beagle, but it can't be, can it? Because it's black."

"That doesn't matter," Sylvan said, finishing his sigh of grief over Norway 433, which he laid for the moment on the roof of his Buick, "every stray dog turns black sooner or later." He cut an angry look at the dog. "It is a beagle. Why?"

"I want to take it inside to wash its head and see his markings. See, I'm looking for a lost beagle for a client, and—I have a feeling—"

"Here." Sylvan took a wet wipe from his belt pouch. "Let's see." Rowe passed him the collar to hold while he scrubbed its forehead. Under the streetlight, beagle markings began to show. The dog flinched and sneezed, but Rowe carefully wiped off the grime to reveal a distinct tan-inside-white blaze, resembling a Doric column.

"Ernest," he said.

The dog wagged its tail.

"Goddamn."

One of Ernest's ears had been torn, and there were a few notches in the other. He'd definitely lost weight.

374

"Gimme back my dog!" demanded the wheelchair guy fear-fully. "He's a service animal."

Rowe told the man in the chair, "This dog is a runaway. The owner wants him back."

"No, he isn't!"

As the feral pack ran in the brush behind the mission, ever closer, Rowe could distinguish individual dog voices, all sharing the joy of late-night aggression.

"He's my service animal," insisted wheelchair dude.

Rowe placed Ernest in the man's lap to calm him. The dog's tattered ears pricked toward the sound of the pack.

"Well," said Rowe patiently, squatting instinctively so that his head was lower than the man's, "the owner is a nice guy, and he has a right to get his pet back."

"Whizzer will be well taken care of," Sylvan put in.

"Yes," Rowe agreed, "he'll get a bath, get cleaned up. Good food to eat."

Wheelchair dude, crestfallen, said, "Back to captivity, eh?"

Rowe said, "Well, yes. But you know, there's a reward."

"How much?" asked the man with sudden alacrity.

"A thousand dollars."

With street instantaneousness, wheelchair dude held out his hand.

"Well, I don't have that much on me at the moment," said Rowe. "Give me the dog, and I'll bring the money to you as soon as I can."

"When?" said the man.

Sylvan watched all this.

"Well—tomorrow," said Rowe. "Or Monday, at the latest, when the banks open."

"No way, man, no way."

Sylvan said, "Tomorrow for this man might as well be next year. What's your name, buddy?"

"Benny."

Rowe said, "Benny, I could—"

Benny broke in, "I give you guys this dog, there's no way you're gonna come back here and give me a thousand bucks."

"Yes, I will," said Rowe.

Quietly, Sylvan asked Rowe, "How much money do you have on you?"

"About a hundred, I guess."

Benny shouted, "I'll sell him to you for a hundred!"

Rowe fished out his wallet and counted out all his currency, $112, and handed it to Benny.

The man folded the money into a wad and shoved it inside his filthy shirt.

The dog looked at Rowe curiously.

Rowe reached for his collar, but Benny pushed the dog's rump and yelled, "Go free!"

Ernest plunged to the ground and bolted for his feral brethren.

"Goddamn!" exclaimed Rowe. *Them again. The pack.*

Benny looked after the dog with a crazy grin. "I'd just as soon he keeps his freedom, like me."

Rowe had never before wanted to punch a handicapped person.

"Goddamn it!"

Benny activated his chair and rolled away into the shadows.

Rowe turned to Sylvan. "I've got to catch that dog!"

"Shit, bro, that pack is vicious!"

"You think they'll kill him?"

"Hell no, he's a hound! They'll kill *us*!"

Already running, Rowe tossed over his shoulder, "They're not so tough! I'll split a hundred grand with you if you help me get him!"

"What!" Sylvan grabbed a noosed catch pole out of his trunk and sprinted after Rowe.

THIRTY-FIVE

Gina and I sat up late into the night, talking as fast as our mouths could move, talking about everything—talking and laughing and crying with relief. We consumed a bar of Cadbury Dairy Milk as an hors d'oeuvre, before starting on the gin and Wheat Thins. Gina had begun a martini thing after she and Daniel and I watched *All About Eve* on cable one night.

I sipped about half of my martini, and Gina got up to make more. "It's so good you have this jar of olives," she commented. "And toothpicks. You're so organized. If this were my house I'd have *had* both things but we'd never be able to find them. I think you should let me wear your aqua Noni Xon dress with the belt to the endowment ceremony tomorrow." She looked at her watch. "Today, I mean."

"*I'm* wearing that dress." A fantastic raw silk number I'd gotten for thirty-eight dollars at Madwoman.

"Oh."

"I like gin," I said, inhaling the juniper.

"It's part aromatherapy." Gina poured the gin over the crackling ice without measuring.

"It's very generous of you to have bought Tanqueray, you know, top shelf."

"I used your credit card."

"God damn it."

We laughed like maniacs and drank more gin.

When the door buzzed well after 3 a.m. and I saw George standing there, I almost fainted. *Standing,* actually, is an overstatement; he was bracing himself against the doorjamb as if his legs were about to buckle.

There was a smear of blood under his nose, and his hand left a blood print on the doorjamb. His plaid shirt was torn, hanging from one shoulder, caveman-style, and he'd—thank God—lost his wig. A bruise was coming up in the exact center of his forehead, and I saw his pale knees, abraded red, beneath the torn cloth of his pants. Deep welts striped his arms like barber poles.

The first thing he said in answer to my speechless stare was, "I'm fine. I figured you two would still be up. Sirius is rising."

That's when I noticed the dog, a weary-looking thing with the head of a beagle and the body of some kind of black hound, tethered to George's hand by a length of clothesline. It panted and looked up at me with pleading eyes.

"Who is it?" said Gina, drying her hands in the kitchen. She got a load of George and said, "Gosh, you look like you tried to get away from a Russian hooker without paying."

He was too tired to crack back, but he was smiling, and I knew he'd won more than one important battle tonight.

"Could you keep this fellow until the kennels open, like maybe ten o'clock? I'll come back for him."

"Oh, for God's sake."

"Let him in. Them in," said Gina.

Once inside, he asked for water for the dog, then drank two glasses himself. He waved off my warm washcloth and box of gauze. He took me to the patio and pointed to a star just peeking above the treetops of West Hollywood. "That's the Dog Star," he said. "Soon it'll go below the horizon and we won't see it again until next year."

"Dogs come and go," observed Gina, wise with gin.

I looked at the star, barely breaking through the night glow of L.A. The mysterious fragrance of night-blooming jasmine wafted along from somewhere.

We went to the living room where, holding the unbelievably smelly, suddenly restless dog by the collar, George sat on the floor and told us about his client and the missing beagle, and an action-movie chase, tonight.

"It's a beagle? The whole dog is a beagle?" Gina was dumbstruck.

George's eyes glazed over as he described dashing after the feral pack through the thorny scrub behind the mission, across the freight yards of Vernon, down the ravine to the Los Angeles River and up again, over bottle-strewn streets, between buildings where ziggurats of discarded box springs had grown. Sylvan had helped him, and between the two of them, they'd managed to head off the pack, cut Ernest from it, and bring him in alive.

"At one point, they led us into a cul-de-sac and then turned on us," he said.

"Good God," I said.

"I never climbed so fast in my life. We made it to a rooftop, then got down a stairwell. We caught up with them in the next alley and used some garbage cans to choke down their flow, so to speak. Sylvan's a master with that noose stick."

"Is Sylvan OK?"

"Yeah, he went home. I went to Hancock Park and tried to return Ernest here to his owner, but the house is locked up and nobody answered my pounding. So, I'll put him in a kennel in the morning until I can find my client."

"What about Gonzalo's place?" I asked warily. "Doesn't he have a backyard over in Los Feliz?"

"Yeah, but he's also got a wolfhound that mangled the last dog who came to visit. I can't take the risk. Please, Rita. Gina? It's only for the rest of tonight. You can close him in Petey's room."

"We could put some newspapers down," suggested Gina helpfully.

"Why didn't Sylvan offer to take him?"

"His kennels are full, and he doesn't want this guy handing along any fleas."

"Fleas, oh, great. Better they all jump off here."

Gina commented, "Yeah, and he could have picked up some other disease or something that Sylvan wouldn't want passed to his dogs."

"Wonderful, wonderful," I said.

Gina volunteered, "I bet I could give him a bath."

"Rita," George pleaded.

My sister piled on, "Don't make it such a big deal, Rita. We can handle this little favor for George, can't we? I mean, he took on the whole feral pack tonight! I'll get the newspapers out of recycling. I sort of forgot to put them out last week!"

WHEN GEORGE CAME by at 10:15 that morning, I was still logy with gin and sleep—the few hours I'd caught—and he grabbed the dog and split fast, spewing thanks over his showered and shirted shoulder.

Gina and I had given Ernest some hamburger, and she had in fact attempted to give him a bath, but in the end couldn't even coax him into the tub. We made a bed for him from an old flannel blanket I'd been planning to take to the mission. Gina had heard him growling in his sleep, but hadn't thought much of it.

When we inspected the small bedroom after first coffee, Gina remarked, "I think that dog's got a personality disorder."

"God *damn* it," I said. "I mean, real God damn it."

The dog had, with careful precision, rubbed much of his stinking black dirt on the rug, on Petey's bed, even the walls along the baseboards. He'd slept, if at all, on Petey's bed, which looked like a bucket of old, old sewage sludge had spilled on it. The last surviving Spider-Man sheet was unsalvageable. The frayed flannel "dog" blanket was untouched.

It took one and a half bottles of Mr. Clean and every rag I owned to clean and deodorize Petey's room after Ernest. It was not a happy job. But at last we were done, Gina threw open the window, and you'd never know a canine had been around.

THE AFTERNOON ENDOWMENT ceremony was a glorious convergence of high spirits, sunshine, TV cameras, music, and potato salad.

Kip Cubitt was at his grandmother's side in a tan suit. He

walked haltingly, but tall and free. No more fear of the Whale, no more fighting off the coercion and the thuggery.

Khani Emberton and Amaryllis B. Cubitt stood on the steps of the mission and said all the things you'd expect about The Heroism Of Ordinary Folks, and How We Can All Make A Difference Together.

I yearned to hear an ethereal pearl or two from Amaryllis's lips, but she kept it all on the surface.

What I did observe, however, was new depth in the Iron Angel's eyes. The old hardness was gone, and with it the guilt, the remorse, the dread—and the empty space left behind was enormous. Amaryllis seemed surprised by this, and I could see her beginning to fill that space with joy. Simple joy. That was what I saw.

I envied her, because I believe she had let go of the past entirely, and was now focused on today like no one I'd ever seen.

It had taken a bullet-studded cataclysm to open that door for her.

I wondered what it would take to open it for me.

As I say, there was picnic food, and perhaps three hundred people—streeties and swells alike—were fed.

Diane Keever, as straight and proud in her wheelchair as Kip was without one, attended as Amaryllis's special guest. George steered her around.

Afterward, Gina and I grabbed trash bags and picked up litter with the rest of the volunteers. We lingered a few minutes with Amaryllis and Mrs. Keever, both of them looking ungodly fresh.

Neneng would soon undergo the first operation of several to reconstruct her nose from her own facial tissue and skin, Mrs. Keever told us. "Doctor make new." The stoic piano virtuoso would be scarred, but she'd have a nose.

"Trouble is, she doesn't have insurance," said Mrs. Keever. "I'd pay for it, except I need—"

"You need what?" Amaryllis broke in, formidably.

"Except I need to give all that money back to your mission."

"No," said Amaryllis, "you use that money to pay her bills, which I predict will add up. That's a good enough use of that money, I judge."

I asked Mrs. Keever how she intended to get by, without Amaryllis's payments.

She gazed up at us with a smile, and suddenly I saw the face of Paramount's Vera Luxon in that terrific photograph. I realized I'd never seen Mrs. Keever's smile except in that shot. Right now her smile was fresh and real and it transformed her whole face, and she said, "I'm going to act again."

"You're joking," said George.

"She isn't," I murmured, feeling my own face lift in a smile.

"First, I'm going to get my knees replaced," she told us in a steady, sweet voice, "then I'm going to refresh my skills with workshops in L.A. I'm moving here with Neneng, after I sell the farmhouse. I'll gain weight, round myself out, and I'll get an agent, and I'll start going on auditions as a character actress. I can play Kindly Grandmother or Evil Grandmother!" She bared her teeth in a snarl to show us, and she was transformed again, and I thought yeah, that character could stir arsenic into your Ovaltine.

"Well—go for it!" was all I could say. "Go for it!"

I thought again of that tremendous photograph of her on the piano. Now, though, she was more beautiful than ever, that was a magical fact.

George watched Mrs. Keever admiringly. *I guess he really goes for actresses!*

GEORGE ROWE FOUND the Japanese gardener trimming a bush in Colonel Markovich's front yard at nine on Monday morning.

After a brief conversation, Rowe learned that Markovich had gone into the hospital for a minor heart procedure and was expected to be home tomorrow.

For his part, the gardener learned that Ernest the plant-digging beagle was coming home and he'd better look for a gardening job that would suit him better than this one. Today.

GINA LEARNED THAT Special Agent Milton Fairbarn, unfortunately, was leaving Los Angeles for a new undercover assignment elsewhere, location not disclosed to us. I asked her, over coffee on Monday morning, if she was sad about that.

Dismally, she said, "Oh, my God, no. I could never date a guy named Milton. I mean, *Milton*? Come on."

I realized his name had nothing to do with it; she was just sour-graping it to save face. Which was OK, I mean, I'd probably do the same thing.

I flew to Wisconsin Monday night.

Petey knocked me on my butt with the velocity of his greeting.

Aunt Sheila had been forced to pay a ransom of twenty-five dollars to the Rawson family for the return of Uncle Fritz's boar's head. Whitey, the puppy, had run away.

"As in, back to the Rawson place," Aunt Toots muttered under her breath.

"We're very, very tired," Sheila said.

They both did look a bit glassy.

Back at home, my boy raced to his room to settle in. Then I heard him calling me.

"What's this? What's this?" he demanded, pulling his toys from under his bed.

I'd forgotten about his stash of toys and lost balled-up socks down there. Moreover I hadn't realized the dog could have squeezed himself under that low bed, but of course he would have taken it as a challenge.

Trikey, Petey's stuffed triceratops, had been chewed thoughtfully from head to tail, especially the head. It had not been decapitated, exactly, but it certainly looked like a much different species now.

"And look at my Lego bag, Mom! Look at my combo snorkel and diving mask! Who's been in here? Mom!"

I didn't have the heart to tell him a dog had been in his room, as in, we had a dog while you were gone but took him away before you came home. I just could not try to explain that, because I knew it would only traumatize him. Gina was at work, or she might have blurted the truth.

So I closed my eyes and lied, "Honey, I don't know. It might have been the vacuum cleaner, you know?" I opened my eyes. "Yes, I was vacuuming under there while you were away."

He stared at me, hard. "A vacuum cleaner did *not* do this. Look—there's like slobber marks on Trikey, see?"

"I just have no idea, honey, it's a mystery. Gosh, that's too bad about Trikey. Maybe we can write to Santa to request a replacement."

Sadly, he said, "I don't want another Trikey, I want a dog."

Hell, hell, hell.

THIRTY-SIX

On Wednesday morning, George Rowe delivered Ernest, bathed and flea-powdered, to Colonel Markovich.

The Colonel was overjoyed, as was Ernest, who wagged so hard Rowe feared he'd snap his spine.

He shook hands with Markovich's retired-RN daughter, who had come from the East Coast to look after him for a couple of weeks.

Rowe had spent a lot of time thinking about the Colonel and his lonely world, and his heart moved with compassion for the old man. He understood what the venerable war hero wanted, and what he didn't want.

"How do you feel?" he asked, taking a seat with the Colonel on the sun porch.

"Wonderful!" Markovich laughed. "I haven't a care in the

world now that I have Ernest back. *And* a clean bill of health! Except for having to find a new gardener! The son of a gun didn't even give notice." He certainly looked chipper.

And he was dreadfully curious.

"I went to China on my own," began Rowe with quiet intensity.

Markovich bolted upright in his armchair, where the daughter had tucked him with a blanket and a cup of tea. "Yes?"

"I realized you were absolutely right about the Chinese situation with champion dogs. You and I had spoken of flying over there together. I didn't want to disappoint you, but the more I looked into it, the more I realized this situation called for speed." Rowe sipped his shot of good whiskey, which the daughter had cheerfully poured for him at her father's direction. Ernest followed her in to the kitchen, thinking treats.

"Aha, of course," said the Colonel. "I understand."

"My contacts in the LAPD put me in touch with CS-35, the unofficial arm of Interpol that operates in places where, for obvious reasons, Interpol can't," Rowe went on. "I'd been building relationships in the State Department on another case, so we were covered there. Between those organizations, I was able to, uh, synergize a strategy using a team of computer hackers operating out of Denmark."

The Colonel's eyes widened. "Very impressive. Even I haven't heard of CS-35. Was there code involved?"

"Oh, yes," responded Rowe. "You know how tricky the Chinese numerical system is, being abacus-based, very foreign to the American mind."

"I never understood it myself."

"It pays to be on the good side of cyber-mercenaries. Well, it turns out there's this cartel based in a village in the upper Yangtze Delta—"

"Brutal region."

"Very," agreed Rowe. "Posing as a veterinarian, I made my way there, only to find out that the cartel runs essentially a clearing-house for abducted champions the world over. I saw breeds from everywhere—Peruvian Hairless, Caravan Hounds, Kai Kens, Redbone Coonhounds—you name it. I was able to trace Ernest with the aid of a freight manifest obtained by the Danish team, starting at the open-air meat market—which term, Colonel, I hate to use, but that's exactly what it was—to a house controlled by one of the old tribal families deep in Manchuria. Intermarriage had resulted in a peculiar strain of aggression among the local people."

"I can imagine! Please go on, Mr. Rowe." The old man's eyes glittered.

"Well, the place was more fortress than cozy home, if you understand what I mean. It took some doing, but I finally made my way in." He paused. "Via—uh, well—," he stammered—

The Colonel leaned forward, his cup and saucer balanced perfectly on one blanketed knee. "Go ahead, I'm unshockable."

"Via the bedroom of the mistress of the house."

"You dog, you!"

Rowe chuckled modestly.

"Was she pretty?"

"Lucky for me, yes."

"Oho! Haha!"

"Yes, yes."

"Well, what happened?"

"Uh, *afterward,* you understand me, she led me straight to the underground kennels. Ernest was there. He'd been in a fight or two."

"Yes, I saw his ears!"

"Judging by the looks of the other dogs, Ernest gave as good as he got."

"I'd expect that of him."

Yes, thought Rowe. A blind date might just work out between Markovich and Mrs. Keever. My God, yes, a possible Hollywood ending. But that could wait.

"Finding Ernest, of course, was merely the tip of the iceberg. I had to get us both out of there safely."

"How did you do it?" The old man clasped his hands. "A fortress in Manchuria! Oh, do go on!"

I WAS SURPRISED to see George at my door again in the middle of Thursday afternoon. I'd just folded a load of laundry and had been reviewing the syllabus for one of my law classes, thinking about getting over to UCLA and buying my books. The doorwall was open, and the sunshine streaming through the plants on the patio brought a hint of autumn coolness, over the fragrance of the madly lush basil. It was September now.

"Actually," he said, "I'm here at the request of Petey." His bruises and welts were beginning to fade, and all of his energy was back.

"What!"

"He called me up."

"He's not supposed to use the phone!"

Petey piped, "I used it at Aunt Sheila and Aunt Toots's! They trained me on it."

"Oh that's right," I said.

"I called people. My friends. Ronnie Rawson."

"Oh."

"I can use the phone and I want my own phone and Mr. Rowe is a private investigator, *everybody* knows that, and he's gonna teach me how to be one too so I can solve what happened to my toys!"

George gave me a wink over his head, and there was nothing I could do.

"We gotta find clues!" Petey tugged his hand.

I felt the cold creep of guilt in my gut, and I realized my boy had crossed a threshold, whether I was ready or not. My free exercise of parental fibbing—well, those days were over.

"Wait," George told him. He eased himself to the living room rug and told the boy, "Before you investigate, you've got to gather your facts."

Petey plopped cross-legged, rapt.

"It'll help when you learn how to write, but until then—"

"Would you like some coffee?" I asked in defeat.

George smiled up at me. "I'd love some, Rita, thank you."

"What's this?"

"I stopped for doughnuts."

"Doughnuts!" shouted Petey deliriously.

I made coffee and poured milk and threw down some pillows, and the three of us ate fresh doughnuts around the coffee table in the afternoon's glad golden light.

"Now, you've got to seize your opportunities," George told my boy. "And a man needs the right equipment." He drew a very nice folding magnifying glass from his pocket. "Here, this is yours." The leatherette was ball-glove smooth.

Petey stared. "For keeps?"

"For keeps. You'll need it. Don't lose it, now."

"No way!" Petey gripped the tool tightly.

I smiled to see that George was just a little awkward with the boy, but Petey loved him. Plainly, it wasn't the gifts: Petey perceived something in George, some quality that resonated with him.

"You can't be reckless," George went on, "but don't be afraid to be bold."

I listened to this man who loved me talk to the son I loved, and I watched the boy's face looking seriously into his. Once, George's knee accidentally touched mine and I felt that *zing*. He pretended he didn't feel it, either.

We helped ourselves to more coffee and milk and doughnuts, and the sun kept piling in, and for a long time that afternoon we talked about truth and secrets and mystery, and the many, many ways there are to get to the bottom of things.

ACKNOWLEDGMENTS

I'm grateful to my family and friends for their love, support, and belief, especially my mother, Carolyn Sims Davis, my brother, David Sims, and my sister, Kathleen Cristman.

Special thanks for excellent expert help to Margaret Baker, M.D., Angela Brown, David and Lesley Hiltz of Starbuck Torbay Beagles, Joy Glover, C.N.M., Philip Lenkowsky, and Monika Lenkowsky.

I'm indebted to my agent, Cameron McClure of the Donald Maass Literary Agency, and to my editor, Kelley Ragland.

Thank you to the Los Angeles Police Department, especially the Narcotics Division, and the Los Angeles Mission, especially the Reverend Larry C. Brown.

Above all, thanks to Marcia, for everything.